LABYRINTH

Labyrinth

Mark Sullivan

For Betsy, Connor, and Bridger, who make every day of my life the best kind of adventure.

Contents

At the bottom of the abyss comes the voice
of salvation.
At the darkest moment, comes the light.

—*Joseph Campbell*

Approach

Thirty-Two Years Earlier . . .

APRIL 22, 1972
12:03 P.M., HOUSTON TIME
6 DAYS, 0 HOURS, 9 MINUTES
MISSION ELAPSED TIME
DESCARTES HIGHLANDS, THE MOON

During their second foray outside the lunar module, James Elder and Howard Kennedy were jolted about as their moon rover lurched across a jagged landscape of boulders and minicraters.

Great view. Kennedy's familiar midwestern accent came crystal clear over the radio headset Elder wore under his helmet.

Elder nodded, mesmerized by the scene unfolding outside his tinted visor. The sun at their backs was as brilliant as a bomb blast. Stone Mountain rose before them in a series of shadowed ridges while Earth hung overhead in a sky of speckled black.

Elder parked the rover, then called into his microphone, *Houston, we're five hundred feet above the Cayley Plains. Highest point ever reached by man on the moon.*

Fantastic, said a voice from Mission Control. The crackling transmission was solid. *Now you boys better get to work.*

Kennedy got out and immediately began to gather samples. Elder climbed farther up the mountain, looking for rocks known as basalts, which would indicate that volcanic activity had formed the Highlands. But all he was seeing were "breccias," stones created by the impacts of asteroids and meteors.

Four billion years ago, the theory went, the moon was pummeled by giant chunks of rock hurled through space by the Big Bang detonation that created the universe. One huge impact created the South Ray Crater on the side of Stone Mountain, five times the size of a football field, more than a hundred feet deep, and covered with coal-and--pearl-colored rocks. As Elder approached the rim of the chasm, he was looking at matter forms from the beginning of time. When studied under a microscope, he thought, these stones might well seem a universe unto themselves.

Elder paused, aware of the suck and whoosh of his breath inside his helmet, then called into his microphone, *Houston, I'm gonna dig a trench up here, see what really made these old highlands.*

Roger... keep... The radio link with Houston broke up under waves of static.

Come back, Houston?

Not reading... flares...

Elder turned and looked downslope eighty yards toward Kennedy, who worked with his back to him.

You catch that, Howie?

Must be a solar storm choking communications.

Damn big one, Elder agreed, holding his hand up to shield his eyes from the sun.

If we lose Houston more than fifteen minutes, we'll head back to the module.

Roger that.

Elder used his rake to dig into the chalk-white dust on the crater's rim. After several minutes of work he felt as if he might not find anything. Then the rake turned over a stone roughly the size and shape of a child's soccer ball. He photographed and gave a number to the find: moon rock 66095, a shock-melted breccia, eleven hundred grams in weight.

Elder used a scooper to lift moon rock 66095 and transfer it to his left hand. Shaking the stone so the dust would fall away, the astronaut held it up to his visor. At first glance, except for its shape, it seemed rather plain, a gray rock composed of concave planes and a few minor extrusions. But closer examination revealed a ragged web of dark crystals embedded in the surface of the stone.

Elder shook more dust off the rock, then tilted it so the sun shone directly on the crystals. The sunlight invaded the black glass, made it flash like a rushing stream. Then it began to vibrate. The crystals' sparkling flared into a welder's blinding arc of light. The astronaut heard the hollow, oscillating roar of something deep and primitive.

A gale of energy, strong and electric, gusted through Elder and he doubled over as if punched. A flare of razored pain seared through his head. For a moment the astronaut could see nothing but that glaring light, hear nothing but that insistent, hushed roar, feel nothing but pulse after bolt of hot, insistent energy passing through him. Elder went to one knee, still clutching the rock in his hand, sure he was about to collapse.

Howie! Elder gasped.

Downslope, Kennedy spun around to see Elder force his hand open and drop something. The second astronaut saw it free of his commander's fingers for only a split second. But it was enough. He stood dumbfounded as Elder collapsed to one side.

Jim! Kennedy cried, dropping his equipment and climbing as fast as he could, bellowing into his headset, *Houston, Houston, Elder's down! Houston, do you read me? Elder's down!*

Nothing came back but heavy static.

By the time Kennedy reached Elder, the mission commander had gotten himself up into a sitting position. The searing, deafening pain that had all but crippled him had eased. His vision and hearing were returning but he was nauseated, dizzy, and panting.

Kennedy crouched by his partner. *You okay? What happened?*

Elder gestured dully behind Kennedy. Like I was plugged into something, like grabbing a live wire, Jim.

But not in the shocking way you'd expect. More like waves of... stuff... going through you, shaking you all up, deep, like in your cells, like...

Elder could not go on; he just shook his head in bewilderment. For a moment, Kennedy gaped at his partner, normally such a strong, even-keeled man. Then again, he himself had seen something from down the slope; it had appeared in his field of vision for a fraction of an instant, but that flashed image had been retained; it looked for all the world like heavily filtered photographs Kennedy had seen of solar eclipses—a dense mass surrounded by a shimmering corona of light.

Now Kennedy followed the line of Elder's gesture to a rock behind his left foot. He picked it up, turned it over, and examined it, a gray stone seemingly no different in appearance from any of the ten thousand others strewn about them.

This?

Yeah. I think I... I don't know.

Jim... Howard? Do you copy, over? The radio link with Houston had returned.

Houston, Kennedy began, *we have a prob—*

Elder reached out and put his hand on Kennedy's arm, stopping him from finishing his sentence. Their eyes met through their visors in silent understanding. They'd been exposed to something. Kennedy had caught a glimpse of it. Elder had been all but overwhelmed by it. But the event was not ongoing and that was the problem.

NASA had cut short several space walks during the earlier Gemini missions because astronauts floating in the void had exhibited symptoms similar to those of anoxia, what deep-sea divers call "the rapture of the deep": disorientation, a feeling of detached well-being, hallucinations. Without evidence to support what they'd seen, the boys back in Houston might cut short their stay on the moon. Both men had spent their entire adult lives preparing for this single endeavor. They did not want to be accused of bugging out.

Come back? the mission commander called.

Jim's feeling a little out of sorts, Kennedy said.

Jim? What's going on?

I'm all right, Elder insisted, forcing himself to his feet. *Just got a little… queasy there for a second.*

There was a long pause, during which both astronauts stared down at moon rock 66095 in Kennedy's glove.

Well, that was one heck of a solar gust that just blew through up there. The docs down here say you could have gotten hit with some radiation, or the rapid change in light could have triggered the nausea.

Elder hesitated. Kennedy nodded. *Rapid change in light,* Elder said. *Must be it.*

We're going to want to run a fall check on you when you get back to the module.

Roger, Elder said. *But I'm good to go now.*

You're sure?

Elder took one last long look at moon rock 66095 before holding out his collection bag to Kennedy. He had already photographed and given the rock a number. The stone had to return to Earth or they would face intense questioning about its absence. Kennedy nodded, then dropped the rock into the bag.

Positive, Houston, Elder said. *Absolutely positive.*

Three months after his return to earth, however, James Elder's behavior turned erratic. He sank into depression, suffered bouts of insomnia, and began to drink. One night he tried to break into the Lunar Sample Laboratory, where all rocks brought back from the moon are kept. He was drunk and belligerent and told NASA security officials that he alone had the right to possess the moon rocks he'd brought back from the Descartes Highlands. In response to the incident, NASA quietly placed Elder on administrative leave and demanded he seek psychiatric help if he wished to rejoin the space agency. He admitted in therapy that he was obsessed by the moon rocks he'd brought back to Earth and that he was haunted by nightmares that all took place on the dark side of the moon. A psychiatrist put Elder on antidepressants and then antipsychotic drugs, but they did not help. In early 1974, despondent and suffering from delusions, Elder committed suicide. An autopsy showed an inexplicable concentration of heavy metals in the cortex of the astronaut's brain.

THIRTY TWO YEARS LATER . . .

JANUARY 12, 2004
1:32 A.M.
UNIVERSITY OF TENNESSEE

The branches of an old, gnarled oak clacked against the clapboards of the small bungalow a mile south of campus. Inside, a world-famous physicist, Carson MacPherson, tossed and turned, unable to sleep. He was approaching fifty and worried constantly about his place in scientific history, more so that night because he had just returned early from a symposium in Geneva, where his most recent research paper had been greeted with a decided yawn.

The wind gusted and the slapping of the branches against the house became intolerable. In frustration MacPherson flipped on the light and got out of bed. A tall man, he had the gaunt build of a mountain climber, one of those who approaches life as a pinnacle to be conquered at all costs. His admirers and detractors alike described him as an imperious workaholic, an egocentric dictator of boundless ambition and drive. Two wives had left him because of these traits. He lived alone now and rather liked it that way. Wives, he had found, just got in the way of work

MacPherson thought about pouring himself a snifter of Courvoisier in hopes the liquor might calm the chatter in his head, but decided instead to take a run. Exercise always seemed to calm him when nothing else would.

The physicist padded over to his closet and pulled on a pair of tights, a turtleneck top, gloves, a windbreaker, and a knit cap. He went into the kitchen, got his keys, went out the front door, down the steps, and onto the sidewalk.

The night was cold, blustery, nearly moonless. Within minutes MacPherson had worked up a sweat and opened up his stride, increasing his pace. He turned onto the university grounds, where most students were still away on Christmas holiday. The campus was virtually empty at that time of night.

He passed the darkened student union, then ran on into the shadows cast by the streetlights and the giant football stadium that dominated the center of campus. MacPherson powered his way up a rise past the Gothic façade of the physics hall and skidded to a halt across the street from the annex building.

A weird, metallic wavering light shone from a window on the third floor. The annex's second and third floor housed the Center for Applied Materials Research, a prestigious facility that MacPherson himself had cofounded and codirected the past nine years, a lab that had become increasingly important as the United States tried to reduce its reliance on foreign energy sources. MacPherson's laboratory was one of many now engaged in the frantic search for superconductors, materials that would allow electricity to flow more efficiently and thus help alleviate that dependence.

MacPherson frowned at the odd light emanating from deep within the main laboratory. He'd never seen anything like it before and a pulse of fear passed through him. Then he found himself wondering what or who had produced such a light and he began jogging, then running, toward the annex, as if he were an ancient Greek sailor attracted by sirens. His mind raced with thoughts as he used his key to open the front door. A few of his colleagues and postgraduate assistants kept strange hours, but, ironically, due to recent budgetary restraints, he'd been forced to order them all out on leave until the following Monday morning.

The physicist entered the dark foyer, ascended three flights of stairs, then turned right down a dimly lit hallway. At the far end, MacPherson unlocked the door to his office and became aware of a vibrating hum echoing from within the main facility. He eased toward the bank of windows that overlooked the lab, a cavernous place strewn with benches, computers, and massive electrical sensors. At one of the benches, with his back to MacPherson, worked a figure of medium height and flabby build, wearing a welder's hood and smock jeans, a red flannel shirt, and work boots. The hooded figure blocked MacPherson's view of the source of the strangely beautiful quivering light that made the whole lab look like a photograph developed in silvertone.

Then the physicist's focus jumped to a bank of computer sensors and data recorders laid out on the bench to the hooded figure's left and right and he was seized with righteous anger. "What the fuck!" MacPherson fumed. He had been using the equipment himself on a promising experiment before his trip to Switzerland.

The physicist wrenched open the door to the laboratory and stomped down the metal staircase. As he crossed the cement floor, the hum that filled the room became a more insistent buzzing and the light surrounding the hooded figure was amplified. MacPherson threw up his arm to shield his eyes and stumbled into a trash can.

The figure at the bench spun around, froze, then slowly lifted the glass-faced hood to reveal a wild shock of dark brown hair above the chubby, acne-scarred features of a man in his late twenties. His cheeks were flushed red with excitement His eyes, however, were distrustful, wary, like those of a dog facing a man who's whipped him before.

"Gregor!" MacPherson bellowed.

"D-Doctor," the young man said. "You're supposed to be in Gen-Geneva."

"Dr. Swain and I gave strict orders that no work be done over the break!" MacPherson roared.

"We're on a tight leash financially. We can't afford to be burning this kind of energy!"

"Yes, uh, yes, sir, I remember you saying that," Gregor said, rubbing his hands together in a washing gesture, his brows tightly knitted. "And you know, I meant to, but m-my work was going so well I couldn't tear myself away and—"

The young research assistant hesitated. MacPherson had turned his attention to the digital readings coursing across the computer screens and a flicker of puzzlement passed across his face.

"Something wrong sir?" Gregor said.

MacPherson thrust his hand toward the screens. "You took these sensors from my experiment without my permission and now you've screwed up the calibrations. Dr. Swain and I had them set perfectly before I left. Look what you've done, you blithering idiot!"

Gregor shook his head. "They're ca-calibrated correctly. I've checked. About one hundred times."

"Impossible!" MacPherson snapped. "Those readings defy—"

The physicist stopped in midsentence. The buzzing noise had ebbed to a hum and the quivering light emanating from behind Gregor had lost much of its force.

"Stand aside," MacPherson said.

At that, Gregor looked like he might throw up. "Please, don't be angry, I—"

"Away from that bench. Now."

Gregor hesitated, then shuffled to his left, staring down at the floor.

MacPherson's jaw dropped. "My god!"

Moon rock 66095 sat atop a Plexiglas pedestal inside a cubicle of glass attached by clamp and hose to a tank of supercooled liquid hydrogen. The glass was completely surrounded by a matrix of thin electrical cables. The surface of the rock crackled with energy. Thin, tremulous fingers of electrical fire whipsawed off the surface of the rock like flare-ups of heated chrome.

"S-sorry," Gregor said in a pleading tone. "I know you forbid me to request a lunar sample from Houston. But as you can see, it—"

The physicist cut him off with a sharp dismissive gesture as his attention jumped from the rock to the numbers flashing across the screen and back again. "You're sure these sensors are working correctly?"

"Yes, sir."

"What's the temperature inside the case?"

"Fifty-six degrees above Fa-Fahrenheit."

MacPherson reacted as if a mule had kicked him in the gut. "Fifty above?"

A triumphant smile appeared on Gregor's doughy face and he began making petting gestures in the direction of the rock. "That's what I was trying to tell you, sir. But it's more than that, it seems to amplify—"

"Who else knows? Dr. Swain? His nephew? Any of the other assistants?"

Gregor shook his head. "Just me, sir."

MacPherson tapped one finger to his lip, his eyes continuing to dart between the source of the light and the sensors. As he did so, his expression changed by degrees from one of awe to something more self-centered. Dr. Swain, the co-director of the laboratory, had no idea of what had occurred here. Neither did the other research assistants. Just this fool, Gregor. "How did you get the sample?" he demanded.

Gregor blinked, swallowed, and looked at the floor.

"Answer me. The truth."

Gregor's lower lip trembled. "F-forged your signature."

The physicist was quiet for a moment, then he said softly, "My signature? You mean *my name* was on the official request to the repository?"

Gregor nodded and cowered as if he expected MacPherson to explode. Instead, his boss leaned back and chuckled as if he could not believe his good fortune. "They're going to give me the Nobel for this!" he said. "The goddamned Nobel Prize! At last!"

Gregor's eyebrows knitted again. He began to blink fast and hard.

Caught up in the sweep of the moment, MacPherson seemed not to notice. "Shut it down, Gregor. I want to do a complete review of the data, energy in, energy out, the protocol followed. Everything transferred to my computer. My office. Ten minutes."

He made as if to leave. Gregor balled his hands into fists. "No!"

MacPherson stopped and stared at him. "No what?"

"You had nothing to do with this, sir," Gregor said. "It's m-my discovery."

There was a moment's hesitation on MacPherson's part, then his facial muscles hardened. "In the world of high science, Gregor, he who runs the lab gets the credit. That's the way it works. You work on my team, not Swain's. This is mine now. You'll be listed as part of the team."

Gregor's shoulders began to tremble. "Not this time. You told me the idea of testing a moon rock for superconductivity was foolish. Called me an idiot in front of the entire lab. Everyone heard you. I d-did this on my own."

The physicist hesitated again, his eyes flickering past Gregor to the stone. "But I changed my mind, didn't I? You said it yourself: My name and my signature are on the formal request to Houston. The paper trail you so cleverly devised will clearly show where the credit is due. Now if you want to continue to work in *my* laboratory, Mr. Gregor, you'll cut off the energy flow to that rock, shut the sensors down, and get that data transferred to my computer. And you'll do it now."

MacPherson turned and made his way across the laboratory floor.

Gregor's jaw quivered as he watched MacPherson go. Tears welled in the young research assistant's eyes. Then his posture dissolved toward defeat and he turned to the stone. The corona was thickening now, obscuring the dark mass of the center. The little flares of energy erupting off the surface behaved like a play of lightning in a late-summer sky.

Gregor could not help himself. He peered fondly at the numbers spitting across the sensor's screen, then back at the stone. Within the electrical storm a single twisting line of energy reshaped itself into a backward S. The shape burst silently and the resultant energy fountained, bathing the young physicist's face in silver light. He beamed.

"You're not what he thinks," Gregor said to the stone as if it were a living thing. "You're more."

For several moments Gregor was frozen, then his neck and shoulder muscles began to shorten, to bunch up, turning bullish and giving the irrefutable impression of pressurized forces about to coalesce and erupt. His nostrils flared and the veins at his temples writhed like worms after a rain. "I'm more than what he thinks," Gregor said.

"Shut it down. Now!" MacPherson bellowed from the top of the staircase.

The research assistant looked over his shoulder and up at his boss from under hooded brows. Then he turned and typed a series of instructions on the computer keypad on the lab table before him. Immediately the energy levels in the matrix of wires around the stone fell, the humming slowed, and in moments the rock turned inert.

Behind him, he heard MacPherson cry, "They won't be ignoring Carson MacPherson in Geneva next December!" Then he heard the door to his boss's office open and slam shut.

Gregor let his attention travel down over the banks of electrical equipment that surrounded him to the cement floor and a piece of thin cable lying there. He stared at it for the longest time. Then he stooped, picked up the length of cable, and wrapped his hands in either end. He slowly marched across the lab floor to the staircase and climbed it.

MacPherson sat before his computer, watching it boot up. Gregor slipped inside, then eased the door shut with a click. Before the older scientist knew what was happening, his research assistant had the cable over his head and cinched tight about his larynx.

"Can't let you do this, Doctor," Gregor snarled without a trace of his lifelong stammer. "I'm the only one who understands that rock's potential. The only one."

Entrance

JUNE 13, 2007
11:30 P.M.
14 VALLEY LANE
TARRINGTON, KENTUCKY

Whitney burke moaned, twitched, and trembled in her sleep. In her nightmare, *muddy water swirled and rose, flooding more of the cave in which she was trapped. She pressed herself back against the underground wall, trying to get away from the water, but it kept surging toward the ledge where she'd taken refuge. There was only two feet of airspace left in the little cavern.*

In the brilliant beam of light given off by the headlamp attached to her helmet, she saw a sudden bubbling in the eddying copper current, as if a large obstruction somewhere downstream had dislodged. The water came up four quick inches. Then up breached the body, facedown, bobbing.

Whitney groaned as the corpse bumped against her boots. She began to shake so hard she felt her purchase on the cave ledge weaken. She slid and plunged into the chill water next to the body. Her light flared, then dimmed. She clawed at the rock overhead, trying to get back up on the outcropping, trying to get away from the body. The body bobbed against her, then rolled over.

The drowned figure was her husband, Tom.

Whitney bolted upright in her bed, perspiration soaking her nightgown. Her strawberry blond hair was matted across her tortured face. She kicked and tore herself free of the covers, then rolled off the mattress and stumbled toward the window, throwing it wide open and gulping at the spiced air of Kentucky in late spring.

She focused on the shadows the moon tossed across the lawn as a way to still the panic attack that had every inch of her shaking. But despite her every effort, Whitney saw the image from her nightmare again: her husband turned around and around in the waters of Terror Hole Cave, cinnamon liquid pouring out the side of his mouth, his eyes as pupilless as those of a blind cave crayfish.

She felt a hand on her shoulder, spun, and screamed, "No! Don't!"

Tom Burke pulled his hand away as if he had touched a live wire. Whitney's husband was forty but looked thirty, with short black hair prematurely shot through with streaks of silver. His blue eyes were flecked with bits of charcoal gray. He wore faded red gym shorts and a yellow T-shirt that advertised Petzl climbing helmets. Every bone, muscle, and sinew in Tom's body looked like it could have been struck from granite. Right at that moment, his face was a carving of fatigue and anger. "Can't even stand to have me touch you anymore, Whit," he murmured.

Whitney's mouth moved, but no sound came out. She kept seeing her husband spinning in the cave water.

The door to the bedroom opened behind them. "Mom? Dad?" The voice was that of a teenaged girl, tired and anxious. "What's going on?"

Whitney's attention jumped to her daughter, standing in the doorway in the ratty blue nightgown she always wore to bed. Like Whitney, the young teenager was pretty, athletic, and freckle-faced, with vivid emerald eyes, naturally crimson lips, a bit too much nose, a narrow, dimpled chin, and a funny left ear that folded over at the top. Whitney felt herself about to break down, but clamped a lid on the emotion. You don't have to go back in the cave anymore, she told herself. She took a deep breath, glanced at her husband's stony face, and said, "We're all right. Go back to bed, Cricket."

"What? The nightmare again?" Cricket said in a defensive, exasperated tone. "Can't you just get over this, Mom? It's been more than a year!"

"What do you know about it!" Whitney cried, looking at her daughter and then her husband. "What do either of you know about any of it?"

"Calm down, Whit," Tom growled. "She's just frustrated. We both are."

"Well, isn't that wonderful," Whitney replied. "I'm the one who's living in hell! But you two are frustrated."

At that, Cricket burst into tears. "I don't even know who you are anymore, Mom." She turned and ran from the room.

"Now look what you've done!" Tom bellowed.

"Me?" Whitney screamed. "I'm not the one taking her into Labyrinth Cave, Tom. You'd think you'd be more sensitive to my situation."

"That's all I've been for thirteen goddamned months," he said. "Sensitive to the point of numbness. Life goes on, Whitney. Our life goes on even if you don't want to be a part of it."

"You're using her," Whitney shot back. "NASA's using her. Have you for one second thought about what might happen to her down in that fucking cave? Has NASA? Or do you even dare to question them? They all but run your life these days, Tom."

"Cricket's an expert," Tom replied. "I'm an expert. So are you, in case you've forgotten. Accidents happen to people who give the cave a chance. We Burkes don't. NASA knows that."

Whitney shook her head violently. "I didn't give the cave a chance, Tom. It came after me. It could come after you, too! Or Cricket. Or anybody on your team. Leave her here with me."

Tom stood there, flexing his hands to fists, then he shook his head. "Cricket's going in for just six hours. It's scheduled, and after everything she's been through the past year, she deserves to go. She deserves the recognition."

"After everything she's been through! How dare you!"

"Cricket will be in and out in six hours," he replied firmly. "Six hours."

They were silent for almost a minute, staring at each other across the abyss. Then Tom held his palms out to her and said in a softer voice, "You know you could still be a part of it, Whit. The most important cave expedition in history. Everything we ever dreamed about. Maybe if you at least came to the site, maybe—"

"No. Never. Haven't you figured that out yet, Tom? That part of my life is over. It's dead and gone. I'll never go in a cave again. Ever."

He stared at her for a long moment, tears welling up in his eyes. "Then where does that leave us?"

Whitney stared back at her husband, seeing in her mind the vision of his body swirling in the cave, and fought at the choking sensation in her throat. "I don't know, Tom. I just don't know."

JUNE 14, 2007
4:25 A.M.
NEAR RAWLINS, KENTUCKY

Five hours later and a hundred miles to the north, the full moon loomed huge in the western sky, casting an ashy glow over the interstate. Tom Burke had the radio in his red Ford F-150 tuned to an all-news station, where a reporter was finishing up a story about the continuing national efforts to create an autonomous source of energy for America to supplant the need for Middle East oil in the wake of September 11, 2001.

Ordinarily when driving long distances Tom preferred music, reggae in particular. The deep throbbing bass notes always put him in mind of the place in Jamaica where he and Whitney had spent their honeymoon. But lately he could not bring himself to listen to anything with a lazy Caribbean beat; such music reminded him too much of the way his life used to be. Before the accident.

He flipped on the blinker and eased by a tractor trailer. Cricket sat beside him, her head against the window, her arms crossed, a look of complete boredom on her face. The news story ended, followed by a brief riff of jazz, then a female announcer came on. "Can a perilous cave expedition provide a resolution to the current national debate over whether to return to the moon? NASA seems to think so. Shortly after dawn tomorrow morning, the space agency will launch its first efforts toward returning astronauts to the Descartes Highlands of the moon in search of rare superconducting ores scientists believe hold the future to our energy needs.

"Tom Burke, widely regarded as the world's greatest caver, will lead the experiment, a never-before-tried traverse of the giant Labyrinth Cave system in east-central Kentucky," the anchorwoman continued. "Burke and his team will attempt to negotiate more than one hundred twenty-five miles of dangerous underground passage in less than five days. NASA scientists will closely monitor the trial, hoping to glean valuable data to be used to design training programs for the future lunar miners.

"In other news..."

Cricket shot upright. "Did you hear that?"

Tom turned to her and grinned. "Told you this was big stuff."

"You sure I can't go the whole way with you?" Cricket pleaded.

"Nope."

"Dad," she said sullenly. "I'm as good as any of those people NASA chose."

"The best young caver I know," he replied. "But we're going end to end in the Labyrinth, sweetheart. Toughest underground trip I've ever heard of."

Cricket got up on her knees on the bench seat and batted at a wayward lock of strawberry blond hair dangling in front of her eyes. "How much you want to bet I'd make it out the other side?"

Tom snorted. "I don't bet against fourteen-year-olds who take third in the four hundred at the state track meet. But being an ace quarter-miler doesn't mean you're going. When NASA asked me to run the Artemis Program, they were looking for data on how *adults* would deal with a rocky environment in total darkness, how *adults* would deal with moon mining. Not *children*."

Cricket threw her hands on her hips and shot Tom a look of incensed disbelief. "I'm not a child! I'm a young woman."

"Technically, no," Tom said.

Cricket turned crimson, then sputtered, "Jesus, Dad, real nice thing to say."

Tom winced, knowing he'd gone too far. His daughter was very sensitive about the whole thing. She was fourteen and had not yet had her period. The doctors said her obsessive running may have delayed the onset of her menstruation. The stress the family was under couldn't be helping things either.

"Sorry, Cricket," Tom said. "I was out of line."

"No one takes me seriously, not even you," Cricket brooded. "Everything—"

"Everything what?"

"It's all just so screwed up. Mom. Me. Everything!"

Before Tom could respond, she turned her back on him, chewing on the inside of her cheek and looking out the window.

Tom sighed at the unfathomable enigma of surging adolescent hormones amid a family in crisis. He knew she was hurting. They were both hurting at the loss of Whitney in their day-to-day life. But he'd been over this ground so many times that he was just sick of it. His mind longed for other things to dwell on than the miserable state of his family, and, geologist that he was, he turned his attention to the physical world.

They had been driving nearly an hour from their home near the Tennessee border. A vast plain on the eastern side of the two-lane highway stretched toward nine distant ridges, barely visible even in the strong moonlight. The plain was laid out in pastures and agricultural fields, but here and there trees grew in clusters around circular depressions called sinkholes that were filled with jumbles of logs, branches, and other debris. Somewhere out there, Tom knew, a brook sinewed across a soft green meadow before disappearing into a deep sinkhole.

Where water goes underground, where sinkholes form on plains, there are always caves. And caves had been a constant part of Tom's life since birth. His father had been one of the original Flint Ridge cavers, a group of intrepid explorers who discovered much of what was then the longest known cave in the world, the Mammoth Cave system—a 346-mile maze of underground passages north of Bowling Green, Kentucky.

As a boy Tom had accompanied his father on hundreds of cave trips. His dad had shown him that caves were grand adventure, intrigue, and mystery all rolled into one; you had to be an accomplished mountain climber, a risk taker, and a detective to survive, explore, and understand them. "There's no greater satisfaction in life than discovery, being an explorer," his father had always preached. "In a cave, that can happen at every turn."

With that kind of upbringing it was no surprise to anyone that after finishing his doctorate in geology at Emory University, Tom set out to find his own cave.

The Mammoth system lay underneath the western slope of what geologists call the Cincinnati Arch, a fossilized, layered pastry of stone put down hundreds of thousands of years ago by a vast sea called the Mississippian. Back in 1999, Tom had been a newly appointed assistant professor at the School of Cave and Karst Studies at Western Kentucky University. As part of his research, he had decided to look for a new cave in the limestone formations to the north and east of Mammoth.

That portion of the Cincinnati Arch had a lot of sandstone in it, which made most cavers discount the area as far as full-scale exploration was concerned. But using satellite imagery as well as old mining-drill logs, Tom had pinpointed a remote series of nine ridges north of Irvine and south of the Furnace River where the limestone deposits seemed deeper and purer than anywhere else in Kentucky.

Every weekend for nearly seven months, Tom, Whitney, and then six-year-old Cricket had walked the ridges and dry streambeds near the Furnace River, searching for cave entrances. They found several small grottoes with leads of hundreds of feet, but ultimately no going cave. Every weekend for seven months they had returned home disappointed and sore. When they told other cavers about their study area, most had just laughed and said everyone knew there weren't any caves near the Furnace.

But on Labor Day, 2000, Tom had decided they should search once again on the north end of the first ridge. They'd been there before, several times in fact, but never found any indication of an underground passage. After many hours of tramping through the brush, Cricket had announced she was too tired to go on.

She sat in the sun on a pile of loose rocks. Grasshoppers buzzed and whirred in the heat. And then Cricket had felt cool, almost cold air puffing at her ankles.

"Daddy!" she'd screamed. "Mommy! The ground's blowing!"

There is only one explanation for the ground blowing air—a cave. What lay under Cricket's rock pile was the first-known entrance to a subterranean environment so vast and complex that Tom christened it the Labyrinth. It became Tom's obsession to explore the find. Relying on mapping technology of his own design, Tom, Whitney, Cricket, and a group of twenty hard-core cave explorers had discovered and charted nearly 180 miles of underground passage within two years.

Within five years, they had expanded the working knowledge of the cave another two hundred miles. The Labyrinth was now the world's longest known cave. In a cover article for *National Geographic* published in August 2004, Tom wrote that he did not believe he had explored the entire system and he speculated that the cave Cricket discovered might someday prove to be a thousand miles of total passage.

Through the windshield of his truck, Tom could now clearly make out the silhouette of the Labyrinth's nine rounded ridges. Each of them jutted nearly a thousand vertical feet above the sinkhole plain.

Forest-clad and articulated along a sweeping curve, Tom thought that the layout of the ridges resembled the crinkled folds of an antique paper fan separated from its handle. Seeing them he felt as if he were coming home to the place where he had always felt most centered.

That thought was followed by one that sobered him. For years he'd always come to the Labyrinth with Whitney. Now she would not even go near a cave. His face screwed up at the melancholy and exasperation that welled within him. She'd always been there for him, through all the tough years. Now they were separated by a single horrible incident that Whitney seemed unable to overcome. He knew he should not feel this way, considering all the sacrifices she'd made for him over the years, but here, at the moment of his greatest triumph, he felt abandoned and angry at her for leaving him.

Focus, compartmentalize, Tom told himself. You've got a job to do. A job that's vital to the nation's future. That thought sent chills through him. He thought of himself first and foremost as a scientist The Artemis Project was not only clearly to the benefit of the nation but to the benefit of mankind. He was part of a team working to solve the world's energy needs. To tell the truth, he was more excited than he'd been at the first discovery of Labyrinth Cave. He was doing something that really mattered. His worries over his fractured relationship with Whitney would have to be set aside for the time being.

Tom turned onto a gravel road that coursed along the southern base of the Labyrinth's nine hogbacks. At the easternmost ridge, he made a left turn onto an even narrower byway that climbed through a series of switchback turns. At the crest of the ridge, he angled the truck onto a dirt two-track and immediately stopped at a gate manned by U.S. Air Force Military Police. A metal sign on the gate read: NASA CLOSED AREA: NO ENTRY WITHOUT AUTHORIZATION.

A burly MP approached their truck with a powerful flashlight, which he shone inside. Then he asked for and examined their identification. "You'll have tent six, Dr. Burke. Directly behind Pavilion A, adjacent to the quarters of the mission commander."

"I'll find it," Tom said. "Has the rest of my team arrived?"

"Last one, a woman from France, came in just before midnight, sir," the guard said, before studying his clipboard. "We have three Burkes on our security list."

Tom stiffened. "My wife isn't coming. She isn't feeling well."

"Sorry to hear that, sir," the guard said offhandedly before signaling the gate man. The metal bar rose. They drove through and onto a darkened lane protected by a thick canopy of oak trees. At the end of the two-track, they emerged into a clearing.

"Old man Jenkins must be rolling over in his grave," Cricket said petulantly.

When the Burkes had first seen the clearing nearly nine years ago it had been part of an old farmstead. A sagging barn. Goats, pigs, and chickens in wire enclosures set about a ramshackle farmhouse. A swaybacked horse named Fred had inhabited the meadow beyond. It was the empire of a hermit named Roswell Jenkins.

After much cajoling, the old man had given the Burkes permission to camp on his property while they explored the cave. The cantankerous septuagenarian normally hated visitors, but he came to look forward to their arrival late on Friday nights. Inevitably the Burkes and Jenkins had become close, but the family had been stunned when the old man died and left them his land in support of Tom's dream of turning the Labyrinth and its nine ridges into a national park

Now the entire farmyard was lit by banks of halogen lights powered by a half-dozen generators. Five television transmission trucks were parked around the huge old elm that shaded the farmhouse. A stage was under construction in what used to be the paddock. A series of large canvas tents of the sort used for outdoor weddings stood on the other side of the farmhouse. The waterproof tent flaps were tied open to reveal mosquito netting through which could be seen row after row of long tables upon which sat dozens of computers. Behind the larger pavilions stood a dozen smaller tents, quarters for the NASA support personnel. Despite the early hour, the place bustled with activity.

They parked and were climbing out of the truck when Andy Swearingen, a sandy-blond-haired man in his early twenties, wearing khaki shorts, hiking boots, and a sweatshirt that read ARTEMIS CAVE PROJECT, trotted out to meet them.

"You're late, boss," Andy called. "Hey, Cricket."

Tom saw Cricket's entire physical attitude change. During the entire drive north she'd been sulking and dismal. Now she blushed and smiled at Andy. Tom felt a twinge of anxiety pulse through him because it dawned on him for the first time that his daughter might have a crush on his assistant and it bothered him. His little girl *was* becoming a young lady. It would not be long now before she began the process of separation. His family was fragmenting, on the point of disintegration.

"How's it coming?" Tom managed to say.

"Everything's right on schedule, but your schedule keeps growing. NASA booked you on the *Today* show tomorrow morning. Helen Greidel herself is flying in to do interviews."

Cricket turned and looked at her father with astonishment. "Dad, that's wild! You're gonna be on national television!"

"You too, Cricket," Andy added.

"What?" Cricket cried.

"Greidel's producers asked that Ms. Alexandra Burke also be available."

"Me?" Cricket said. "On the *Today* show? Oh, I don't know about that."

Andy leaned over and gave her a big kiss on the cheek. "You're gonna do great."

Cricket's skin turned red with embarrassment and confusion. "I don't know if I want to do this, Dad."

Tom sighed. "We need you, Cricket. It's for the good of the project. It's good for me, too, okay?"

Cricket stared at her father for a long moment, then nodded. "Okay, Dad. But only for you."

5:15 A.M.
EDDYVILLE PENITENTIARY

Three hundred and ten miles to the west, the full moon still loomed high in the sky, even as the sun began to rise over Lake Barkley and the long four-story front of the state penitentiary at Eddyville, Kentucky.

More than 150 years before, convicts under the direction of Italian stonemasons erected the prison atop a peninsula that jutted out into the deep waters of the lake. With its limestone ramparts, the battlement treatment along the prison's roofline, and its six hexagonal gun turrets, the rugged façade suggested not so much a penal institution as a medieval fortress. Indeed, prisoners doing time at Eddyville still referred to the Gothic structure by its nineteenth-century nickname—The Castle.

At that moment, deep within The Castle, a guard stepped into the grid of shadow and light cast by the steel bars of a cage painted a warning red. Lieutenant William "Billy" Lyons stood there for a moment, swigging coffee, his face screwed up in concentration.

"Coming in, Andrews," he called out.

"Coming in, Lieutenant."

A steel sally door clanged open before him and Lyons stepped through. He was thirty-six, a dark-skinned black man. Six feet tall, 180 pounds with a weight-lifter's chest, powerful hands, and a boxer's broken nose, features made all the more imposing by a pair of intelligent, wary eyes.

Inside the cage, three other guards sat on metal chairs around a Formica-topped table, reading the previous day's edition of the *Louisville Courier-Journal.* The headline read: CONGRESS FUNDS RETURN TO MOON. A fourth guard stood next to an open metal box attached to the far wall of the cage. Rows of green lights glowed inside the box. Old-fashioned keyholes occupied positions below each light.

The Kentucky penal system is tiered according to the types of criminals and the levels of security they require. The most hardened convicts are sent to Eddyville. Within The Castle itself is a similar tiered system of security units. Lyons looked beyond the guards, out through the back bars of the cage, into the segregation unit home for the worst in the state. The hall, at this early hour, was silent.

"Kind of an odd hour for a visit Lieutenant," said one of the guards, an older man named Keith Wilcox.

Lyons rubbed his chin and looked away before replying, "We got positive tuberculosis readings. Segregation, lower unit."

"All of them?" Wilcox said, one eyebrow raised.

"You know the rules," Lyons said. "If one has it, they all go to Louisville."

"Don't tell me we're the transfer team," Wilcox grumbled.

"You are," Lyons said, handing Wilcox a large white canvas bag. Then he turned, hesitated at the chance he was about to take, and nodded to Arnold Jarrett, a beefy guard in his late twenties.

Jarrett threw a switch. The cage's far sally door slid open. Lyons stepped through, sniffing at the stinging scent of industrial cleansers that tainted the air. Wilcox followed. Like Lyons, Wilcox was dressed in navy-blue pants and a matching short-sleeved shirt. The guard was in his late fifties, with rheumy eyes and busted red veins across his nose and cheeks. Both men wore black soft-soled boots and baseball hats embroidered with the emblem of the Kentucky Department of Corrections.

"Who do you want first?" Wilcox asked.

Lyons ran a shaky finger down a list on his hand-held computer. "Kelly," he said. He highlighted Inmate 3309 on the list and pressed Enter.

Edward Kelly, the screen now read. *Convicted 2004, first degree murder, four counts. Sentence: death by electrocution.*

Inside the cage, Jarrett pushed a key into the hole under the first green light on the panel's upper right quadrant. He twisted the key. The green light died. The scarlet lamp beneath turned electric. Out in the segregation unit, the first door rolled back to reveal a cramped cell with a narrow bunk and stainless-steel toilet and sink. There were shelves on the upper wall stocked with dog-eared paperback mystery novels and several on emergency medical techniques. On the bunk lay a swarthy, thick-featured man. Curly brown hair. Wrists and forearms as stout and powerful as bridge cables. Hands huge, with gnarled, meaty fingers. Kelly roused, sat up, looked at the clock on his sink and groused, "What's this shit? It's three fucking hours to inspection."

"Out on the line, Kelly," Lyons said. "You're being transferred."

At that, Kelly came fully awake and snapped his head to the right, revealing slate-colored eyes. "No lie? Test came back pos?"

Lyons swallowed hard. "Everyone on the unit's been exposed. Early-stage TB. Can't risk the chances of you boys infecting the rest of the population."

The big guard grew more confident in his deception. He rocked forward, unclasped his hands, pulled out a billy club, and waved it at Kelly. "You get six weeks' sanitarium time at the hospital prison at Louisville in order to keep our Castle clean. Now out on the line, before I drag you out."

A trace of a grin crossed Kelly's face. The convict rolled off the bunk toward the open cell door, provoking an instant change in Wilcox's level of vigilance. Kelly was of average height and weight, but the way he moved, low and centered, suggested a great ape trolling the jungle. He came out on the line, hooked left, and looked straight ahead.

"Strip, motherfucker," Lyons said.

Kelly climbed out of the yellow scrub bottoms and top and boxer shorts and left them in a heap on the floor. It was the arms Lyons took note of, abnormally long for Kelly's chiseled torso, bulging with weighted gangly power, a grappler's arms. Wilcox snapped on rubber gloves, probed Kelly's mouth and rectal area, then said, "He's clean."

Lyons held out a pair of flip-flops and a bright orange transfer jumpsuit. KENTUCKY DEPARTMENT OF CORRECTIONS, INMATE TRANSFER had been stenciled in large black letters across the back and chest of the coverall. After Kelly put the suit on, Wilcox handcuffed the inmate. Then from the canvas mason's bag the older guard pulled out what looked like the back-support belt weight lifters wear for their workouts—except for the small black box attached to the back of the belt.

"You gotta use that?" Kelly asked as Wilcox strapped the device around his waist.

Lyons waved a black cylindrical device with green buttons and an antenna in Kelly's face. "Not unless you try to run."

"C'mon, Lyons, you know I wouldn't do that," Kelly replied. "If I've told you once, I told you twice, I like it here. Why would I want to leave now?"

Lyons looked away from Kelly's smirk, trying to make his own face a mask of intense concentration.

"You're done," Wilcox said, locking the hasps on the belt. "Stand ahead."

Lyons glanced at his watch, then called to the bearded guard still sitting at the table inside the cage, "Peterson, get in here. We'll take them two at a time."

"Two at a time?" Peterson said. "That's not protocol, Billy."

Lyons hated himself for what he was about to do, but he did it anyway. "I don't give a shit about protocol right now," he retorted. "Do it."

Peterson shrugged and came through the sally door toward Lyons, who said, "Wilcox and I handle the searches. You shackle."

Up and down the unit Lyons saw eyes showing at the windows set in the white cell doors. The entire unit was awake now. Lyons's job had just become more difficult Jarrett twisted the skeleton key twice. Two green bulbs faded. Two scarlet bulbs lit

First out was a man in his early twenties who looked more like he belonged in a *Vanity Fair* advertisement or on a lounge chair by the pool at a country club than in a prison cell. He ran delicate fingers through dirty blond hair and winked at Wilcox.

"I was having a lovely dream," he said. "A blonde. Large breasted and—"

"Shut up and strip," Wilcox said.

Quentin Mann, Lyons's computer read. *Convicted 2005. Serial sexual assault. Sentence: twenty-five years to life.*

"I feels fine," called out a second man in a sleepy voice that was thick and southern. He slunk out of the cell next to Mann's. Rawboned, he sported a tattoo of a burning trident spear at his Adam's apple. *Leonard Pate. Convicted 2002. Arson. Five counts. Sentence: thirty-years.*

"Test says you're sick, Pate," Wilcox replied. "You're sick."

"Yeah, right," Pate drawled. "And next you'll be telling me the moon man's not off his rocker. But, what the hell, old Lenny'll take the change of scenery."

Lyons, meanwhile, had eased up to the window of the last cell on the unit. Inside, by the glare of a single naked bulb, the guard could make out a poster of the moon taped to the far wall. His eyes went left and right, seeking the cell's inhabitant. But there was no one on the bunk or on the toilet or at the sink; and for a moment, Lyons almost panicked.

Then a fist smashed into the bulletproof glass. Lyons jumped back. A man appeared at the window: completely hairless, skin so colorless it seemed waxen, several thick swatches of dingy scar running across his neck and cheeks as if he'd been burned at one time. The rest of his facial skin was leached of color. But his eyes glowed like embers ready to take fire.

"Let me out of here!" he screamed. "You have no right to hold me like this! It's a plot to keep me from what's mine!"

Lyons shivered, then he hit Enter on the computer. *Robert Gregor. Incarcerated 2005. Convicted one count first degree murder. Sentence: life.*

The lieutenant took a deep breath, then barked, "Gregor! Stand back from the door! You're being transferred to the hospital unit. I told you it might be coming."

For a moment, Gregor regarded Lyons with complete and abject hatred. Then he blinked and the incessant twitching at his temples softened. "Transfer?" he said.

Lyons set his teeth and nodded. Gregor stepped back and held up his hands in surrender.

"Let him out," Lyons called to Jarrett

"You don't want to wait for backup?" Jarrett asked anxiously.

"No time," Lyons said.

The white metal door slid open. Gregor weighed barely 135 pounds. Even so, every guard, including Lyons, drew his baton. "Ease out slow, Gregor," Lyons ordered. "Hands where we can see them. You don't want to fuck this up. Not now."

Gregor hesitated, then nodded at the lieutenant, padded out onto the yellow line, and stripped. His skin was so pale it was almost opaque and drawn so tight against his rib cage that to Lyons he appeared to be the victim of some wasting disease. Wilcox searched Gregor, then handed him the orange transfer suit.

"Check his pulse and blood pressure before we put on the belt," Lyons said. "I don't want him stroking out on us before we get to Louisville—where the guy should be anyway. I mean, shit, look at him."

Gregor's jaw stiffened. From the mason's bag, Peterson came up with a stethoscope and blood pressure gauge. He went to attach the cuff below Gregor's left biceps. At his touch, the wan inmate reacted as if he'd been struck with a cattle prod. In one motion, Gregor changed his entire carriage, spun, and rammed his elbow into Peterson's solar plexus. The guard doubled over. Gregor brought his knee straight up into Peterson's face. His nose exploded. Two teeth broke free of his gums. Peterson crumpled to the floor.

"Keep your hands off me," Gregor seethed. "I'm a respected researcher. A scientist. I'm not like you, you fucking hillbilly."

"You stupid shit!" Lyons cried. He hesitated, then chopped his baton down between Gregor's neck and shoulder. The convict buckled to his knees. Lyons raised the baton again.

"Don't do it, Lyons!" Kelly shouted.

The lieutenant glanced at Kelly, then back at Gregor, who was making as if to rise again. There was a split-second's pause on the guard's part, followed by resolve, and he struck Gregor twice more between the shoulder blades. The inmate sprawled next to Peterson.

"Get the doctor!" Lyons roared. "And the strait-jacket!"

Wilcox sprinted for the cage even as Jarrett was picking up the phone. On the floor at Lyons's feet, Gregor was moaning, "I'm a scientist. A respected scientist."

6:45 A.M.
NEAR CENTRAL CITY, KENTUCKY

An hour and a half later and fifty-five miles east of Eddyville, the transfer van sped along the Western Kentucky State Parkway, which was flanked by thick stands of hardwood trees. The moon hung low on the western horizon behind them. Ahead, the sun tried hard to burn off the ground fog that shrouded the hilly landscape. At that hour the parkway was almost empty, and overall the guards and inmates were making good time.

The transfer van itself was a rolling cell block. Keith Wilcox drove. Lieutenant Billy Lyons rode shotgun. Heavy metal screens separated them from the inmates, seated and ankle-chained to bars welded horizontally along the floor.

Wilcox had the radio tuned to US 101, which was featuring a Dwight Yokum retrospective. The guard tapped his boot in time with Yokum's sulky twang. Next to him Lyons put on a pair of thin brown driving gloves, then shifted restlessly in his seat, clearing his throat several times, telling himself he could do this.

Then he turned and stared through the screen at the inmates. On the bench seat directly behind Lyons, Robert Gregor was wrapped in a straitjacket and propped up against the passenger-side window. There was a livid welt along the back of his neck where Lyons's baton had struck him. Gregor's eyes were slightly unfocused. Saliva dripped from the corner of his mouth. Leonard Pate occupied the middle bench seat next to Quentin Mann. Edward Kelly sat in the rearmost seat. He was cracking his knuckles and staring bullets at Lyons.

"You thinking on how hard you hit him?" Kelly asked. "You thinking on what you may have done to us back there?"

The tendons in Lyons's neck stood out like stretched rope. "My thoughts are my own, Kelly," he snarled. "You got that?"

"You done checked his pulse?" Kelly demanded. "How 'bout his blood pressure?"

"He'll be fine," Lyons insisted, twisting around to face the windshield.

Puzzled, Wilcox glanced over at Lyons. "What's with you?" he asked.

"Nothing. Fuckin' Kelly knows just how to get under my skin."

"Lieutenant, you should have developed calluses against guys like Kelly by now. You ain't been—?"

"No," Lyons said, shaking his head. "I'm solid, Keith. Haven't put a bet down in more than a year now."

"You're sure?" Wilcox asked.

"Said I'm cool," Lyons insisted, then he pointed to an empty Styrofoam coffee cup on the dashboard. "Too much of this swill just gets me on edge."

"Try this, then," Wilcox said, tugging a pint of Maker's Mark bourbon from a black gym bag on the seat "Sure to calm the jangled nerves."

Lyons raised his hand against the offer. "Didn't see that, Keith."

"Don't care if you did, Lieutenant, wouldn't care if the warden himself did," Wilcox chuckled. "I'm twenty-five days from retirement. What're you all gonna do, fire me for taking a snort?"

"Look at the moon!" Gregor whispered suddenly. Lyons turned and saw that the pale physicist had pressed his face against the window so he might watch the moon sinking from sight. "It calls to us with its mystery."

"Why don't you shut the fuck up with that fantasy again," Pate groaned.

The mobile radio suddenly crackled in the front of the van. "Eddyville transfer, do you copy? This is Kentucky State Police dispatch five."

Lyons felt sweat trickle from his armpit down his rib cage as he snatched up the microphone. "Eddyville transfer."

"Your position?"

Lyons looked at Wilcox, who said, "Coming on to Central City."

The black guard repeated their location and the dispatcher came back: "We've got a gas tanker turned over and on fire parkway eastbound near the Peabody WMA. A mess. You can wait it out or take sixty-two as a detour."

The lieutenant closed his eyes for a second. This was it, the chance he had been waiting for, the chance to be bold. "Roger that," he said. "But you're saying sixty-two's clear?"

"'Cept for fog, that's a ten-four."

"You copy, Andrews?" Lyons said into the microphone.

The chase vehicle's headlights on the highway behind them flipped on and off. Once again, Lyons found himself turning to look back through the screen at the inmates.

Gregor smiled dreamily at him. "The Descartes Highlands," he whispered. "See them, Lyons? That light gray ridge above the dark plain in the orb's upper hemisphere? That's where they found it."

"Uh-huh," Pate snorted. "One day, Cap'n Kirk and Mr. Spock beamed down to Kentucky from the starship *Enterprise* and found a moon rock, that—"

Kelly crushed one manacled hand against the other. "Leave him alone, Pate, hear?" he said. "Guy's a genius."

"Nutcase, more like it," Pate replied.

Wilcox steered the van onto the Central City exit ramp. In the front seat, Lyons felt his breath go shallow and quick, then he reached into his right pants pocket, feeling for the two steel-wool pads he had placed there before coming to work. Tiny beads of sweat appeared on his dark brow and he yelled back at the inmates, "Not another word! I want silence back there now."

The van soon cleared the fast-food joints and twenty-four-hour stores of Central City's south side and disappeared onto the lonely back road that was state highway 62. As the road climbed they encountered dense fog. A doe and her spotted fawn bounded out from behind a sign that read ENTERING PEABODY WILDLIFE MANAGEMENT AREA Lyons removed his hand from his pocket to gesture out the window to the south where a bright glow showed through the mist.

"Must be that tanker on fire," Lyons said.

Wilcox took another swig of bourbon. "Must be."

A minute passed and now they were traveling through deep forest. The trees were all slick black from fog. They had not seen another car since leaving Central City.

Lyons shifted in his seat. "Hate these damn holsters," he announced. "Pistol butt gets you right on the hipbone every time."

Wilcox's grunt was noncommittal. His eyes never left the road.

Lyons unbuckled the strap that held his .38 caliber pistol in its holster and made a show of sighing with relief. Then he glanced over his shoulder. Gregor was sitting upright, lucid now, staring at him intently. *Do it,* the inmate mouthed silently.

Lyons's eyebrows tightened, then he nodded and turned away. The guard held his breath, looking down at his own hand lying on his thigh. As if by force of will, the hand traveled to his pocket and eased out the two steel-wool pads.

"Gotta take a piss," Lyons said. "Pull over up ahead there."

"Got a full balloon, too," Wilcox said, plying the brakes. "Alert Andrews."

Lyons leaned forward as if going for the radio, but instead he drew his pistol and stuck the muzzle into the steel-wool pads. His face carried a sickened expression of inevitability and doom. "Sorry, Keith," Lyons said. "Nothing personal."

Wilcox frowned at the unexpected statement and looked over just in time to see that Lyons had jammed the barrel of the .38 up against the side of his chest. Silenced by the steel wool and the point-blank target, the gun's report was no more than the rim shot of a snare drum. Wilcox slammed sideways against the driver's door, where he slumped, glazed-eyed. Blood and whiskey drooled from his mouth. The van lurched into the other lane, tires squealing.

Gregor flung back his head and crowed, "Yes!"

Shaking with adrenaline, Lyons grabbed the wheel and steered the vehicle back to the right side of the road. He kicked Wilcox's limp leg out of the way and got his foot on the brake. An alarmed voice came over the prison radio frequency: "Lyons! What's going on up there?"

Lyons dropped the pistol on the seat and grabbed the radio microphone as he wheeled the slowing van onto the shoulder of the road. "Blew… blew a front tire," he said, his voice quivering. He steered the van past the faint beginnings of a logging trail that led off into the forest. He braked to a halt and shoved the transmission into Park. Before any of the inmates could say a word, Lyons was out the door, holding the pistol and stumbling toward the white cruiser that had pulled up behind the van. Jarrett and Andrews climbed out of their vehicle.

"Want some help?" Andrews asked, looking beyond Lyons toward the van.

"Won't be necessary," Lyons said. He put his left hand on the hood of the cruiser for support, then raised his pistol and aimed it shakily at the middle of Jarrett's chest

"Hey!" Jarrett said, taking a step backward, raising his palms.

Lyons pulled the trigger. The beefy guard was punched straight backward and landed on the wet tarmac.

"What the—!" Andrews roared. The second corrections officer had twisted at the shot and was trying to run, get his body down, and unholster his gun all at the same time. Lyons's two shots struck Andrews high in the spine. The guard arched, then dropped and rolled off the road into a ditch. For a long moment, Lyons just stood there, his ears ringing from the pistol reports, staring at the bodies sprawled on the damp ground.

"I'm cut off," he whispered to himself. "There's no turning back now."

"Lyons! We've got to get out of here!" Gregor screamed from the van. That ripped him from the shock of what he'd just done. His consciousness seemed to narrow and he went forward with the plan because it was the only thing he could do now. He hobbled toward Jarrett's body and grabbed the man's pistol. Then he took Jarrett under the armpits and dragged him around the rear of the cruiser, where he rolled him into the ditch next to Andrews.

He climbed down into the ditch and got hold of Andrews's weapon.

Lyons was feeling more confident now. He scrambled back to the van and yanked open the driver's door. Wilcox's body sprawled onto the pavement. He steeled himself, then tugged off Wilcox's gun belt and tossed it onto the front seat

"Let me out of these irons," Pate cried from behind the metal screen.

Lyons ignored him and dragged Wilcox back and dumped him into the ditch. The chase vehicle's engine still idled. Lyons slid into the front seat, working the mechanism to release the riot shotgun from its post even as he peeled rubber back up the road fifty feet before jamming the car into Drive and spinning onto the logging two-track. Mud spat through the air. Pebbles ricocheted off the under-carriage. Out of sight, he killed the engine, jumped out, and sprinted back toward the highway, holding the shotgun at port arms.

As he reached the near side of the van, the headlights of a pickup truck appeared out of the fog from back toward Central City. Lyons froze in the shadows, his heart pounding in his throat. The road was supposed to be empty. That was the plan. The rig slowed and for an instant he thought the driver, a middle-aged woman with a beehive hairdo, had seen the blood in the road. Then she noticed the men sitting inside the van and just went on by.

Lyons waited until he could no longer see the pickup's taillights, then went to the van and opened the side door. "Let me out!" Pate demanded.

"We're going for Gregor's stone," the guard replied. "Everybody agreed that if I could fake the tests, we'd all have to go."

"I didn't agree to jack shit, remember?" Pate said. "I told you before. I don't fucking believe there is a stone. Never was. Never will be. I just want out!"

"What about the rest of you?" Lyons demanded.

"I'm with Gregor," Kelly said. "All the way."

Mann hesitated, then nodded. "Me too. I want that fortune."

Lyons hesitated. Letting Pate run wasn't part of the grand design. But he didn't dare bring him along if he was not a believer, and he didn't want to kill anyone else. He jumped inside the van and unlocked the handcuffs and ankle irons that held Pate to the bench seat. Freed of the shackles, Pate said, "Gimme a gun."

The guard hesitated, then looked down at his pistol three shots spent, and tossed it to the arsonist. Pate stuck it in his waistband, turned, and sprinted for the forest in his orange jumpsuit and flip-flop sandals. Lyons threw the van in gear and spun back out onto the highway. For several moments, all he could do was drive.

"It went perfect," Gregor called from behind him. "Now get us lost, fast."

Lyons shook with sudden fury then looked over his shoulder. "One thing I'm making clear, Gregor—I don't take your orders. You squeezed me into this play. I upheld my end of the bargain. But I don't take your orders. This is a business now and

I'm your partner. So shut the fuck up while I take care of business, partner."

Lyons grabbed the radio. "This is Eddyville Transfer."

"Copy you, Eddyville."

"We'll be back on the parkway in a minute here. Had a flat tire and it's kind of foggy, so the going's slow. I'll check in when we get to the hospital. Figure on at least two more hours until we make contact."

"Roger that."

Lyons slid the microphone back onto its holder, then glanced in the rearview mirror and saw Gregor glowering at him.

"Which way to this stone of yours?" Lyons demanded.

Gregor held the glare for a moment. "Head due east, Lieutenant. Back roads. I'll tell you when to stop."

9:12 A.M.
JENKINS RIDGE LABYRINTH CAVE

Cricket burke threw her duffel bag onto the cot in the canvas tent behind the big Mission Control Pavilion her father had disappeared into moments before with his assistant, Andy Swearingen. She stood there looking all around, feeling very alone.

She felt like that a lot these days—severed from the ties that bound her to childhood. It was unfair, she decided. All of it was unfair. She was only fourteen and everyone seemed to have forgotten her needs, her hopes, her fears. Everything was always about her mother and the accident. Or her dad and the Artemis Project. There had been days in the past few weeks when she swore neither of them knew she was even on the same planet.

And almost every night there was either her mother's recurring nightmare or her parents arguing over the time her dad spent away from the house, working for NASA. This morning had been the worst yet. When she and her father had gotten up early to leave, her mother had refused to come down and see them off. Cricket missed her mom, missed all the time they used to spend together just talking. She felt a hollowness open up in her stomach and wanted to throw herself on the cot and cry herself to sleep. Or grab her things and hitchhike home. But in her mind, home seemed a dark hole in the ground where you might get lost and never find yourself again.

When had that happened? she asked herself. Home had always been such a happy place. Jenkins farm had always been such a happy place. Now it seemed to be just a setting for her dad's next big career move.

A bug fluttered in the air and she caught it. She was surprised. A firefly. During the day?

She smiled sadly at the bug moving across her palm, its antennae waving. She flashed on a memory of herself at seven years old. She had been pestering her parents all week about catching fireflies when they got to Jenkins farm to explore more of Labyrinth Cave. But there were no glowing bugs in the air when they got to the farm around dusk, and Cricket had fallen asleep disappointed.

Several hours later, however, her mom and dad had gently shaken her shoulders. "You've got friends here to see you, sweetheart," Whitney had said.

Yawning, Cricket had gone out into the wet meadow grass in her nightgown. Hundreds of fireflies danced in the night air. She caught dozens in a jar and placed the jar near her pillow. The last thing she remembered that night was her mom and dad smiling down at her, both their faces lit by the glow of fireflies.

"Cricket?" Tom said.

Cricket turned and wiped away the tears streaming down her cheeks. "Yeah?"

"You okay, honey?" Her father came into the tent with his duffel bag of gear.

She hesitated, wanting to tell him what she'd been thinking about, then decided against it. Her dad could be absentminded and self-absorbed, but he was essentially a good person. She knew that. And he was under a tremendous amount of pressure these days. How many men were asked to lead one of the most important experiments in the history of NASA? He did not need to hear the pining of a young girl. Not now.

"I'm fine, Dad," she said, rubbing at her red eyes. "My allergies are just bothering me again."

9:40 A.M.
14 VALLEY LANE
TARRINGTON, KENTUCKY

Two hundred sixty-five miles to the southeast, Whitney paced from the kitchen to the den and back again inside the restored post-and-beam farmhouse where she, Tom, and Cricket lived.

Her bowed head swung to and fro. She plucked strands of terry fabric from the sleeve of her faded turquoise bathrobe and flicked them into space. Dozens of the threads already lay on the pine-plank floor like blaze marks on a well-worn trail between the TV, the computer, and the staircase. The television showed in split screen, one side tuned to the Weather Channel, the other to NBC.

For the eighty-seventh time since her husband and daughter had departed for Labyrinth Cave, Whitney found herself at the bottom of the stairs. She gazed upward, then glanced at a mirror on the wall. Her tangled hair hung in her eyes.

"Looking lovely, Whit," she told her reflection. "And why shouldn't you? You haven't slept well in months. Your daughter's not talking to you. You and your husband haven't made love in…who knows when? Tenure review's coming in September and you haven't written a paper in a year."

She paused on the precipice of a full-blown anxiety attack, then shook her head. "Go upstairs, get showered, and get your butt to the office. Cricket will be home tomorrow night. You'll go out to dinner. Laugh and talk like you used to."

Fortified by those notions, Whitney made a goofy face, stuck her tongue out at her disheveled self in the mirror, pivoted, took a step toward the stairs, then stopped. The computer on the desk caught her attention. She crossed to it and jiggled the mouse. The screen activated to an Internet web page posted by the National Meteorological Service out of Memphis. The Kentucky forecast—largely clear skies with high, thin cloud cover predicted to move in over the next twenty-four hours.

Whitney made one keystroke and the national weather map came up, revealing two cold fronts active in the west: one moving south-southeast out of Idaho, the other gathering momentum over southern Kansas and the panhandle of Texas. As of 11:00 A.M., the weather service was giving no clear indication of either front's anticipated path.

For a moment her mind whirled with possibilities, all of them adverse: If either of those storms came through when Cricket and Tom were in the cave ... She felt herself begin to shake and once again had to talk herself down from the brink of a panic attack. They'll be fine, she told herself. Everything will be fine.

She forced herself away from the computer, trudged through the kitchen to lock the back door, and exhorted herself to go upstairs to shower. She flipped the dead bolt, then crossed back through the kitchen toward the family room and the staircase.

Drip!

Whitney froze at the sound. Her palms turned clammy. *Drip!* She turned, hunting for and fearing her quarry. From the kitchen faucet a bulge of water distended and fell. *Drip!* And a second bulge. *Drip!* And a third and fourth. *Drip! Drip!*

Despite her every effort to remain in control, Whitney's vision distorted, went kaleidoscopic, and she felt herself sucked away into a maze of memory. She saw a ridge rising fifteen hundred feet off a lime jungle of a valley floor, all choked with kudzu, and the nightmare of the accident seized her again.

A muddy river called the Washoo rolled in from the east and disappeared under Ayers Ridge for several miles before popping up on the other side and continuing its torpid course toward the Gulf of Mexico. Ayers Ridge was four miles long, a half mile wide at its base, and occupied the geographical center of a region known as TAG, short for the Tennessee-Alabama-Georgia karst country, an area that contains some of the most formidable pit caves in North America.

High on the side of Ayers Ridge lay a bench cut into the hillside by thousands of years of wind and rain. There, in the dappled early-morning light, the forest gave way to a gaping hole in the ground some twenty-five feet across—a darkened pit, the entrance to another world.

Mist steamed up out of the hole. Mist blackened the oaks that clung to ledges above the entrance. Mist turned the red soil on the pit's mantle as treacherous as watered ice.

Whitney maneuvered her way along the rim with the concentrated agility of a city cat that has crept out an apartment window onto the narrow ledge of the thirtieth floor. She wore a yellow jumpsuit, a red helmet with headlamp, and a waist harness. A pack was slung bandolier-style across her left shoulder and cinched at her hip by a waist belt.

She rocked her ankles into the slope so her boot treads bit the mud, then eased her way out over the exposed tree roots, focused, confident, and yet all too aware of how close she worked to the lip of the hole. It was more than three hundred feet to the bottom. One misstep and Whitney would suffer a four-and-half-second fall and certain death.

She scrambled to a rope lashed to one of the oaks. The line disappeared over the rim. She straddled the rope and began the complicated task of rigging herself to it. She called over her shoulder, "ON ROPE!"

"On rope!" answered a woman from somewhere far below.

Whitney glanced back into the abyss and grinned in anticipation of the adrenaline rush that always accompanied her going over the edge in what cavers call a "pit drop." Then she recited a cautionary principle Tom taught her years ago: Never, ever give the cave a chance. *"On rappel!" Whitney yelled.*

"On rappel!" the woman hollered back."

Whitney had dropped down ropes into scores of such shafts in the past. Still her heart beat faster. But that, she knew, was a *good thing: it meant she understood the consequences of her actions. The experts she had known who died caving became accustomed to the danger, grew dull in their perceptions, and gave the cave a chance.*

Whitney created slack on the rope in order to arch her body backward until it was almost horizontal above the three-hundred-foot pit. Then she squatted, blew all her breath out in a burst, and kicked free. She dropped ten feet before the stiff soles of her leather boots contacted rock again.

Luscious ferns sprouted from the ledges around her. Small white flowers with magenta seeds grew from cracks in the wall. The place smelled like freshly crushed nutmeg. She made a second kick and dropped another ten feet and a third ten feet. She bounced off the wall a fourth time and dropped into the cave's expanse, where the walls become underhung and she could no longer maintain contact with the rock.

Whitney slowed herself to a stop and leaned back, twisting lazily in space. The morning sun angled into the top of the shaft, cutting through the swirling mist, creating clouds of rose-tinted glitter. Her mouth hung agape and she yelled, "God, I love this! Where's my camera when I need it?"

"Down here, where you should be by now!" the woman below answered.

High in the Alabama sky, a small cloud passed into view. Whitney's delighted expression sobered as she inspected it. A powerful spring storm, not uncommon in this part of the south, could flood the lower reaches of the cave. But she had searched the Web on her laptop only moments before leaving her truck. The latest forecast called for blue skies with occasional fair-weather clouds.

Whitney eased the tension on her rappelling rack, a rectangular metal device, the bars of which interlaced with the rope. She began to slide, spinning around and around in long, descending spirals that allowed her a panoramic view of the cave's interior. Narrow, limpid waterfalls plunged fifty feet, splattered off rock outcroppings, then plunged again and again in a series of shimmering cascades. Moss covered much of the pewter-colored rock, which appeared carved by the hand of a genius.

Twelve seconds and one hundred feet down, the sunlight splintered into three shafts that shone weakly against the west wall of the pit. The vegetation dwindled. At a half minute and two hundred feet, Whitney spun down the rope into what cavers call the twilight, and the mist cleared. At three hundred feet, Whitney shivered; the cave air was a constant fifty-six degrees and saturated with moisture. She was twenty feet off the bottom now and her headlamp revealed a brackish brown floor littered with boulders, scree, and moldering logs. In the left wall of the cave was a black six-foot-high slot of an opening.

A young Asian woman stood next to the opening, adjusting the flame of a carbide lamp, the kind miners used to wear. Jeannie Yung was Whitney's research assistant. Jeannie was eight years Whitney's junior, strikingly beautiful, with flawless skin, shiny black hair, and a constant expression of bemusement on her face.

"Fancy meeting you here!" Whitney said as her boots reached the floor.

"Well, it is the best place to meet confirmed troglodytes," Jeannie replied, snapping her helmet in place. And you know I have this thing for slimy blind creatures."

"Think they'll mind us crashing the party?"

"Are you kidding? They'll be thrilled to have a couple of babes like us show up."

Whitney laughed as Jeannie came across the wet stone to help her.

"Great ride, huh?" Jeannie asked.

Whitney leaned back to stare at haw, way, way up in the tube, the mist seemed to create a backlit opaque ceiling separating the world above from the world below.

"Absolutely beautiful," she said, unfastening her rack from the rope, then unhitching her climbing harness. "What moron named this place Terror Hole?"

Jeannie shrugged. "Cavers love melodrama. What do you figure for time inside?"

"Why, you got a hot date?"

Jeannie blushed. "Well, Jim's coming in from Purdue for the weekend. I wanted to be at the Nashville airport by four."

Whitney smiled. Jeannie had been working for her for nearly three years and was just a thesis away from her doctorate in environmental science. Her assistant was as devoted a young scientist as she had ever known, but, in Whitney's opinion, Jeannie paid too little attention to her personal life. A weekend with Jim was a step in the right direction.

"No problem," Whitney said. "I promised Cricket I'd be there for her track meet. We'll be in and out in four hours, tops."

"Great," Jeannie said. "Now what do you say we go crash that crayfish orgy!"

Whitney was still laughing as she turned on her headlamp and entered the black slot in the wall of the pit.

Immediately, her visibility was reduced to a cone of soft light. The cave walls turned slick, close, and mottled gray. Her helmet bumped against the smooth ceiling and she slowed, casting her beam forward into inky darkness. The cave ahead was becoming smaller, tighter, wetter, a place saturated with the threat of claustrophobia.

10:24 A.M.
LOUISVILLE, KENTUCKY

The bedroom phone in the suburban home of Damian Finnerty, the U.S. marshal for eastern Kentucky, jangled.

"No," Finnerty groaned.

At that moment, the marshal and his wife, Natalie, a nurse-anesthesiologist who had just ended her overnight shift at a local hospital, were engaged in a bout of vigorous midmorning love-making, both of them sweating and building toward climax.

"Don't answer it," Natalie pleaded. "God, don't answer it."

The couple had been trying desperately to have children for the past two years. A simple test taken an hour before had shown she was ovulating. She had called her husband at the office and ordered him home.

"I've got to," the marshal moaned, rolling off his wife. "I said only call in an emergency."

He sat up on the edge of the bed, noting how remarkably sexy he found his wife even after seven years of marriage, and snatched up the phone. "This better be good."

"The opposite, I'm afraid," replied Mark Boulter, a Kentucky State Police captain.

Finnerty was a good-looking Irishman, six feet tall with reddish brown hair, fair, freckled skin, and a hard build. Relaxed, he could be an engaging man with a quick wit, an easy social manner, and an appreciation for books. But Finnerty was not relaxed. Not now. He stood up beside the bed, listening intently.

"Around forty-five minutes ago, a woman named Margaret Afton came on duty with Kentucky State Police central dispatch," Boulter went on. "She noticed a Post-it the prior shift worker left on her computer screen. The note said that the Eddyville Penitentiary inmate transfer van was scheduled to arrive at the prison hospital at Louisville at 9:45 A.M. and that the guards had promised to confirm their arrival with the dispatch office.

"When Afton still hadn't heard from the transfer van at quarter past ten, she attempted to raise them on the state police frequency they were supposed to be monitoring, but got no reply. She placed a call to the prison hospital and was informed by the admitting officer that the van had not come in yet. She called Eddyville and was told there had been no contact with the van or the chase vehicle for more than three hours.

"Afton pulled up a computer log that detailed the previous dispatcher's radio transmissions and found a record of the last communication with the van, somewhere east of Central City."

"Get to the point," Finnerty said, ignoring the scowl developing on his wife's pretty face.

"Afton patched herself through to the Central City sheriff's office, which in turn contacted Sheriff

Michael Arnet, who was having breakfast at a truck-stop," Boulter continued. "Afton told Arnet she had no troopers in the area and asked if he would cruise the fifteen-mile stretch of state highway sixty-two that would have served as the natural detour around the flaming tanker truck. Arnet entered the Peabody Wildlife Management Area at 10:24 A.M., crested a ridge, and noticed fresh skid marks leading to dark, pool-like stains near the side of the road. Arnet left his cruiser to inspect the splotches and discovered blood. He followed the blood into a deep ditch and saw the bodies of three guards. Bugs were already swarming."

"Jesus Christ," Finnerty said. "How many are loose?"

"Four inmates," he said. "They've got a guard with them."

"Hostage?"

"We assume so."

Finnerty moved away from his wife, going for his pants. Natalie picked up a pillow, pressed it to her mouth, and screamed in frustration. In the mirror, he saw why. He had that expression on his face, the expression that said he was going hunting.

The marshal had grown up the son of a dentist in a small town outside the Adirondack Park in northern New York State. His father and grandfather were white-tail-deer hunters and they had taught him that to hunt well, you had to think like your quarry.

He was a good student and an excellent athlete, playing lacrosse at Dartmouth. Upon graduation, he accepted a commission with the Marine Corps and served six years, the last two as a military police captain, where he employed the hunting philosophy his father had handed down to him to establish a reputation for tracking down young Marines who'd gone absent without leave. The U.S. Marshals Service have made a specialty of manhunting since the mid-nineteenth century and enthusiastically recruited Finnerty. During stints as deputy U.S. marshal in Kansas City, Dallas, and Baltimore, he further established his reputation as a man who would absolutely not quit when it came to pursuing fugitives.

Now, struggling into his clothes, the telephone smeared against his ear, Finnerty finished listening to a description of the murder scene and brief biographies of the four inmates at large.

"Okay," Finnerty said at last. "I'll meet you at Louisville International in twenty-five minutes. We'll take the chopper. In the meantime I want an all-points bulletin put out for Kentucky, Missouri, Illinois, Indiana, Ohio, Virginia, West Virginia, and Tennessee. These men should be considered armed and dangerous. Treat this guard, Lyons, as a hostage for now. Contact the prison. Have them transmit whatever they can on the inmates. Call Sanchez and Two-Elk. I want complete workups on these guys."

Finnerty hung up the phone and looked over at his wife, who was sitting upright, sulking, her arms folded across her breasts. "Sorry, Nat," he said softly. "Gotta go."

"What about our baby?" she asked. "What about us?"

Finnerty hesitated. Natalie was the smartest, most beautiful woman he'd ever known, and now she looked defeated. They'd been through so many disappointments in the past year, so many tests, so many different fertility methods. The toll of it all showed clearly on his wife's face and it made him feel helpless, a feeling deepened by the fact that the doctors had told them the week before that he was the problem. His sperm count was 60 percent of the norm. He'd been ordered to wear boxers, placed on a regimen of Chinese herbs, and told to keep trying. Now it seemed he couldn't even do the trying when it really counted.

"I'm sorry," he said again. "We'll give it a go again next month, okay?"

For a moment, Natalie looked ready to explode. Then she seemed to catch something in her husband's face, something besides that hunting expression she knew only too well.

"This is a bad one, isn't it, Damian?" she asked.

"Very," the marshal replied, nodding grimly. "And I have the feeling it's only going to get worse."

10:37 A.M.
14 VALLEY LANE
TARRINGTON, KENTUCKY

Whitney paused ten yards inside the entrance to the horizontal part of Terror Hole Cave, remembering how tight the way ahead would soon become, then she shrugged off the looming claustrophobia. Caves had forced her to deal with the fear of narrow places a thousand times before. It never went away completely, but she knew it could usually be managed.

She went ahead and within a minute the ceiling got lower. She and Jeannie got down on all fours and crawled their way deeper into Ayers Ridge. One hundred yards farther on, the floor disappeared into a chimney some twenty feet deep and about half the width of an elevator shaft. They descended it by bracing their feet and backs against either wall and shimmy-sliding down.

At the bottom of the chimney, for nearly seventy-five yards, the cave became a twisting, muddy crawlway about twenty inches high. The tube was so small that Whitney and Jeannie could not crawl; they had to lie on their sides and slither like snakes, pushing their packs along in front of them. It was exhausting work made worse by little nubs of rock that grabbed at their boots, ankles, and knee pads, making them think for an instant that they had finally been thrust into every caver's worst fantasy—getting stuck.

It took thirty minutes to negotiate the tube, then descend another fifteen-foot chimney and emerge into an oval-shaped passage. Water dripped off stalactites into an easy-flowing stream that ran down the center of the passage. Whitney and Jeannie moved down the rivulet looking for blind crayfish.

With two claws, a segmented tail, and long antennae, the crayfish looked like lobsters. But their skin was without color. And their eyes were pupilless, like freshwater pearls set on either side of their beaks. At each pool where they found crayfish, the women inserted a triangular orange flag to mark the spot. They planned to return to the same lagoons in a week to count and observe the crayfish again.

Whitney was a marine biologist as well as a speleologist, a specialist in cave ecology. More specifically, she was an expert on how pollution, especially agricultural pollution, affected life in underground rivers. She wrote her Ph.D. thesis on the ecology of subterranean rivers. She believed the delicate health of such ecosystems was as much an indicator of man's effect on Earth's environment as the size of the hole in the ionosphere above the South Pole. She and Jeannie were in the bot-torn of Terror Hole Cave because this was the breeding season for Cambarus aculambrum, *blind crayfish, and she was trying to determine whether chemicals from irrigated fields upstream were disrupting the reproductive cycles of the endangered species.*

After an hour of working their way along the underground watercourse, counting crayfish as they went, they reached a broad, shallow pool. Mud slicked the sides of the pool. Gravel and stones that looked like polished marbles covered the bottom. On top of the stones, blind crayfish milled about. "I count seven," Whitney said.

"Same here," Jeannie replied.

"Twenty-eight pools. A solid sampling."

"I'm hungry."

"Me too," Whitney said. "Lets eat something before we head out."

Jeannie nodded and slumped against the wall of the cave. Whitney took a seat on the other side of the pool, against the wall opposite her assistant. She stowed her notes in a Ziploc bag, then fished in her pack for tins of boneless cooked chicken and fruit cocktail, a commercially manufactured energy bar, and a water bottle filled with Gatorade. As she ate, she let her light wander about the little grotto. More of those amber-colored stalactites clung to the ceiling. Beyond them, the passage drifted to the northeast, shrouded itself in shadow, then disappeared into perpetual night.

Oddly, Whitney took solace from the solemn environment. She never got tired of being in caves. As her late father-in-law always used to say, "Where else can you go these days, other than the bottom of the sea or another planet, where you have the chance to walk where no human has been before?"

That notion caused Whitney to think about Tom. She and her husband had planned an evening out after Cricket's track meet. Whitney's thoughts wandered to the black negligee she'd bought on impulse the other day. She imagined herself appearing before Tom wearing it and couldn't help but grin.

"Hey, check this out," Jeannie said, breaking Whitney's reverie. Her assistant was on her hands and knees, the flame of her carbide lamp inches above the surface of the pool.

"What's going on?" Whitney asked. Jeannie looked up, puzzled, worried. "I've never seen the trogs act like this."

Whitney came over and aimed her headlamp at the placid cave lagoon. Twenty minutes ago the crayfish had been gathered at the pool's center. Now three of them were crawling at a frantic clip across the streambed. Two were already at the banks, clawing into the smooth brown muck.

For a moment, Whitney seemed suspended in time. No future. No past. Sheer inertia. Then she felt disbelief followed by gut-wrenching fear. Blind crayfish are usually as active as tortoises. One of their odd characteristics is that they will bury themselves in mud. They do it to survive being washed away in the rushing waters of early spring. But even then their pace is sluggish. These crayfish were acting as if they sensed a tidal wave roaring at them.

"Oh, Jesus, no," Whitney whispered.

"What?" Jeannie demanded. "Why are they doing that?"

"Flash flood!" Whitney cried, leaping across the pool, going for her gear.

Lying there on her kitchen floor, Whitney held her hands over her head and moaned, "No. I don't have to go back in the cave anymore." She forced open her eyes, took deep breaths, and twisted the stray lock of hair that hung in her eyes. "I don't have to go back in the cave anymore."

Whitney sat up, breathing and telling herself to imagine azure skies over prairie grass kissed by a summer's wind. She conjured up the pungent smell of summer fields and the clicking sound of grasshoppers in flight

To her relief, the waking nightmare of the cave gradually faded and the familiar objects of her kitchen took on clearer focus. The pine table Tom had built her for their fifth wedding anniversary; the framed photograph of Tom crawling through a deep tube inside the Labyrinth on the cover of *National Geographic*; the snapshot of the family on vacation at the beach off Nag's Head; the watercolor painting of the magical place where they had honeymooned in Jamaica.

Looking around at the relics of her past, it was as if Whitney could see her husband right in front of her. Then she realized with a gasp that she was seeing him. There on the muted television on the kitchen counter, Tom was walking through the woods holding a helmet.

Whitney sat up, fumbled in her robe pocket, and hit the Mute button on the remote. Another video clip of Tom showed now, this one somewhere deep in a cave, his headlamp glowing, his face grimy, his big toothy grin flashing. And the announcer was saying, "Coverage of NASA's Artemis Project will begin on the *Today* show tomorrow seven A.M. Eastern Standard Time."

The anchorman stopped and pressed his hand to his earpiece, frowned, then looked up at the cameras. "We have late-breaking news. Four prisoners have escaped from a maximum security prison in western Kentucky. Three guards were killed during the daring daylight escape and—"

Whitney punched the Mute button again. She looked up at a framed photograph of herself with Jeannie Yung on a research project in the Dolomite Mountains of Italy three summers ago. Her assistant had her arms spread wide before a huge pink stalagmite, throwing the camera her contagious smile. Whitney crossed the room and looked out the window into the morning sky.

"I know I don't deserve it after what happened," she whispered, "but watch over them for me, Jeannie. Please?"

11:40 A.M.
PEABODY WILDLIFE MANAGEMENT AREA, KENTUCKY

The U.S. marshal for eastern Kentucky climbed from a helicopter that squatted like a dragonfly in the middle of state road sixty-two. The fog had burned off and the sun's glare and the incessant blue flashes from the police cruiser cast the scene in an unsettling metallic tone. A tow truck pulled the chase cruiser out of the woods.

For a second, Damian Finnerty stood there, feeling strangely impotent. Low sperm count. His life up to now had been all about testosterone. How the hell had this happened? Then he shook his head, took a deep breath and told himself to focus. He could not allow his mind to be back there in the bedroom with his wife. He had to catch bad guys. At least that was something he still knew how to do, right?

Sheriff Michael Arnet, a pudgy man in his early fifties, came up and shook the marshal's hand but would not look him in the eye. "What a mess, huh?" Arnet asked.

"Looks it," Finnerty agreed. "Where are the bodies?"

Arnet hesitated, swallowed, then shrugged. "Gone, Marshal. FBI took 'em out of here half an hour ago."

"The FBI?" Finnerty replied, puzzled. "What's their jurisdiction?"

"Hell if I know," Arnet said, throwing up his hands, still unwilling to look directly at Finnerty. "They were feds, they had documents, and they said they were taking control of the bodies. Who am I to argue? They loaded 'em in ambulances and skeedaddled."

The marshal shook his head and made a note to himself to figure out what the FBI wanted with this case. Then he took off his aviator sunglasses and wiped the sweat that beaded his brow and made his black polo shirt stick to his back.

An evidence technician walked up to them. "Not much here, Sheriff. Footprints coming out of the woods. No bullet casings. And we got partial prints on the steering wheel of the chase vehicle, but most of them were smudged by someone wearing gloves."

"Gloves, huh?" Arnet said, and he spat out a wad of snuff on the ground. "Now why would them guards be wearing gloves in the heat like that?"

"You figure that one out, Sheriff," Finnerty said. "My job's just to catch them."

The marshal turned away and went to the hood of the nearest cruiser. He opened a map of the area, then picked up a handheld radio.

"This is Finnerty," he began. "I want roadblocks at Lewisburg, Elizabethtown, Rockfield, and Owensboro. If we get no sightings in two hours, I want the circle widened. Put them up at Corydon, Mumford, Burksville, and Somerset. And I want the media to have their pictures. It's too late for the papers, but I want their mugs on every television station from Cairo, Illinois, to Cincinnati and out into Huntington, West Virginia. The Clarksville, Bowling Green, and Nashville stations, too."

Finnerty paused, his jaw set hard as he studied the map. Even with the dragnet he was erecting he could see hundreds of back roads that the escaped convicts might take.

"Got those bios, boss," a deep male voice called. "Preliminary stuff from the warden's office at Eddyville. Just came in over the computer."

Finnerty snapped his head up to find Kentucky State Police Captain Mark Boulter striding toward him. Blond, buzz-cut, a square-jawed brute of a man, six-foot-four, 230 pounds, Boulter wore dark clothes and a badge on a lanyard around his neck just like Finnerty. The state police captain was one of the best fugitive-response men in the Midatlantic. Finnerty had tried several times to get him to join the U.S. Marshals Service, but the trooper was a Kentucky boy through and through, played four years at defensive end for the university, was married to his high-school sweetheart, and did not want to risk being transferred out of his beloved home state.

Finnerty took the printouts. "Do me a favor. Talk to dispatch. Make sure they're getting these pics in the hands of every cop in Kentucky, Ohio, and Tennessee. West Virginia, too."

"You got it," Boulter replied, then he jogged back to the helicopter.

Finnerty opened the printouts. At first glance, the most dangerous of the escaped inmates appeared to be Edward Kelly. He had enlisted in the army as a medical corpsman at seventeen. The day before his twenty-first birthday, he was court-martialed and served two years at Leavenworth for his part in the sale of contraband Demerol and codeine stolen from the base hospital at Fort Bragg. Upon his release, Kelly returned home to the backwoods of Kentucky and busied himself bringing organization to a group of marijuana growers, many of whom were his relatives. After two years under Kelly's ruthless leadership they became one of the major pot distributors on the middle eastern seaboard. When Kelly learned that four members of his organization, including two of his cousins, were attempting to craft their own network and cut him out of the profits, he knelt them down on a remote Kentucky hill, tied them up, and strangled each one to death with his bare hands.

"Wonderful," Finnerty said, turning to the next printout.

Quentin Mann: twenty-four, the son of a Lexington newspaper editor and a domineering socialite mother. Raped nine coeds in and around the University of Kentucky campus. Prior to his attacks, Mann had made phone calls in which he hummed and sang children's songs to each of his intended victims.

"Psychopath," Finnerty murmured. "Good. He'll make a mistake."

Then the marshal turned to the next page and frowned. A brief biography of the missing guard, William Lyons: thirty-seven, divorced, father of two, prison guard in Mississippi for ten years before joining the Kentucky Department of Corrections as a supervising lieutenant fourteen months ago. Lived alone outside Eddyville on the lake. Liked to fish for bass in his off hours.

Finnerty glanced over at the bloodstains on the highway and found himself praying that he would not find Lyons's body somewhere down the road. He couldn't stand the idea of having to explain the death of their father to the guard's children. Then he looked at the next biography and remembered the case from the newspapers.

Robert L. Gregor: a promising young physicist who'd become a cold-blooded murderer. No known father, mother died when he was eight. For much of the next four years, Gregor was raised by Elvin Loring, his maternal grandfather, a petty criminal and alcoholic who lived in the backwoods of eastern Kentucky. When Gregor was twelve, the grandfather died and the boy was turned over to the state. He was shy, sullen, and saddled with an extreme stammer.

A court-appointed psychologist discovered, however, that Gregor had a remarkable aptitude for mathematics and science. The psychologist had him placed in a foster home run by the wife of a physicist at Bowling Green State. For the first time in his life, Gregor was challenged, and he excelled at academics, finishing high school a year early.

He completed his undergraduate degree at twenty and was accepted into the doctoral program at the University of Tennessee that same year. He got his Ph.D. with distinction in less than five years and was awarded a prestigious postdoctoral research position at the university's Center for Applied Materials Research.

Two years ago, a Kentucky state trooper pulled Gregor over on a routine traffic stop and discovered the corpse of Carson MacPherson, Gregor's research supervisor, stuffed in the trunk of his car. The subsequent investigation revealed that MacPherson had been garroted into unconsciousness in his lab, then taken across the state line into Kentucky, bludgeoned to death, and left in the car trunk to rot.

"Damian!"

The marshal looked up. Boulter was hanging out the side of the helicopter.

"We've got one of them," the big man yelled. "Pate. The arsonist"

"Where?" The marshal was already weaving in and out of the cruisers and ambulances, running back toward the chopper.

"In an ambulance en route to the hospital at Madisonville."

"Shit, what happened?" Finnerty asked, climbing into the passenger seat.

"Chicken farmer about twelve miles north of here heard noises in his yard about forty minutes ago, thought it was foxes, and Went out with a shotgun," Boulter said, firing the engine. "Caught Pate trying to hotwire his truck. Pate shot at him twice at close range and missed. Farmer didn't miss. Hit him with two rounds of number sixes. They're taking him into the OR."

"I want to be there when he wakes up," Finnerty said.

They lifted off. Finnerty pulled out his map as they gained altitude and headed west. He studied it for a moment, then said, "Relay dispatch to change my order on those blockades. Let's put them at Roundhill, Hadley, and keep that one at Mumford. And tell Sanchez we need more information on all these guys. Those bios the prison sent were worth shit."

9:00 P.M.
JENKINS RIDGE
LABYRINTH CAVE

Tom Burke stifled a yawn and set a bulging file folder on the table beside the computer.

"I think that's everything," he said. "We all clear on tomorrow's schedule?"

Andy Swearingen, Cricket, and seven other men and women gathered in chairs in a corner of the NASA Mission Control tent before him nodded. Beyond them were row after row of tables covered with computers. A giant glowing screen hung from light stancheons near the front of the tent. On the screen a confusing series of lines showed—a map of the internal passages of Labyrinth Cave's nine ridges.

"Everyone's gear set?" he asked.

They all nodded again. "We're ready, Tom," said a pretty redheaded woman with a French accent.

"Then get some sleep," he ordered. "You're going to need all you can get for the next five days."

One by one the men and women gathered notebooks and packs and shuffled out through the tent flaps into the night. Cricket hesitated. "You coming, Dad?"

"In a minute, sweetheart. I just want to go over a couple more things with Jim. Andy? You take her to our tent?"

Tom's assistant nodded and led his daughter outside. Tom turned to a man with a thick torso, muscular neck, and flattened face that made him resemble a pit bull puppy. "We got it all covered, Jim?"

"That's what we're about to find out," replied the man, lighting a cigarette. "The tracking system's a go. Burst transmitters and relays from the supply dumps are all functioning. Guess it's time to see if it all works."

Jim Angelis's formal title was Director of Adaptivity and Training, Artemis Project, NASA. He was charged with figuring out which earth-mining technologies might best be adapted to the lunar model as well as how to train future astrominers. Using a cave as a physical and psychological proving ground had been his idea. Thirty years earlier, Apollo astronauts had prepared for their missions by enduring brutal survival trips in the California and Idaho deserts. It had been Angelis's conviction that a similar challenge in an underground maze would reveal which candidates were tough enough to burrow into the surface of the moon. He'd approached Tom with the idea nearly fifteen months before and found the cave scientist wildly enthusiastic. Indeed, aside from the time he'd spent with Whitney after the accident, Tom's every waking moment since that first meeting in Houston had been dedicated to the details of the mission.

Most of their time had been spent designing and implementing a system that would allow NASA scientists aboveground to track the caving team as it negotiated its way through the nine ridges of Labyrinth Cave. All of Tom's cavers would carry electronic beacons about the size of a candy bar inside their packs. The beacons would emit a location signal that would be relayed through a series of burst transmitters set up throughout the cave complex. Because rock is a powerful insulator and therefore limits the passage of radio waves, NASA scientists believed that the future astrominers would have very little direct communication with their surface support teams. Tom's cavers, Angelis believed, should face the same limitations. Indeed, the only way they'd be able to contact the surface was via computer link from one of two supply dumps deep inside the cave. Other than that, once inside, they'd be on their own. Angelis and the rest of the NASA scientists gathered on Jenkins Ridge would act essentially as observers.

"This is it, then," Tom said.

"Get some sleep, Tom," Angelis replied. "You've done everything you can to prepare. Now it's show time."

"Country's counting on us," Tom said. "The President's counting on us."

"We're ready," Angelis said. "Get some sleep."

"My wife's not happy about Cricket going in the cave tomorrow."

Angelis frowned. "I thought we all agreed on that. The P.R. people think it's great."

"We did agree and it is great," Tom said. "But Whitney—oh, never mind."

Angelis put his beefy paw on Tom's shoulder. "She's not coming up to see you off, then?"

Tom shook his head. "Says she can't get near a cave. Never again."

"I'm sorry." Angelis studied Tom. "This isn't going to affect your focus, is it?"

Tom looked up at the mission commander with a steely expression. "Not underground it won't. I never give the cave a chance."

"What I wanted to hear," Angelis said. "Now get some sleep. This is all going to go like clockwork."

Tom nodded, then picked up a pile of three-ring binders and left the tent. It was still hot and humid, even at this late hour. Cicadas buzzed in the night and there was a pepper scent to the air that made him think of Whitney. The buzzing of cicadas and the pepper air had been present the first time he'd kissed her, nearly fifteen years ago. Tom sighed again at the fact that here, at the peak of his professional career, his wife and research partner was nowhere to be seen.

He wove his way through a long line of canvas tents, stopping now and then to talk with NASA scientists involved in various aspects of the mission. By the time Tom reached his tent, he was jittery and wondered if he'd be able to sleep at all. He came through the flaps to find Cricket lying on her back on top of her cot, dressed in running shorts and T-shirt, a thin sheen of sweat on her brow, staring at the ceiling.

"Thought you'd be long gone by now," he said.

Cricket shrugged, chewing on the inside of her cheek.

"Still nervous about the interview with Helen Greidel?" he asked.

"No," she said, not looking at him. "Maybe."

"Tell you a secret?" he said.

Cricket shrugged again.

"I'm nervous, too," he said. "Biggest day of my life tomorrow. Besides meeting your mom and the day you were born."

She shook her head. "You've never been nervous about anything, Dad. Everything goes just the way you planned it, always."

Tom studied his daughter for a long moment, then went to the side of her cot. "What's going on with you?" he asked.

Cricket looked away from him toward the wall of the tent. "Nothing."

"I know you're a young lady and all," he said. "But I thought we were still friends. Friends talk, Crick."

Cricket did not reply for several moments and her fingers worried the outer liner of her sleeping bag. "Wish Mom was with us."

Tom forced a smile, sat down on the side of the cot, and took her hand away from the sleeping bag. "I do too, honey," he said.

Cricket's eyes filled with tears, "You two gonna get divorced?"

Tom was stunned by the question but remained cool. " 'Course not. What would make you ever say anything like that?"

"I don't know, doesn't seem like you two like to be with each other much anymore," Cricket said, tears rolling down her face. "I miss her, Dad. I mean, I miss the way she used to be. The way we all used to be."

Despite his wanting to be strong for Cricket, emotion choked Tom's voice when he answered, "I do too, honey. But the doctors say what she went through was as tough as being in a battle zone or witnessing a murder. That's what her nightmares are all about, why she won't go near caves anymore: shock amplified by guilt."

"What's she got to be guilty about!" she replied, grimacing furiously.

"Your mom was the one who wanted to go into the Terror Hole in the first place," Tom said, stroking her hair. "She feels responsible. She's just gotta work it all out."

A long moment passed. "But she's gonna get better?"

Tom closed his eyes. "I hope so. I can't imagine life without her."

"It's like Grandpa used to say, right?" Cricket asked.

"Your grandpa used to say a lot of things."

"Together we Burkes can get through anything?"

"Oh, that one." Tom smiled wistfully. He leaned over, kissed his daughter on the cheek, and tucked her sheet up under her chin. "Go back to sleep now."

Tom got up and crossed to his cot. He lay on his back, hands under his head, staring up at the roof of the tent for the longest time, wondering whether he and Whitney could get through this together or whether that kind of mutual support had been shattered forever.

9:35 P.M.
CAMPBELLSVILLE, KENTUCKY

"Nobody move a muscle," Billy Lyons said. "We're gonna watch awhile."

He and the three escaped inmates were spread on their bellies in the weeds below the lip of a creek bank that ran behind the gravel parking lot of a low cinderblock building. A garish neon sign that read SOAPY SUDS LAUNDROMAT cast the twilight scene in a thin yellow light. An aging green Dodge sedan was parked closest to the deserted road. Deeper into the lot sat a tan panel van adorned with a magnetic sign advertising the laundry business. From their angle, the laundry appeared empty.

After escaping early that morning, Lyons and the inmates had driven an hour and a half east of Central City, keeping to the gravel roads. By mid-morning, the guard had become nervous that they'd be spotted if they kept driving, so they sank the transfer van in a remote pond outside of Jonesville.

They passed the next twelve hours dozing and keeping watch from a thicket beyond the pond. As the sun began to sink, they'd walked four miles across farm fields and through small woodlots to the creek bottom that had led them here, to the Soapy Suds. Gregor had labored hard coming across the last field. Even now the pale physicist's eyes were closed and his breathing was shallow.

"You okay?" Lyons whispered.

"Just get me to that stone and I'll be fine," Gregor rasped.

For a moment Lyons paused, wondering if what Gregor said was true, whether any of it was true. He'd put his life on the line for this man. He'd done things for this man that made him question his own morality, his own sanity. It had to be true. If not, the past two years had all been a terrible waste. Then he nodded and once again took in the parking lot in a glance before turning to the others. "Here's the plan: Everyone stays here but Gregor. We're going to grab that Suburban, hot-wire it, and swing around to get you all."

"Fuck you are," Mann said. "You're not cutting out on us."

"Mann's right," Kelly said. "Gregor stays behind. I'll go with you."

"I murdered three men to get you all out," Lyons said, thinking fast.

"Yeah, you did," Kelly replied with a soulless expression. "Which is why I believe you'd ditch us if you got the chance."

Lyons hesitated, then spat in disgust. "Fine, you and me, hotshot. Don't fuck up."

The two men jumped to their feet and ran in a crouch across the gravel parking lot, the neon sign throwing stretched green shadows behind them. Lyons went to the Suburban. Meanwhile, Kelly peered inside the panel van. "Key's in the ignition!" he hissed. "And there are bags of clothes in here, too."

Before Lyons could reply, a door squeaked open and closed, followed by scuffing footfalls. The guard and Kelly looked up to see a tired-looking woman in her midtwenties halfway between the Dodge and the front door of the Laundromat. She carried a yellow plastic basket piled high with the clothes of young children. Kelly immediately sauntered toward the woman. "Don't you worry none, miss," he said, laying on a thick southern drawl. "My driver done lost our keys."

The woman backed up a foot, staring hard at the words stenciled across the chest of Kelly's bright orange short-sleeved jumpsuit: KENTUCKY CORRECTIONS. INMATE TRANSFER.

Lyons offered an awkward smile. "I'm a guard. We broke down."

The woman's attention flickered between the men She focused on the badge on Lyons's chest and relaxed. That so?" she said. "Y'all from Eddyville, then?"

"That's a fact," Kelly said, smiling at her.

"Got a cousin did time in Eddyville," she said.

"Poor bastard," Kelly said. He continued to slip toward her. "I'm sick myself. Tuberculosis. They're sending me to the prison hospital. Your cousin ever go there?"

"Can't say… we, uh, wasn't that close," she said. "Well, I best be going now. Got to get some sleep. Five-thirty rain or shine my twins are up making a racket. Tony's on a two-week haul and they're down now, so I took the time to do the laundry while I had it." She paused, as if realizing that didn't sound quite right, then she shook her head. "I mean, they're not alone, the twins, I mean. My sister Margie's there."

"Course she is, Mrs …?" Kelly said.

"Cox," she replied. "LaValle Cox."

"Go on home now, Ms. Cox," Lyons called out, not liking where this was going.

Kelly stiffened, then made a slight bow in her direction. "That's right. You get back to your kids and Margie."

LaValle Cox dropped her head and made as if to hurry past. But when she came abreast of Kelly, he took a step in time with hers, then hooked his bear-like forearm across her throat and arched her over backward. The basket crashed, spilling little T-shirts and patched overalls across the cement "No," she whimpered. "Please. My boys."

"No, Kelly!" Lyons cried. "Don't do it!" Kelly's eyes flickered to the guard, then he smiled and reached under the flat of her neck with his free hand, as if he were about to set her free. Lyons, however, read Kelly's true intent and rushed him. Before he took two steps, Kelly's arms embraced each other. He thrust her head up sharply and to the right. The still, humid night was broken by the sound of bone snapping below the flange of her skull. The young mother's body collapsed like a marionette severed from its strings.

10:30 P.M.
MADISONVILLE, KENTUCKY

Ninety-four miles to the west, in the hallway outside the intensive care unit of the Madisonville Memorial Hospital, U.S. Marshal Damian Finnerty stared incredulously at a buff Latino man in his early thirties with a shaved head and a single weird eyebrow that reached from one side of his face to the other. Then he reached out and snatched a set of folders from the younger man, demanding, "What do you mean, sealed?"

"Sealed, as in no-looky," replied Deputy Marshal Amador Sanchez in an annoyed tone.

Deputy Lydia Two-Elk, a short, powerfully built Native American, glared at Sanchez, then stepped in front of him to speak directly to Finnerty. "A good chunk of the testimony at Gregor's murder trial, specifically the details of the research he and his supervisor, MacPherson, were doing was heard in closed chambers and then zipped up tight at the request of the U.S. attorney general."

Finnerty rocked back on his heels and ground his fingers against his temples. He felt like he'd been spinning his wheels since he'd left the escape scene. The operation to repair Pate's gunshot wounds had taken nearly six hours and he had not yet regained consciousness. During all that time, the marshal had made no headway whatsoever on the FBI's interest in the case. Agents in Louisville said none of their men had picked up the bodies, and when Finnerty tried FBI headquarters in Washington, D.C., he'd been given the bureaucratic brush-off. Since the escape there'd been no sightings of the inmates or their hostage. His wife was not returning his phone calls. And now there was this sealed testimony.

"That's not the worst of it," Two-Elk said. "This guard, Lyons, is a mystery man. Beyond a certain point, he doesn't exist."

"What are you talking about?" the marshal demanded.

Two-Elk said that the warden at Eddyville told her that up until five years ago Lyons had been a guard with an excellent record working in Mississippi's maximum-security prisons. Then he developed a prodigious gambling habit. His wife and two kids left him over the problem. And when prison officials discovered he was in debt for fifty thousand to a Gulf Coast bookie, they fired him. Lyons drifted awhile, then started attending Gamblers Anonymous meetings before applying for work in Kentucky. The state, stretched thin for experienced ranking supervisors, took a chance on Lyons and hired him to work the segregation unit at Eddyville two years ago.

"Warden said he figures Lyons must have started gambling again. The convicts found out, used it as leverage to get him to help them escape," Two-Elk said.

"Gambling debts?" Finnerty said, flipping through the folders. "Is that enough of a threat to make a guard kill three fellow officers and help four inmates escape?"

"That's where the story begins to fall apart," Two-Elk said, nodding. "We spent most of last night trying to track down where Lyons lived in Mississippi. No luck. Can't find a record of him at the department of corrections there. We even e-mailed a photograph of him to every medium-and maximum-security prison in Mississippi."

"And?" Boulter asked.

"No marriage certificate," Two-Elk replied. "No kids' birth records. No school records. No nothing."

"The department of corrections never checked?" he cried.

"Guess not," Sanchez said. "And now they're faced with the biggest prison break in years."

Before Finnerty could react to that news, a bearded doctor emerged from the ICU. "Pate's awake, but weak," he said. "You can have five minutes."

Finnerty and Boulter went through the double doors and into a room where Pate lay back in a raised bed. He was naked from the waist up, his chest wrapped in bandages. Bags of intravenous fluids ran into his arms. A nurse checked a monitor attached to the wounded arsonist. A sheriff's deputy sat in a chair next to the bed.

"Leonard Pate?" Finnerty said.

Pate opened his bleary eyes. "Who's asking?"

"Damian Finnerty, U.S. marshal for—"

"Fuck you. I ain't talking without a lawyer."

Finnerty's eyes narrowed. He put a hand on the nurse's shoulder and looked at the deputy. "Would you excuse us a minute?"

The nurse hesitated, then went out. The deputy followed and Boulter pulled shut the curtains. Finnerty said nothing but made a show of pulling on latex gloves. He smiled, leaned over Pate, then grabbed a piece of tape holding the convict's dressings in place. He tugged hard on it. The inmate howled.

Finnerty grabbed Pate by the chin. "Listen, shit-for-brains," he said. "I have three dead corrections officers and one suspect in custody: you. From where I'm standing, you're looking at an extreme change in your miserable circumstances—from twenty years' hard time for arson to a death sentence on three counts of premeditated murder."

At that, Pate stopped howling. "Didn't kill no one."

Finnerty started to peel off another piece of tape.

"Lyons did it!" Pate gasped.

"The guard?" Boulter asked.

"Shot 'em all point-blank."

"Why would Lyons do that?" Finnerty asked.

"I'm in pain here. Chest feels like it's burning," Pate groaned. "I need meds."

"Answer my questions. Then you get your drugs."

"That's brutality," Pate protested.

"One of my specialties," Finnerty said, reaching for the tape again. "Why?"

Pate scowled at him, fought for breath. "The moon man."

"What the hell are you talking about?"

"Gregor," Pate said. "Killed his supervisor at the U of T, carried the body around in the trunk of his car for weeks. Real fucking whacko."

Finnerty glanced at Boulter, then back at Pate. "Keep talking."

Pate grimaced, then went on, his voice hoarse with effort. "Gregor got Lyons and the others believing in this bullshit story that he killed that guy—his supervisor—because he got onto Gregor's big scientific discovery about this moon rock and the supervisor was going to steal credit for it. Says he hid the moon rock where no one would ever find it. Gregor convinced Lyons to help him escape so they could go get the moon rock. Lyons bought into the story and faked the results of a TB test to get us all in the transfer wagon to the hospital at Louisville. I didn't know he was gonna kill 'em."

"What's so important about the moon rock?" the marshal demanded.

Pate snorted and closed his eyes. "It's horseshit."

"What did Gregor say about the rock?" Boulter pressed.

Pate shrugged. "Said he figured out that it could, you know, do special stuff."

Finnerty squinted down at Pate. "Keep going."

"Most of it was mumbo jumbo to me," Pate said, swallowing hard. "But from what I could understand of it, Gregor says the rock's like a magnifying glass for energy. Says it can change things."

"The hell do you mean, change things?" Boulter asked.

Pate chortled and coughed. "Change things," he said. "Like one molecule into another. Lead into gold or rock into diamonds or whatever else you want. Total horseshit, but Gregor's got them convinced that—"

Sanchez stormed into the hospital room. "They've surfaced."

Finnerty spun. "Where?"

"Little town called Campbellsville, about forty miles from here," the deputy said. "Killed a woman at a laundry and stole a vehicle no more than an hour ago."

"We're out of here," Finnerty cried. The three men rushed for the ICU doors.

"Hey," Pate called after them. "What about my meds?"

A minute later, Finnerty and his team were jumping into the helicopter on the roof of the hospital. Boulter revved the chopper's engine.

"I want the blockades pushed east," said Finnerty as they lifted off. "Somerset. Lancaster. Danville. Frankfort in case they go north."

"I'm on it," Boulter barked into his headset.

Finnerty looked over his shoulder at Sanchez and Two-Elk sitting in the backseat of the chopper.

"What was Gregor working on when he killed his supervisor?" Finnerty demanded.

"We don't know," said Sanchez. "Case was sealed, remember?"

The marshal rubbed his hand over his face. "What kind of researcher was he?"

Two-Elk said, "Materials science and superconductors. But his Ph.D. dissertation was on the geological composition of moon rocks."

"Moon rocks!" Finnerty groaned, as the helicopter banked east toward the full moon glowing high in the night sky. "Someone get on the horn to the duty officer at the A.G.'s office in D.C. Tell that son of a bitch I want that testimony in Gregor's case unsealed and I want it unsealed now!"

June 15,2007
6:55 A.M.
14 VALLEY LANE TARRINGTON, KENTUCKY

"Flash flood!"

Jeannie dove to her knees and shoved gear into her pack, muttering, "Fucking weathermen! Fucking weathermen!"

Whitney ignored her assistant, leaping across the pool, going for her own things.

In less than thirty seconds, both women were tightening their packs into position. Then they heard it: a distant, guttural bubbling noise. Somewhere outside the ridge, the Washoo, the surface river into which the underground stream flowed, was breaching its banks and backing up into its tributaries.

"Run!" Whitney screamed.

Their headlamps sliced the gloom as they tore back down the passage toward the chimneys. Their footfalls splashed against the sound curtain of water rising behind them. Two hundred yards down the passage, a mound of sediment blocked their way and they had to crawl around it. The handprints and knee prints they'd left in the sand earlier in the day were almost washed away. "It's up four inches!" Jeannie shouted.

They scrambled up the bank and raced on. In fifteen minutes they reached the bottom of the first chimney. The water in the channel was up eleven inches.

Whitney grabbed at a crack in the wall, hoisted herself up into the first shaft, and started to climb.

"C'mon," Jeannie urged. "C'mon."

"I'm going as fast as I can."

"It's up twenty inches, "Jeannie yelled after her. "We're ten minutes from pipe-full. I'm not waiting for you to clear. I'm coming up."

"Do it," Whitney said, then clenched her jaw and forced herself to go faster, to try not to focus on the extraordinary pace at which the water was rising. But it made no sense. For Terror Hole Cave to flood this fast, the storm outside had to be a deluge of at least five inches an hour and it had to have been raining that way from the moment they had

entered the first horizontal shaft *of the cave. Impossible. She had checked the meteorological data herself. But there was no denying the facts—this was a hundred-year flood, maybe a thousand-year flood. And she and Jeannie were in the worst possible place to survive it.*

Whitney reached the top of the chimney with Jeannie right behind her.

"You think it can come up and flood the next level?" Jeannie panted. The water roiling up into the chimney below them had a reddish tint. The lower passage in which they had counted crayfish was pipe-full, flooded to a sump.

"We're not waiting around to find out," Whitney said.

With that, she ripped off her pack and darted into the 225-foot crawlway. The second chimney beckoned at the far end, the only way to higher ground. They got on their sides and dragged themselves into the tube. The cave floor was covered with ridges like thousands of scallop shells, which caught on their clothes and boots.

After fifteen minutes of dragging herself against the scalloped floor, Whitney collapsed and lay gasping on her side. Sweat gushed off her brow, seeped into her eyes, stung, and turned the world a hazy yellow. "Give me a sec."

Jeannie was still right behind her, puffing hard. "Take a minute," she said. "We're a third of the way there already. We're gonna make it."

Here, some hundred feet down the crawlway, the cave roof was barely four inches over their heads and the walls pressed in a mere six inches from their torsos. The light of the headlamp in that confined place seemed hypnotic. Whitney stared into the light and realized that she had let Cricket go to sleep last night without telling her daughter she loved her. And Tom had been away at meetings in Houston all week; they'd barely spoken.

Then Whitney noticed something out of the corner of her eye, something that erased all thoughts of family and home. There were two of those scallop-shell formations on the floor right in front of her. Muddy dollops of water filled each of the stone divots, which were separated by a fringe of limestone. The water in the rear scallop was lapping hard against the rock separation.

"Jeannie, are you moving back there?" Whitney demanded.

"Give me a break," Jeannie replied, still breathless.

Whitney looked back at the cave floor. The two pools had become one pool now, a pool that was eating up the bottom of the crawlspace with every second that passed.

"It's in the tube!" she screamed.

"For God's sake, go!" Jeannie shrieked. "Go!"

"NO!" Whitney shouted.

She jumped out of bed and ran into the hallway before she knew she was even awake. The scent of the flooding cave, that mud stench, filled her nostrils and threatened to gag her. She clutched the banister. "You don't have to go in the cave again," she whispered through her tears. "You don't!"

She suddenly realized that morning sunlight was streaming through the window above the staircase and shook her head in confusion. She had lain down for a nap around five after coming home from yet another fruitless day in her office. What time was it?

Whitney tore downstairs into the family room, saw the grandfather clock, and was shocked to see it was nearly 7:00 A.M. She'd slept nearly fourteen hours.

She noticed the television still running in the family room, still muted on split screen, NBC on the right, the Weather Channel on the left. The meteorologist gestured excitedly at large swirls of cloud cover over the Rocky Mountains. Whitney found the remote and smashed her thumb down to release the mute. The sound blared on just as the Weather Channel cut away to commercials. She threw down the remote in disgust, inadvertently switching the sound to NBC.

Whitney went to the computer, shook the mouse. The National Meteorological Service web page appeared. The two storm fronts had moved significantly since she'd last checked; the northern storm now coursed over Wyoming tracking southeast on a path that made it seem as if it would collide somewhere over Arkansas, with the second storm gathering strength over the Texas panhandle. The local forecast read: *High pressure giving way as unstable masses forming over the plains move east. Possibility of severe weather for eastern Kentucky rising toward week's end.*

In her mind, Whitney heard the rush of water. She grabbed the phone and punched in the number for Tom's cellular. It rang several times, then—

"Hello?" Tom yelled over the background noise of people talking.

"Thank God I got you!"

"Whitney?"

"Yes, Tom, I…"

"Cricket and I were going to call you in about fifteen minutes."

"The weather stations are warning about severe rain in eastern Kentucky."

"There isn't a cloud in the sky up here."

"It's not supposed to hit until later in the week."

"Well… what do you want me to do?"

"Postpone the experiment."

A long pause, and then in an angry, exasperated voice Tom said, "Look, those meteorological models only say what might happen and… I can't call off a twenty-five-million-dollar experiment on the basis of a 'might'."

"Tom, it could be a huge storm—"

"I've got to do an interview right now. We'll call back in half an hour, tops, okay?" He hung up.

"Tom? … Tom! You shit!" She slammed the phone down, then slouched forward on the desk, pissed off and unsure of what to do. Suddenly she was aware of the grating of stones in a vast and resonant chamber. Then she heard it: *Drip!* Whitney looked up at the television and saw the image of water slipping off the tip of a cave stalactite. She crammed the forearm of her terry robe into her mouth but could not take her eyes off the image, which jumped to Helen Greidel, a stylish blonde in her midthirties. Greidel strolled out the mouth of a cave, wearing a shiny new helmet and headlamp.

"Welcome to a special edition of *Today*," she began. "We're here in the backwoods of eastern

Kentucky, a landscape dominated by dense woods, high, steep ridges, and caves—lots of caves. Not exactly the kind of environment where you'd expect to find NASA scientists researching the potential rigors of mining the moon, is it?"

The camera angle widened and there was Tom wearing a navy-blue jumpsuit with a gold waist belt. Under his arm he held a red helmet. He had a caver's pack slung across his shoulder. Greidel removed her helmet to reveal a fashionable hairdo.

"Say hello to Tom Burke," she said, "a spelunking scientist as it were, who has convinced NASA that a cave is indeed the ideal location to prepare for moon mining. Tom, why a cave?"

The camera zoomed in on Tom's face as he replied, "Moon miners will face some of the most unforgiving terrain imaginable, Helen. Endurance caving—long, uninterrupted subterranean trips with little or no support—is the closest we can come to precreating the lunar mining experience here on Earth. Let me show you what I mean."

The screen cut to an aerial shot of a broad green valley. The farms that dotted the foreground adjoined a dense forest bisected by the Furnace River. The watercourse was perhaps fifty yards wide, a silted green color and lazy in its current. On the far side of the river, nine distinct ridges rose steeply out of the mist. All the ridges were laid out perpendicular to long bends in the river. Upstream, the river met a low earthen dam, beyond which lay a lake some five miles long and two miles wide.

"What you're seeing here is the northern approach to the Labyrinth Cave system," Tom said. "What makes this cave perfect for NASA's purposes is that the known entrances are so far apart—about twenty-three miles as the proverbial crow flies, more like one hundred twenty miles underground."

A computer graphic of the Labyrinth area replaced the aerial shot. One of the animated ridges split to reveal a maze. "Inside," Tom explained, "are level after level of tubes, tunnels, pits, canyons, and great underground halls, places just as unforgiving as the surface of the moon. Negotiating these obstacles will be fantastic training."

"What about food and water?" Greidel asked as the camera returned to them.

"We'll carry enough for thirty hours," Tom said, patting his hip pack. "And we can resupply at two different cache sites we've set up inside the cave."

Greidel smiled, then shot him a perplexed look. "I understand your young daughter will make the first part of the trip. Isn't that kind of dangerous?"

Tom shook his head. "Cricket may be just fourteen, but she's already one of the most experienced cavers in the world. And she'll only be accompanying us for the first six hours. Besides, we—and by that I mean NASA—wanted the youth of America to get behind NASA's new mission. What better way than to bring along someone like Cricket?"

His answer seemed to satisfy the anchorwoman because she smiled again, then looked offstage and made come-here motions. Cricket shuffled out.

The sleeves of her cave suit were tied around her waist She carried her helmet and wore a white long-sleeved polypropylene undershirt.

Whitney's hands sought her lips; seeing her daughter this way, through the separating lens of the television camera, forced her to realize that her beautiful daughter was on the cusp of womanhood. She felt a terrible throb over the time they had not spent together the past year.

"You really like it in there?" Greidel asked Cricket "I get the heebie-jeebies in a closet."

"Caves are great," Cricket replied, swatting at the strand of hair that dangled in her eyes. "I mean, it's like my granddad always used to say: 'Where else can you go, other than the moon or some other planet, where you could be the first person to ever walk there?' "

Greidel laughed. "You're a natural, Cricket," she said, delighted. "Will you come back and share your experiences with us when you come out of the cave this afternoon?"

Cricket looked at her father, who nodded. "Okay," she said.

Greidel turned and threw the camera one of her patented expressions of concern and sincerity. "Today will return to its coverage of NASA's first efforts toward putting man back on the moon, after a station break."

Whitney continued to hold her hand over her mouth as the image of her family faded. In her mind she saw Tom, not as the ruggedly handsome man on her television set, but as the dead man in her recurring nightmare, floating in a muddy, headlamp-lighted chamber, faceup, water draining from his mouth. Cricket's body floated beside his.

Fingers of pressure formed around Whitney's throat She glanced over to see the gray swirling clouds spinning on the computer weather map. The fingers tightened. Her hands flew to her temples. Then the panic became overwhelming and she began to choke. Whitney understood she was being irrational, but she knew she had to act or the pressure around her throat would throttle her.

She grabbed her car keys and went tearing out the back door. A moment later, she burst back into the kitchen and skidded to a halt in front of the dryer. She ripped off her nightgown, then hopped into jeans, hiking boots, and a T-shirt In seconds she was behind the wheel of her beat-up Toyota Land Cruiser, had the four-wheel-drive vehicle rammed in reverse, and was squealing backward down the driveway.

7:20 A.M.
NORTHWEST OF HERMES FOUR CORNERS, KENTUCKY

The laundry truck careened up a dirt road through a forest that the rising sun had cast in shades of copper. Inside, Billy Lyons pounded his fist on the steering wheel.

"You didn't have to kill her!"

Kelly kneeled next to Gregor in the back of the van, taking his pulse and blood pressure. "Said it twenty times, bitch saw us," he replied. "And when our pictures appear in the papers and on the TV, she'd call the troopers."

They'll know anyway," Lyons fumed. "These people aren't stupid, you know."

"What's your problem?" Gregor asked in a raspy voice. "You killed to get here."

"That was different," Lyons said.

"Yeah, you tell yourself that," Kelly snorted.

Lyons glared out the windshield at the road and the rolling forested terrain they passed through. All the men had changed their clothes. The guard's uniform and the orange transfer jumpsuits had been stuffed away in the laundry bags, replaced by jeans and work shirts. For a second, Lyons thought of stopping the van and going after Kelly. Then he took a deep breath and told himself to be calm. Killing Kelly now could throw his whole plan into jeopardy. Getting to Gregor's stone was what was important—the *only* thing that was important. A stone that could amplify energy and alter molecular structures was more valuable than anything on Earth. He had to get it. Nothing could stop that. Nothing. But deep inside himself he made a promise: At some point Kelly would pay for killing that poor woman. He glanced in the rearview mirror and saw Gregor looking at him.

"How you feeling?" he asked.

"I'll live," Gregor replied. "I've got a reason to now."

Mann, meanwhile, leaned over the passenger seat. "C'mon, Lyons," he complained. "You said there'd be food when we broke into that army-navy store. We got boots, clothes, flashlights, but nothing to eat. Now, dammit, when we going to stop?"

"He's right," Gregor said. "We'll need food and water. I'll need painkillers in addition to my normal meds to endure the long walk ahead of us. There's a store just up the road a mile or two. Stop there."

" 'Bout time," Mann said.

"I don't give a shit about food or water, hear?" Kelly said. "I want that gold and that platinum. There'll be enough for everyone; right, Gregor?"

Gregor smiled weakly at Kelly and said, "If my calculations regarding the energy input and subsequent amplification were correct and you could carry it all, you might give old Bill Gates a run for his money."

Mann slapped his thigh and chortled. "I'll tell you where this dog's going—Bora Bora. Rum. Hammocks. Palm trees. Beaches. Polynesian babes with big old cinnamon-brown butts and silver-dollar-sized nipples."

Gregor got up on his knees and looked out through the windshield. "That's the store, Lyons. Pull in there."

Lyons hesitated. The last thing he wanted now was for some civilian to catch sight of them. Not now, when he felt they were close. But Gregor had said they needed supplies. It went against the plan, but he had to take the chance.

He slowed and turned into the parking lot of the Hermes General Store, which occupied the intersection of two rough roads that wound through a mountainous, unincorporated area hard by the border of the Daniel Boone National Forest. It was a two-story, white-clapboard affair with rocking chairs and a porch overlooking the gas pumps. An old bloodhound slept on the stoop.

"Everyone stays here," Lyons said. "I'll get the food and anything else we need."

"No way," Mann replied, yanking open the side door of the van. "I haven't been in a store in four long years. I'm going in."

"Me too," Kelly said. "I want orange juice, fresh squeezed."

Gregor did not say a word but climbed out after the inmates.

"Fuck," the guard said, then jumped out and jogged to catch up behind them.

They went through a screen door and Lyons found himself in a low-ceilinged room with rows of goods and a wide-planked floor. An older man with slicked-back gray hair sat on a stool behind the cash register, smoking an unfiltered cigarette, sipping coffee, and watching a television bracketed to the ceiling.

Mann moved down the center aisle, grabbing cracker boxes, doughnuts, and tins of meat. Kelly went straight to the upright cooler and pulled out a carton of orange juice and several bottles of water. Gregor walked toward the front counter and a rack of nonprescription medicines. Up on the television screen, Lyons noticed Helen Greidel sitting in a director's chair on a stage erected before a pair of large white tents.

"Welcome back to a special edition of *Today* live from the site of the Artemis Project," she was saying.

Lyons ignored the broadcast and squatted before the newspaper rack. The headline on the *Louisville Courier-Journal* read: FOUR ESCAPE EDDYVILLE. THREE GUARDS KILLED. FOURTH GUARD SUSPECTED AS ACCOMPLICE. Under the headline were mug shots of all of them. The guard put the paper back and then, with his head cast down, sidled over to Gregor. "We're front page," he muttered. "Pictures of all of us. Even you."

Gregor glanced at the paper. "We've got to get out of here. Pay and we're gone."

Lyons nodded. Mann and Kelly arrived at the counter and put the food and beverages on the counter. The store owner said nothing as he rang up the purchases.

"That'll be twenty-seven fifty," he said.

Lyons handed the man a fifty and the store owner grimaced. "I'll have to get you change for something that big." He turned and disappeared into an office.

"Let's go," Lyons whispered.

"We leave that kind of change behind, he'll remember us," Kelly said.

"Look," Gregor said before Lyons could reply. The black guard turned and saw the pale scientist, frozen, shaking and staring up at the television screen where a photograph of the moon had appeared. Then, through computer animation, a large area of the photograph lifted and spun. The camera zoomed and slowed over a mountainous region of the lunar surface.

"This is the Descartes Highlands," Greidel was saying in voice-over, "where NASA hopes to have miners working within the next three years. The area is believed to contain dense concentrations of ores that scientists have determined are crucial to the field of so-called superconductors. Such ores allow energy to flow through them with almost zero resistance. Scientists say the ores will revolutionize technology here on Earth as well as ease America's dependence on foreign oil."

"Those ba-bastards," Gregor whispered. His sickly body began to quiver and sweat. "They're trying to bury me!"

"Let's go!" Lyons insisted.

But Gregor was frozen, staring at the screen. The picture had jumped to that aerial shot of the nine ridges again. The camera's eye zoomed in on the northern end of the easternmost ridge, then hovered over a plume of thick mist belching up out of a gaping wound in the earth. At the sight of it, the breath caught in his throat. The snowy skin on his bald head furrowed and ticked as if he were suffering the remnants of a stroke.

"Burke's team will enter Labyrinth Cave here at the Orpheus Entrance within the hour," Greidel was saying in voice-over. Then the camera pulled back again and zoomed toward the eighth ridge. "The original plan called for the team to eventually exit at the Virgil Entrance way out on Tower Ridge, the eighth of the nine. But a roof collapsed inside the cave six weeks ago and that entrance is now buried under at least one hundred fifty feet of rubble and Burke's team now plans to leave the cave—"

Gregor doubled over, racked by spasm. "No. No," he moaned.

"What's the matter?" Lyons demanded.

But Gregor was unable to speak. The air kept catching in his throat and Lyons was afraid he might have a stroke right there inside the old store.

"Oh, shit," Mann said.

Lyons looked up to see that the local Lexington station had broken into the *Today* show broadcast. An earnest young man in a suit and tie sat before a desk. An electronic logo that read PRISON BREAK was splashed on the screen beside him

"One of the largest manhunts in Kentucky history is under way this morning," the local anchor began. "Four inmates from the state penitentiary at Eddyville escaped from a transfer van yesterday morning near Central City. One has been recaptured. Authorities say the inmates escaped with the help of one of their guards, who is believed to have killed three other corrections officers assigned to the transfer. If you see these men, contact the Kentucky State Police."

The screen jumped again and their mug shots appeared.

Kelly elbowed Lyons in the ribs. The guard looked down to see the store owner standing in the doorway of his office. He slammed the door shut. Gregor stumbled toward the front door. Kelly jerked his pistol from his waist belt and started toward the office. Mann took off after Gregor.

"We got no time for killing!" Lyons yelled at Kelly, who was stepping back as if he meant to shoot off the office door handle. "Gregor's running for it!"

Before Kelly could turn, there was the roar of a shotgun and the store office door six inches to the left of his abdomen exploded outward. Kelly threw himself to the right just before a second shotgun blast blew another ragged hole in the door. Somewhere behind the door they could hear the store owner ramming another shell through the mechanism of a pump-action. Lyons got low and scrambled toward the front door. Kelly took two shots at the light streaming through the holes in the office door, then raced after the guard.

Lyons burst out the front door with Kelly right behind him. Gregor was already in the driver's seat The scientist jammed the vehicle in Drive, squealed forward ten feet, then slammed on the brakes. Mann slid open the side door. The old store owner appeared at an open window, aiming down the barrel of his shotgun.

"Get down!" Mann yelled.

Lyons and Kelly dived into the van. Gregor floored the accelerator. The store owner fired. The blast took out the passenger side window, spraying them all with glass. Kelly stuck his pistol out the window and took another shot, even as Gregor spun the wheel and the big utility vehicle heaved about like a yawl changing tack in a gale. The tires squealed and smoked. The van skidded onto the two-lane highway and roared off to the south. Blood trickled from cuts on Gregor's face and scalp. He hunched over the wheel, his boot still jammed down on the accelerator, fighting for control of the vehicle around a tight curve in the forest.

"Slow down," Lyons yelled. "You'll roll us."

"We've got to get up there before it's too late," Gregor bellowed back.

"Get up where?" Lyons asked, looking at the dense forest that hemmed the road.

Just then they crested a ridge in the road. The forest ended and the land fell away toward a wide plain of farmland leading to a lazy river. A ferry chugged across a ford in the river. On the other side, nine distinct ridges rose through the morning mist

"Up there," Gregor panted. "We're going up there."

8:07 A.M.
NEAR SOMERSET, KENTUCKY

"National security, my ass!" Damian Finnerty shouted into his headset "That's crap and you know it Jerry. I want that testimony from Gregor's case unsealed ASAP! I want to know why the FBI took those bodies. And I want someone from the attorney general's office to get on the phone with me or better yet to get their butts down here to tell me what the Christ it is I'm dealing with! Cut the crap, Jerry. And cut it now!"

Finnerty angrily clicked off the radio link with his liaison in Washington. From the helicopter, he could see below him a line of honking cars, eighteen-wheelers, and pickup trucks that stretched more than a half mile from a police barricade back to the west along the Cumberland Parkway. The throughway ended at Somerset Beyond the town, to the east crisscrossed with serpentine two-lane highways and a vast network of dirt logging roads, lay the Daniel Boone National Forest as rugged a land as any in the Appalachians.

"That line's getting pretty long, boss," Boulter said. "You still want them checking every car?"

"Every damned one," the marshal snapped. Then he gestured to the open file in his lap. "As a kid Gregor lived out in this area with his mother and then his grandfather. This forest is one of his comfort zones. He's coming here. I can feel it in my gut."

The second Finnerty said it, he caught his reflection in the windshield of the helicopter and felt doubt surge through him. What if he was wrong? He'd always trusted his hunting instincts before. But somehow things were different now. He wasn't the man he'd been the week before, was he? Even Natalie looked at him differently. If he didn't have what it took to father a child, maybe he didn't have what it took to be a marshal anymore. Maybe—

A voice broke him from these depressing thoughts: "Fugitive one?"

Finnerty put a hand to his headset. "Roger, dispatch."

"They've been spotted at a town called Hermes Four Corners about sixty miles from you. A store owner was in a gun battle with them about ten minutes ago."

"Jesus Christ!" Finnerty fumed. "I'm two steps behind these guys!"

The marshal ripped open a map and found Hermes Four Corners just south of the Furnace River. Sanchez leaned over Finnerty's shoulder from the backseat, looked at the map, then jabbed a finger just below the Hermes Reservoir.

"Gregor lived with his grandfather in a shack at the west end of that lake!" Sanchez crowed. "That's gotta be where he's taking them!"

"Get us to this road, one-eighty-eight—south of Hermes Four Corners," Finnerty told Boulter. "Then we'll swing over the lake."

The nose of the chopper dipped, then they arced with gathering speed northeast across the meadow and out over the long exit ramp that led off the parkway and the troopers who were already pulling the barricades.

8:22 A.M.
NASA ENCAMPMENT JENKINS RIDGE LABYRINTH CAVE

Sixty-seven air miles away, the sound was deafening and the klieg lights were blinding as Tom Burke,

Cricket, and the rest of the NASA team entered the cave.

Behind him, Tom heard Helen Greidel announce: "The United States of America prepares to return to mine the moon, the most expensive and ambitious project ever undertaken by man. And the early fate of the program rests on the shoulders of these men and women."

The cave that Tom and his team entered for the cameras had no known connection to the Labyrinth complex. The entire thing was staged. A media charade. The little grotto in the woods just beyond the pasture of the old Jenkins farm was no more than one hundred feet long, with entrances at both ends, similar in layout to the tunnels pedestrians use under busy urban streets.

Tom thought the entire thing was ridiculous, but he had agreed to it in order to placate a media horde turned testy by his refusal to let them accompany his team to the real entrance site. The ingress his cavers would actually use, the Orpheus Entrance, lay at the far end of a footpath that coursed two miles north out the spine of Jenkins Ridge before slabbing off the steep east face in a curved descent toward the Furnace River

Tom had reasons for having his people walk to the cave alone. He wanted the clear separation from civilization to have its effects on the team. Moon miners would face the same sort of physical and psychological disconnection when they left the safety of their lunar stations.

Indeed, a mile into their hike, Tom noticed with satisfaction that the five male and two female cavers he had chosen for the traverse were quieting, checking their equipment, turning subdued in anticipation of the rigors to come.

Now that they were under way, Tom allowed himself a gloomy recollection. Before leaving the Mission Control grounds, he and Cricket had tried to call Whitney twice at home and then on her cell phone, but there'd been no response. It was almost like Whitney was a completely different person now. When they'd met in college, all she'd talked about was her dream to do great science. For years they'd been partners in that effort. And now? He shook his head and wondered whether Cricket was right: Were they heading for divorce?

They crossed through an opening in the forest, and, to get his mind off the travails of his marriage, Tom once again turned a critical eye toward his gear. The subject had been an obsession with him the past three months as he'd tried to winnow out the things they carried.

Each of Tom's team members wore a blue or yellow ballistic-cloth coverall adorned with red and white NASA mission patches. Their red helmets had been retrofitted to handle a powerful headlamp system called a SuperGlo 5000, which could run a solid fourteen hours on a slim battery roughly the size of a baseball card. Underneath their coveralls they sported polypropylene shirts and midweight leggings that fit into thin wool-poly-weave socks. Over the socks they wore Gore-Tex booties. Rubberized padding protected their shins, elbows, and knees.

In their packs, his cavers carried three backup sources of light—small electric headlamps, mini-flashlights, and several fluorescent loops. They also toted replacement batteries for the SuperGlo, an ingenious dry suit NASA had developed for the wetter portions of the cave, a silk bandana to use as a filter should they encounter dust, and packets of electrolytic salts. Each caver also carried a tube of fluorescein dye, which scientists with the U.S. Geological Survey had asked them to carry and dump into the water as part of an experiment to determine how long it took for water to leave the interior of Labyrinth Cave and reach the Furnace River. Every pack also contained a one-liter plastic bottle equipped with a built-in filtration system, emergency heat packs that activated when exposed to air, and a Leatherman tool.

NASA had provided food packaged in plastic tubes. At two thousand calories per tube, each ration was designed to provide a third of the cavers' daily nutrition.

In addition, each caver wore a small microprocessor attached below the left collarbone. The processor would gather and store basic physiological data—heart rate, oxygen saturation, blood pressure, temperature, and glucose and adrenaline levels. The NASA engineers planned to download Cricket's and Andy's data when they emerged from the cave later that afternoon. Tom and the rest of the team would transmit their physiological information into the computer links at the two supply dumps.

As they entered a glen of mature pin oaks, Tom was jolted from his thoughts by the sight of Cricket trudging along with her head down. He frowned and hurried up to her side. "C'mon, kiddo," he said. "You'd think you were carrying the weight of the world on your shoulders. You're famous now. Every kid in America knows you. Helen Greidel wants to talk to you when you come out this afternoon. You're going to be our spokesgirl... er... spokes-young-lady... on the world's most widely watched news show."

Cricket shrugged. "I'll probably make a total baboon of myself."

Before he could reply, the terrain dropped off steeply, forcing Tom to concentrate on his footing. Far to the north, he could see the ferry that took cars across the Furnace River at Cronin's Landing. The barge was at midstream, its side wheel cranking madly.

The trail turned west toward the edge of a brush-choked ravine. On the far side of the ravine, a hole gaped in the mountainside. Thick steam belched from the hole. Tom felt a surge of energy pulse up his spine. This was the original entrance to Labyrinth Cave, the one Cricket had discovered all those years ago. He quickened his pace and soon they reached the gated entrance. He tossed his pack to the ground and struggled into the sleeves of his cave suit. Cricket did the same, but with little enthusiasm.

Tom got a key from his pack, set it into the lock, then swung open the stainless-steel gate. The rest of the caving team scrambled now, snapping on helmets, darting into the woods for last-minute urination.

"Everybody check that their locator units are transmitting," Tom called out. "You should see a green LED light flashing on the upper left corner. Cricket?"

Cricket rolled her eyes, then looked in her pack and cupped her hand around the device. "Mine's on," she said.

"I think you should go in first," Tom said. Your cave."

She stood there for a moment, then shrugged, picked up her pack, and slung it over her shoulder. Tom felt a wave of frustration and anger toward her. If this was her attitude, he didn't know if he wanted her inside the cave. Going underground demanded focus and eagerness. It was the only way you survived. Then he thought, She'll be better once she gets inside. Caves are in her blood.

He turned to his assistant "I'm going in right after her," he told Andy. "We'll head straight through the anteroom, then down the ladder into Christmas Tree. Send the others on in as they get ready. Don't help them. I want to see where their caving heads are at, whether they can read the place yet Lock up when the last one enters."

"These guys are good," Andy boasted. "They'll be right behind you."

Cricket, meanwhile, was already moving toward the gate and the mouth of the cave. Usually, she felt a great deal of anticipation heading underground. And she knew she should be excited at the honor of entering first on such a historic mission. But all she felt was tired and left out somehow.

As she went by Andy, he reached out and squeezed her arm. "Hey, Miss Happy. I'm looking forward to coming out together. It'll be fun."

A week ago, having Andy say he was looking forward to spending time with her would have induced a bout of the giggles and a reddening of the skin, but all she did was nod. "Yeah," she said. "Fun."

She went inside the mouth of the cave. It was cool here, midfifties, and very humid. The floor slanted at a steep angle down and to the right before it disappeared into blackness. A layer of dried black guano covered the floor and when she stepped on it, there was a crushing noise. A sour smell filled the air. Several hundred bats clung in the crevices of the cave's ceiling. The bats rustled and shifted at her passing. The walls around the bats were discolored by mineral seepage, iron most likely, from the rusty quality it gave the limestone. Long-legged cave insects, creatures the color of sand, crawled across every plane of the rock

Cricket reached around to the padded neoprene belt that fit snugly at the small of her back and snapped on the SuperGlo. A boulevard of light flared out from the powerful electric headlamp attached to her helmet. Then she turned down the lamp's power to approximately half its capacity, got on her hands and knees, and crawled into a black plastic culvert placed there to allow access to the greater cave. The culvert was thirty feet long and tilted down into the earth at a twenty-degree angle. She slid through the culvert into a world of complete and total darkness, a world where she immediately sensed the weight and pressure of tens of thousands of tons of rock all around her.

Cricket had spent so much of her young life underground that the closest she could come to describing the experience was that it was similar to what she felt during summer vacations when she donned a mask and snorkel and went skin diving in the ocean—she immediately found her senses altered and muffled. Sight became crucial but was limited by the power of the headlamp. Sound was thrown by the ever-changing acoustics. And touch was buffered by the heavy gloves and coveralls she was forced to wear.

Her father came out of the culvert behind her with a big smile on his face. "Isn't it great that this will be the proving ground for the lunar miners, Crick?" he said. "Caves strip people to their essence, exposing their strengths and weaknesses as glaringly as an electron microscope reveals the inner workings of a molecule."

"I guess," she said.

"You know why I love caves?"

"No, but I suppose you're going to tell me."

He frowned. "You're right. I am going to tell you. I love caves because the silence is so complete you can listen clearly to your heart, which is not always a pleasant thing, but a necessary one now and then. You know?"

Cricket looked up at her father and told herself that he was a nerd, but essentially a good nerd. "Yeah, I guess you're probably right, Dad."

"Course I'm right," he said. "Let's get going."

She followed her dad under an overhang into a vast cavern shaped like an apse. At this setting her lamp was incapable of lighting the vast blackness; instead, she saw the place in shadowy slices. The floor was strewn with small blackish boulders. At the far end of the subterranean room, a towering pile of rubble reached nearly to the ceiling, some sixty feet above.

A chill breeze turned against her cheeks, a steady wind her dad often called "the Labyrinth's breath." The scent of the cave wind usually had a calming effect on Cricket; it had always reminded her of fall nights after a gentle rain. But at that moment the underworld's breath seemed to carry an odor that surprised her. Two years ago, she and her mom and dad had gone to visit relatives in Savannah, Georgia. They had gone to the famous Bonaventure Cemetery and toured some of the mausoleums. The Labyrinth's breath now carried the same acrid mustiness she'd smelled in the crypts. That graveyard scent was not one she had ever associated with the Labyrinth before and its strange presence put her on edge.

Her wariness heightened as she and her father crossed the cavern toward the large rubble pile. Her dad was always telling people in interviews that caves were living organisms composed of soluble rock, air, and water instead of flesh and blood. But she knew from English class that that was only a metaphor, a way of giving a geological formation a personality that people who'd never been in a cave might appreciate. Now, however, Cricket felt something weird about the cave; it seemed to be pressing in on her, as if the rock that surrounded her had indeed been changed into a living, dangerous force. In return she had the cutting thought that she and her dad should go back outside.

Then she glanced over at her father moving so effortlessly through the cave, and she shook off those feelings, telling herself that she just hadn't gotten enough sleep the night before, that she was letting her mom and their family problems get to her.

Her dad reached the rubble pile and began scrambling up. She hesitated for a moment, then went up after him. The pile was fifty feet high and it took her three minutes to reach the top. Then she followed her father down the steep backside of the pile, navigating her way over the rocks as if they were a pressurized jigsaw puzzle, using her headlamp to pick her way down over hundreds of stones all shifting and grumbling against one another. Below her, Cricket saw a narrow, cockeyed V of a gash in the rock at the cliff's base. The prongs of an eighteen-foot aluminum ladder stuck up out of the hole at the bottom of the V.

They reached it and her father said, "Young ladies first."

Cricket grabbed the ladder's top rung, swung around to get her feet positioned, then pumped her way down, studied and focused in her every move. The floor she dropped through became, in turn, the ceiling of a lower cave passage. The base of the ladder was surrounded by what looked like a stand of frosted Christmas trees growing from the bottom of the cave. There were dozens of the stalagmites, all coated in powdery white gypsum crystals. Cricket had seen these speleological formations at least a hundred times and they still amazed her. When she reached the bottom, she called back up through the hole, "Clear!"

In less than a minute, her dad reached the bottom. "They'll be right along," he said to her. Cricket went and sat next to one of the frosted cave formations.

"You know, even after all these years, I'm still head over heels in love with all of this," her dad said. "The grit, the adventure, the challenge, the beauty. But you know what I love most of all?"

Cricket shook her head. Her dad was always talking like this, asking questions and then answering them before you could get a word in edgewise.

"It's the science and the possibility of new discovery," he said. "It's being the first, Crick. It's being—" Something terrifying reverberated down through the hole in the ceiling above her dad's head. From far back, toward the anteroom beyond the gate, Cricket heard the echo of Andy Swearingen yelling and then the unmistakable flat slap and roar of a gunshot.

8:55 A.M.
SOUTH OF HERMES FOUR CORNERS, KENTUCKY

Nearly three-quarters of a mile below the Orpheus Entrance and one hundred feet in the air, Boulter flew the helicopter across the Furnace River roughly paralleling a narrow mountain road that led south from Hermes Four Corners. Finnerty and his two deputies were using binoculars to search for any sign of the escaped convicts.

When they swept over the southern shoreline, the marshal dropped his glasses, adjusted his headset microphone, and said, "Two more minutes and we go try to find Gregor's grandfather's cabin out on that lake."

"No, we don't," Sanchez yelled suddenly over the thrum of the rotors. "I've got the panel van. Right there!"

Finnerty raised his binoculars and saw the van pulled in under brush at the mouth of a ravine that cut into the mountainside. Ahead of the van he saw broken branches where someone had passed.

"They're climbing," Finnerty yelled. "Get us up that hill. Try to spot them."

Seven hundred yards up the hill, Billy Lyons held his hand to his forehead and moaned at the sight of the young man lying just inside the metal gate to the cave. Blood trickled from his mouth and nose. His eyes were filmy and lifeless.

"Goddammit," Lyons murmured. "Another civilian dead."

All day, ever since LaValle Cox's body had slumped to the sidewalk in front of that Laundromat, Lyons had promised himself that no more civilians would perish. But it had all happened so quickly that the guard had been powerless to intervene. Lyons and the inmates had been climbing up the brush-choked ravine with Gregor in the lead. They reached a steep lip and had to push the pale scientist, gasping and sweating, up and over onto a wide ledge that encircled the mountain. Lyons peeked over the top of the ledge just in time to see the young man in the red helmet and blue coveralls pick up a pack and start toward a stainless-steel gate that barred the way to a gash in the mountainside.

For a moment, Gregor stood there wheezing and studying the young man and the opening to the cave as a nomad coming out of the desert might an oasis. The young man heard Gregor wheezing and turned, hesitating at the sight of the scientist eyeing him murderously. The young man pointed at Gregor and said, "This is a restricted area, sir. Turn around. Go back the way you came."

Gregor sneered and pulled his pistol. The young man panicked, spun, and ran toward the cave. Gregor tore after him. The young man got inside the mouth of the cave, pulled out a key, and tried to shut and lock the gate, yelling "Help! Someone help!" But even in his weakened physical state, Gregor was too quick; he reached the young man, raised his pistol, and shot him right in the throat. Then he kicked open the gate, flipped on his flashlight, jumped over the body, and disappeared into the cave.

Lyons saw it all from the lip of the ravine and something expired inside of him. This was not the way it was all supposed to happen. Innocent civilians were not supposed to die. This was not part of the grand scheme. But before another thought passed through his mind, he heard the deep throb of a helicopter coming up the mountain behind him.

They're after us!" Kelly screamed as he vaulted by Lyons up onto the ledge, with Mann right behind him. The guard hesitated, then scrambled up after the escaping inmates.

As he and Mann reached the cave entrance, the helicopter achieved altitude and was two hundred yards out from them, closing fast. The blade wash threw a storm of pebbles that pinged against the metal gate. Mann dived in beside the young man's body, plucked the key from his lifeless hand, shoved the gate shut, and locked it. The helicopter swung sideways in space.

"*U.S. Marshals. Do not move!*" Finnerty barked over a loudspeaker. "*Lay down your weapons or we will use force.*"

The side door of the chopper opened. A Latino in a blue baseball cap was on one knee, bracing a woman who sat before him, legs crossed, elbows draped over her upper shins in the classic sniper position.

"Fuck!" Lyons bellowed. For a second he didn't know what to do. Then, overriding all other thoughts, came the absolute, inviolate conviction that he had to stay with Gregor no matter the circumstances. He had to get to that stone, no matter the cost to property or life.

He spun on his knees and began scrambling toward the plastic culvert into which Gregor and Kelly had already disappeared.

From the helicopter, Finnerty saw the dead body and Lyons moving. In his headset he heard Two-Elk, calm, controlled: "Target acquired. Permission to fire."

"Fire!" the marshal yelled.

The black guard was now halfway into the culvert. Two-Elk touched the trigger on her .270. There was a roar, then a clang and a whine as the 130-grain bullet ricocheted off the bars of the gate. Lyons disappeared. Then the marshal saw the flash of a pistol in the shadows of the cave entrance and heard two flat cracks above the thumping of the chopper. The window beside him shattered. The marshal jerked away from the shower of glass then came back up just in time to see Two-Elk swing the muzzle of her rifle toward another of the inmates running for the culvert.

"He's going for the hole!" Finnerty cried.

Mann, pistol in hand, dived into the culvert just as Two-Elk fired again. Her shot struck rock right next to the escaped inmate's boots and then he was gone, too.

"Son of a bitch!" Finnerty bellowed. "She missed them both! Put us down. We're losing them!"

Boulter's massive hands pulled back and to the left on the helicopter's flight stick. The bird swung into space over the ravine, the wind howling in the shattered window, then did a 360-degree loop back toward the narrow ledge. The blades scalped the tips of pine branches that overhung the cave entrance.

"Goddammit, Captain, put me on the ground!" Finnerty yelled

"Ledge isn't wide enough!" Boulter yelled back. "I'll shear a blade!"

"We'll drop in by rope. Climbing gear on!"

The chopper rose twenty feet and hovered. Two-Elk and Sanchez slung ropes out the side door. Finnerty unbuckled his safety harness and was trying to get into the backseat of the chopper when he heard Boulter whisper over the headset, "Holy mother."

The marshal froze, then looked back over his shoulder. Rising over the spine of Jenkins Ridge was a second helicopter and then a third, both of them military gunships with bold black lettering on their flanks: U.S. AIR FORCE/NASA SECURITY.

An unfamiliar voice crackled in the marshal's ear: "Unidentified aircraft, you have entered restricted NASA airspace. Identify yourself and withdraw immediately or you will be fired upon."

9:10 A.M.
ANTEROOM
JENKINS RIDGE
LABYRINTH CAVE

Tom heard two more gunshots as he scrambled off the ladder and began to climb the backside of the rubble pile. Cricket was right behind him. He turned and whispered, "You stay here."

"No, Dad," she said. "I'm coming."

He hesitated, then said, "Stay behind me and get ready to run."

Ahead he heard the clash of voices in the cave on the other side of the rubble pile. Tom turned off his headlamp and motioned to Cricket to do the same. He eased up behind jutting rock slabs that in the glow of the gathered headlamps below looked like chunks of melting ice.

"Move," a sickly-looking man carrying a flashlight ordered. He was waving his pistol at six of Tom's NASA cavers, who were now stripping as fast as they could.

There were three other men, one black, with the sickly-looking man, and as each piece of caving gear hit the ground, one of them swooped in to put it on. Marie LaCroix, the petite, redheaded French woman and longtime friend of Tom and Whitney's, sniffled, as she kicked off her boots and zipped down her coverall. The colorless man slapped on knee pads, elbow pads, and helmet like a seasoned caving veteran. The others were more hesitant, following his lead.

"What do we do?" Cricket asked in a voice that hovered on the verge of hysteria.

Tom shook his head, bewildered. The men had guns. Where was Andy? "Don't move," he commanded.

Now the ashen-skinned man was dressed and standing before the members of Tom's team, all kneeling on the cave floor in their underwear. He shone his headlamp in each of their faces. "Where's Burke?" he demanded. "The guy who was on television?"

The cavers glanced furtively at one another.

"Where the hell is he!" shouted a swarthy-looking man beside the sick one.

Marie LaCroix began to sob. "We do not know this! Tom, he goes on first into the cave, then he waits for us to come up and we was to begin!"

The pale man cocked the pistol and aimed it at the woman's forehead. "Please, no, I am just married," she said, her voice shaking.

"Then your life will be as much a tragedy as mine," he replied. He looked from the begging woman into the shadows and rocks where Tom and Cricket hid. "Come out, Burke!"

"How does he know who you are, Dad?" Cricket whispered.

"I don't know," Tom replied, shaken.

"Come out or she dies!" the feeble-looking man roared.

Tom grabbed Cricket by the upper arm and whispered, "You stay hidden, you hear? Whatever happens, you stay right here."

"No, Daddy!"

But Tom was already up and stepping out of the shadows. He raised his hands. "Don't shoot!"

"Excellent decision, Burke," the pale man said.

Tom eased down the slope, his attention passing over the members of his team, who shivered in the chill, humid air. When he reached the bottom of the rubble pile he looked at the pale man. "Why are you doing this?" he demanded. "You're ruining one of the greatest science experiments of all time."

A spasm of mirth crossed the man's face. "You wouldn't understand greatness if it stared you in the face. Now, you're going to guide us into this maze."

"Hell I will," Tom said, defiantly.

His tormentor's face went flat and ugly and he swung the pistol toward the kneeling cavers. "Shall I shoot another like the one at the gate?"

"Andy?" Tom mumbled in shock.

The black man stepped from the shadows, holding a shotgun leveled at the pale man's stomach. "Don't do it, Gregor," he said. "Too many folks died for that stone already."

Gregor's eyes narrowed and the hand that held the pistol tensed.

The swarthy man stepped between the black one and the sick-looking one. He held a burlap sack in one hand. "Be cool now, Lyons, Gregor," he said to them. "What we need is a more subtle form of bending him to our will, hear?"

From the sack, the swarthy man drew out what looked like the sort of belt that weight lifters wear, only this one had a narrow black box attached to the back. The swarthy man faced Tom.

"Put it on, fucker, or they all die right now."

Tom hesitated, then saw the tears streaming down Marie LaCroix's face, and passed the belt around his waist. The fourth man, the one who looked like he'd just walked in from a country club, stepped up to Tom and snapped shut a lock on the belt

"Do as he says now," Pretty Boy said. "This sucker'll give you fifty thousand volts through the tummy."

Tom blanched. He understood that he was facing not men but animals. That understanding triggered the survivor instinct in him, an instinct honed over years spent navigating the bowels of the Earth. He felt himself turn to iron inside. He looked around at them all. "You sick bastards. I promise you, you'll pay—"

Gregor backhanded Tom across the mouth. "I'm coming to get what's mine. I don't pay for that."

A stone zinged out of the darkness and caught the pale man flush in the rib cage. He grunted at the blow, lurched sideways, and almost dropped his pistol. A second stone caught Swarthy in the kidneys and he dropped the belly-belt transmitter. The third rock found its mark on Pretty Boy's shoulder; he spun and wailed with pain.

"Run!" Cricket screamed. "Daddy! Run!"

There was a flash of movement high in the rocks atop the slope and the men all swung their headlamps toward it. Cricket was rising from her hiding place to launch a fourth salvo when Gregor found her with his light and raised his gun.

Tom panicked and shouted, "Don't! She's only a girl."

"She called him Daddy," Swarthy mused, his expression curving into a smile. "Tell her to come down, now, Burke, or she might suffer a serious mishap."

Tom gazed up the rock pile toward Cricket, who stood with her arm cocked behind her, ready to throw. "Drop the rock, honey," he called out

"I won't," Cricket cried, shaking the rock

"It's over," Tom insisted. "Come down."

Cricket hesitated, then started down, still gripping the rock, her headlamp bobbing, slicing the gloomy interior of the cave. The black man stepped out when she got close. "Give me the rock, kid," he said softly.

She grimaced, handed it to him, then ran to her father and held on to him, tears dripping down her cheeks.

"Belt her, too," the swarthy one said. "Gives us more control."

"Do it and then we move," the pale man said. "Those fucks in the helicopter will be coming for us. Leave the others. They're useless to us now."

The swarthy man held up what looked like the transmitter to an electronic dog collar and snarled, "Now get moving. Like Gregor said. Take us west."

Tom looked at Cricket the horror of what had just transpired unfolding through him like fire catching wind He flashed on an image of Whitney the day before, begging him not to take Cricket into the cave.

"Do what they say, sweetheart," he said. "No matter what. Do what they say."

10:20 A.M.
NASA ENCAMPMENT
JENKINS RIDGE
LABYRINTH CAVE

In the field opposite the Mission Control tent, Helen Greidel pressed her earphone to her head, then nodded into a camera lens with a studied expression of shock and concern.

"We interrupt your normal programming to bring you an update on an unfolding crisis at the site of NASA's initial efforts to return man to the moon," she began. "What started out earlier this morning as an intriguing experiment designed to give NASA crucial insight into the potential rigors of moon mining has turned into a deadly hostage situation here near rural Hermes, Kentucky, site of the largest cave in the world.

"As members of a NASA expeditionary force entered Labyrinth Cave, they were attacked by four armed and dangerous inmates who made a daring and bloody escape from a state prison hospital transport van yesterday morning," she went on. "The four fugitives have killed one member of the cave team, taken hostage Artemis Project leader Tom Burke and his daughter, Cricket, and appear to have disappeared into the bowels of the Labyrinth."

Greidel glanced down at a piece of paper she clutched in her left hand, which was visibly trembling.

"Six other members of the NASA team were rescued from the cave about an hour after the attack," she continued. "But my sources have just confirmed a stunning piece of the story. U.S. marshals were engaged in a pitched gun battle with the escaped inmates right outside the cave entrance. But before the marshals could enter the cave to recapture the fugitives, and possibly save the Burkes, NASA security forces intervened."

"You fuck-ups!" Finnerty yelled. "We had them. We were right there and we had them and you stopped us."

Jim Angelis, the NASA chief, looked as though he wanted to bite the marshal's face off. Instead, he jabbed Finnerty in the chest. "You entered NASA restricted airspace and opened fire with high-powered weapons!" Angelis shouted. "One of my people was lying there dead inside the gate to the cave. What'd you want my men to do, lay down the red carpet? Who the hell do you think you are, buddy?"

The two men, six Air Force security personnel, and Finnerty's entire team were gathered in what passed for a conference tent just off the Mission Control pavilion.

Finnerty stood there, shaking from head to toe, aware of Boulter, Sanchez, and Two-Elk watching him, aware of feeling the way he had when the doctor had broken the news to him that there was a problem with the mobility of his sperm—emasculated, a shell of the man he'd always believed himself to be.

"I'm the U.S. Marshal for eastern Kentucky," Finnerty said, doing everything in his power to regain control of the situation. "And all I wanted was for your people to let me do my job. I'd appreciate it if you let me do it now."

"This is a NASA show," Angelis retorted. "Our people will take it from here."

"This is not a NASA installation," Finnerty snapped. "This is a cave under public land that you just happen to be using for your experiment. I am going after those fugitives, *Mr. Angelis.*"

"Bullshit," Angelis said.

Finnerty took a step closer to the NASA chief. "My team trains to deal with hostage situations. Does yours? You've got two dozen reporters outside and I guarantee there are dozens more on the way. Do you want to be the one, after the Burkes turn up dead, who has to explain why an inexperienced team was sent in while my people, trained in hostage rescues, stayed above ground?"

Angelis's hands gathered into fists and for a second Finnerty thought the Mission Control chief would strike him. But Angelis just walked away and sank into a chair behind a small desk in the corner of the tent, ashen-faced. He ripped open a cigarette package and fished one out. "What a goddamned mess," he said wearily. "Why's this happening? What the hell do they want to be in this cave for?"

"We didn't chase them in there, if that's what you're asking," Finnerty replied. "And frankly, we don't care why they're in there. We just want to capture them and rescue Burke and his daughter."

Angelis nodded in resignation. "How can we help you?"

The marshal gestured toward a computer screen atop Angelis's desk that showed a smaller version of the grid representation of the cave that hung in the main pavilion. A blob of bright yellow pulsed inside the horizontal and vertical lines. "I assume that's some kind of locator map."

Angelis nodded. "Linked to low-frequency transponders in all the cave packs."

Finnerty leaned over, peering at the electronic chart. "They seem to be heading toward the next ridge west. Is there a way I can get in there and cut them off?"

"The next entrance is out on Munk's, the third of the nine that make up the cave," Angelis replied. "Then you'd have to backtrack."

"Fine," Finnerty said. "I'll need someone to lead me in there."

Angelis grimaced, took a deep drag off his cigarette, then kneaded the back of his bullish neck. "Gonna be a problem."

"Why?" Finnerty demanded.

"There are people here who know sections of the cave, but not all of it," Angelis replied. "That's part of the reason we sent cavers on this first traverse rather than potential moon miners—we needed to train guides for future training missions."

Boulter, who had been standing by quietly, piped up. "You're saying there's no one else who knows Labyrinth Cave as well as this guy Burke?"

"Well, there's one, but…"

"But what?" Finnerty demanded.

At that very moment, a commotion erupted outside the tent. "Ma'am? Ma'am!" a woman's voice cried. "This is a restricted area, ma'am! You can't go—"

Finnerty spun in his tracks to see a disheveled woman with strawberry-blond hair and wild eyes bursting into the tent. Her denim shirt was soaked with sweat. Blades of grass and dandelion stalks hung from the laces of her boots. She was gulping air as if she'd been running a very, very long way.

"Thank God I got here in time!" she gasped in Angelis's direction. "Bad storm coming. You've got to send in a team to pull Tom and Cricket before they get in too deep. How long have they been in? Three? Three and a half hours?"

The woman strode by Finnerty as if he weren't there, going straight to the computer screen on Angelis's desk and put her fingers on the gathering of blinking yellow icons. "See! That puts them maximum in the passages near Monroe's Slide, maybe almost to the Orchid Grower's Way. Level two. Still dry cave. No problem."

Finnerty glowered at Angelis. "Who the hell is this woman?"

Angelis cuffed his hand around the back of his neck again. "Damian Finnerty, meet Whitney Burke, Tom Burke's wife," he said. "The only one who knows Labyrinth Cave well enough to guide you."

Descent

NOON
MONROE'S SLIDE
JENKINS RIDGE
LABYRINTH CAVE

The belly belt had metal nubs that dug into Cricket's sides and back. She stumbled along, wincing at the pain, still stunned and benumbed by what had happened. Andy Swearingen was dead. Really dead. These men had taken her and her dad hostage. And they would not tell her father where they were going.

"Take us west into the second ridge," the sick-looking man, the one they called Gregor, kept saying. "I'll tell you where to go from there."

"How far are we, Gregor?" the dark-featured one, the man called Kelly, said behind her.

"I don't know," Gregor said.

"How can you not know?" the large black man called out. "You've been here before, right?"

Gregor shook his head. "I came into the cave a different way, Lyons, a way that can't be used anymore. So we're going to have to come at it from a different angle."

"But you know where the stone is, right?" Lyons asked.

"Trust me," Gregor said. "I know."

They were 350 vertical feet down inside the hollow core of Jenkins Ridge now, hugging the right side of a curving slope, creeping ever deeper into the earth. Cricket followed Gregor, who followed her father. The soft-faced one, Mann, she thought they called him, was right behind her. Kelly and Lyons brought up the rear. Their headlamps bobbed and sliced the gloom, revealing water dripping from the ceiling high over Cricket's head and, forty yards ahead, a spot where the curving slope they walked met a cliff and fell away into darkness. Tom slowed and crept sideways across the slope. Every few minutes he turned to seek her out and nod in encouragement. Cricket smiled grimly back at her father. Every negative thing she'd thought about him in the past few weeks had disappeared. Now she looked to him at every chance for support.

As she inched her way along the slope after her dad, she remembered the blinking green liquid display of her location transponder deep inside her pack. Someone on the surface had to be tracking them. A rescue effort had to be under way. Someone had to be coming. Didn't they? And who were these men? She knew from the newspaper coverage of the Artemis Project that there had been threats from ecological activists opposed to mining the moon.

Were these men terrorists? No, she decided. They kept mentioning a stone, which they obviously believed was hidden somewhere in the cave.

"Pay attention now, Cricket," Tom called out, breaking her from her thoughts. They had reached a spot on the thirty-degree incline covered with dozens of rock plates. Most of the slabs were the size and shape of medieval castle doors, she thought; they lay loosely one on top of the other at odd directions.

Cricket watched as her father crawled out onto the stones first, making his way slowly down and at an angle over the plates of rock toward the edge of the cliff. Ten yards shy of the edge, he scrambled to his left and stood on a flat spot. Gregor went next. Cricket waited until Gregor stood next to her dad, then began to move. She got low and eased out onto the first slab, then hopped to a second, which rocked up under her weight. She crouched for a moment to regain her balance and swallow her fear.

Behind her Cricket heard someone climb out onto the first plate. She turned and saw Mann leering at her. "Hey," she said. "One at a time. Wait until I get down."

"Screw that," Mann said, and he took another step and immediately lost his balance. He lurched forward. The sole of his boot slammed hard on the edge of the plate where Cricket crouched. Whatever wedge had held the tablet in place the last couple of thousand years cracked free. Cricket felt herself thrown on her back. The slab took off beneath her, shrieking, grinding, and clanking like an imbalanced bobsled. She looked up and almost vomited. She was zooming toward the cliff.

"Daddy!" she screamed.

Downslope, Tom knocked Gregor aside, took two strides uphill, and lunged toward Cricket with his arm outstretched. As the front edge of the slab cleared the rim, he saw Cricket throw herself toward him and reach. There was a sickening moment of inertia, when Tom was sure his daughter was doomed. Then her fingers caught his. The slab sailed off into the inky darkness and crashed to the bottom, sixty feet below.

Cricket dangled from his hand off the edge of the cliff. "Don't drop me!" she cried.

"Never," Tom said. He reached down with his other hand, got her wrist, and hauled her back up onto the slope. He stared at her for a second, struck by how much she looked like her mother, then crushed her in a hug.

"God, that was close," he whispered. "Can't lose you. Ever."

It was taking everything Tom had to beat back the hysteria that threatened to cripple him. His thoughts kept jumping all over the place, and then, strangely, to the memory of yellow buttercups in a meadow one early summer afternoon a long, long time ago. Cricket had been no more than four that day, running barefoot into the wildflowers. Whitney had chased her, laughing. Their strawberry-blond hair shone gloriously in the June sun. Whitney scooped up Cricket, laid her in the grass, and tickled her under the chin with one of the flowers. For a few moments, the memory and the feeling of Cricket safe in his arms filled Tom with a sense that somehow everything was going to be all right. But then the feelings of well-being mutated into a startling awareness that he might never see his wife again.

"Let's go," Gregor said, pushing at Tom with the barrel of his gun. "She's fine."

Kelly, Lyons, and Mann stood behind him now.

Tom's initial reaction was to go after Gregor. Instead, he forced himself to look down at Cricket and contain his rage. In the three hours they'd been held hostage, Tom had come to the conclusion that although these men needed him, they would kill his daughter without a second thought. Cricket's safety was all that mattered to him right now. He had to play it smart to make sure she survived. That meant giving them whatever they wanted. At least until the opportunity for escape came.

"Can you keep going?" he asked Cricket.

She looked ready to dissolve, but nodded. "As long as I'm with you, I can keep going, Daddy."

Tom kissed her on the forehead and then pulled away from her and set off again, climbing down through the pitch-black hall, going deeper and deeper into the bowels of Jenkins Ridge.

He noticed a musty, vinegar odor in the air, the sweat scent of the men who held him captive. The sound of their footfalls slapped and echoed all around him, a constant reminder of his predicament.

Now the passage leveled and increased to the size of a subway tunnel.

Despite the danger he was in, Tom's mind whirled. Like most of Labyrinth Cave, he knew, the ancient subterranean byway had started hundreds of centuries ago as a crack in the rock through which seeped a dribble of water tainted by humic acid. Over the aeons, the mildly corrosive water poured through the crack, acting like a chainsaw, cutting, smoothing, and flushing the opening until it became a streambed and eventually a river. All along the walls Tom could see where thousands of years of water flow had created large, shell-like depressions in the limestone. These were the landmarks he was constantly reading, using them to navigate through the cave.

On the cave ceiling he was suddenly aware of curled petals of pallid gypsum mineral brushed by hints of rose. Within the petals, the white crystals grew into tendrils shaped like flower stamens, both ribboned and straight. Drifting from the tips of the most stunning orchid stamen were wisps of blond minerals so fine they stirred in the breeze like pollen threatening to take flight.

Kelly reached up and snapped off one of the formations just behind the flower. He sniffed it, then flicked it against a wall, where it shattered into a hundred pieces.

Tom couldn't help himself. "Stop that," he yelled. Those are some of the rarest formations in the world!"

Kelly's swarthy face tensed at being challenged. He snapped off another orchid and smashed that one, too. "Tell it to someone who gives a flying fuck," he said.

Behind Kelly, Tom saw Cricket shake her head, fear twisting her face. Once again, Tom was forced to swallow his anger. He moved them quickly forward to where the ceiling rose to almost twelve feet and the gypsum orchids grew out of reach.

"What about those guys in the helicopter?" Mann demanded. "How are we going to get out of here without being caught?"

"It's all taken care of," Gregor replied. "Let's just get to the stone first. If I get there, everything will be all right."

Tom's mind spun at the conversation. They kept talking about a stone. He wanted to know more, to understand what these men really wanted inside the Labyrinth, but decided the best thing he could do right now was keep quiet and make discoveries about them passively. Once he knew exactly why he and Cricket were being held, he might be able to use that information to help them get away.

For Tom, the next two hours were characterized only by the dull thud of boots on bedrock and the squeak and swish of packs against nylon suits and the clashing swords of light from helmet lamps; and the shadows in his peripheral vision, the dripping of water off the ceilings, and the constant, overriding thought that he had to save Cricket.

Then, somewhere in the line behind him, Tom became aware of one of the men humming. It was a tune he'd heard before but could not place exactly. Then he understood that it was a children's melody, one Cricket used to hum, but it was being delivered not with joy but with such understated menace that Tom stopped and turned.

The pretty boy, the one they called Mann, was ambling along behind Cricket His helmet hung off to one side of his head. Mann was humming and leering at his daughter. His hand was rubbing at his crotch.

"Get the fuck away from my daughter, you sick bastard," Tom roared as he weaved by Gregor, Kelly, and Cricket going for Mann.

But before he could get there, a girdle of electricity cinched itself around Tom's abdomen. Spikes of heat sliced inward from the girdle where they joined at his back, then twisted and ran up and down his spinal column, chopping him down. The last thing he remembered before the blackness took him were his fingers lashing the air as if he were keying an invisible piano.

12:22 P.M.
NASA ENCAMPMENT
JENKINS RIDGE
LABYRINTH CAVE

Jeannie's body kept bumping against Whitney in the darkness. The gritty water dripped down Whitney's throat, making her gag. She had to get back up on the ledge, out of the water. Her only chance. The water was robbing her of heat. She had to get out of the water.

But every time she got a handhold on the ledge, the corpse bumped her and knocked her hand free. Whitney plunged under the water for a second, then surfaced, sputtering and crying. She looked at her best friend's body in the dim light and, furious, began to strike out at it again and again and again…

"Can't go back in the cave again!" Whitney sobbed as she flailed her arms. "I can't! I can't!"

Then Whitney felt her wrists caught and taken in a strong grip. A voice, a steady, sure voice that reminded her of Tom's, said, "Mrs. Burke! Please, stop!"

Whitney struggled against the grip, which only became tighter and tighter until she relented and let the energy go out of her muscles. Then she hung her head, blinked several times, and breathed slower; and the waking nightmare faded and the redheaded Irishman who'd said he was a U.S. marshal, who'd told her what had happened to Tom and Cricket, came into focus.

Finnerty was on his knees, holding her by her forearms, a look of concern and understanding on his face. Whitney looked around and saw that she was sitting in a canvas-backed chair inside a tent. There were people she didn't recognize and then she saw Angelis, the mission commander, standing behind the marshal; and she knew it wasn't a dream.

That it was real and terrible. Finnerty was talking again and she turned her head in his direction. "That's better," he was saying. "Much better. Would you like some water?"

Whitney shook her head, then she felt tears streaming down her face. "They're gone," she mumbled. "Tom. Cricket. Gone just like Jeannie. Just like I said. I told him. And he didn't listen. I told him."

"No," Finnerty soothed. "They're not gone, Mrs. Burke. We're getting a strong signal from the locators they're carrying. We know where they are and that they're alive, but as I said before, we need your help to rescue them. We need you to take us into that cave."

"I can't," she blubbered. "When I go in caves, people die."

"Mrs. Burke... uh, Whitney," Finnerty said. "If you don't help us, your husband and daughter may die. You don't want Tom and Cricket to die, do you?"

Whitney stared at the marshal for the longest time, struggling to understand exactly what he was saying. Then she rubbed her sleeve across her nose and shook her head. "No. I want them to live. I want them to come home."

Finnerty smiled. " 'Course, you do. We all want them to come home. We all want them—"

"Boss," another voice said. Whitney turned and saw a shaved-headed Latino with a badge hanging on a lanyard around his neck.

"I'm sorry," Sanchez said. "But two guys with Justice Department clearance just came through security. It's about that sealed testimony."

Finnerty closed his eyes for a second, then let go of Whitney's wrists. "Can you wait here for me, Whitney, while I go talk with these men. What they have to say could be very important."

Whitney sniffed and nodded, then said, "Important to Tom and Cricket?"

The marshal frowned. "Could be."

Whitney flashed on the image of Tom and Cricket standing in her bedroom two nights before, all of them upset in the wake of her nightmare. "I want to be there. I want to talk to them."

"That's not a good idea," the marshal said. "You're upset and—"

Whitney stuck her chin up at him. "If you want my help, I want to be there."

For a long moment the marshal said nothing, but studied her with his hands clasped prayerlike in front of his face. Whitney felt a part of herself she thought she had lost a long time ago surface, and she met his gaze and did not let it waver. Finally, he let a smile creep onto his face and nodded. "Okay, Whitney. We'll play it your way."

Finnerty patted her on the leg, then stood and turned to Sanchez. "Call the gate. Have them send the Justice guys up."

Sanchez did not reply, but went straight out through the tent flaps.

The marshal nodded toward Two-Elk. "Get her something to drink and eat. She's gonna need it."

Then Finnerty motioned to Angelis. Together the two men walked outside the tent and toward the tree line. The sun was high overhead. The air was as thick and misty as a steambath. In the distance, the marshal saw the klieg lights of reporters covering the events. He thought of Natalie scowling at him the morning before, thought of all that it meant, then shook it off, stopped, and turned to the mission commander. "You want to tell me what the hell was going on in there?"

Angelis got a pained expression on his face. "Whitney Burke's suffering from post-traumatic stress," he replied. "She was involved in a horrible caving accident last year. Her best friend died. She was trapped with the body for nearly seventeen hours in a flooded cave before she was rescued."

"Jesus H. Christ," Finnerty moaned. "There's no one else who can do this?"

"No one with her level of experience," Angelis said. "I think if you just keep her focused on her husband and daughter, she'll be okay."

"Damian!" Boulter called from back near the tent. "They're here. The guys from Justice."

12:30 P.M.
JENKINS RIDGE
LABYRINTH CAVE

"Daddy!" Cricket cried, rushing to Tom's side. He writhed on the cave floor, his eyes rolled back in his head. His tongue arched backward and sought his throat.

"Do something!" she screamed at the men standing around her. "He's dying."

"Don't worry, kid, he ain't dying," Lyons said, squatting down next to her. "He just took a shock. Last a minute or so. He'll come around. Be weak awhile, but okay."

Cricket looked down at her dad, whose spasming had already ebbed. "I hate you," she told Lyons. Then she looked up at Gregor, Mann, and Kelly, who held the belly belt transmitter. "I hate all of you."

Mann smiled smugly down at her. "I don't hate you, Cricket. In fact, I think we can be real good friends."

Lyons stood and got right in Mann's face. "Leave the kid alone," he growled.

"I don't think so," Mann replied. "I haven't had a whiff of it in two years and she smells so ... ripe for the picking."

Lyons stuck the muzzle of his shotgun into Mann's belly. "I said leave her alone."

Mann hesitated, then batted his soft blue eyes at the guard. "Sure, Lyons. Suit yourself."

"Crick?" Tom said in a thick slur.

Cricket looked down at her dad and started to cry. His eyes were focusing, but there was a trickle of blood coming out the corner of his mouth.

"Don't talk, Dad," Cricket said. "You bit your tongue, bad."

Kelly got down next to them and tapped Tom on the shoulder with the antennae of the belly belt transmitter. "Control that temper a' yours, hear? Or next time I'll buzz you so hard, you'll bite that tongue a' yours clean off."

"I want my daughter with me," Tom managed to say.

"Can't do that," Kelly replied. "Separation keeps you compliant"

Tom tried to sit up and groaned at the effort.

"Lay down, Daddy," Cricket said. "Just stay there a minute."

Gregor stepped forward, shone his light into Tom's eyes, then snarled at Kelly, "Shit, I been hit twice that hard. Get him up. Now. We're losing time."

Kelly got his arm under her father's armpit and yanked him roughly to his feet. He almost collapsed, but Cricket grabbed him and held him upright. She'd never seen her dad like this, so helpless, and it scared her worse than anything that had happened so far. "I'll be okay," he said to her. "Just give me a minute."

"Daddy," Cricket said, then began to cry.

"Shhh. I'll be okay."

Then Tom looked from Kelly to Gregor to Lyons. "Keep that fucking pervert away from my daughter," he said. "Or I won't lead you another step."

Kelly said, "We'll keep Mann away from her and the belly belt away from you if you keep doing what we want."

He glared at Kelly, then said, "And Cricket gets to sit with me when we rest."

"No way," Kelly said.

"Deal," Lyons said.

"What are you, out of your mind?" Kelly demanded. "That's against the protocol of handling dangerous prisoners, Lyons. You know that."

"Fuck you, Kelly," Lyons said. "I said, deal."

"Gregor?" Kelly asked.

Cricket saw Gregor study Kelly and Lyons. Then he nodded and stared straight at her and her father with the coldest eyes she'd ever seen. "Sure, long as he takes us to the stone, she can sit with her daddy. But one more stunt like that and I'll kill the girl. Understand?"

12:40 P.M.
NASA ENCAMPMENT
JENKINS RIDGE
LABYRINTH CAVE

Whitney drank from the tumbler of ice water Two-Elk had given her. "Do you have children?" she asked.

The deputy marshal shook her head. "Never had the time."

"When they're born it makes you feel like you're connected to infinity, like you have all the time in the world," Whitney said. "But you don't. You have no time at all."

She started to feel herself reel toward the edge of the abyss, but she fought against it, closing her eyes, talking herself down. Then she heard the flaps of the tent rustle and the big Kentucky State Police captain, the U.S. marshal, and Angelis came in, followed by two men she didn't recognize.

The tall one wore shorts and a denim shirt and carried a battered leather satchel. He had a silver ponytail, and from the lines on his face appeared to be in his early fifties. Despite his age, he had the broad shoulders, pumped chest, and tapered waist of a competition swimmer. The second man was much younger, in his late teens, early twenties at best, Whitney thought. He was blond and blue-eyed and should have been quite handsome, but his features were obscured by a heavy layer of fat. The younger man wore baggy khaki pants and a white polo shirt stained with coffee. He was sweating so hard in the hot humid air that his eyeglasses were slightly fogged and Whitney immediately felt sorry for him.

Finnerty pointed at her. "Professor Swain, Whitney Burke."

The pony-tailed man strode to her with confidence. "Jeffrey Swain," he said. "Chairman of the Physics Department. University of Tennessee. This is my assistant Chester Norton."

The young man looked at his boss the way a slave might a demanding master, then smiled shyly and stuck out his hand. "Sorry we couldn't have met under better circumstances, ma'am," Norton said.

Finnerty said, "I gather we set off alarms with our request to see Gregor's trial record?"

"Alarms we've been waiting almost three years to hear," Norton said.

Swain smiled in a way that reminded Whitney of other academics she'd known who did everything to put forth the air that they suffered fools lightly. "I'm afraid my assistant has a penchant for the dramatic," he said.

Whitney saw Finnerty react as if he'd gotten a whiff of something he didn't like. "We've got hostages in that cave, Dr. Swain. Mrs. Burke's husband and daughter. If you've got something to say, something that will help us, I suggest you get on with it. These men are vicious. Lives are at stake."

"Just so, Marshal," the physicist replied. Then he took a deep breath and went on. "What I am about to describe is one of our nation's most guarded secrets, and at the request of the attorney general of the United States I must ask you all to sign these forms before I continue with the briefing."

He reached into the leather satchel and pulled out a thick sheaf of papers. Whitney took one in confusion and perused it. It was a legal document, the equivalent of a gag order, drafted under the auspices of the attorney general's office, demanding that she never reveal what Swain was about to tell her.

Finnerty took his copy and said, "What the hell is this all about?"

"Sign," Swain replied. "Then you'll hear it all."

"Does this concern my husband and daughter?" Whitney asked.

"It does now," Swain said.

Whitney took a pen and signed the document immediately. She watched as Angelis, Boulter, Two-Elk, Sanchez, and then Finnerty did the same.

"Very good," Swain said, taking the documents and handing them to Norton, who tucked them back in the briefcase. "Now, what do you know about superconductors?"

"Superconductors?" Finnerty said. "What does that have to do with this?"

"Everything, I'm afraid," Swain replied haughtily.

Angelis shrugged. "Superconductors are materials that channel electricity with virtually no resistance," he said. "Without resistance, electronic devices become infinitely more efficient and powerful. Scientists believe that superconductors may solve our energy problems and result in great economic gain for the nation. The most powerful superconductors, the ones we're going back to the moon to mine, were discovered at... " He suddenly looked intently at the physicist.

"The University of Tennessee," Swain said, finishing the thought.

Whitney gazed at Swain with newfound appreciation. She'd heard of him. Everyone had. "You were the one who figured out that certain materials in moon rocks superconduct at room temperature," she said. "You're responsible for all of this, the Artemis Project, everything. They say you're going to get the Nobel."

"It is what they say," Swain replied, grimacing. "Unfortunately, I was not the real discoverer, only the one who got the public credit."

"What?" Angelis said, stunned.

Finnerty shook his head. "I'm not clear on any of this."

Swain began to pace up and down in the tent. "Yes, I can see that, Marshal, and it's important that you be clear, very clear, to understand exactly what it is you're dealing with here. So a bit of history first: Superconductors were first discovered in 1911 by a Dutch physicist named Onnes, who found that the electrical resistance of a frozen mercury rod and thousands of other materials suddenly disappeared when cooled to near zero Kelvin, or two hundred seventy-three degrees below zero Fahrenheit.

"But for nearly seventy-five years, no scientist ever found a material that superconducted other than at those extreme temperatures," Swain went on. "Then, in 1986, scientists at the IBM Research Laboratory in Switzerland found that a ceramic material made of various ores would superconduct at the unusually high temperature of thirty degrees above absolute zero, or negative two hundred forty degrees Fahrenheit. Soon scientists around the world, including me, began experimenting with ore mixtures, and by the early 1990s they had driven the temperature for superconductivity up to nearly one hundred forty degrees below zero Fahrenheit."

"Okay," Whitney said. "But what does this have to do with—"

"It will all become clear if you just listen," Swain insisted. "During this same time, scientists at the University of Houston discovered another, more mysterious superconducting system that they called a Fullerene. The name came from the late designer-author Buckminster Fuller, inventor of the geodesic dome, a structure roughly the shape of a soccer ball. The scientists did not understand why, but they found that when specific compounds were formed at the molecular level in the shape of soccer balls, they, too, acted as superconductors. Are you with me, Mrs. Burke?"

Whitney saw from the expression on Swain's face that these facts might be crucial to her family's survival. For the past year, ever since the accident, she'd accepted life passively, mostly out of fear. Now, something deep inside her turned active. She was all scientist, listening intently to the nuances. "I'm with you," she said, nodding.

"Me too," Angelis replied.

But Finnerty and Boulter shook their heads in confusion.

Chester Norton pulled off his glasses and wiped them on his sweaty polo shirt. "The point is that even up until a few years ago, the highest known superconducting temperature was still staggeringly cold. The grail—zero-resistance energy transmission at room temperature—was still a pipe dream."

Swain frowned at the young man. "Are you going to tell the story, or am I?"

Norton cringed. "Sorry, Uncle Jeff."

" 'Uncle'?" Angelis said.

Swain got a pained expression on his face. "Yes, uncle, and my impetuous nephew is quite right. After all, I chased the dream myself. Carson

MacPherson, my late partner, did as well. We were materials researchers. We founded a laboratory at the University of Tennessee together. Like thousands of other scientists who tried to achieve room-temperature superconductivity, Carson and I spent most of our time experimenting with various exotic ceramic compounds."

Norton laughed. "He's making it sound like rocket science. Like most researchers, their methods were haphazard in the extreme; they would take darts, throw them at the periodic table of elements taped to the wall of their lab, then mix the compound and measure its superconductive properties."

Swain's face tightened in annoyance. "True. But by 2004, after nearly ten years of work, we were still having very little luck and our funding was being threatened. Enter Robert Gregor."

Whitney saw Finnerty become very alert and she leaned forward in her chair as the physics professor continued.

"Carson and I had been following Gregor's career for several years," Swain said. "He got his Ph.D. in materials science from Tennessee, then went on to an assistantship at the Planetary Geo-Sciences Institute, another research laboratory at the university that specializes in the study of asteroids and moon rocks. In the spring of 2004, Gregor came to Carson looking for a job, said he was interested more in applied research than pure science and wanted to work in the superconductor field."

The physicist smiled sourly at the memory. "Carson balked. His impression was that Gregor was smart but not exceptionally brilliant. There was also the way he looked and took care of himself. His clothes. His personal hygiene. The stammer. But Carson had heard stories about Gregor's childhood and knew what he'd overcome, so he gave him a break and hired him."

Whitney couldn't take it anymore. She felt that this was all irrelevant. Tom and Cricket were being held hostage inside the cave. "What does this matter?" she cried.

"It matters a great deal," Swain snapped.

Norton stepped in. "What my uncle's trying to get at, Mrs. Burke, is that within a few weeks you could tell Dr. MacPherson had it in for Gregor. Like a lot of these big-time physicists, he liked to badger people he considered intellectually inferior to him."

"That's not true," Swain said, indignant.

"Hell it isn't," Norton shot back glaring at his uncle in a way that surprised Whitney. "And you could see Gregor just taking it, or when he tried to defend himself, getting so crippled by his stammer. He'd turn beet red with frustration."

"This still doesn't give us the connection," Whitney said.

Swain sighed. "The connection, Mrs. Burke, is that Gregor's doctoral thesis focused on lunar rocks brought back by the Apollo astronauts. In October, after he'd worked for Carson for about ten weeks, Gregor suggested at an open staff meeting that he begin to focus some attention to the possible superconducting qualities present in the rare ores that make up asteroids and moon rocks."

"Sounds reasonable enough, given your methodology," Angelis said.

"Not to Dr. MacPherson," Norton retorted. "Uncle Jeff was in Japan at a meeting, but I was there and MacPherson dumped all over Gregor's idea, all but called him an idiot. You could just see the disbelief and hurt in Gregor's face." He pointed at Whitney and Finnerty. "But the real story, the one you're looking for, is based on research logs Gregor secretly kept between October 2004 and mid-January 2005."

"If you don't mind, Chester," Swain cut in. "You should know that NASA's Lunar Sample Laboratory in Houston safeguards every rock brought back from the moon. Getting samples to test is a complicated procedure. For a junior researcher such as Gregor, a written affidavit of support from the head of a recognized facility is required. Unbeknownst to me, Carson refused to sign the affidavit.

"According to the research logs Chester mentioned," Swain went on, "Gregor continued to think about the hundreds of stones that had been brought back from the moon during the Apollo missions. He wrote that he knew that several dozen of the rocks had never been touched. NASA had set these aside to be tested as technology advanced."

Whitney said, "So, what? Gregor got hold of one of these rocks anyway?"

"Very good, Mrs. Burke," Swain replied. "In mid-November, Gregor forged Carson's signature on his application to test one of those untouched moon stones. After a review of the request, the curator of lunar samples went to a liquid nitrogen tank and with long metal tongs plucked out a Teflon bag that had been sealed in 1972 and marked 'Moon Rock 66095.' According to Gregor's logs, the rock arrived at our laboratory in a small crate six days before the Christmas break."

Norton said, "It was finals week. Very chaotic. Everyone trying to finish up work before Christmas. It's easy to see how Gregor could have intercepted and hidden the stone before anyone knew of its presence at the lab."

"You got this all from his research logs, right?" Finnerty asked.

Norton nodded. "Say what you want about Gregor. But he was very detail oriented and a visionary."

Swain snorted. "Gregor was and is a madman who just got lucky. My nephew has a fine mind, but remains a shitty judge of character, I'm afraid."

Norton reddened and shook his head, but his uncle seemed not to notice and went on with his story. "Gregor waited to work on the rock until the dead of night the first evening of the Christmas break Carson had left for Scotland, where he would spend the holiday week before pushing on to a conference in Geneva. Chester and I had gone back to La Jolla, California, to visit my mother.

"Anyway, Gregor's logs show that his initial analysis of the stone indicated that it was made up of whitloctite, a calcium carbonate that contains low levels of uranium, and two oxide ores—illemnite and armalcholite—that are rare on Earth, but abundant on the moon.

"About two o'clock in the morning of Christmas Eve, he crushed a tiny bit of moon rock 66095, then created a film and ran an electric current through it at one hundred degrees below zero. It superconducted."

Whitney saw Finnerty shrug. Norton saw it, too, and said, "He'd raised the temperature of superconductivity nearly fifty degrees, Marshal. I mean, he's already got the Nobel at this point, but he tells no one. Doesn't e-mail Uncle Jeff or Dr. MacPherson. He goes on alone, basically living in the lab round the clock. His head isn't on prizes. It's on the boundaries of the thing."

Whitney nodded, understanding how easy it was to get swept up in the power of a new discovery. It had been exactly the same way in the first years she and Tom had explored Labyrinth Cave. She flashed on an image of Tom and herself hugging each other when they'd found the entrance into Christmas Tree Lane and almost broke down again.

"Yes, well," Swain said. "For the next five days, Gregor continued his experiments, altering the composition of the ore compound. On his twentieth try, on New Year's Eve, he took the temperature of superconductivity to an astounding fifty-eight degrees above zero."

Angelis shook his head in awe. "Room-temperature superconductivity."

"Closest you'll ever come," Norton agreed.

Now Whitney allowed impatience to creep into her voice. "Fascinating. But my family is underground with a bunch of animals. What does this have to do with—?"

"Please, Mrs. Burke, I'm almost finished," Swain interrupted. "On January third, Gregor made a cryptic notation in his logs that reads: '66095 equals composite Fullerene'."

"Which means what?" Finnerty demanded.

Norton cleared his throat "We take it to mean that because the rock itself was roughly the shape of a soccer ball, Gregor was hypothesizing that the stone *as a whole* might have superconductive properties."

The physicist's nephew then described Gregor's activities on January 6, 2004: "He built a spherical matrix of electrical wire around the stone, then ran a substantial current through it. He had sensors, recorders, and computers arranged around the rock." At that Norton stopped, ran his fingers over his cheeks, and stared at the floor.

"Well, what happened?" Whitney demanded.

Swain shook his head as if he couldn't believe what he was about to say. "Gregor's notes indicate that under the presence of the electrical matrix, the rock seemed to enter a state beyond what we would call superconductivity. The data he recorded indicates that it somehow fed on the energy, breaking it down into its base parts, then accelerated the speed and power of certain of those parts to stupefying levels, causing them to act in a way we've never seen before."

"What way?" Angelis asked.

Swain said, "Do you all know what a quark is?"

Whitney and Angelis nodded, but Finnerty said, "No."

"It's a subatomic particle, one of the most basic building blocks of matter, never known to rot or break apart before," Swain said. "But Gregor wrote that the stone showered off huge quantities of energy, including quarks that appeared to be disintegrating. Gregor wrote that it showed up on his sensors as bizarre spiral markings girdling the main flow of accelerated energy. He called the phenomenon 'quark decay'."

"Extraordinary!" Angelis said.

Whitney did not understand all of this, but grasped enough to nod in agreement.

To her surprise, a look of disappointment crossed Swain's face. "Yes, it is extraordinary," he said. "About the most extraordinary thing to happen in the world of physics since Einstein postulated relativity, and it was discovered by a poor boy from the backwoods of Kentucky."

"But he told no one about this?" Whitney asked.

Norton said, "Not one person. He just kept experimenting and over the next six days he developed a theory. He wrote that the quark decay, because of its effect on the energy flow, seemed to be the key to the stone's power. He believed that if he could figure out a way to control the quark decay, he might be able to make the stone act like a cannon, battering the subatomic composition of elements around it."

"To do what?" Whitney asked, confused.

Swain laughed caustically. "To transmute them. To change one element into another. At the subatomic level."

"Impossible," Angelis said.

"Completely," Whitney agreed. "Elements cannot be broken down and reconfigured. That's why they're called elements."

"Yes and no," Norton interjected "Back in 1941, three Harvard scientists showed that elemental transmutation was feasible. They bombarded four hundred grams of mercury with a blizzard of high-velocity neutrons. The neutrons knocked about the mercury at a subatomic level and the mercury was changed into isotopes of gold."

"Jesus H. Christ," Finnerty moaned. "Gregor convinced the guard and the inmates that escaped with him that he had a moon rock that could turn things into gold."

"That belief is unproven, at least according to the logs," Swain said. "Before he could attempt transmutation, Gregor was surprised by Dr. MacPherson, who had arrived home early from his conference in Switzerland. According to Gregor's notes, Carson was going to steal credit for the discovery and therefore control of the stone."

Norton said, "Gregor just couldn't take it. He couldn't take the idea of Dr. MacPherson, this man who'd belittled and run roughshod over him, taking credit for his discovery. We figure he just snapped, went nuts, and decided to kill Dr. MacPherson."

Swain nodded sadly. "Gregor's repeated exposures couldn't have helped his mental state."

"Exposure to what?" Whitney asked.

"The quark decay," the physicist replied. "Essentially it's a form of radiation we've never seen before, Mrs. Burke. You study Gregor's logs and you realize that he took very few precautions to protect himself."

"Because he didn't know what to expect," Norton interjected.

"That's your theory, Chester," Swain said, waving his hand dismissively. 'The point is, he kept exposing himself. Gregor wrote that he put Carson in the trunk of his car, then drove north with the stone and hid it in a place where he believed it would never be found. He wrote that he designed an entirely new matrix and energy source for the rock and let it run in his presence without adequate precaution for almost a week before leaving it to get resupplied.

"A state trooper pulled Gregor over January 22 near Louisville," the physicist went on. "He was driving as if he was drunk. The trooper said Gregor was in a terrible state mentally and physically. Grossly dehydrated. Lost all his hair. His skin was completely leached of pigmentation and—"

"That's when the trooper noticed the smell," Norton cut in. "Dr. MacPherson's decomposing body was in the trunk of Gregor's car. The research logs were in there too. But no stone."

There was a prolonged, heavy silence in the tent. Whitney struggled to digest everything the physicist and his nephew had said. It was all so fantastic. It must have struck Finnerty the same way, because he asked, "You believe everything Gregor wrote?"

"Initial skepticism was my reaction as well, Marshal," Swain admitted. "But at the government's request, I repeated Gregor's experiments with mixtures of armalcholite and illemnite gleaned from other rocks from the Descartes Highlands. There's no doubt about it. The composite ore superconducts at close to room temperature and because of that, we're returning to the moon. Because of that we're all here right now, trying to find out if Gregor's stone still exists."

Whitney saw the connection. "You think Gregor hid the stone here, in the Labyrinth, don't you," she said, then pushed on before either Swain or Norton could answer her. "You said the moon rock enters a superconducting state at just below fifty-eight degrees Fahrenheit. Labyrinth Cave has a constant temperature of fifty-six degrees. And then there's the insulating qualities of the cave. Two hundred feet of rock makes it darn tough to use sensors to detect it, doesn't it? Gregor's taken Tom and Cricket hostage because he wants them to lead him back to wherever he's hidden his moon rock. Isn't that right?"

"Yes, Mrs. Burke," Swain said. 'That's exactly right."

At that, it all became overwhelming and Whitney hung her head and began to shake it back and forth like someone who's just suffered a concussion. Then she felt a hand on her back and a presence by her side. Finnerty knelt next to her once again. "You see now you've got no choice, don't you, Mrs. Burke?" he said. "Without you to lead me, I can only guard the entrances and hope that after Gregor gets to his stone, he allows your husband and daughter to emerge alive. Given his ruthlessness in the past, I'd say that's a big if."

Whitney felt the irrational need to pluck at the fabric of her sleeve, but she couldn't allow herself to dissolve. Not now. Not when her child's life was at stake. Not when her husband's life was at stake. Not when their future as a family was at stake.

She raised her head and gazed at him. "Guarding the known entrances may not be enough, Marshal," she said. "There may be more than four ways into the cave."

"How many more?"

"I don't know. But Tom was convinced that we hadn't found all of the entrances and we might not in our lifetime. The Labyrinth lies under a large area, more than two hundred fifty square miles, and the ridges are so steep, and the hollows between them so choked with vines and thorns, that he believed there could be dozens of ways in and out of the cave we don't know about."

"What would you do if you were me?" Finnerty asked. "To save Tom and Cricket, to recapture these men?"

Whitney swallowed hard and looked all around the tent, petrified by what she was about to say. "If I were you, I'd go inside," she said, her voice shaking with emotion. "I'd go inside, ambush those bastards, and rescue my family before it's too late."

1:30 P.M.
JENKINS RIDGE
LABYRINTH CAVE

For the next six hours, Tom kneaded at his aching stomach muscles while leading the inmates and Cricket slowly west through dry subterranean canyons. Every minute or so he'd look back to make sure Cricket was all right. That had become a fixation, making sure that Cricket came out of this cave safe and sound. He'd promised Whitney that. He owed Whitney that. He didn't know if Whitney could tolerate anything but that. He wondered how she was coping. He imagined she knew by now and prayed that the news had not sent her into another tailspin.

In the early evening, they came to a grotto nearly two hundred yards long and one hundred fifty feet wide. The cavern's ceiling was nearly forty feet high and smooth. The walls were dull flat gray. The floor was covered with thousands of small rock disks. The disks themselves were coated by thousands of years of dried bat guano, which lent the air a chemical quality. Alert for any slip that would cause a snapped ankle, Tom led them across that treacherous place. For many minutes, the sound of the cave wind was drowned by the inmates' cursing and the noise of the rocks clunking together underfoot.

At last they reached the end of the loose disks and rested before a giant, floor-to-ceiling mineral formation that resembled a waterfall. Some of the individual draperies that created the petrified cascade were a dull white, but most carried a red or bluish gray tone, which lent the place its name: Patriot Falls.

Cricket came toward Tom. He noted to his satisfaction that she seemed barely winded by the rigors of the long hike. But the toll was clearly beginning to surface on their captors, who were covered with dust and sweaty grime. Mann, Kelly, and Lyons held themselves this way and that to cradle the bruises the cave had scrimshawed on their bodies. Score one for us, Tom thought. It's a particular skill to be able to move your body cleanly over stone, and none of them yet had it.

Except for Gregor. If Tom had to point to the one who had obviously been in caves before, it was this physically contorted albino of a man. Despite his sickly appearance, he moved with economy and balance. He used his headlamp to plot a way forward before he took any steps; he checked his handholds constantly; he never crawled when he could stoop; he never stooped when he could walk upright

But what interested Tom more was the sense he'd gotten that Gregor's entire being seemed to ebb and flow as if it were a tide connected to the pull of the moon's gravity. At times he seemed about to explode with nervous energy. At other moments he turned sullen and spent and appeared on the verge of collapse. Every hour or so, Kelly would take Gregor's blood pressure, his temperature, and his pulse. The vital signs he called out were wildly erratic. Lyons kept feeding Gregor pills in an effort, Tom supposed, to level out his system. But from what Tom knew of basic physiology and emergency medicine, the pills were having minimal effect. The guy could have a stroke at any moment.

Then Tom asked himself if he might create enough stress to cause Gregor to have a stroke. The thought chilled him. But he had to defend himself, didn't he? He certainly had to defend Cricket by any means necessary.

Cricket sat down and rested her chin on Tom's shoulder. "You okay, Dad?"

"Stomach feels like a truck plowed into it, but I'm fine," he said. "You?"

"I'm okay," she said, then knitted her brows. "You think Mom knows?"

"She must."

Tears welled in Cricket's eyes. "You think we'll ever see her again?"

Tom put the knuckle of his index finger under her chin and stared directly into her eyes. "We'll see her again because we're coming out of this alive. Don't you dare ever think different, you hear me?"

Cricket snuggled into the crook of his neck. "I hear you," she whispered.

Ten feet away, Tom caught Lyons watching them, then turning when Mann asked Gregor, "How far we gotta walk? My feet are killing me."

"How far would you journey to hold the universe in your hands?" Gregor said.

"What kind of answer is that?" Mann grumbled.

"An answer that could make you a very rich man," Gregor snapped.

"What is it exactly you guys are after?" Tom asked.

"None of your fucking business," Kelly said. "Shut up unless you're spoken to."

But Gregor said, "You're a scientist, Burke. You might just comprehend it."

"Hey," Kelly warned. "It's just like back in The Castle, Gregor. Keep him dumb, ignorant, and happy, and we won't have no problems."

The pale man ignored Kelly, his face suddenly flushing. "It's best understood mathematically, but I'll give it to you in laymen's terms," he said, then went on in the tone of a young professor addressing an upper-level class. "It goes back to the Egyptians. They were the first to refine metal ores. They were the first to make alloys, mixing gold with silver to create the jewelry Pharaoh wore.

"At the same time," Gregor continued, "the Greeks were refining their method of logical inquiry, culminating in Aristotle's first science experiments. These two forces—Egyptian metallurgy and the Greek rational-thought process—collided in Alexandria, which was then the greatest center of learning on Earth. And so was born the great arcanum, the science of alchemy."

Tom stared at Gregor for a long moment, then rolled back his head and laughed. "Alchemy?" he chortled. "What, you think you have some philosophers' stone or something in here that can change lead into gold? Is that what this is about? Ridiculous!"

He continued to chuckle and Gregor's entire body twisted with fury.

"I... I was speaking in a metaphorical sense, you dimwit," he retorted. "The first scientists were seeking to manipulate the building blocks of the universe. What all those crackpots back in medieval times did not understand was that the philosophers' stone was not some substance that could be isolated. It was unbridled energy, transformative energy. That's what the Big Bang was, fool: an outpouring of the creative force of the universe. That's what I harnessed, that creative force. And that's what we're in here to recover: the harness."

JUNE 16, 2007
4:15 A.M.
MUNK'S RIDGE
LABYRINTH CAVE

Dr. Jeffrey Swain looked through the bars of the locked gate at the Nautilus Entrance to Labyrinth

Cave. Cool steam bearing the faint scent of rot billowed up from the dark slot in the ground bordered by two knobby arcs of gray limestone that jutted out of the earth like spire whorls on a crustacean.

"Check it out, Chester," Swain said.

Heaving and sweating from the forty-five-minute hike up the side of Munk's Ridge, the third of the Labyrinth's nine, the physicist's plump nephew pushed his glasses back up the bridge of his nose, took several steps toward the cave entrance, reached into his pack, and took out an electronic device about twice the size of a minicassette tape player. It was cased in green metal and fitted with a thick nylon lanyard, two small screens, and a stubby rubberized antenna.

Swain slid up next to his nephew. In the dawn light, Chester looked so much like his mother it made Swain's heart hurt. The physicist's sister had raised the boy herself after a miserable short-lived marriage. She'd been a brilliant attorney who died of leukemia when the boy was nine. Chester had gone to live with Swain because there was no one else capable. For the physicist it had been a long period of adjustment. His only commitment in life up until that point had been to science, and then there was this responsibility shoved upon him. But Chester was an intellectual prodigy as Swain himself had been, and he had spent the ensuing years pushing, prodding and driving his nephew until now the nineteen-year-old was just a semester away from obtaining dual master's degrees in physics and computer science. At this rate he'd have his doctorate before he turned twenty-five. Swain knew that at some level Chester resented his relentless goading, but he told himself it was all for the good. True scientists were interested in one thing: immortality through achievement and discovery. And Chester, so young so brilliant, so masterfully guided, was positioned to do exactly that.

"Motherfucker," Chester said, startling Swain from his thoughts. "It's for real."

Swain looked at the sensors. On the lower screen, an elongated infinity symbol floated serenely in a sea of digital cobalt. A baffling series of numbers spat themselves across the upper screen below a multicolored, bell-shaped bar graph. For a moment, the infinity symbol lay inert, then almost imperceptibly it began to pulse. And the bell-shaped bar graph began to rise and fall, as if in rhythm with someone's breath.

"Unbelievable," Swain said.

"What's unbelievable?" Finnerty demanded behind them.

The physicist turned. The marshal, Sanchez, and Two-Elk were now dressed in ballistic-cloth suits colored mottled gray. On slings around their necks they carried small machine pistols mounted with glow-in-the-dark tritium sights. Cave packs hung at their hips. Mrs. Burke wore the same outfit, minus the weapon. She was sitting on a log forty yards down the slope, her head in her hands. Captain Boulter was busy positioning a crew of FBI snipers who had flown in overnight.

They had begun climbing the mountain in the pitch dark after getting just three hours of sleep. The plan that he, Finnerty, and Mrs. Burke had put together during the long night was twofold. The physicist, his nephew, and Boulter would use sophisticated sensors at the various entrances to the cave to try to triangulate the moon rock's position. Mrs. Burke would lead Finnerty, Sanchez, and Two-Elk into Munk's Ridge. The theory was that unless Gregor managed to retrieve the rock within twenty-four hours, the inmates and their hostages would be forced to get food and batteries and use the sleeping bivouacs at the supply dump deep within the far northeastern corner of the third ridge of the Labyrinth's nine. From the Orpheus Entrance to the cave, where Cricket and Tom had gone in, it was a minimum of twenty-two hours to the supply cache. But Mrs. Burke believed she could get Finnerty and his team to the dump within just six hours by going in through the Nautilus Entrance. Leaving at dawn, they should make it to the cache site in plenty of time to prepare for the ambush.

But Swain's immediate concern was the stone. He looked at Finnerty and pointed to the sensor his nephew held.

"It's the exact electromagnetic signature Gregor said he measured coming off the moon rock," he explained. "Staggeringly high energy output. Low photon surge. Incredible neutron exchange, not to mention the quark decay. That rock's definitely in this cave.

"Now, whatever you do," Swain went on, "do not attempt to deactivate the stone should you happen upon it. The way Gregor's log notes read, he believed there's a risk of destabilization should the stone be disconnected from its power source too abruptly."

"Just frigging great," Sanchez said. "We're gonna go play hide-and-seek in a cave with some kind of atomic bomb inside."

"Perhaps one of us *should* go inside with you, Marshal," Swain said.

Finnerty shook his head. "It's bad enough I have to take one civilian."

Norton reached into his pack and handed the marshal a second sensing device. "At least take this with you. It'll give you an idea if you're at all close."

Finnerty took the sensor as if it were a live grenade, then handed it to Two-Elk, who put the lanyard around her neck and tucked the machine into her cave suit.

The woods were waking up around them. Mosquitoes whined, squirrels chattered, owls hooted, crows cawed, and in the distance wild turkeys gobbled. Then the moist breeze turned gusty, spinning the live oaks around them like thousands of green pinwheels. The forest fell silent. The dawn sky showed the patina of hammered brass. Far off on the southwestern horizon, puffer clouds rolled steadily east, violent through their bellies, the first portent of distant unrest.

Finnerty turned away from the physicist and his nephew and looked up at the threatening sky. "How bad could this storm get?" he asked Boulter.

The state police captain chewed at his upper lip. "Latest report says we could be feeing two inches an hour, maybe more, sometime after midnight. But you get in and out quick, you should be okay, Damian."

The marshal hesitated, then said, "Do me a favor, Mark"

"Anything."

"Natalie. I just tried to call, but she was in the OR. Would you call her, give her reports on our progress?"

"Absolutely," Boulter said. "But don't worry, you're going in and out clean."

Finnerty hesitated again, then said, "Tell her I love her, Mark. More than anything. And if something should happen to me, there's a letter in my—"

"Knock it off. You're gonna be fine."

"I got a bad feeling about this one," Finnerty said.

Boulter glanced over at Whitney Burke. "Think she can do this?"

"We're about to find out," the marshal replied, then he called out, "Mrs. Burke? Whitney? We're ready."

Whitney had intentionally kept her head down, studying the moldering leaves and branches on the forest floor, unwilling, unable, to look anywhere near the distinctive seashell shape of the Nautilus Entrance.

At Finnerty's call, she got to her feet with the movements of an arthritic. She tied the red silk bandana she always wore when caving around her neck. She snapped her helmet in place, then got her pack and started shuffling toward the cave. Every snap of twig, every cry of bird, every tremble in the forest canopy around her seemed more distinct than it should have. Finnerty, Sanchez and Two-Elk, Boulter, and Swain and Norton stood aside to let her lead. She went right by them without a word and stopped just short of the cave's mouth, throwing her arm out against the frame of the open gate. Her vision tunneled, then went kaleidoscopic.

She heard Two-Elk murmur to Sanchez, "This is gonna be like the disturbed leadin' the blind."

"Knock it off," Finnerty growled. "You okay, Whitney?"

But Whitney could not answer. She felt herself falling into the darkness of her mind.

"It's in the tube! The flood's in the tube!"

"For God's sake, go!" Jeannie screeched.

Whitney battled the hysteria surging within her and by sheer will pulled herself along. But with every foot of passage gained, she felt the power of something wild, savage, and uncontrollable take possession of her. She had an overwhelming desire to get up and run, wanting nothing more than to smash the walls of her confinement and escape into sweet, clean, open air.

Whitney reached a section of the cave that doglegged left and then immediately back to the right. The water was six inches deep now. Her hands and forearms were submerged. A foot of air remained. Whitney made it through the contortion, glanced up, and saw what looked like the arched interior of a belltower about three feet wide and ten feet high. She ducked down to tell Jeannie. The crown of her assistant's white helmet poked around the second dogleg.

"There's a shaft ahead," Whitney called, "with a ledge that should get us above flood level."

Jeannie squirmed forward a foot, stopped, then splashed and pulled herself along another ten inches. Suddenly her eyes widened and widened again. "Whitney, I'm caught!"

Whitney jerked at the dread that swept over her. "Where?"

"My left boot. It's locked in a crack in the floor!" Jeannie's face turned crimson as she struggled to free herself, then she stopped and heaved in frustration. Water reached the corner of her mouth and she sputtered at it.

"Try to go backwards," Whitney soothed. "Caving 101, remember? Whatever you can get into, you can get out of."

Jeannie nodded. She braced her hands against the ceiling and pushed, arching her body in a grotesque limbo move. She strained, let out a grunt of exertion, strained again, then all at once she let herself slump. "No way."

"I'm coming in there!"

Whitney stood into the belltower grotto. She threw her pack up onto the little ledge, then ducked back into the lower passage. Jeannie had twisted her face toward the ceiling to keep her mouth out of the water. The flame of her carbide lamp burned a black tongue on the roof of the passage. Whitney reached Jeannie in three pulls and said, "I'll push on three, okay?"

Jeannie seemed not to hear. She stared at the black scorch on the roof of the cave.

"On three!" Whitney yelled.

"Okay."

"One, two, three!"

Whitney got her left hand against Jeannie's shoulder and pressed forward with all her strength. She felt the muscles in her assistant's upper body bunch for the longest time and then sag again. "It's no good, "Jeannie said.

They rested helmet to helmet, panting, watching the water swirl in the lamp glow. Then Jeannie started to cry. "Whitney, I'm so scared."

Whitney fought off the urge to sob. She thought of her daughter, sitting in school, and her husband, on his way home from Houston. She gazed into Jeannie's eyes. Over the years they had become the sisters neither of them had ever had.

"I'm gonna try one more thing, okay?"

Jeannie could not speak.

"When I tell you to, you're going to arch your body as high as you can against the ceiling. I'm going to try to get under you and see if I can untie your boot. Ready?"

Jeannie managed to nod.

Whitney took a big breath and dropped into the water. With the light of her headlamp it was all harshly bright and bubbling brown. She found Jeannie's coverall and got a shoulder under her assistant's torso and stretched her arm as far as she could. Her fingers brushed Jeannie's thigh, her knee, her shinbone—Whitney struggled, shifted, and stretched again. Her lungs felt as if a torch were burning inside them.

She breached back up. "I can't reach it. I… "

The water pressed against their lips. Jeannie stared at Whitney. "Save yourself," she said.

"No. I won't leave you."

"For Tom and Cricket. You do it for them. You hear me?"

It was all beyond her comprehension now, but at some deep survival level Whitney knew she had to leave or they would both drown. Robotically, she began to back out of the passage. Jeannie bent her head back to keep her mouth and headlamp flame above the water. When there was only an inch of air left, she called out, "Tell my mom and dad and... Jim... that I loved them."

"Oh, God, Jeannie, I... "

But Jeannie's flame was gone, swallowed by the food.

"Whitney!" Finnerty said, shaking her by the shoulder. "Are you okay to do this?"

"No," she said. Then she twisted on her headlamp. "But I'm going in anyway."

She moved carefully through the open gate, as if it were electrified, then pressed both her hands out to the rock walls beyond. The limestone was slick and cool and had the consistency and color of molten pewter. The opening spiraled left and steeply down.

Whitney took one step, then shakily another, and the full force of the cave's rotting breath came whistling up the stone staircase at her. She saw dots before her eyes, and when her vision returned it was as if she had somehow disconnected from her body and the anxieties that dwelled within it. But she kept thinking about Tom and Cricket and reminding herself that she had come this way safely dozens of times before the accident. Her body moved stiffly down a third step and another and then five more. The limestone walls seemed to close in around her. She wanted to scream. She wanted to scream, turn, and run. But she forced herself to keep going footstep by footstep, even as she realized that the dimensions of her fear were becoming circumscribed as her headlamp replaced the fading sunlight behind her.

The passage bent again to the left and Whitney moved completely out of the cave's twilight zone. She slowed, letting her eyes adjust to the graduating cone of beamed light that was now the only thing separating her from complete and permanent darkness. The tone of the cave wind changed, turned broader and more muted, almost like the undulating hollow roar of a distant crowd. It all seemed as if she were doing it for the first time and she was hating every moment.

"I don't have to go back in the—" Whitney stopped, realizing that this would no longer do. She seized on an older mantra, one that had supported her through miles and years below ground: "Okay, Whit, never give the cave a chance."

8:00 A.M.
JENKINS-HAWKINS CONNECTION ROUTE
LABYRINTH CAVE

"This is crazy!" Mann cried. "How much more of this we gotta go through?"

Tom was concentrating too hard to answer. They were in a floorless canyon, a passage without a bottom. Looked at in cross-section, it was like a series of stacked figure eights with no closure between the loops. They were in the uppermost loop, feet braced against one curved wall of the cave, shoulders pressed back against the other. Their butts and thighs hung in space above a twenty-five-foot fall through jagged rock outcroppings to rushing water below. Worse, honey-colored mud caked the curved walls. As they started to inch sideways over the chasm, the ooze avalanched. The saturated soil splattered off the ragged stone teeth and fell like dirty hail into the Whitewater. The sound echoed all around them. The air in that confined space turned thick with the stench of muck and the sweat of fear.

They were negotiating one of several connection routes between Jenkins Ridge and Hawkins Ridge. Over the years, Tom had come to equate going through a cave connection as akin to slithering down a rotting sewer drain—it got tighter and nastier the deeper you went. And he had chosen the nastiest way he could think of to get from this part of the cave to the next.

It was part of his strategy. Ever since seeing how upset Gregor had become when he'd challenged him about alchemy, Tom had come to realize that keeping the inmates off-balance might be the best way to fight back. Caves are among the most unforgiving environments on Earth; they have a way of punishing people who are too tired or too preoccupied. If Tom could get his captors to make mistakes, the odds of him and Cricket escaping would rise dramatically.

He glanced over his shoulder to see the inmates spread out behind him on the slick ledge. They were coated waist to toe in a film of mire. There was a glazed quality to the way they took in their surroundings. It was happening: They were learning that the cave was a living thing, the skin of which changed at every moment. Keep them going at this pace, Tom thought, and one of them will screw up soon.

They reached a dead-end wall in the passage. Tom paused to adjust the strength of his headlamp beam, then dropped his feet through the serrated cavity beneath him. The rims of the pinched canyon caught him under both armpits and for a moment he dangled there, his feet free in space above the long drop through the rock teeth to the water. Then he began to swing back and forth like a gymnast on the parallel bars until, on the fifth upstroke, his toes found an unseen ledge. He leaned way back, limboed his way under the rock face, and found himself in an oval-shaped chamber. Cave onyx—calcite deposits that looked like grape-sized pearls—lined the walls of the grotto.

"Clear," Tom called back.

One by one, Gregor, Kelly, Cricket, Lyons, and then Mann accomplished the tricky maneuver. One by one, they collapsed against walls of the grotto, all of them gasping for breath, almost overcome by the particular horror of crawling a slick wall three miles underground.

Cricket went over to Tom and lay against him. They had stopped for only two forty-minute rests since entering the cave nearly twenty-four hours ago. She fell asleep immediately. Tom gazed down at her, sleeping so peacefully, and the whole cavern seemed to melt into the night she was born.

Whitney had been two weeks overdue. It was raining hard. He was still working on his doctoral thesis and had fallen asleep at his desk, so at first he didn't hear Whitney calling him from the bedroom. Then a crack of thunder woke him and he heard her yelling. He ran into the bedroom and found her already in hard labor.

"I'll get the car started!" he cried.

"I won't make it," Whitney screamed.

"I'll call the paramedics!"

Twenty minutes later, a fire truck pulled up in front of the house, and Tom, for the first time in his life, lost his cool. He raced down the steps, yelling, "There's no fire! Go back! I don't need firemen! My wife's having a baby."

"Calm down," the mustached chief told him. "We came with an ambulance."

The ambulance pulled up a second later, followed by the local sheriff, a notorious hard-ass who'd given Tom several speeding tickets. Then the whole crew—firemen, paramedics, and sheriff—all marched in to find Whitney spread-eagled on the bed.

Whitney stared up at the crew of handsome men and moaned, "Oh, God, why me?"

A half hour later, with the paramedics holding her from behind, Whitney sat up and pushed, and Tom caught Cricket in his arms. All the firemen cheered. The hard-ass sheriff started crying.

"I'll make sure she's okay, Whitney," Tom murmured. He had dozed and now he came awake and looked around. The three inmates were asleep. Lyons, the guard, sat just two feet away with his headlamp on low power. His dark skin glistened with grime. He was looking right at Tom.

"Be cool, Burke," he whispered. "There's a lot more at stake here than you know. Gregor may seem a nutcase, but he's a genius. The rock's for real. It's the most valuable thing on the planet."

"I don't give a shit," Tom replied evenly. "I just care about my daughter."

"Like I said, you care about her, you be cool, we all get what we want."

Cricket stirred. "Dad?"

"Right here, sweetheart," Tom said, drawing his attention away from Lyons. "I know you want to sleep. But you need to eat to keep your strength and give your body enough fuel to ward off the cold."

Cricket forced open her eyes, nodded, sat up groggily, then dug into her pack for food tubes. Lyons gave Tom one last look then began shaking Kelly, Gregor, and Mann awake.

As they ate, Gregor coursed up on one of his manic highs. He stood and tugged tight the straps of his pack. "How far is it to the next ridge?" he demanded.

"Four hundred yards, if we could go straight through the rock," Tom replied. "But it gets tricky up ahead, there are lots of switchbacks and pits—"

"Whaddya mean, pits?" Kelly demanded. His swarthy face was caked with drying mud.

"Shafts," Tom said. "Deep holes."

"Hate this place," Mann grumbled.

"Don't think about the short-term pain, Mann," Gregor said, waving his hands about. "It will be worth it. Soon the untold riches created by the stone will be yours."

"Uh-huh," Kelly grunted. "What I wanna know is, who gets the stone?"

At that Gregor's entire being went on high alert. "The stone is m-m-mine," he said. "I discovered its power. I alone understand it."

"Sure," Lyons said, his eyes sweeping the other inmates. "We wouldn't even know what to do with it, now, would we? How to handle it, I mean. That's all yours, Gregor. Let's just get there and get the gold, right?"

Gregor eyed them all distrustfully, especially Kelly. "Right," he said at last.

Cricket watched the men who held her and her father hostage with growing despair. They didn't care about her or her dad. She was sure of that.

They'd do anything to get the gold and this stone they were talking about. Gregor had said he'd kill her if her father tried to fight back again. Then she thought, But he didn't think about me trying to fight back. The thought startled her and then filled her with dread. What would happen if she did fight back? Wouldn't they just kill her anyway?

Before she could continue in this vein, her father began to move into a dismal crawlway that led off the western end of the onyx grotto. Gregor followed Tom, then Cricket followed the pale scientist. It was dank in that closed space. Ahead somewhere she heard the echoes of water falling. She crawled toward the sound on all fours, trying to keep pace with the soles of Gregor's boots. A headlamp lit up her lower torso from behind. During the first hundred yards or so, Cricket thought Lyons was directly behind her. Then they reached a tight spot where Gregor had to wait for her father to move through.

She lay there, head down, focusing on the dust. She was thinking how tired she was and how much she'd love to be held by her mother right then. A whistle began in the crawlway behind her. A softly blown, jaunty whistle that gave over to murmured singing. *"When there's too much to do, don't let it bother you, forget your troubles... do, do, do."*

The singing turned to menacing laughter. It was Mann. He was singing "Whistle While You Work" from *Snow White and the Seven Dwarfs*. Coming out of the oval chamber where they'd eaten and rested, he had somehow gotten behind her in line.

Gregor began crawling again. Cricket scurried after him around the curve in the cave passage and out of Mann's reach. But his murmured singing did not stop even when they reached the first pit and she heard Gregor grunt with alarm.

Cricket saw Gregor's torso sticking out of the wall near the top of a hollow, prism-shaped pipe that drilled thirty feet deeper into the earth. She knew from experience that the right side of the tubular grotto was perhaps twelve feet across. On the left, nine feet from Gregor's position, it cinched to a black crack in the wall. Water bubbled and dribbled down the rift. The sides of the pit and the floor three stories below were spiked with slanted formations that looked like the upturned heads of giant axes. It was known as the Turbine Blade Shaft because when you looked down into it, under the glare of a headlamp beam, you got the sickening impression of peering into the throat of a revving jet engine.

Crossing the shaft demanded an icy will, Cricket knew, especially for the first caver in line. She craned her head to watch her dad ease onto a narrow ledge at his right, then stand and brace one arm against the ceiling, ever mindful of the glistening blades below. He leaned out over the void to grab a nylon loop anchored in the ceiling many years ago. Then he inched his way to a balcony at the far side of the pit, turned, and looked back.

"Get out on the ledge, then reach for the loop," her dad called to Gregor.

With excruciating slowness, Gregor crept out onto the narrow rock outcropping. There was a moment of distress and then he leaned out into space, caught the loop, and made it to the far side.

A gloved hand reached up and cupped Cricket between her legs. Mann's thumb began to rub at her as he sang, "*I know we'll be alone sometime soon, Cricket, and when we do… Imagine that the broom is someone you love… where hearts are high the time will fly, do, do, do, do.*"

A scream choked in her throat and she kicked back at him, but couldn't get loose of his grip. She scrambled forward, finally freeing herself from Mann's grasp, and got out onto the ledge. She looked over at her dad, tears streaming down her face. She was shuddering, barely holding on to the side of the pit. Mann's face was at her feet. He was whistling again.

"Make him stop!" Cricket screamed.

"Knock it off, you asshole!" Tom yelled. "You'll kill her!"

Cricket looked down at Mann. He stopped whistling but still smirked.

"Calm yourself down," she heard her dad say. "Then look for the loop. You've done this before."

Cricket blinked back her tears, swallowed, and nodded. Then she looked down again at Mann's face leering up at her. She got very pissed off and told herself she was not going to fall, not because of a sicko like him. She got herself turned just enough to see the nylon loop dangling from the ceiling. A small piece of ledge under her foot crumbled.

Cricket threw her body flat against the wall, listening for the entire edge to give way. It held. She raised her head. She squinted at her father's headlamp shining at her from the other side of the pit.

"You can do this," he said.

"The ledge. It's weak."

"I can see that. But the loop is what really matters."

Cricket nodded, adjusted her footing, took a breath of faith, and went for it. She caught the anchored webbing and in fifteen seconds was at her dad's side, sobbing, "He grabbed me, Dad. Between the legs."

From the slot on the opposite wall, Mann's face was splotched with grit. His helmet was cocked to one side. He grinned across the shaft, then let his headlamp aim down into the gloom toward the turbine blades and his expression sobered.

"I hate him," Cricket whispered. "I want him to die."

Tom looked at her, then back at Mann. He waved his hand in the direction of the sling dangling from the piton. "Get out on the ledge. Get the loop."

Mann hesitated, then the chamber was filled with voices issuing from the passage behind him—Kelly and Lyons—urging him on. At last he forced his body out into the tube and up onto the narrow outcropping of rock. He smeared his trembling body into the wall.

"Reach for it," Gregor yelled. "It's not that bad."

"I'll fall," Mann said.

"Do it," said Kelly, whose face was now poking out the far end of the cave passage.

Mann hesitated, then shuffled left. More of the ledge crumbled. Fragments of stone careened away, pinging off the sharp rocks that jutted off the shaft wall.

"Break off," Cricket muttered. "Break off."

But Mann made it across the rotted worst of it and onto a stronger section of ledge. He grinned at his success, then twisted his upper body, his eyes searching for the nylon loop. Cricket knew with certainty then that Mann would make it across to torment her in the hours to come, rape her if he had the chance. She experienced a moment of internal blindness, of no possibility, of shrinking inward. Then a voice she had never heard before began talking in her head, an angry voice, a woman's voice that she recognized as her mother's, then strangely as her own, commanding her to act.

Mann arched his body, readying his fingers to cross through space. Cricket puckered her lips. She began whistling that melody he'd been taunting her with. Out of the corner of her eye, she saw her father startle, look at her, then begin whistling along with her.

By the time Mann registered their whistling, he had already committed himself. His legs were uncoiling and his upper body was crossing out over the shaft, his hand lifting toward the loop, two feet away. For a split second Mann's attention left the loop and sought Cricket and her dad. Their eyes met. Then a look of panic flashed across Mann's face and he jerked his head back toward the loop.

It was too late. He had leaned too far at the wrong angle. He batted impotently at the bottom of the nylon loop. He made frantic swimming motions with his arms, then screamed and pitched headlong after his headlamp beam.

A blade along the wall caught Mann's outstretched right forearm, causing him to list to one side before falling again. He glanced off two more wall blades, then rolled in space. He struck the floor sideways with a nauseating thud. Mann shuddered a moment, impaled on the spikes of angular rock, then he crumpled and lay perfectly still. Blood poured out on the wet limestone, and Cricket felt triumph pulse through her.

11:30 A.M.
MUNK'S RIDGE
LABYRINTH CAVE

Whitney, Finnerty, Two-Elk, and Sanchez emerged into a cavern with a low ceiling and walls thirty yards to either side. The floor looked like a deep lake of oil, shimmering against the cave's breath. The ceiling appeared rippled.

They were six hours into the Labyrinth now and all of them were covered in a fine gray dust. Despite their superb physical conditioning, Whitney could see that the marshals' confidence had been shaken during the time they'd been maneuvering in the harsh, rocky environment. They had not anticipated the cave's unforgiving nature. They had not expected to be mountain climbing underground.

"Disturbed leading the blind, huh?" Sanchez said to Two-Elk.

The tough little woman tugged off her helmet to ring out the blue bandana she wore, then glanced at Whitney. "Sorry about giving you a hard time back there at the entrance, Mrs. Burke."

"Don't worry about it," Whitney said. "I wouldn't have trusted me either. I'm still not sure if I do."

"Where are we?" Finnerty demanded. "How far to the dump?"

Whitney knelt on the sediment and with her finger drew three overlapping ovals. Around these she drew a single elliptical ring.

"We're at the southern end of three interconnected caverns," she said. "The entire complex is known as the Halls of the Mountain King. We're here at the outlet of the Lake of the King; next one north is King's Castle, and the last one's The Keep. The supply dump's in the northeastern corner of the Castle, just beyond the breakdown pile."

Finnerty adjusted his machine pistol and said, "What's a breakdown pile?"

"Huge caverns like these are created over tens of thousands of years of having water cut tunnels this way and that, searching for a way down to what's called master base level—the water table, effectively," Whitney explained. "Eventually the honeycomb becomes too fragile and the whole thing collapses. Water normally flushes out the sediment leaving these big caverns. But in certain places, the rubble stays and builds up in crazy jumbles called breakdown piles. The one we're going to climb is a good eight hundred vertical feet, the biggest I've ever heard of, a subterranean mountain, really."

Two-Elk eyed the lake. "How far we gotta swim to get to this mountain?"

"Who said anything about swimming?" Whitney said. She picked up her pack, slung it over her shoulder, bent low, and took two steps across the sediment before stopping and looking queasily at the water.

Don't think, she told herself. Just go. She stepped out onto the surface of the lake. It was something of an illusion, a film of near-stagnant water spread over pitch-black sediment in a way that gave the perception of inky depths. The lake held barely five inches of water at its deepest point. Most of it was less than two inches deep.

The marshals followed Whitney. The sounds of their splashing footsteps echoed from the rock overhead to the water and back again. Their boots kicked up dregs of sediment that boiled up to the surface and scented the air with a stale, hoary odor. The ceiling lowered and she had to duck to keep her helmet from scraping. She swore she could feel the thousands of feet of stone above her and the tens of thousands below her like opposing grindstone wheels ready to reduce her to chaff. As that image became paramount in her mind, slowly, inexorably, the panic began to reassert itself.

Her calves cramped, her joints began to ache, and she felt the urge to lie down in the shallow water, to curl up in a ball and close her eyes to the nightmare. But Whitney knew that if she stopped, dread would freeze her solid and she might never move again. So she forced herself on at a frantic pace, arms extended in front of her, legs wide, hips shifting side to side, her attention centered within the cone of light cast by her headlamp. She would not allow herself to look into the shadows beyond the light for fear of what her imagination might conjure.

Think good thoughts, she kept telling herself. Positive thoughts.

Whitney's mind leaped to her sophomore year at Emory University. On a lark one autumn weekend she decided to go on an outing-club trip—an introduction to caving and the caves of TAG, led by Tom Burke, who was, at the time, a second-year graduate student in geology.

When she followed Tom underground that first time, the beauty, power, and complexity of the subterranean world had stunned her with its possibilities. There, stripped of the sensory overload of the surface world, Whitney had felt as if, at every corner, she was heading into the core of something. Shy and retiring on the surface, below ground Tom was confident to the point of cockiness, willing to take terrible risks while climbing, descending and crawling through the dark passages. By the end of the day, some of her fellow neophyte cavers had nicknamed him Batman. Others were calling him Tommy Death, as in "Tommy will be the death of us."

Whether by nature or nurture, Whitney was not a person who opened up easily to other people, especially men. An only child, her mother had died of ovarian cancer when Whitney was ten. In his grief, her father, a taciturn aeronautics engineer to begin with, had shut himself off from her and retreated into his work. There'd been a succession of nannies and long stretches spent with various relatives. She could remember every time she had to leave someone to whom she'd grown attached. At each parting, there was that tearing, that feeling of once again being made alone in the world. And so Whitney had taught herself to keep others at arm's length, to barricade herself with the knowledge of books and the rhythms of athletics.

But the evening after that first cave trip, sitting on the front porch of the cabin where they were staying Whitney found herself talking easily with Tom Burke. She'd meant only to ask a question before turning in for the night, but their conversation had lasted four hours. One on one he was reserved, but he smelled fantastic, had a rock climber's physique, and—she had noticed it before—was damn good-looking. Tom's father was an engineer, as was hers. His mother had died in a car accident when he was twelve. They both had a burning desire to be great scientists. He seemed more than a bit lonely.

For Whitney, there was a flush of uneasiness as the hours wore on. She felt walls coming down, leaving her exposed and vulnerable to that tearing sensation she hated. She told herself to go to bed before Tom got too close. And she had done so.

But the next evening, after another incredible day belowground, she found herself on the front porch of the cabin again, watching the rain fall, listening raptly to his stories, and telling him more about herself than she'd ever told anyone. Approaching midnight, the rain stopped. In the moonlight they walked away from the cabin toward the stream, the comforting smell of wet woods surrounding them. Tom stopped her under a hemlock tree. "Can I tell you something?"

"Guess so," Whitney said.

He stuck his hands in his back pockets and craned his neck around before blurting out, "I've never been scared of anything before, but I'm scared of you."

"Me?" Whitney said, surprised. "But why?"

He looked at the ground. "It's like I spend all this time in caves, you know, and I'm always right down there, never afraid of getting lost… "

"And?"

"I feel like I could get lost forever inside you and I'm petrified of that."

"Don't be afraid," she whispered, turning up her lips to his.

This warm memory calmed Whitney in ways she hadn't expected: the panic attack receded, and for the first time since entering the Labyrinth she felt herself begin to engage with the subterranean world. She still knew how caves worked. Each had its own personality. To move through them fluidly, you had to remold yourself to suit their personalities. All these familiar thoughts and instinctive movements returned in a flash.

Suddenly, the ceiling above her seemed to vanish. A dark, drab wall appeared at her back, abrupt and towering. Even on full power, the beam thrown by her headlamp could not reach the ceiling. The vast blackness simply swallowed the light. Only one known cavern in the world, the Sarawak Chamber in Malaysia, was thought to be larger than the one in which she now found herself. It was tall enough to hold an eighty-story building and long enough to let a bush pilot land a single-engine prop plane.

"This is creepy," Two-Elk said.

"Like being in the bottom of the Grand Canyon on a moonless night," Sanchez agreed.

Whitney took a compass reading, then set off into the great void, heading north-northeast across the lake.

Twenty minutes later, she felt it before she saw it, a looming presence there in the blackness before her. Whitney slowed and adjusted her headlamp to peak intensity. The light pierced the dark to reveal a thin beach just ahead of them and beyond it the base of a soaring, anarchic tower of shattered rock plate, block and pillar. It put her in mind of the two World Trade Center towers after the terrorist attacks, the buildings all fractured and collapsed onto each other in an almost incomprehensible ruin of cavity and harsh angle. The rubble pile looked friable and unstable, as if one false move might disturb the strange physics that held it together, bust it apart like one of those children's games whose object was to remove as many pieces of a tower as possible before it fell apart and smashed to the ground.

"Son of a bitch," Finnerty muttered.

"We're gonna climb that?" Sanchez asked incredulously.

"Not without ropes," Two-Elk said.

"We don't have any ropes; you said you wanted to travel light, remember?" Whitney said, swallowing hard. "So, like it or not, we're free climbing."

NOON
WALKER RIDGE
LABYRINTH CAVE

On the surface, halfway down the southwestern slope of the ninth ridge, Dr. Jeffrey Swain gasped for breath. The physicist had grown up in Southern California and been a competition body surfer while attending Cal Polytech. He still kept in shape by swimming a mile in a pool at the university every day. But he was not used to hiking in steep terrain, especially splattered with drizzle under a jungle-hot forest canopy.

Ahead of him, Captain Boulter was almost sprinting down through the bracken-choked hardwoods, using his combat shotgun to push aside the vines and branches that got in his way. The state trooper had been going at this possessed pace for nearly seven hours now and showed no signs of slowing.

Thirty yards behind Swain, his nephew staggered along. Chester's white polo shirt was soaked with sweat and smeared with blotches of red clay and bits of vegetation. Mosquito bites pocked his face.

"Slow down!" Chester called. "I can't keep up."

The physicist turned. "If you'd started exercising last year as I'd asked, you'd be able to keep up."

Chester stopped and glared at his uncle. "Do I do anything that pleases you?"

Swain set his jaw and crossed his arms. "I'm trying to make you into the person your mother would have wanted you to be, Chester. You'll thank me for it someday."

"You're doing fine, kid," Boulter called back. "We're not far from the truck now. Just one foot in front of the other."

"I don't have feet anymore," Chester snapped as he limped by his uncle. "I have two pieces of meatloaf attached to my ankles."

After placing guards around the Nautilus Entrance, Boulter and the physicist, his nephew, and a second group of snipers went to the Orpheus Entrance. As they had done earlier in the day at the Nautilus Entrance, while the state police captain positioned the snipers, Swain and Chester ran the sensors at the cave's mouth. The electromagnetic readings emanating from inside Jenkins Ridge were similar in magnitude to those found coming out of Munk's—distinct, but weak.

Midmorning had found them high on the side of Tower Ridge, the eighth of the labyrinth's nine hogbacks and site of the collapsed Virgil Entrance. Due to the 150 feet of rubble that sealed the ingress, the sensors had not registered a reading. Boulter had not bothered to leave a guard.

Now they were on their way down off Walker Ridge, which contained the westernmost portion of the cave. Boulter had placed a third band of snipers up there around the Paradisio Entrance. The sensors had picked up an electromagnetic deviation at that ingress strong enough to indicate that the stone was probably somewhere within the last five ridges of the Labyrinth. But the reading was not potent enough to position the moon rock exactly.

Swain felt the frustration swell inside him as the thick woods they'd been traveling through opened suddenly to reveal a cliff top that offered a panoramic view of the sinkhole plain. Towering thunderheads darkened the southwestern horizon. A bolt of lightning ripped the sky about three miles out in front of them, followed almost immediately by a clap of thunder that vibrated through his chest. The wind gusted again, tearing leaves from the oaks overhead and sending a cloud of pollen up into his nose. He sneezed, then steady rain began to splatter down.

"Storm's coming right at us!" Boulter yelled. "We'd better get off this hill fast."

Swain saw agony course through his nephew's face. "Mind over matter, Chester."

His nephew turned without a word and staggered after Boulter. For a second Swain felt he should go and comfort the boy. But empathy was not an emotion that came easy for the physicist. Even in the months after Chester's mother had died, he'd been unable to go into the boy's bedroom when he heard him crying at night. Swain was used to bucking up when things got tough. That was the way the world demanded he be. Why should it be any different for Chester? These thoughts did battle within him for the next quarter mile until they reached Boulter's four-wheel-drive vehicle. They got in just as the rain started to pelt

Swain climbed into the passenger seat Chester got in back, took off his sneakers, and rubbed his blistered feet. Swain was aware of him brooding as they began to drive back toward Jenkins Ridge. Finally, the silence got to be too much for the physicist

"Chester, for these sensors to help us, we simply need to find other openings into this cave," he said. "Another two or three and I think we could have that stone's position positively triangulated."

Chester acted as if he hadn't heard.

"Chester?"

"I heard you," he grumbled. "But that's easier said than done, Uncle Jeff. Mrs. Burke said she and her husband looked for years and hadn't found any but the four ways in. And one of those is now collapsed."

"I know what she said," Swain replied, trying to restrain the testiness he felt. "She also said she was sure there were others that haven't been found yet I was wondering if you had any ideas."

Chester sat there stunned, then blinked and looked up. "You're asking me?"

"I'm asking you," Swain said. "I saw you studying the electronic cave map last night and talking with the engineers and—"

"It's too crude," Chester said.

"What is?" Boulter asked. The state trooper was hunched over the wheel, peering through windshield wipers that were doing a poor job.

"The digital grid map NASA's using to track everyone's position," the teen replied. "It's crude, Uncle Jeff, just a vector graphics bit-map—you know, a line drawing."

"Okay?" Swain said.

"But one of the engineers said it was based on more complicated measurements Tom Burke made using a sonar emitter and an accelerometer."

"What's an accelerometer?" Boulter asked as he turned the rig left down the two-lane country road that paralleled the southern base of the nine ridges.

"It's a fist-sized device originally used in the inertial guidance systems of missiles," Chester replied. "It has the ability to measure three-dimensional displacement from a specific reference point, such as the entrance to a cave. The sonar emitter has the ability to gauge the distance from its holder to walls, ceiling, and floor."

"I still don't see your point," Swain said.

Chester rolled his eyes. "The point is, Uncle Jeff, that the data that created the map of the cave we're looking at is much richer than the end product I bet if we can remanipulate the raw data to create a raster graphic—a three-dimensional version of what's underground here—we'd find the other entrances."

Swain wanted to grin but would not allow himself. "The idea has some merit" he said at last "With refinements—"

"Kid," Boulter said impatiently. "Ignore the old man. What the hell's a new map gonna do us?"

Chester looked away from his uncle and said, "If I'm right Captain, it might put us on top of that rock."

1:00 P.M.
HAWKINS RIDGE
LABYRINTH CAVE

"Take them out," Kelly said, going for his pistol. "That's what I say, Lyons. They killed Mann, they'll try to kill us all. Take 'em both out."

Kelly, Lyons, and Gregor were crowded in around Tom and Cricket, their faces frescoed in grime. The flesh under their bloodshot eyes drooped and showed darkened sockets. They were way up inside Hawkins Ridge now, the second of the Labyrinth's nine. Cricket knew they were in terrible danger, but her mind would not release her from that memory—that instant when Mann wavered in space, shocked by their whistling, his fingers slipping past the nylon loop, the comprehension of his own doom erupting across his smug face.

The exhilaration that had exploded through Cricket was different from anything she'd ever felt before. She and her dad hadn't just beaten the filthy bastard. They'd outwitted him. They had defeated him. They had killed Mann. And part of Cricket was very glad he was dead.

But now it seemed that the whole thing might backfire and get them killed.

"Go ahead, big guy, pull the trigger," Tom suddenly told Kelly. "And I guarantee you'll have absolutely zero chance of getting out of here alive."

Lyons knocked Kelly's gun aside. "He's right. Don't be an idiot. He's the only one who knows the way."

Kelly's face screwed up in anger. "Bullshit. Gregor must know where we are by now. Don't you?"

Gregor shook his head. "Not in the least. Lyons is right. We need Burke. But we don't need the girl."

"That's more like it," Kelly said, grinning as he cocked the hammer on the pistol and began to raise it toward Cricket.

Cricket shrank back against the wall, sure she was about to die, only to see her father step in front of the gun. "Kill her and I don't care what you do to me," he said. "Shock me, beat me, torture me. I won't move another inch. I'll sit here until we all die."

Kelly's face contorted and for a moment Cricket was sure he would shoot or strike her dad or zap him again with the belly belt. Then Lyons put one of his huge hands on Kelly's arm. "Don't forget what we're really after, Kelly," he said. "That stone means more than your lust for revenge right now."

Kelly scowled. "Who made you honcho, Lyons?"

Lyons stuck his face in Kelly's. "Just speaking common sense for the sake of the partnership. Am I right Gregor?"

Gregor's attention flashed between Cricket's father and the large, dark man. Then he shrugged. "He's right. We need him to get to the other end of the cave."

Kelly raised his eyebrows in confusion. "Other end of the cave? That's seven more ridges! You never said nothing about that!"

"I'm saying it now," Gregor replied.

"We're goners," Kelly said.

"Take that attitude and you—you'll never achieve greatness," Gregor replied, his eyes flaring. "My grandfather was a drunken lout, but he always said you have to fight for what's yours because there'll always be someone trying to take it. Considering what's at the other end of this cave, Kelly, you should be willing to suffer. I know I am. I can see Lyons is, too."

Gregor suddenly began to cough and choke from the effort the speech had taken out of him. He swayed for a second, then dropped to his knees, his breathing shallow and forced.

Lyons jumped forward. "What's going on?"

Kelly ripped off his pack and pulled out a blood pressure kit and strapped it around the pale scientist's arms. Gregor slumped to one side and his eyes rolled back in his head. "Shit, he's one eighty-five over ninety, pulse one thirty," Kelly said. "We've got to get those meds in him or he'll stroke out."

"He's gonna die, Dad," Cricket whispered in Tom's ear. "Two down. Two to go."

For a single, wonderful moment, Tom thought Cricket was right and they had succeeded in eliminating another of their captors. Then Lyons dug into his pack and came out with a syringe and a vial. Kelly drew five ccs from one vial and shot the liquid into Gregor's arm. Gradually, the emaciated man's breathing came back and he opened his eyes, but he looked lethargic.

"We should rest here awhile," Lyons said. "Let him sleep a couple of hours."

Tom's thoughts raced. Letting Gregor or any of them recover was the last thing he wanted. "We sleep now, we all die from hypothermia," he blurted. "The cave's a constant fifty-six degrees with one-hundred-percent humidity. It'll have us chattering in less than an hour. You want to rest, you've got to reach the cache inside Munk's Ridge. There are sleeping bags there, dry clothes, more food. It's set up as a bivouac."

Lyons studied him. "You better not be fucking with us."

"It's true," Cricket said. "They even talked about it on television."

"How far?" Lyons demanded.

Tom hesitated before answering. NASA had to know they'd go to the cache eventually. He wanted to keep the pressure on Gregor, on all of them. On the other hand, he wanted to give any rescue operation enough time to get into position. "Three hours," he said at last.

"And how long to the other end of this shithole cave?" Kelly demanded.

"Eighty miles of passage. Three days minimum."

"Three days!" Kelly looked at Gregor, whose breathing was stronger now. "Why the hell didn't we go in the way you did? It couldn't have been this far."

"Because," Gregor gasped, "according to Burke, that entrance collapsed six weeks ago."

Gregor had been in the Virgil Entrance out on the eighth ridge? Tom thought. How was that possible? It had been gated for years. Then he remembered an incident a couple of years before when he and Whitney had discovered that someone had dug underneath the old iron gate and they'd been forced to replace it with a stainless-steel version that was sunk deep in the dirt. They had figured that whoever broke into the cave was out to steal rock formations. Could it have been Gregor?

"Then how are we going to get out of here if the way you went in is collapsed?" Kelly demanded. "They've got to be guarding the other entrances."

"My grandfather showed me a secret way out," Gregor said. A tinge of color had returned to his cheeks.

Tom looked at him sharply. "What secret way? There aren't any other ways in."

Gregor snorted. "You think you know everything about this cave, Burke. Guess what? You don't. Others had been in here long before you found it."

"Why didn't we just go in your secret way?" Lyons asked, annoyed.

"Because I've never used it from the outside, I just know where it starts inside the cave," Gregor replied testily, then he turned his attention to Tom. "Keep your daughter in line, Burke. I know we need you. But sooner or later we'll come to the end of the line. And there'll be either mercy or hell to pay."

Tom looked at him, calculating whether to keep the pressure up. But he could see the dead certainty in Gregor's expression. "Okay," he said.

As soon as Gregor could walk, they began to trudge west through the dry portions of Hawkins Ridge. Cinnamon-colored crystal flakes, each no bigger than a fingernail, filled the floor of the cave. The granular silica was so deep, arid, and sifted that it seemed to have loft. As they set their boots into the exotic sand, they broke through pockets of air, releasing barking noises that resonated down the chamber. It was hard going and the sound of their passing was a din.

At one point, Lyons left Gregor's side and fell in alongside Tom. "What'd you two have to go and kill him for?" the guard murmured. "You almost got your daughter snuffed. In case you hadn't noticed, I'm watching out for you and for Cricket."

Tom looked up quizzically. For the first time he felt there was more to Lyons than met the eye. For some reason, that made him angrier than ever. "Yeah, you were doing such a sweet job of it," Tom hissed. "That pervert was all over her."

"He got ahead of me," Lyons said. "I admit it. I screwed up."

"Then we did what we had to do, didn't we?" Tom said.

"You don't understand what's at stake here, Burke," Lyons whispered. "If you can keep yourself under control I'll make sure you and your daughter get out safely."

Tom studied Lyons. He saw something conflicted in the man's face. "You're not like them. Why don't you just help us get out now?"

At that, Lyons's expression hardened. "You must think I'm a better man, Burke. Well, I'm not. My job is to get that stone. I'll do whatever it takes to get it. Kill Kelly, kill Gregor. Kill you, too. But you stay out of my way, I'll continue to watch over you and your daughter. But get in my way, keep me from the stone, I'll make you and Cricket suffer."

3:20 P.M.
MUNK'S RIDGE
LABYRINTH CAVE

Whitney, Finnerty, Two-Elk, and Sanchez clawed their way up over the massive rock slabs and stone rafters that jutted from the underground mountain's chaotic core. There were fissures between the large pieces of fallen limestone that threatened to snap their ankles and buckle their knees. Pockets of rounded gravel on the slabs acted like ballbearings; whenever they stepped into one of these pockets, their boots skated toward the edge and the long fall to the subterranean lake.

Whitney talked herself through the climb, forcing her body and mind to work in ways they had not in nearly thirteen months. She was hardcore caving now. In the flow. Which is not to say that the anxiety of being there had left. But somehow the threat of panic had been transformed; when she had entered the Labyrinth nearly eight hours before, fear had been like a poisonous mist that saturated the air around her. Now it was a manageable weight she carried like a yoke across her shoulders.

She paused five hundred feet up the breakdown pile, so high that her headlamp beam no longer reached the lake surface and yet not high enough that her light could reach the ceiling. It was as if she were climbing a cliff at night in the fog and with that sensation came a blow to her equilibrium and a rattling of her sense of up and down. Her progress and the progress of the marshals behind her slowed to a crawl.

Whitney used memories of her family to help her forge on. One in particular kept coming back to her the higher she climbed. It was the image of an oddly shaped sand castle—a cone inside a circular wall. The simple formation, circle and cone, made up a symbol only Whitney, Tom, and Cricket understood. When Cricket was a little girl, no more than three, Whitney and Tom still called their daughter by her real name, Alexandra. On her first trip to the beach, however, Tom made a large version of the circle and cone in the sand. Alexandra asked what he was doing. Her father announced that he was building a cricket trap.

"Why?" the little girl asked.

"People all over the world, especially in Asia, believe all that is good follows a cricket," Tom explained. "You build one of these and the cricket comes and brings luck and happiness to whoever traps it. My design, of course."

She stared at the circle for the longest time. Then, without warning she jumped the barricade, landed inside the trap, and threw up her hands while letting loose a joyous smile. And so Alexandra had come to be called Cricket. And the circle with the cone had become the family's private totem; when one of them was having a tough time, the others would make a cricket trap out of whatever was handy so that it might gather luck and happiness for whoever needed it.

Whitney's lamp revealed the top of the breakdown mountain some hundred feet above her. The sight broke her from her thoughts. Another twenty feet of climbing and she could make out the coffered roof of the cavern itself. There was an outcropping above her as well, about thirty vertical feet above her position and eighty feet below the ceiling. Seeing it, she called down to Finnerty, "We're gonna get on that ledge up there, then traverse it. At the other end, we'll enter a chimney that'll take us to the top."

The marshal looked up at her. He was covered in grit and there was a gauntness about him that she had not seen before. "Make it quick. We're losing time."

Whitney glanced at her watch and felt sick to her stomach. They were supposed to have reached the supply dump by now. What if Tom and Cricket got there first?

She climbed hand over hand and finally reached a spot where she could stand upright beneath the ledge. Then she cut to her left, out from under the rock balcony, toward a series of handholds that would allow her to get around and up onto the ledge itself. She was reaching for the first of those handholds when it began.

A quiver at first. Then a distinct vibration that fluxed through the entire breakdown pile. Accompanying the vibration was a noise like the distant caterwauling of rusty train wheels forced to roll across bent rails. The wailing immediately deepened into the locomotive grind of boxcars unbuckling their hitches. Then the entire breakdown pile pulsed and shifted. The grinding noise became a deafening primordial bellow of things elemental giving way. Far above Whitney, the ceiling coughed out boulders.

"Rock!" she screamed. She threw herself back under the ledge, just as the first chunk of rock smacked off the craggy exterior of the outcropping.

The boulder burst in two, scoring her with BB-sized pebbles. Another boulder struck, disintegrating a slab on the slope just below her. Shards of the slab ricocheted downslope.

Finnerty and Two-Elk dived for cover. But Sanchez was caught in a tricky place and was helpless to react. The barrage of tumbling debris caught him flush in the chest. The deputy flung his arms up and out then he flew backward off the face of the breakdown pile. His throaty scream and the arc of his headlamp swept through the hollow darkness above the lake.

2:25 P.M.
HAWKINS-MUNK CONNECTION ROUTE
LABYRINTH CAVE

Lyons, Gregor, and Kelly were all pressed back against the cave wall, stricken with vertigo. Cricket was beside them, equally unnerved. She had never been to this part of the cave before and had to fight the urge to crawl back into the passage behind her.

"Welcome to Dante's Tubes," her father said. "You've each got a harness in your pack. Put them on."

He stood ten feet from them, near the edge of a crescent-shaped projection of rock that jutted out above black emptiness. With rock bolts, carabiners, and bowline knots, a rope had been rigged to the ledge behind him. The rope disappeared over the side. A strong wind blew up out of the hole.

Somewhere far, far below, over the sound of the wind, came the crash of water falling.

"Is this the only way?" Kelly demanded. "You better not be dicking with us."

"It's the only way into Munk's Ridge," Tom insisted. "We either go down, or we go back. Your call."

Before Kelly could reply, Gregor said, "We go down." In the hours since his collapse, Cricket had noticed, the physicist seemed to get stronger with every step.

One by one, the men reached into their packs, got out the harnesses, and, following her father's directions, closed the screw links that held the legs of the device together.

Cricket did the same. Her sweaty hair hung in her eyes. Her cheeks were splotched with grime. Her legs felt as if she were dragging chains. Every muscle, sinew, and bone in the young teenager's body cried out for more sleep, but she forced herself to listen to her dad's explanation of what they had to do to get into Munk's Ridge and reach the supply cache.

The vertical shaft before them dropped 340 feet, roughly twice the height of Niagara Falls. A waterfall that had gone dry about two thousand years ago created the tube. About 200 feet down, it connected through a horizontal passage to a second shaft, in which a second torrential waterfall still ran. Viewed in profile, the system of joined vertical caves had roughly the shape of an off-kilter H where the right leg was longer than the other and the connecting rock sagged steeply to the left. The challenge was to descend 170 feet down the first tube, then switch to a second rope that traversed the crossbar of the H, then switch to a third rope and drop 400 feet down the second shaft.

"How we gonna change ropes fourteen stories in the air?" Lyons demanded.

"Very carefully," Tom said.

"Ah, for fuck's sake," Kelly grumbled.

Tom went over to Cricket and kissed her on the cheek. "Be smart now on rope," he said. "Don't give the cave a chance."

Cricket studied her dad. His beard was coming in. All salt and pepper. Despite the fatigue in his eyes, there was still such a solidness about him that she smiled and said, "Never do, Dad."

He nodded, tickled her under the chin, got on his knees, and rigged his rappel rack to the line. Then he worked his way over the sharp cliff edge. "You won't be able to see me stop at one seventy, honey, so keep your hand on the rope until you feel me unload, then send the next person."

Before Cricket could reply, her father disappeared. She heard a zinging noise above the moan of the wind and the distant roar of the waterfall. She lay down and peered over the lip, watching his helmet and shoulders drop away. The rope quavered in the parasol of light thrown by his headlamp. Lit that way, the bore hole of the cave below her dad seemed to collapse in dizzying, concentric circles that diminished toward a vanishing point. Within seconds, he became a fingernail of light that eclipsed into darkness. It was the first time Cricket had been alone with the men and she felt a pang of unease wash through her.

"Show us again how you thread the rope," Gregor demanded.

Cricket did not want to take her fingers off the nylon line her father rode deeper into the earth, but she forced herself to stand, turn, and use a safety line on her harness called a cat's tail to demonstrate how to feed the rope through the three bars of the micro-rappel rack. She did it quickly, hoping that at least one of her captors would miss the intricacies of the lesson and make a deadly mistake. Out of the corner of her eye, Cricket saw the tension in the rope ease.

"You're next," she said to Lyons.

Lyons, oddly, seemed familiar with the principles of rope rigging and performed it flawlessly. He went over the side and disappeared. Gregor soon followed And Cricket was left with Kelly. "Your turn," she said

"Ladies first," Kelly replied, shaking one of the belly belt transmitters at her. "I wouldn't want you running on us."

"I wouldn't leave my father," she said.

"Just the same."

Cricket let her hatred of Kelly show openly as she attached herself to the rope. Then she willed herself to go over the side; she had been rappelling into caves since she was a little girl, but never in a place as scary as Dante's Tubes. In fits and starts she slid down the rope. The deeper she descended, the louder the waterfall in the parallel chamber became until it rumbled like kettle drums. Soon there was a drizzle all around her that made the ropes slick. And the gusting wind kept pushing her toward the walls.

At last the rope turned a solid red. Cricket braked to a halt and tied off. The shaft fell away into dim light between her legs. Behind and below her about eighty feet, Cricket could make out the jagged floor of the crossbar that connected the two vertical tubes together into that lopsided H.

"Good job," she heard her father say.

Cricket spun herself around to see him about twenty feet away, hanging from the wall near the ceiling of the horizontal passage where it met the western rampart of the first vertical tube. He was clipped by a safety line to a metal carabiner bolted into the stone wall. His boots were snugged into the rungs of a nylon webbed ladder called an etrier that was also bolted into the wall. Beyond him, interconnected arcs of rope were draped horizontally along the wall of the crossbar passage heading west. At each point that the rope tied into the wall, there was another carabiner hanging from a bolt and another one of those webbed etrier ladders. Lyons and Gregor were already well out along that spider's web, heading toward what looked like one of those wind-eroded spires of reddish sandstone she'd seen in pictures of Bryce Canyon National Park in Utah. And beyond the spire, the glimmer of the waterfall.

"Get your feet on the wall there, squat, kick off, and swing like a pendulum across to me," her dad said. "It may take you a couple of kicks. When you get close, I'm going to catch you so you can switch to this traverse rope."

Cricket felt her stomach turn over at the fact that she was hanging 150 feet in the air, 500 feet underground. But she had no choice. "Okay," she said.

Cricket knew that the danger of penduluming on a high rope presents itself when riders fail to commit to the move. They thrust halfheartedly and come off the wall at an angle, which can lead to a broadside collision with rock, a possible loss of contact with the rope, and a fall to certain death. But Cricket went for it 100 percent and in two big kicks she'd traveled far enough that her dad was able to grab the rope and haul her in.

"Way to go," he said, kissing her on the cheek. "Now you're going to slide yourself sideways across these arcs of rope. When you get to that tower of rock out there, clip your harness to the anchors so you don't pitch off the other side into the waterfall. Send Lyons and Gregor down to the bottom. I'll be along after Kelly."

Cricket hesitated for a moment, then gestured into the abyss below. "Why don't we just drop down this rope and escape that way, Dad?"

"There's no way out down there, sweetheart. I know. I've looked. So has your mother. Besides, we're in these electric belts, remember?"

"Is it bad?" she asked. "The shock, I mean?"

"Godawful," he replied.

Twenty-five minutes later, Cricket reached the next to the last arc on the spider's web. Lyons and Gregor lay panting atop the tan, flat-topped tower of rock. The waterfall on the other side was a thick column of emerald and white. There was a steady shower of droplets in the air. The noise made her ears hurt

Cricket fought her way up onto the ledge, clipped herself to a safety anchor, then lay back and closed her eyes, enjoying the way the mist cooled her face and the way the waterfall created a cocoon of sound around her.

"What now?" Lyons asked.

Cricket opened her eyes and scowled at him. "You go down the next rope and try to stay out of the water."

A half hour later, Lyons reached the bottom of the second shaft and yelled, "Clear!"

Gregor rigged himself to the rope and went over the side. Kelly rested against the back wall of the outcropping. Her father had just climbed up onto the ledge. Cricket was getting herself organized to begin her descent, doing her best to avoid eye contact with Kelly, who had been watching her constantly ever since they'd whistled Mann to death.

She glanced down the shaft and saw that Gregor had reached the first directional, a contraption designed to keep the rope out of the waterfall. She was turning back to tell her dad of Gregor's progress when the entire steeple of stone beneath her lurched sideways as if bludgeoned by some monstrous hammer. A tremendous grinding noise filled the cave. The jolting and milling jumped in amplitude. She was thrown backward into the waterfall shaft, the rim of the cliff flashing by her head and her father's face twisted in horror as he flung himself after her, screaming, "Cricket!"

**3:54 P.M.
NASA ENCAMPMENT
JENKINS RIDGE
LABYRINTH CAVE**

Jeffrey Swain stood in the open entrance to the Mission Control tent. Bolt after bolt of lightning scribed the sky over the nine ridges of Labyrinth Cave. The wind gusted at sixty miles an hour, causing the tent canopy above the physicist to cavitate and strain at its braces. The rain sweeping across the encampment looked like hundreds of gray full-bellied sails.

Just behind Swain, Boulter, Angelis, and the NASA mission commander were hunched over a computer that showed the digital grid map of the cave.

"Still transmitting strong," Angelis noted with satisfaction. "See there? Whitney Burke and Finnerty's team are no more than six hundred yards from the supply dump now. Gregor's people are still at least a half mile away in Dante's Tubes. One of the toughest parts of the cave."

"Damian's gonna get there first," the trooper agreed, slapping Angelis's back.

Swain turned and looked beyond the trooper and the NASA official. Chester sat at a second computer terminal typing furiously. An open Diet Coke and a half-eaten doughnut lay on the table beside the keyboard. The physicist told himself he might speed up the process of transforming Burke's data into a better map if he guided Chester. Swain believed, however, that isolating people brought out their creativity. The crucible was where great scientists were forged and he was leaving Chester to face the fire alone. But what Swain could not bring himself to admit to was the simple fact that his nephew knew far more about computer programming than he ever would.

Suddenly, Chester leaned in closer to the computer, then typed in several more commands and sat back, picked up the soda, drained it, and grinned. He picked up the doughnut and stuffed the rest into his mouth, then looked over at his uncle.

"Now we give the supercomputers back at the university a few hours to do those calculations, and in the meantime the laser prisms I ordered should be arriving from the lab and we should be in business."

"You're sure in your calculations?" Swain asked. "In your coding?"

Chester threw his uncle a look of irritation. "Yes, I'm sure."

"We'll see then, won't we?"

Before his nephew could come back with a retort, a flash of lightning lit up the entire tent, followed by a walloping thunderclap that made them all jump.

"Son of a bitch, that was close!" Angelis cried.

"Are these tent poles metal?" Swain asked, then he stopped, puzzled, as if hearing something confusing from afar. A rumbling noise, but not thunder. He recognized the sound from his childhood. "Earthquake!" he yelled.

The pulverizing roar of the first shock wave built and pulsed through Jenkins Ridge. The porch of the dilapidated farmhouse swayed, then tore away. The roof of the main structure lifted and bucked inward. The meadow crested and troughed like a stirred-up sea. All along the forest edge, trees uprooted, tottered, and fell. The generators providing electricity to the encampment convulsed. Several detonated. The explosions threw fireballs high into the sky.

Twenty miles upstream on the Furnace River, deep within the rammed earth dam that held back the waters of the Hermes Reservoir, fourteen of the eighty-seven pilings supporting the structure cracked under the incredible pressure and moved nine inches off-center. Water rushed into the cracks and began to gnaw at the base of the destabilized embankment.

Inside the Mission Control tent, Swain saw Boulter tossed through the air like a rag doll. A wire whipped Chester across the face. A light stanchion struck Swain in the head and upper back, knocking him to the floor. Then the tent's ridge-support poles, guy wires, and stake lines all snapped at once and the whole thing came crashing down.

The shaking went on for eleven seconds, then stilled. Clouds of black noxious smoke billowed above crackling electrical fires. Hundreds of birds, spooked from their roosts, circled and called madly in the pouring rain.

Swain got to his hands and knees, choking on the electrical smoke, shaking his bleeding head from side to side like a prizefighter who's just taken a devastating uppercut to the jaw. All around him he heard the cries and moans of the wounded.

"Earthquake in Kentucky," he mumbled. "How the hell is that possible?"

Then he flashed on the image of his sister and panicked. "Chester!" he yelled. "Chester, where are you?"

4:10 P.M.
KING'S CASTLE BREAKDOWN
MUNK'S RIDGE
LABYRINTH CAVE

Whitney curled on her side beneath the ledge that ran below the summit of the underground mountain. She gazed after her headlamp beam, which disappeared into the cloud of fine white dust that now hung over the lake in the great cavern.

In her mind, she kept seeing Sanchez arch backward off the breakdown pile, the incredulity at his coming death etched across his face. Sanchez's visage became Jeannie's and then Tom's and then Cricket's. Whitney clenched her eyes shut against the sobs that erupted out of her.

She heard the sound of rocks clopping and sliding against one another again and she curled up tighter, thinking an aftershock might be under way. But the jolt never came. She heard rocks move again, opened her eyes, and was blinded by two headlamps shining at her from just below the ledge.

"Mrs. Burke?" Finnerty called out "Whitney?"

A fragment of stone had gashed the marshal above the left eye and it was swelling shut. He was coated in the white dust. It made him look like a bleeding ghost. Two-Elk appeared alongside him her left hand badly discolored.

"People who go underground with me always die," Whitney said dully.

"You didn't kill Amador," Finnerty said in a voice filled with emotion at the loss. "He was done in by a freak of nature, trying to save your husband and daughter. We've got to honor him by pushing on."

In her befuddled state, Whitney gave scant attention to a question that flashed through her brain: How was it possible that an earthquake had hit Labyrinth Cave? Tom's research had revealed only the slimmest of fault lines in the area.

"How do I know Tom and Cricket aren't dead, too?" Whitney asked in a choked voice. "How do I know they weren't chewed up by this god-awful hole in the ground?"

Finnerty shook his head and turned angry. "Whitney, you're sounding to me as if you're willing to give up without even trying. Don't Tom and Cricket deserve more? Don't they deserve for you to keep trying, no matter what the odds?"

Whitney tried to see Tom and Cricket in her thoughts, to imagine them still alive. Cricket's image surfaced as if in a cloud. Her daughter seemed lost frightened, and alone. Then the image changed. Cricket was just born and Whitney was holding her to her breast while Tom and a half-dozen firefighters looked on.

"Okay," she murmured, getting to her knees.

In a stupor, she inched her way along the ledge to the east. All around her the breakdown pile groaned and shifted as the rocks settled into new positions. Where the overhang ended, Whitney stopped, scared to move beyond its protection should the ceiling cry and the stone rain fall once more. She saw again the image of Cricket as a baby. Only this time Tom was giving Cricket her first bath, carefully swabbing the area around her umbilical cord. Those memories enabled her to ease out into the chimney that led to the top of the breakdown. Once she was in the shaft, she summoned all her skills and started to climb. Below her, Finnerty and Two-Elk watched her every move, then mimicked them exactly.

When Whitney at last reached the top of the underground mountain, she lay on her back, gasping for air, taking in the venous fractures in the cave's ceiling not four feet over her head. In the glare of her headlamp the dust was as dense as the smoke coming off a greenwood fire. She coughed and hacked, the fit in turn triggering a foreboding she did not grasp at first.

Finnerty hoisted himself up out of the chimney, then turned and reached down to grab Two-Elk below the wrist of her injured hand. The marshal grunted, pulled, and soon his deputy was lying on the crest as well.

"Where now?" Finnerty asked.

"Back that way," Whitney said, throwing her thumb over her shoulder.

Two-Elk shook her head. "Nothing but rock back that way, Mrs. Burke."

Whitney rolled over and shone her light into thickest part of the dust cloud. She crawled forward, searching for the passage that led to King's Castle Cavern. But all she saw was fresh rubble. And then she understood that foreboding generated by the dense grime that just seemed to hang there in the air, unmoving.

"The cave's stopped breathing," she said in disbelief. "The passage collapsed."

Finnerty stared at the cloudy pile of rocks. Then he smacked his open palm on the wall and shouted, "Dammit! This is the goddamned story of my life these days. Close but not enough!"

Whitney stared into the rubble and dust. Then she turned away from the choked passage. She walked toward the chimney she'd climbed to get to the cliff top. She stopped several feet short of the edge and aimed her headlamp out into the void of the great cavern. The light from her lamp picked up the dust still swirling in the pitch darkness. She watched it fall and waft Hypnotized.

She cast her headlamp up and saw where the big boulders had coughed free of the ceiling. She thought of Sanchez. She thought of Jeannie. She thought of Cricket and Tom somewhere on the other side of that caved-in passage. For a moment, all Whitney felt was despair, then her gloom mutated into fury.

"*Haven't you done enough?*" she screamed at the cave. "*Haven't you taken enough of me?*"

She stood there shaking and thought of throwing herself over the cliff. Then the anguish that swirled within her fed itself with adrenaline until it became an overwhelming desire to fight She pointed her finger toward the fractured ceiling.

"You're not taking any more of me," she vowed. "Nothing more."

She reached inside her cave suit and pulled up the silk kerchief she always kept tied about her neck when underground. She wrapped it around her mouth, then clambered back into the depths of the dust cloud and began pulling away rocks with the possession of a peasant woman whose husband and child have been buried in a landslide.

4:11 P.M.
DANTE'S TUBES
LABYRINTH CAVE

Tom leaned over the edge of the flat-topped tower of rock, yelling, "Cricket! Cricket, can you hear me?"

She dangled by her safety line against the tubular cave wall. The shaft fell away four hundred feet below her boots. The subterranean waterfall rushed a yard way.

"Can you hear me, Cricket?" he called again.

But she did not move. From far below her, just audible against the sound of the waterfall, Tom heard Lyons bellow, "What's going on up there?" His headlamp beam shone up from the bottom.

"Cricket's hurt!" Tom screamed. "She's unconscious and—"

Cricket tilted her helmet back and looked up at him, dazed. "Dad, what—?"

"It's okay," Tom said. "Earthquake. Unbelievable. But it doesn't matter. Nothing matters but you're alive. Thank God you attached your safety line."

Tom looked back over his shoulder at Kelly. "Hold my ankles," he ordered, then he reached down and got a grip on the safety rope and hauled his daughter back up onto the spire. He bear-hugged her, then laid her on her back Kelly came around on the other side. His face was scraped and raw from being hammered against the cave wall during the earthquake. "Get away from her," Tom said.

"I used to be a medic," Kelly said.

"I don't care," Tom said. She was coming fully conscious now. "Stay away from her."

"What happened?" she asked, sitting up and resting her elbows over her knees.

"Earthquake, I think. Extraordinary, isn't it?" Tom said. He was very concerned about her condition, but as a geologist, he was flabbergasted at the scientific implications of the event. "There isn't a major fault within two hundred fifty miles of here. The last known earthquake to hit anywhere in Kentucky was way out west near the Ohio border almost two hundred years ago. We're just lucky you weren't on rope when it hit."

"Who was on rope?" Kelly demanded.

Cricket startled. "Gregor."

Kelly darted to the edge with Tom right beside him. Together they shone their lights down the length of the wriggling rope to where it disappeared into the ripping emerald curtain of the waterfall. Tom grabbed the static line and tugged on it. The shaking on the rope turned intense. Then, weakly, from out of the din of the cascade, they heard Gregor yell for help, followed by Lyons's frantic exhortations from far down the tube. "What the hell's going on up there!"

Tom leaned over the edge. "Gregor's caught on rope!" he yelled. "He's conscious, but getting pounded by water. Even with the NASA suits, he's only got minutes."

"Save him!" Lyons roared. "Whatever you do, save him!"

Tom looked down the rope and shook his head

"You heard Lyons," Kelly said. "Save him before it's too late."

"Can't save him," Tom retorted. "We don't have another rope."

"Then go down the rope he's on."

"Not a chance," Tom said. "You've got to get three bars of a rappel rack onto a rope to be safe. That can't be done with a loaded line—you can't bend it."

Kelly drew his pistol and stuck it in Tom's face. "I didn't come all this way, take all these risks, not to get that gold," he said. There's got to be a way to save him. Either think of one or the two of you die. The girl first."

Tom said, "You kill us, you die too."

"So what?" Kelly sneered. "I got nothing to lose. You got everything to gain."

"Okay, okay," Tom said, pounding one gloved fist into the other.

"You can save him?" Kelly said, brightening.

"No," Tom said. "You can. You're lighter than me. I'll talk you through it."

Kelly glanced at the rope. Tom's hopes soared. If Kelly took the bait and went over the side, he and Cricket would be free to run. Lyons could never climb the rope, not with two men already on it. It would be tough, but he and his daughter could rig a climbing system and go back out the way they had come. Their rations were dwindling. But at least they'd have enough water to survive the trek back to the Orpheus Entrance.

Kelly gestured at Cricket. "She's lighter than me," he said. "She goes."

"No!" Tom protested. "She's too shaken up."

Kelly pressed the muzzle of his pistol between Tom's eyes. Then he glared at Cricket. "Go down that rope, girl, or I'll shoot your old man where he stands."

4:58 P.M.
NASA ENCAMPMENT
JENKINS RIDGE
LABYRINTH CAVE

Outside, in the distance, the fading rumble of thunder sounded against the thrum of the driving rain on the canvas roof of the Mission Control tent. The caustic stench of electrical fire still tainted the air inside the pavilion. And everywhere rescue workers shouted and the wounded groaned, ambulances wailed and helicopters chugged to landings out in Jenkins meadow.

Dr. Swain winced as a NASA medical tech sewed the nasty gash on the back of his head. "Hurt, huh?" Chester asked. His nephew had been one of the lucky ones. He'd survived the earthquake with no more than a raised welt across his face where the guy wire had whipped him. Swain had found the teen within minutes, hiding under the computer table.

"Forget what hurts," Swain snapped. "What have you got on the earthquake?"

"Jesus, so much for caring, Uncle Jeff," Chester said.

"I need information, not emotion, Chester," the physicist replied. "I need to understand what's happened and why."

Chester opened his mouth, then shook his head and slammed himself down in front of one of the few computers still capable of running.

The tech stuck a needle deep into the cut and Swain almost cried out, but bit his cheek instead. Ten feet to the physicist's left, Boulter wrenched off his headset, reached up gingerly to touch his broken nose, then looked over at Angelis. A second medical tech was working on the shoulder of the Mission Control chief, which had suffered a third-degree separation.

"My men are reporting complete collapses at the Orpheus and Paradisio Entrances," Boulter said. "Nautilus is still open, but just barely. They don't dare try to dig yet; the rubble's still settling. Any change in the position of the burst transmitters?"

They'd managed to get part of the big tent back up in the first minutes after the quake, but the electronic map that had hung on the lighting stanchions had been destroyed. Angelis glanced at a tiny version of the map on a computer screen next to him, then shook his head. "Still getting no signals from Burke, his daughter, or the inmates," he said. "Weak signals from Finnerty's team, but they haven't moved in almost an hour."

"What does that mean?" Boulter asked. "Or don't I want to know?"

"I can't answer that," Angelis said. "They could be trapped. They could be hurt."

"What you're saying is that they all could be dead," Boulter said, closing his eyes. "How in God's name am I going to tell Damian's wife?"

Swain said, "We have to proceed on the assumption they're alive."

"Absolutely," Angelis said. "I'm betting the quake destroyed some of the transponder repeaters, so the signals we're getting could be garbled."

Chester turned in his seat and nodded. "The size of that quake, that's a real possibility."

The tech finished applying a bandage over the twelve stitches in the back of Swain's head. The physicist stood immediately and walked to his nephew. "How big are they calling it?"

Chester gestured at a web page up on the screen. "National Earthquake Information Center at Memphis is pegging it at 6.2 on the Richter Scale. Here's the weird stuff, Uncle Jeff—the only known fault line east of the Rockies capable of producing that magnitude of quake is the New Madrid system more than two hundred miles west of here. But they aren't calling the epicenter anywhere near the Ohio-Indiana border. They're saying it's roughly 37.37 longitude, 83.912 latitude, at a depth between three hundred thirty-two and six hundred fifty-seven feet."

Angelis pushed away the medical tech who was trying to work his arm into a sling. "That's right here, somewhere inside the cave."

"That's right" Chester pushed his eyeglasses back up the bridge of his nose. "Now take a look at this: NEIC records show minor seismic activity in the same area three months ago. And here's the strangest thing of all: check out the quake graphs."

They all huddled in behind him as he typed in several commands. Swiftly, a drawing like an EKG printout appeared on the computer screen.

Swain frowned and leaned in for a closer look. "That's not normal seismic activity."

"No, it isn't, Uncle Jeff. You'd expect to see long, undulating waves, wouldn't you? These are short. Whippy. Like an explosion."

"An explosion?" Boulter said.

"What's going on down there?" Angelis demanded.

"I have no idea," Swain replied, perplexed.

"I do," Chester said. "Wild theory, just a crazy guess."

Swain stared at his nephew, feeling an irrational sense of irritation rising inside him. "What could you possibly—?"

"Don't listen to him, kid," Boulter said. "Out with it."

Chester looked at the trooper and smiled, then sobered and looked back at his uncle. "Remember Gregor's log notes, Uncle Jeff? His theory was that moon rock 66095 had the ability to amplify and accelerate energy."

"I remember," Swain replied, now openly peeved.

Chester pointed out through the open flaps of the Mission Control tent. Lightning flashed, followed by a thunderclap. "If a lightning bolt hits any of these ridges, it goes to ground, right? But the ground here isn't solid. It's hollow. There was a big lightning bolt just before the quake, remember?"

"The kid's right," Boulter said to Swain. "You asked if the tent poles were metal."

"Yes, yes," Swain said. "Get to the point. I assume you have one."

"I do have one, a good one," Chester shot back. "Lets say that just before the earthquake, that tremendous bolt of lighting hit the right ridge, the ridge where the stone is hidden. Let's say all that energy reached the stone, got amplified, broken down, and re-formed by quark decay, and then accelerated—"

Swain saw what his nephew was getting at and his irritation gave way to unbridled dread. The physicist's face turned as gray as his ponytail and he had to sit down because he thought he might faint.

Boulter caught the transformation in Swain and moved to stand in front of him. "What's the kid saying?" he demanded. "You obviously think he's right."

Swain sat there stunned for a moment before looking up at the trooper. "He's saying that if we don't find that rock soon and this storm gets as bad as they're predicting, we could have Hiroshima beneath our feet."

5:02 P.M.
DANTE'S TUBES
LABYRINTH CAVE

Cricket wanted to puke. Below her in the shaft, Gregor shook and bucked, his jerky actions echoing up the slick rope to where she and Tom tried to attach her rappelling rack to the line.

"Get her down the rope," Kelly yelled, waving the pistol at them. "He's dying down there."

"We're trying but this is fucking tricky," Tom shouted back at him. "And we don't need you in our face while we're doing it."

Tom kept trying to get the third bar closed over the rope, but it wouldn't bend because of Gregor's weight. "You'll have to go with two bars and a hot seat," he said, a sickened look on his face. "If anyone can do it, you can."

Now Cricket wanted to puke and cry. To descend safely on a climbing rope you needed to weave the line through at least three metal bars so they could then be squeezed together to create enough friction to control your speed. It was the first rule of vertical rope work. She knew it was theoretically possible to descend a rope by loading it on a diagonal through just two bars, and then bending part of the rope back around the hip and butt in a "hot seat" rappel. But the technique was absolutely unsafe according to every modern climbing protocol. Cricket knew that if she made any mistake, she would go zipping down the rope in near free fall. But her dad's life was at stake here. She had to save Gregor to save him.

"I'm scared," Cricket said.

The stricken look on her dad's face deepened. His chin quivered and she understood his thoughts. Cricket was all he and her mother had, all they would ever have. A year after Cricket's birth, Whitney had developed a fibroid tumor in her uterus, making any more children an impossibility. And now their only child was being forced to do what most adults would not even consider. Her dad had to be thinking, What in God's name was he going to do if she screwed up and he somehow survived?

Then he gritted his teeth, put his hand on her shoulder, and looked her in the eye. "I'm scared too, sweetheart," he said. "But that's not going to change the fact that you've got to do this. I want you to imagine you're at the starting line at the state finals. You shut everything out except the right now. Focus on the now. Okay?"

Cricket swallowed and nodded, then got on her knees before the fright they shared could paralyze her. She immediately became hyperaware of everything around her: the way the toes of her boots scraped against the slick edge of the stone platform; the way the waterfall threw mist against the back of her neck; the way her arms quivered with the appalling concentration required to run an unsafe climbing rig.

The rope slipped across her butt, around her rib cage, and up, under and over the two brake bars of the rappelling rack mounted above her seat harness. She watched the rope pass through the gear works inch by inch until only her head projected above the edge of the platform and her feet hung free of the wall, out in space.

"Go just that speed," her dad said. "When you get to the falls, don't look up, the water pressure could blind you. Once you get to him, you tie him into your rappel rack, then get yourself swinging on the rope. You've got to get yourself to that nylon ladder on the wall down there. I left it there years ago when hanging this rope."

Cricket glanced down between her legs, seeing the purple nylon etrier that was bolted into the wall about twenty feet below her. She looked back up at her dad and nodded, but she could feel hysteria worming its way up her spine. Before it could possess her, she pressed the rope below the rack against her hip as hard as she could and began to descend again. The rack shuddered under the strain. Her outer thigh began to burn. The mist from the waterfall became a fine rain and she had to squint to see.

In seconds, she was just above Gregor. She could see him, or rather the blurred outline of him, there inside the three-foot-wide roaring cascade. The water ballooned out around him like rapids around a boulder. She eased her way down until they were only eight feet apart. Her boots were inches from the waterfall. The crashing of the water against the cave wall hurt her ears.

"You're doing great," her father called down.

Gregor must have heard him. The rope below Cricket began to twist and toss.

"Stop!" she yelled.

But Gregor's thrashing turned frantic. Cricket felt the rope slide across her hip. "For God's sake, stop!" she screamed.

In desperation she tried to pull the line up onto her rappel rig to arrest her descent, but Gregor's weight made that impossible. Her right hand slipped. The rope jumped free of her hip and snapped toward the center of her rappel rack. All friction was lost. She plunged into the falls and expected to die.

The water burst around her head, a raging white experience. It buffeted her from all angles, pounded in her ears. She slammed into something and stopped falling. Her senses were all but extinguished by the ungodly weight, pressure, and noise of the falling water that rammed her chin down against her chest and beat against her back.

At least it wasn't in her eyes; the flange of her helmet acted like an umbrella, giving her about two inches of clear vision. She moved her head and saw that her rappelling rack had collided with Gregor's, stopping her fall. The pale scientist's arm was crooked across his forehead. He was oriented toward her, but she could not tell if his eyes were open or not. She reached into the space between them and did what her father had told her to do, re-rigging her rack to his. They were one now on the rope.

She knew if they stayed much longer in that position the water, ripping at the seams of their dry suits, would rob them of precious body heat, even as the webs of nylon about their thighs acted as tourniquets, cutting off their blood supply, killing them both. Then she remembered what her dad had said.

She needed to kick free of the waterfall and try to get hold of that webbed ladder somewhere behind her.

"Can you hear me?" she yelled at Gregor.

He nodded weakly.

"Can you help me get us swinging?"

Gregor nodded again.

"Okay, here we go. On three. One, two, three!"

They missed their timing on their first attempt and succeeded only in spinning themselves around inside the cascade. On their second try she and Gregor rocked together and swung deeper into the water. On the third try, Cricket felt her boots meet the cave wall. She squatted and kicked off.

They swung backward through the waterfall and came free of it for an instant. Cricket took a deep breath just before they plunged back into the roaring cascade. She extended her feet, anticipating contact with the cave wall, squatted, and kicked again. Gregor did the same, and with his added thrust they flew much farther out the other side of the plume. Cricket managed to twist her head to throw her light to the wall to seek out the purple nylon climbing ladder. Just as they began to swing back toward the subterranean cascade, she located it.

"One more time!" Cricket yelled.

They splashed back into the ripping water, boots and knees raised. Cricket tensed as they met the rock, then kicked off it with every ounce of her remaining energy. They broke free of the waterfall again. She arched her back, her left hand seeking the nylon ladder. It seemed an eternity, that crossing of space, waiting until her fingers were in range. She felt the rope reach the apex of its swing, then let loose a scream of frustration as her fingers missed the ladder and clawed wildly at the air, just as Mann's had done the day before while falling to his doom.

But Gregor's longer arm shot out and snagged one of the rungs.

They hung there gasping for several seconds before Cricket had the presence of mind to open the carabiner on her cow's-tail safety line and clip herself to the nylon ladder. Then she grabbed Gregor's safety line and did the same thing. She got him to step into the nylon ladder, then followed him, taking all their weight off the rope.

She heard her dad whoop with joy above her, then yell, "You've done the tough part, Crick. Now re-rig the racks and take him down slow."

"Take me down s-s-slow," Gregor said. He was drunk with the cold.

For an instant, Cricket fantasized about unclipping his safety line and watching him tumble into the abyss. Then she remembered Kelly and the gun.

"If you want to live, you're going to do exactly what I say," she said.

"You have the knowledge," Gregor replied. "I don't."

It took Cricket ten minutes to get her rappel rack properly loaded on the rope and then Gregor's harness attached to her own. She disconnected the carabiners holding them to the wall anchor and they began to drop down the rope facing each other. Gregor was so grossly waxen up close like this that Cricket swore she could see the blue of his veins under his skin. The whites of his eyes were a root system of blasted red capillaries.

"You despise me, d-don't you?"

Cricket did not reply

"Doesn't matter," Gregor said. "For great science, you must sacrifice everything. What people think of you, what they expect of you. Everything."

His head rolled to one side. Cricket just kept working the rope through the rappel rack. She wanted to get to the bottom of the shaft and away from him as fast as she could. His breath was horrible, as if he were being eaten away from the inside and this was the smell of that deterioration.

"All the great minds are ha-hated in their day," Gregor said, chattering as well as stammering now. "Copernicus. Galileo. Oppenheimer. The revolutionary minds are the most threatening, they're the ones the world tries to smash. But my due will come soon. History will judge me. Then nothing else will matter."

"I just want to go home and be with my mom," she said.

At that, Gregor blinked, and his focus became unscrewed, as if he were looking through Cricket and off into a great distance. He didn't say anything for almost a minute. When he did, it was with the hardest stammer Cricket had heard from him yet.

"M-my mother was a fragile person," he said. "Always tottering at the edge of life. She died one night in this cabin we lived in with my granddad. I was eight. No—no one else there. Granddad was in the county j-jail. I knew I should go tell someone. But I knew they'd take her away from me. Granddad always said they'll ta-take away the things you love. They did eventually. Social worker came. Found me. Found my mother. They buried her in a pauper's grave."

He chuckled bitterly. "So you see, a loving home life is a myth. The only secure thing in life is knowledge. Only armor in life is knowledge. Protects you. Tran-transforms you. The only thing they can't steal from you."

His head lolled, then rocked back, and he lost consciousness.

Now a light shone up from below. Cricket looked away from Gregor and, despite her exhaustion, kept them descending at a steady pace. Lyons waited where the rope ended beside a wide aquamarine pool that emptied into a stream running north. The big prison guard stepped up, caught her by the waist, and lowered her the last few feet. "You saved his life. You're an amazing girl, Cricket."

She stared at Lyons with utter hatred. "I hope he gets pneumonia and dies for what he's done to us. For what you've done to us."

Then she struggled free of the harness, her entire body trembling with fatigue and chill. She staggered and collapsed against the wall of the shaft. Her arms, shoulders, and hips felt like they'd been struck with bats. Her teeth chattered. Lyons came after her and reached out his hand.

"Get away from me," she said. "I'll take care of myself until my dad comes."

The guard stared at her for a moment, then turned and went back to Gregor. He stripped the comatose man to his waist and applied to his torso heat packs that activated upon contact with air.

Cricket had never been so tired and cold in her life. She had to sleep, if only for a few minutes. But she knew she had to get warm. She got out a heat pack of her own from her knapsack and stuffed it down the front of her suit. Then she rolled to her side, using her knapsack for a pillow, drowsily aware that the rope from above was already wiggling.

5:45 P.M.
KING'S CASTLE BREAKDOWN
MUNK'S RIDGE
LABYRINTH CAVE

Whitney clawed at the earthquake debris, burrowing her way into the choked passage rock by rock. Her knees and shoulders ached. The tips of her fingers felt hammer struck from all the digging, but she did not stop. In the past hour and a half she'd managed to penetrate four feet into the collapse. By her reckoning, she had to be less than eight feet from breaking through to the other side and King's Castle Cavern.

She squinted into dust as thick as coastal fog and fought against a loose boulder. Finnerty squeezed in beside her, a handkerchief up over his mouth. Together they reached up and tugged at the rock.

After nearly five minutes of hard work, it came free. But more wreckage slid down to replace it, shooting additional dust into the air. In seconds they were coughing so hard, they had to back out of the tunnel.

"We'll take turns working in there," Finnerty said.

"This is a waste of time," Two-Elk complained. "Mrs. Burke was right, boss—they're probably all dead. If they're alive, they've reached the supply dump and gone."

Whitney jumped to her feet before Finnerty could reply, shaking with rage. "Don't you dare say that. Don't you dare. We've gone through too much the last year for it to all be over now. Life's cruel, but it's not inhuman. I can't believe it's inhuman. My husband and daughter are alive. And we're going to beat them to that dump and rescue them. Do you understand? Do you!"

Two-Elk shrank back, stunned. "Okay, Mrs. Burke, calm down," she said. "I'm sorry. I understand."

They worked like a firemen's bucket brigade, passing the tailings back out of the tunnel, then throwing them off the cliff, where they clattered down the underground mountain before splashing into the lake some eight hundred feet below.

Whitney tried to keep her attention on clearing the passage. But troubling thoughts kept intruding. What if Two-Elk was right? What if they were dead? She shook her head, unwilling to let that idea fester. The cave could not do it to her twice.

Finnerty backed out from the collapse. He removed his helmet and wiped his sleeve across his brow, smearing the chalky grit that caked his face. His eyes were bleary and his hands trembled with fatigue. "Got a problem," he said. "You better take a look"

It was the first time that Whitney had heard anything but a resolute attitude from the marshal and she crawled to the head of the excavation with nervous anticipation. She cocked her head to shine her light on the rubble pile that still blocked the passage and understood Finnerty's concern at once: During the earthquake two enormous chunks of rock, each nearly a half ton, had become dislodged from the cave ceiling. The giant boulders rested against each other, supported and balanced atop three blocks the size and shape of microwave ovens. The middle block was badly fissured.

"See it?" Finnerty asked when she'd backed out

Whitney nodded. "You could pull the pieces of that middle block and both boulders might come down. Or the two big boulders could push against each other and leave us a way forward beneath them."

"Or we could just forget this and could go back the way we came," Two-Elk offered quietly, looking at her disfigured hand.

"And we might find that way collapsed, too," Finnerty snapped.

"I'm not listening to negativity," Whitney said.

"I'll go try," the marshal said.

"No," Whitney said. "This is my family. If anyone's taking the chance, it's me."

Before Finnerty could stop her, she ducked into the tunnel and scrambled forward to where she could run her fingers down the deep lines that fractured the middle stone, felt her throat go dry, then crammed her fingers into the cracks and yanked. Nothing budged. She picked up a rock about the size of a goose egg, gave the block a rap, and saw a piece of it move ever so slightly. She hesitated, then reached into the fissure and yanked again. A good-sized piece of the block came free. She handed it back to Finnerty. And then another. And then a third. But as she began to work at the fourth piece, the two slabs over her head began to moan and grind against each other.

7:30 P.M.
NASA ENCAMPMENT
JENKINS RIDGE
LABYRINTH CAVE

Swain lay on his back, attaching a power cable to one of three black boxes Chester had arranged on metal stands set in an equilateral-triangle formation. Fish-eye lenses stuck out the end of each box, aimed toward a fourth box suspended on wire about four feet above a white rectangular board lying flat on the ground to the physicist's right. A crystal-grade prism about seven inches long brought up from the university lab, hung out of the bottom of the suspended fourth box.

Swain finished the task, then sat up and looked at his chunky young nephew, busy at the computer terminal. There was no denying it. In the past few hours, Chester had grown, become more mature and sure of himself. As much as Swain hated to admit it, he had been very little help in designing this holographic system. It had been Chester's concept from the start and he had put the device together in what would have taken days for men twice his age and experience.

The physicist sighed at the feelings of guilt that coursed through him. Perhaps he was too hard on his nephew. Perhaps he had been for a long time. He thought of Carson MacPherson and how Chester had said his late partner had treated Gregor. Swain asked himself if he was blameworthy of the same insensitivity. Then he asked himself if the way he treated his nephew was born of jealousy. He had been around academics long enough to hear all the stories of older, established scientists who worked hard their whole lives, yet never achieved the big breakthrough. Then one of their students would stun the community with some discovery and they would crumble into bitterness. The world thought Swain had discovered room-temperature superconductors. He had been lauded in the press, lionized by his peers. Less than a dozen government officials, all sworn to secrecy, and Chester knew the real truth. Was this why he was so hard on the boy? Could he not stand the idea of being upstaged by youth once more?

"Chester, I have something to tell you," Swain began.

Chester turned around in his chair. He hadn't had a shower in days. His hair was oily and flew in twenty directions. His polo shirt was covered with so many food stains it could have belonged to a smorgasbord chef. "Yes, Uncle Jeff?"

Before the physicist could complete his thought, Boulter rushed into the Mission Control tent. The state trooper's SWAT uniform was soaking wet and splattered with mud. In the past two hours the electrical storm had abated, but the rain had intensified; a half inch an hour pelted the canvas roofs of the tents. Jenkins meadow looked like a rice paddy in a monsoon.

"We getting signals?" Boulter demanded.

Angelis, who had been busy the past four hours trying to repair the computer system, shook his head. "The earthquake damaged those repeater relays. If any of them are alive and moving underground, there's no way we'd know. But right now we've got worse problems. The U.S. Geological Survey has hydrostatic gauges on the Furnace River. The damn river's running at twenty-five thousand cubic feet per second, almost ten thousand cfs above normal. If it continues to rain like this, the lower levels of the cave could be flooded within thirty-six hours. And we're getting reports of damage at Hermes Reservoir. They're attempting to shore it up, but it's not looking good."

"Son of a bitch!" Boulter shouted. He paced, rubbing his beard-stubbled jaw, then stopped and looked at Swain and Norton. "What's that thing?"

"Watch," Swain said. "Chester's ready, am I right?"

Chester nodded. "I'd stand back if I were you, gentlemen, and put sunglasses on if you've got them," he said. "Your retinas could get damaged by the lasers during entanglement."

All three men took several strides backward, fishing in their pockets for sunglasses. Chester typed in a long string code on the computer keyboard, then struck Enter. At once a low-frequency tone competed with the sound of the rain thrashing the roof of the tent. An intense red saber of light shot out of the box at the head of the triangular formation and struck the prism. A second, midrange pitch sounded and a blue laser burst from the box on the right side of the triangular formation. A high, piercing note arose right on the heels of that, creating the musical discord of a child smashing his fists on a piano, and a searing yellow light zoomed out from the third box. It collided with the two other colored beams inside the prism.

There was a moment of searing brilliance that caused all four men to squint and turn. Then, from the bottom of the suspended prism, green light poured forth. The light cascaded downward and reflected off the white board on the floor below it. It rebounded rose, gathered volume, and then became a discernible shape.

"I'll be a son of a bitch," Boulter muttered. "The fat little shit's a genius."

"I would not go that far," Swain said. "But it's a good step."

"Good step?" the NASA mission commander cried, shaking his head in wonder. "It's incredible."

Hovering there above the white board, cast in shades of opaque green, was a three-dimensional holograph of Labyrinth Cave. At first glance, it looked like a school of a hundred jellyfish doing battle with a miserable assembly of octopuses and squid; the thousands of tentacles seemed to hang, arch, and coil off the scrum of geologic mollusks in an almost incomprehensible tangle.

Swain crouched to study it and soon saw structure within the morass: nine distinct, elongated, hump-shaped gatherings linked together by filigreed appendages sprouting from their bases. High on the sides of four of the humps were gaping holes, like hungry beaks searching for food: the main entrances to Labyrinth Cave. There were similar mouths at the bottom of the north end of each hump. From each of these mouths emerald liquids spilled into one common, slow-moving stream.

Chester snapped his fingers. "Why didn't we think of it before?"

"What?" Angelis demanded.

Chester slapped his thigh and chuckled to himself.

"What is it?" Swain demanded.

"Can't you see it, Uncle Jeff? It's right there in front of your nose. Remember what Mrs. Burke told us? Caves are formed by water seeking its tortured way through soluble rock to base level, where it flows to a common drainage and eventually to the sea."

"Okay?" Boulter said.

Chester gestured at the four openings high on the sides of the holographic representation of the cave. "We've been running the sensors only at the entrances humans could use."

Then he pointed at the nine spots on the holograph where the emerald liquid poured into the single stream. "The point is that there are nine other ways into Labyrinth Cave, or actually nine ways out of it, all of them submerged beneath the Furnace River. We have to go to these outflows and lower the sensors into the water. Wherever the readings are strongest, we'll find the stone."

"Not bad, Chester," Swain said. "B-plus."

6:40 P.M.
KING'S CASTLE CAVERN
MUNK'S RIDGE
LABYRINTH CAVE

Tom knelt next to Cricket. She shivered violently despite the heat packs. He picked her up and held her to his chest. She opened her eyes and looked at him. Tom smiled. "You were unbelievably brave up there."

"So tired, Daddy," she mumbled.

"We all are," he said. "But we're real close to the supply cache now. Half hour, tops. You can eat and get into some dry clothes. C'mon, honey, we've got to get you dry. I know you can do it."

Tom could tell that Cricket wanted nothing more than to sleep for hours and hours. But she nodded, and with his help got to her feet. Half an hour, he thought. Was he right? Would a rescue team be there at the cache? It was the only logical place.

"Be ready to run when we get to the cache," he whispered.

Cricket came wide awake at that. "Okay," she whispered back.

Tom turned and, to his astonishment, found Gregor already shouldering his pack. He looked weak, but far better than Tom thought possible given the circumstances. Gregor glanced his way and their eyes met. Tom saw in him no flicker of consideration for what Cricket had done. Indeed, he saw such callousness that he realized that Gregor regarded him and Cricket as nothing more than tools. Kelly saw them the same way. But Lyons. Despite his vow to kill them all if they got in the way of his retrieving the stone, there was something about the man, something that told Tom he was not as ruthless as the others. Right now, however, none of that mattered. They had to get to the cache site.

"Let's go," Tom said.

He set off at the head of the line once again, circumventing the aquamarine pool and the underground channel fed by the waterfall, then headed west into an easy-walking passage with a gently rising grade. The cave's breath blowing at him was strong and soon its sound replaced the cascade.

It took only twenty minutes for Tom to lead them into a cavern of immense proportions. The wind ebbed and all was a fantastic silence save the crunch of their footsteps echoing off the ceiling somewhere in the darkness high overhead. King's Castle was the second of the three gigantic grottoes that made up the hollow interior of Munk's Ridge. The underground mountain lay on their left.

Tom slowed as he approached the gigantic breakdown pile. He swung his headlamp all around like a beacon. Any rescue team NASA might have sent would have to come through the low passage that led over the peak of the underground crag. He glanced over his shoulder at Cricket and she began to wave her headlamp beam around as well.

"What the hell are you doing?" Kelly asked.

"Just, ah, just making sure the pile there's stable," Tom replied. "The earthquake could have weakened it."

He threw his light higher up the side of the underground mountain. But his beam revealed only jumbles of rock and dun flowstone in the shape of castle turrets. No noise. No light. No sign of rescue. Nothing. Nothing but silence.

For a second, Tom was flooded with the same sort of marooned feeling that had overpowered him when he first received word that Whitney and Jeannie Yung had gone missing in Terror Hole Cave. Then he noticed the tears in Cricket's eyes.

"We're going to be all right," he told her. "The cache is up here two or three hundred yards. Okay?"

"Okay," Cricket said, her chin trembling.

They had taken no more than five steps when they heard it. High overhead and to their left. Way, way up the face of the underground mountain. The muffled grating of rock against rock. A silence. Then the grating again. Louder this time. Followed by the rhythmic cracking of stone upon stone.

The inmates heard it too. And the whole line of them halted, training their headlights up the north face of the breakdown pile.

"It ain't another earthquake, is it?" Kelly asked, the concern plain on his face.

"Shut up," Gregor ordered. He stepped forward, the veins at his temple twitching, his gun held loosely before him. Kelly pulled out his weapon as well and cocked it. Lyons put his index finger on the safety of the shotgun but did not ease it off.

For almost a minute there was just the fan of their lights against the shadows and the shallow, rapid sibilance of their breath. And then it came a third time. The clacking of rocks somewhere in the darkness, just beyond the range of their lights.

Gregor hissed, "That's no aftershock. Someone's digging up there!"

"Help!" Tom bellowed into the darkness. "We're down here!"

Kelly struck Tom so hard at the nape of his neck that he buckled to his knees. Cricket spun, intending to scream up the slope, but Gregor threw his hand over her mouth and pressed the pistol barrel into her ear. "One peep and you're over," he growled.

Tom rolled over and looked up blearily at Lyons. "You said you'd make sure we were safe. Why don't you help us, for God's sake?"

Lyons looked up the slope, then at Gregor and Kelly, who were glaring at him, watching every line in the big man's face. "I lied just to keep you helping us," Lyons said. "Ain't my job to help you. Now get up and get moving!"

Supply Cache 1 lay off the northwest corner of the main cavern in a sandy grotto about twenty feet across and ten feet high. Ten red rubberized cargo bags of the sort canoeists use on long trips were stacked against one wall of the grotto. Next to the waterproof bags lay a medical kit and a slim, blue plastic box.

"Where's the food and the sleeping bags?" Kelly asked.

Tom said nothing.

"Tell us," Lyons ordered.

"In the bags," Tom replied, feeling defeated. Cricket slumped to the floor of the cave. He saw her take off her gloves and put her index finger into the sand.

"There's no time to stop," Gregor said. The physicist was jumpy, looking over his shoulder into the broad tunnel that led back toward the north flank of the underground mountain. "Everybody grab a bag and we go. They could be right behind us."

Tom, meanwhile, was staring at the blue plastic box. He hesitated, keenly aware of the bruise rising at the nape of his neck. The box held a computer linked via repeater transmitters to the surface. If he could get a message out…But if they caught him…He glanced at Cricket, her head down, more depressed than he'd ever seen her, running her finger through the sand. Tom felt terrible anger rising inside him that these men had been able to break her like this. He had to take the risk. He knelt and undid the hasps on the box. There was a laptop computer encased in soft foam inside. He raised a long whip antenna, then flipped a switch and the screen glowed to life.

"What he's up to?" Gregor demanded. Kelly rushed toward the computer and made as if to kick it. But Tom held out his hands to protect the box.

"We're about to head into an area of the cave that's almost impossible to navigate without help," he said. "Even I get turned around in there. I've got to download the map into my navigation unit."

Kelly stopped, studying him and the box. "Take it with you. We gotta go."

Tom shook his head. "Doesn't work that way. The central processor functions off repeating transmitters calibrated from this specific location. If I move the computer, everything will be thrown off. It will only take a minute to download the way points."

"We don't have a minute," Gregor snarled.

"Without the coordinates, we'll be heading in blind," Tom insisted.

Lyons's attention jumped from Tom to the passage that led to the underground mountain and back again. "Get your coordinates," he said.

The computer screen sprang to life. Gregor got behind Tom as he called up the electronic map, then made a show of taking his transponder out of his pack and holding it toward the machine with one hand, while triggering a function key with the other. In the screen's top right-hand corner a red light came on. A tiny fiber-optic camera built into the frame of the machine was now activated and recording.

"C'mon, c'mon, hurry up," Kelly snapped.

"Thirty seconds," Tom said, looking directly into the camera lens. "And I'll have a fix on the confluence of the Forgotten and No Return Rivers. With a little luck we'll be through the rinky-dink and there at midnight tomorrow."

"He's up to something," Gregor said.

Tom struck another function key, the one that sent burst transmissions to the repeaters he and NASA engineers had installed throughout the cave. "Done," he said, standing up. "Let's go."

"You sure you got it?" Lyons asked, giving Tom a probing look.

"Positive."

Just then, far out in the main cavern, they heard a tremendous crashing.

Gregor pulled his pistol. Lyons spun with his shotgun.

"Go!" Kelly cried.

Tom stalled, wanting to hear the sound of running feet.

Kelly yanked Cricket up and held the belly belt transmitter under her nose. "Move or I'll hit her with it."

Tom took one last look at the dark passage that led back toward the underground mountain, then grabbed two of the rubberized supply bags and stumbled toward the far end of the grotto.

10:25 P.M.
KING'S CASTLE
CAVERN MUNK'S RIDGE
LABYRINTH CAVE

A steady drip of sweat rolled down between Whitney's eyes and dangled off her nose. It was ghastly work trying to remove the final pieces of the fractured rock beneath the two boulders over her head without triggering a total collapse of the passage.

The tension had gotten so dizzying fifteen minutes ago that she swore she had heard Tom shout to her for help. His voice had seemed so real and so close that she'd begun to hyperventilate and then to pound at the last locked pieces that blocked the passage. She'd stopped and listened again, eager for his voice. But she'd heard nothing.

"How's it going?" Finnerty asked. The marshal was in the crush up to his shoulders just behind her right boot.

"This one piece just won't budge," Whitney said. "Maybe Two-Elk's right, we should turn back."

"Weren't you the one who gave us a lecture on positive thinking?" Finnerty asked. He passed her his combat knife. "Use this as a lever."

Part of her just wanted to lie there and let sleep come and whatever would come after that. But something inside—the memory of how Tom had seemed to call to her through the rock—caused her to take the heavy-bladed tool from Finnerty and jam it under the lower edge of the blockage and press down hard. Pebbles rang off her helmet. Grit and dust swirled around her.

She waited for the debris to settle, then tried to pry the rock toward her. No luck. She inserted the knife into the gap she'd created and worked at it a third time. The pebble shower became a torrent and she had to duck, holding her kerchief tight to her mouth. When the debris settled again, the stone blocking the passage remained.

"Dammit!" she cried, smacking the heel of her palm against the rock

It moved. Not much, but it had definitely slipped forward. Whitney braced her boots against the walls of the tunnel and rammed the heel of her palm against the rock again. It slid ahead two inches this time.

"What's going on?" Finnerty asked.

"Give me a second," Whitney said. She picked up a chunk of limestone the size of her fist and smashed it against the last piece of the fractured block of stone. It popped free and clattered away. Whitney felt a puff of air on her face.

"We're almost there!" she cried. "I feel it. We're—"

She stopped at the high-pitched whine of the two boulders grinding against each other. A fist-sized piece of rock was all that now supported them.

"Get out! Get out!" Whitney screamed. "It's caving in!"

The last stone holding up the two boulders disintegrated under their weight. Sediment and rock avalanched into the tunnel and for a moment she thought she'd be stamped. But when the boulders were dislodged, they crashed forward, exploding away from her, clattering and booming into the darkness down the north slope of the underground mountain.

Whitney raised her head. A strong cool wind bathed her face and cleared the dust. Eight feet in front of her was an exit hole the size of a beach ball. She turned, looked back at Finnerty, and shook the knife in triumph. "We're through!"

Twenty minutes later, Finnerty and Two-Elk stormed into the supply cache while Whitney remained hidden outside. There was a long period of silence, followed by the sounds of their murmuring before she could not take it anymore and, despite their demand that she remain safely behind, she turned on her headlamp and went in after them. Two-Elk was on one knee, examining the tracks in the soft sand that covered the grotto floor. Finnerty stood beside her.

"We must have spooked them out of here when those boulders fell," Finnerty said. "They got here first."

Whitney rolled back her head. "How long ago?"

"Minutes," Two-Elk replied.

"Where would they go from here?" Finnerty demanded.

"Ah, shit, I don't know," Whitney said, throwing up her arms in frustration and disappointment. "In the next thirty miles of cave ahead of us, there are a half a dozen different ways you could go and still end up in the same place."

"One of them's dead, boss," Two-Elk suddenly announced.

Whitney froze. "Who? How do you know that?"

Two-Elk gestured at the pile of red waterproof bags. The NASA people said there were supposed to be ten of these bags at each supply dump. There are five left now. If the Burkes, Lyons, and the three inmates came through here, there would only be four left. One of them's not with us."

Whitney fought a rumble in her stomach. "Which one?" she asked.

"Can't tell yet." Two-Elk returned her attention to the footprints in the dust "I'm sure it's not your husband. They could not have gotten this far without him."

Whitney went over next to Two-Elk and looked around the floor. She was searching for a small boot print. Instead, her attention locked on a circle about six inches in diameter that had been dug by a slender finger in the sandy cave bottom. In the middle of the circle was a rudely crafted cone.

"Cricket's alive," Whitney whispered.

"How do you know?" Finnerty asked.

She pointed at the sand carving and tears welled in her eyes. "Cricket trap," she said. "A family thing."

"Good," Finnerty said, smiling. "Very good. Not only is your family still alive, but there's one less of their captives. The odds are tilting in our favor."

Whitney nodded, smiling through her tears.

"Where's the next supply cache?" Two-Elk asked.

"Nyrens Ridge," Whitney replied. "Four ridges west of here. Forty miles of passage."

"Are there enough supplies in these bags for us to get there?" Finnerty asked.

"Well, yes, but how do we know if that's where they're head—"

Whitney stopped. She had noticed the faint blipping light showing under the loose cover of the blue box next to the cricket trap. She knelt and lifted the cover. The computer screen came to life. On it was a section of the vector grid map of the Labyrinth. Overlaying the map were the words TRANSMISSION ERROR.

Whitney looked up, excited. "They tried to send a message to the surface, but it didn't make it," she said. "I think there's a record here of what they tried to send."

She gave the computer another command. An orange bar appeared on the darkened screen followed by a grainy digital movie of Tom. His skin was blackened and streaked with grime. His eyes were sunken. Great strain showed everywhere about him.

Whitney watched him talk to the screen, but barely heard his words because she was dumbfounded at the fact that minutes ago he had held the computer. The picture twisted suddenly. Cricket was there, too. The picture twisted again and she caught glimpses of Gregor, Lyons, and Kelly, all of them hangdog with fatigue.

"They're in worse shape than us," Finnerty said. "We can catch these guys."

Two-Elk was already standing to follow him, but Whitney didn't move. She was replaying the movie, listening to what Tom was saying.

"Stop!" she yelled after the marshals. "Tom said they'd reach the confluence of the Forgotten and No Return Rivers at midnight tomorrow after they go through the rinky-dink."

"Rinky-dink?" the marshal said.

"It's an old-time caving term for giving someone the runaround."

The marshal looked at her, still puzzled. "What are you trying to say?"

"The next few ridges are so riddled with passages that there are literally dozens of places you could lead someone in circles and come back on course and eventually make it to Nyrens Ridge, the seventh of the cave's nine, where two underground rivers converge."

"Okay?" Two-Elk said.

Whitney felt hope surge through her at the audacity of Tom's plan. He was still fighting for his life. For Cricket's life, too. How could she have doubted him? How could she have doubted his love?

"Tom's going to run these men in circles for the next thirty hours," she explained, excitement giving a quiver to her voice. "He's going to try to completely break them down before leading them to the confluence of those two rivers at midnight tomorrow. If you're still intent on an ambush, Marshal, there's no place in this entire cave that would be better."

Deep Cave

June 17, 2007
7:00 A.M.
NASA ENCAMPMENT
JENKINS RIDGE
LABYRINTH CAVE

For the third morning in a row, Helen Greidel reported live from the Artemis Project. Wearing a bright red rain parka, she hunched under her umbrella before the wreckage of the old Jenkins homestead. Rain pelted her face.

"A story that has gripped the world in the past few days has now turned grimmer," she began. "In the wake of the powerful earthquake that struck eastern Kentucky yesterday afternoon, NASA now admits that it has lost all signals from the electronic location beacons carried by those still trapped in Labyrinth Cave—escaped prison inmates, two hostages, and a team sent in to rescue them."

The screen cut away to Angelis, the Mission Control chief, standing before a bank of microphones, the effects of the ordeal showing everywhere in his face.

"NASA has lost the signal being emitted from the beacons carried by Tom and Cricket Burke and the four men we believe are holding them hostage," Angelis shouted over the calls of reporters. "We have also lost contact with the rescue team—Burke's wife and three U.S. marshals."

"Are they dead?" a reporter yelled.

Angelis stopped, sobered. "We are proceeding on the assumption that they are alive."

The screen switched to a still shot of what looked like a gigantic drill mounted on the back of a flat-bed truck Greidel spoke in voice-over: "Angelis also announced that the U.S. Bureau of Mines is rushing a rescue boring machine to the site. The machine will be used to reopen the entrances to the cave that collapsed during the earthquake and perhaps allow a second rescue team to enter the cave in search of survivors."

The picture jumped a third time, to a black-and-white newsreel film showing filthy men working on mining equipment, over which Greidel spoke: "The effort under way here appears to be the largest and most complex underground rescue attempt since the one undertaken back in 1925 to save Floyd Collins, the famous Kentucky cave explorer who was trapped in a cave about one hundred miles to our southwest.

"Rescuers managed to reach Collins and kept him alive with food and heat for five days before a landslide blocked the passage to him," Greidel went on. "It took twelve more days for engineers to sink a shaft and reach Collins a second time. All they found was his body."

The camera returned to Greidel huddled under her umbrella. She opened her eyes wide in sympathy. "We can only pray that the rescue efforts now under way here at Labyrinth Cave prove more successful than those undertaken on behalf of poor Floyd Collins."

Two miles north, the Furnace River had turned into a boiling maelstrom replete with whirlpools and the sort of standing waves big western rivers spawn at the height of the spring runoff.

Swain stood on the bank above the ferry, hunched over against a gale that drove the rain in sheets so thick that the Furnace's north shore was but a dim gray line. He wore a yellow rain slicker, bib pants, and high rubber boots.

Boulter came up behind the physicist, wearing a similar outfit. "The kid just checked the USGS web site," he said. "River's running fifty thousand cubic feet per second and rising."

"And I don't think we've seen the worst of it," Swain agreed.

Indeed, before leaving the Mission Control pavilion, the physicist had seen the latest satellite imagery, which showed the freak storm moving northeast across southern Appalachia and gathering enormous strength. Rain was already falling at one and a quarter inches per hour. Wind speeds were roughly fifty-two miles per hour, with gusts approaching sixty-five. The front was some two hundred twenty miles in breadth. Its center was rotating over northern Mississippi while its southern edge sucked moisture from the warm waters of the Gulf of Mexico. Barometric pressure readings at dawn were 28.5 and falling. Over the next fifteen hours, the barometric pressure was predicted to drop at more than a millibar an hour. Hurricane statistics.

In the area surrounding Labyrinth Cave, thirteen hours of rain had all but liquefied the thin soil atop the limestone substructure. Trees whose root systems had been weakened by shock belowground toppled in the gusting wind. Others snapped halfway up their trunks. The fierce weather had made flight in the area all but impossible. Helicopters had been grounded, slowing the final medevacs of the earthquake's wounded. The dirt road approach from the south had been turned into a trough of red clay gumbo. Ferry traffic had halted at midnight. The only thing preventing a full-scale flood was the damaged rammed-earth dam at Hermes Reservoir, twenty miles upstream of the cave, where repair crews were working around the clock.

"You sure we want to be doing this?" Chester asked.

Swain turned to see his nephew peering out from under the hood of his rain suit, a look of pure terror on his face. He held on to a life preserver. "Couldn't we wait for the storm to die down a little?"

"Your call, Dr. Swain," Boulter said.

"I don't think we have a choice," Swain replied. "The sooner we locate that stone, the better."

"Let's do it, then," Boulter said. He climbed down the bank and into the cab of a pickup truck. He backed it and the boat trailer it was towing toward the river. The boat was a seventeen-foot whaler normally used by state police scuba divers when searching for drowning victims. The raging current slammed into the boat's stern and threw it off the trailer. Swain ran into the shallows, grabbed the bow rope, and held on for dear life.

"Give me a hand, Chester!" the physicist yelled at his nephew. But the teen did not move. He seemed transfixed by the whitecaps in the middle of the river.

Boulter pulled his rig up to dry ground, then ran to Chester and Swain. "Get in!" He splashed out into the muddy water and jumped aboard. Swain was right behind him. He turned and saw Chester just standing there.

"C'mon, Chester!" Swain yelled.

"I can't swim."

"What?" the physicist said, bewildered. "Impossible."

Now Chester got furious. "No it's not! You and Mom had me in school every day since I was two. I never learned, Uncle Jeff. I never learned. You were always in the pool, but you never gave me lessons."

At that, Swain felt as if everything he'd done in the past ten years had been for naught. Body surfing and swimming had been his refuge, his solace, the thing that kept him sane in the insane world of big-time physics. And he'd never even thought to give Chester swimming lessons.

"Chester, I..." Swain called from the boat. "You've got the life preserver. You'll be fine."

Boulter fired up the 120-horsepower outboard. "He's right, kid. That's the best preserver on the market."

The chunky teenager still did not move. "Please, Chester," Swain said.

Reluctantly, the young man at last waded out, hoisted himself onto the lunging craft, then threw himself into the passenger chair, shaking like a fish thrown on the sand. Swain helped him tighten the straps on the orange life preserver. "You're gonna be okay."

"No, I won't," he grumbled. "I'm going to drown because of you and some stinking moon rock."

Before Swain could reply, the trooper turned on the depth finder and loran unit and yelled, "You got those coordinates, Doc?"

Swain tore himself away from his nephew, unzipped the top of his yellow rain suit, and peered inside at a list of longitude and latitude measurements, then called out the first. Boulter typed the numbers into the loran, jammed the prop in Reverse, and backed the boat into the current. The small craft was flung sideways. A wave burst over the gunwales.

Boulter spun the wheel of the whaler and gunned the engine. The boat pitched and threatened to roll abeam before the big outboard caught and they moved upriver, tentatively at first, then with more authority. The hull slammed off the roiling surface of the river. At each lift and fall, geysers of spray broke across the bow.

"Help me watch for debris," Boulter shouted.

Swain got up on one foot, was thrown hard to the side, then managed to get both feet under him, legs spread wide, hands grasping the windshield struts. The rain was falling so fast that it seemed not to have motion, only sound, color, and temperature. The river writhed like thousands of copperhead snakes dumped in a pit. Tree trunks, broken branches, and pieces of crushed lumber from destroyed buildings upstream flashed by in the cataracts. So did a washing machine, a derelict car, and what appeared to he the spar of a windmill. But with Swain's help, Boulter managed to avoid them all and ten minutes later the shrouded mausoleum of Jenkins Ridge came into view.

"Get those sensors ready, kid," Boulter yelled at Chester. But the physicist's nephew clung, catatonic, in the passenger chair.

"Chester, for God's sake, the sensors," Swain yelled. "We've got to do the readings!"

The teen's eyes focused, but his hands shook as if with palsy as he unzipped the top of his rain suit and brought out the handheld device. Boulter began shouting out the river's depth: "Twenty-two feet... twenty... Forty-five feet! That's gotta be your outflow! Do your reading, kid. I can't hold her here for long."

7:20 A.M.
EASTERN CAVERNS
BAILEY'S RIDGE
LABYRINTH CAVE

Deep within Bailey's Ridge, the fifth of the Labyrinth's nine, the passages were like hallways in an opera house, with high arched ceilings and dripping chandelier formations. The sediment that lined the floor was firm but had a bounce to it, like packed sand or padded carpet. Off the side of one of these grand hallways was a grotto roughly the shape of an igloo with a long entrance tunnel leading into a rotunda, where Cricket lay snuggled deep in the cocoon of her NASA sleeping bag.

As grumbling and shuffling noises echoed in the darkness around her, Cricket came to the edge of consciousness. A light flashed against her closed eyelids and then died. She heard fading footsteps. Two days in the cave had destroyed her sense of night and day. She had no real understanding of how long she'd been sleeping, only that it felt like a long, dreamless time. It was so warm and cozy inside the bag, she started to drift off. Then whispers began somewhere behind her.

"Once we get the rock we don't need Puff Daddy, hear?" Kelly whispered. "We won't need any of 'em."

"Who says I even need you?" Gregor replied.

"You need someone," Kelly insisted. "Last time you ran it alone, you ended up in The Castle. Besides, you're sick. I know more about medicine than Lyons."

"I won't be sick much longer," Gregor said.

Cricket came wide awake, eyes open. She strained to see her father beside her. She could hear his rhythmic breathing, but didn't dare move to wake him. There was a long silence and then Gregor murmured, "Lyons and the two of them?"

"After we get to the rock what do you need any of 'em for?" Kelly said.

Light flared out of the darkness and the two men fell quiet. Cricket saw Lyons approach, carrying his shotgun. She closed her eyes. The guard kicked at her sleeping bag and then at her dad's. "Get up," he said, then called out, "Gregor. Kelly. It's time."

Cricket made a show of waking, then looked around. Gregor and Kelly were only yards away, climbing from their bags. Her father sat up, his eyes filmy with sleep. She wanted to tell him what she'd heard, but didn't dare. Not with Lyons standing right there, watching them. She'd have to wait until they got a chance to be alone.

Minutes later, she crept out of the side passage into the grand hallway. The inmates were on alert, pistols drawn, looking for the source of the noise they had heard back in Munk's Ridge and fled from all the way through Smith's and Bailey's, until Lyons had thought it safe to stop and sleep. Gregor led, keeping his back to one wall of the cave, shielding himself behind Tom from what might be hiding in the shadows. Kelly moved the same way behind Cricket. Lyons brought up the rear, toting his shotgun.

After a half hour of walking with no encounters, Cricket noticed that Gregor, Kelly, and Lyons gradually dropped their guard and the way they moved ahead through the caverns became less restricted. They reached the end of the series of grand hallways, proceeded under a low vault and through a stooped passage, and found themselves overlooking a canyon about twenty feet across. Some sixty feet deep, the bottom of the canyon looked like a western creek bed with eroded brownish walls and water sluicing over a narrow track of smooth cobbled stones. The gorge curved away from them to the north. The bank that formed the east side of the chasm was level and wide, almost a road. Forty yards out that byway was a stout arched bridge of stone that spanned the canyon. Beyond the arch, on the western wall, loomed a gaping wound of passageway. Her dad halted at the foot of the bridge. He pointed across and then again up the road.

"Both routes lead to the same spot west of here inside Parker's Ridge," he said. The way right takes a solid six hours. You go across the bridge, it's tougher going, but you save two hours. I don't care one way or the other. Your call."

"We cross," Gregor said. "Every step closer to the stone, I feel better."

Cricket did her best not to smile. She had heard about this place, about the two routes. The way across the bridge might save two hours, but it was supposedly beyond tough; it led through the sort of cave that could crush a man's spirit.

"You up for it?" her dad asked.

Cricket nodded and her dad turned away.

"You're first, Gregor," he said.

"I'll go after him," Lyons announced.

The sickly physicist took two uncertain steps out onto the narrow arch of rock that spanned the gorge, then got down on his knees and crawled. When he was halfway across the span a harsh, concussive sound coughed from the stone beneath him.

Gregor's face contorted. "W-what the hell's that?"

"Don't know," Tom said, confused as well. "Never heard that kind of noise in a cave before."

"The quake weaken that span?" Lyons demanded, rushing to the edge.

"I don't know," Tom said again. "It looks okay from here."

Gregor said, "G-go back or—?"

"Keep going, you're almost there."

Gregor put his head down and scrambled to the other side. Lyons followed.

"Kelly now," Tom said.

The swarthy inmate looked across the bridge, then shook his head. "I'm not letting you stay with the kid on this side," he said. "You first."

Her father shrugged, then got down on his knees and began to crawl across the arch. Cricket watched her dad glance over the side at the long fall into the chasm and shudder. He slowed as he crossed the middle of the span, leaning his head closer to the rock, trying she supposed, to understand the source of the sound Gregor had triggered.

He crawled several more steps and his face blanched.

"What's the matter, Dad?" she called.

"The limestone out here—it looks like cracked porcelain," he said. "Oh, shit."

Even from fifteen feet away, Cricket could see more fine cracks appearing on the side of the arch, like dominoes racing through the rock.

"Go, Daddy!" Cricket shrieked. He scrambled forward. But the cracks became too complex. The stone ruptured, fragmented, and crumbled. Just as the center of the bridge disintegrated behind him, he threw himself forward, his arms and fingers outstretched. He caught the rim of the cliff and dangled there while an eleven-foot section of the arch crashed into the canyon below with an ear-hammering roar.

The whole thing happened so quickly that no one moved at first. Then Cricket threw herself onto her belly at the edge of what had become an outcropping on the near cliff face. "Hold on!" she screamed.

She could see her dad's fingers slipping over the fine granular pebbles along the ledge above him. He grunted and kicked at the wall of rock, trying to find any toehold. Then Lyons and Gregor grabbed each wrist and dragged him up over the ledge to safety.

"Thanks," he gasped, looking from Lyons to Gregor.

"No problem," Lyons said.

"We need you," Gregor said, shrugging. Then he looked back across the canyon at Cricket and Kelly. "So three of us now."

Cricket saw her father jerk his head to look across the chasm at her and their eyes locked in horrible understanding. Their worst fears had come true. They were separated. Fourteen, maybe fifteen feet at most. But it might as well have been an ocean; there was no way anyone could jump it and they had no ropes.

"Say your good-byes, Burke," Gregor said.

"No, Daddy," Cricket said, feeling the panic well inside her. "Don't go."

"Hey!" Kelly yelled from behind Cricket "You can't leave me. We had a deal."

"Deals change," Gregor said.

"Burke!" Kelly cried. "You said this way ends up in the same place."

Through the tears welling in her eyes, Cricket saw her father nod. "Eventually it does."

"Tell us how to do it then," Kelly yelled. "It's the only chance you got of getting your daughter back, hear?"

For the first time in her life, Cricket saw her dad exhibit true, gut-twisting fear. He had broken out in a drenching sweat and the muscles in his neck quivered. "You can do this, Cricket," he said.

"No," she whined. "I want to be with you."

"I want you to be with me, too, but you can't," Tom said.

Lyons said, "You listen to your father now, Cricket. Your life depends on it."

She ignored him, never taking her attention off her father. "Please, Dad. There's got to be another way. I'll get lost."

He shook his head and pointed a finger at her. "You're not getting lost and I'm not losing you now. We're getting out of here and we're gonna see Mom. And we're going to all be together again, you and me and Mom. This is just a little detour. You hear me?"

Cricket nodded through a wash of tears. "Yes."

"Okay, now listen close," he said, the waver in his voice echoing all around her. "The entire route is mostly big booming cave with one tight spot in the connection into Parker's Ridge. At every major junction for the next two hours, you're going to use your compass and you're going to trend north-northwest. After two hours, you should find yourself in a crawlway that will slope west and down in elevation. When you feel the crawlway rise again, you'll be in Parker's. You'll climb up into a big cave, almost below the caprock of the ridge. The passage there is dry, good walking, and you'll head due south for almost a mile and a half. I'll meet you somewhere along there. I promise."

"How long should it take?" Kelly demanded.

"Five and a half, maybe six hours," Tom said. "Give me the directions back"

Cricket recited them until she had them down pat.

"Good," Tom said.

"Let's go," Gregor said, tugging on Tom's pack.

He got to his feet, still looking at Cricket. She could see that the words he was about to utter were going to be the toughest of his entire life. "Go on now, Crick."

Cricket got up off her belly robotically She was barely aware of Kelly beside her when she reached the level bank above the gorge. She turned and stood there for a long moment, letting her light dwell on her father's face.

"You keep whistling, you hear?" she said.

"I will," he said. " 'Bye, sweetheart."

Cricket stood there thinking that her dad had always had such a sure sense of direction that he hardly needed a compass underground. But right then he looked completely lost. Seeing him like that almost crushed her, but she told herself that her mom had been in a worse predicament than this one and had survived. Damaged, but had survived. " 'Bye, Daddy."

8:15 A.M.
FURNACE RIVER

"C'mon, kid! Take the goddamned reading!" Boulter roared at Chester, still frozen in the passenger seat of the whaler, insensible with fear.

Swain let go of the windshield struts to reach for the sensor himself, when his pudgy nephew suddenly spun out of the seat, and crawled along the deck beneath the low gunwale.

"I've got you," Swain said, grabbing the teen by the webbing of the life preserver. "We're in this together."

Chester looked over his shoulder at his uncle. "Okay," he said, then tossed the sensor over the side, letting fifteen feet of a nylon tether slide through his hands. He waited ten seconds, then retrieved the device and threw himself back away from the gunwale, peering at the screen. "Nothing stronger than what we got at the Orpheus Entrance!"

"Give me the second series of coordinates, Doc," Boulter ordered.

It took them nearly an hour fighting the raging current to check the outflows at the next three ridges—Hawkins, Munk's, and Smith's. At each of these locations, the sensors revealed no discernible difference in the electromagnetic readings they'd been getting at the dry ingresses to the cave.

"We're no closer to that stone than we were before," Chester grumbled. "The three-dimensional map didn't help us one bit."

"Nonsense," Swain insisted. "We've still got five outflows to measure, Chester."

They were almost nine miles above the ferry crossing now, approaching the most remote section of the river, in the deepest part of the Labyrinth wilderness. The storm was still intensifying. The Furnace was like a wild foaming sea before them. The whaler pitched and rolled. And then a huge wave blasted over the hull, soaking all of them and forcing Boulter to initiate the automatic bailing device.

"Maybe we should turn back and wait for the storm to subside before checking the rest of the outflows," Chester moaned.

"No," Swain retorted. "We're finishing this. Now."

"You're sure?" Boulter demanded.

Swain looked at his nephew, so wan and shaking. "Yes," he said. "We can do it."

The outflow of Bailey's Ridge occurred at the tightest point of the great bend in the river. The underwater cave exit lay at the bottom of a sheer cliff that rose nearly ninety feet. The river beat at the cliff as Boulter tried to tease the boat close enough for Chester to get a reading. Again, while Swain held him about the waist, the teenager leaned over the side and dropped the sensor into the chill water of the cave outflow. When he drew it up, the golden infinity symbol pulsed larger than it had at any of the other cave exits. "We're getting closer!"

"You sure it's not in there?" Boulter demanded.

"Could be," Chester admitted. "But if it is, it's in there awful deep. We need to keep going, take readings at the next four ridges to give us a comparison."

The outflow at Parker's Ridge, the sixth of the Labyrinth's nine, issued an even higher reading than the one at Bailey's. The pulse at the outflow at Nyren's Ridge was stronger still. With a sense of heightened anticipation, they pushed on toward Tower Ridge, the second-to-last mountain that contained the great cave system.

The river conditions below the soaring semicircular rock outcropping that gave Tower Ridge its name were the worst encountered so far. The current and the wind battered the whaler so hard that its momentum ground to a creep. The outboard screeched and squalled trying to make headway. Finally, Boulter aimed the boat toward the river's flooded north shore, where he found a back channel that allowed them to forge upstream parallel to where they believed the outlet lay.

But between them and the submerged cave exit stood a series of what whitewater guides call haystacks, semi-static arches of seething water that form when flooding rivers pass over gigantic glacial-cast boulders. The biggest haystack before them was some fifteen feet at the base and more than twelve feet high. Three others below that one were almost as large. Between them twisted whirlpools.

"Take the reading here," Boulter yelled. "I don't think we can make it across."

"No good," Chester cried. "We need to drop the sensor right into the outlet"

"Take the wheel," Boulter barked at Swain. The physicist reluctantly grabbed the steering wheel, which wrenched and hauled against his grip. Boulter got out a pair of binoculars from inside his rain slicker. He cupped the objective lens with his right hand to ward off the rain and studied the pattern of the river between the four haystacks and beyond. After several tense moments, he turned and said, "This is gonna be tight."

Boulter took the wheel again, then mashed the throttle. The boat sprang forward and now they were battling their way upriver roughly parallel to the haystacks.

They passed the first standing wave and the second. Boulter drove the whaler at an oblique angle past the third coming wave. White foam showed at the crest of the wave's swirling brass flanks. Boulter cut hard toward the passage between the third and fourth waves and laid the throttle down. There must have been placid water in the current there because they surged forward so fast it caught them all off guard.

The bow of the whaler bounced off an eddy, rose, and slammed down, throwing Chester from his seat. Swain reached for his nephew but missed as he tumbled toward the stern. Boulter tried to compensate at the wheel and throttle back, but it was too late; the powerful outboard had already thrust them straight up the steep face of the fourth standing wave. The boat climbed and almost made the crest before the prop lost purchase. The vessel hesitated, then slid back down into the trough at the base. The whaler jackpoled, standing nearly straight up on its stern, threatening to flip.

Chester was ejected from the boat. He screamed as he flew through the air and into the churning river. Boulter wrenched the steering wheel hard to port. The boat crashed sideways into the gap, nearly capsizing, but then, incredibly, righting itself.

Swain caught a glimpse of his nephew's terrified expression as the river swept him away. Without thinking, the physicist dived into the raging water.

8:22 A.M.
BAILEY'S RIDGE
LABYRINTH CAVE

"Slow and quiet now," Finnerty whispered. "We don't want to bump them, let them know they're being stalked."

Whitney winced at his choice of words. Stalking implied that, for the time being anyway, the marshal had put aside the idea of trying to rescue her family by ambush. She knew very little about Finnerty's background, but there was no mistaking what was going on now: The marshal was acting as if he were still-hunting in a forest; he was getting whispered navigational instructions from Whitney, using Two-Elk to read the footprints left in the dust, and then moving all of them as a single, elastic unit through the cave.

The marshal eased forward into the stooped passage off the last of the grand-opera hallways. Whitney slipped after him, followed by Two-Elk. They'd been moving in this caterpillar way for a little more than an hour. It took a maddening amount of concentration, and despite the fact that she'd slept a fitful seven hours, Whitney was already feeling the strain.

"Feel totally exposed with these headlamps," Finnerty whispered. "Let's turn them down as low as we can."

They all adjusted their lamps until they could barely see one another.

"Up ahead here," Whitney murmured, "the way forks and doesn't come back together again for nearly six hours. I'm betting Tom took them across the bridge into Endless Crawl. Terrible place. Could drive you crazy."

The marshal looked at her. "But everyone's holding together just fine here though, right?"

"Right," Whitney said, feeling angry at the comment and surprised by that anger.

"Just want to be sure," Finnerty said. He took a deep breath, squatted, then scuttled out onto the rim above the narrow gorge. Whitney waited ten seconds, then followed to where he crouched behind a boulder. Their lamps barely lit the room.

Whitney could feel the emptiness break away to the north, cast in deep charcoal shadows. As Two-Elk slipped in beside her, she strained her eyes, peering out there into the curtains of darkness, catching sight of something that shocked her to her core. She jumped up and ran forward, cranking her headlamp beam to high power.

"Mrs. Burke!" Finnerty hissed.

But Whitney ignored him and sprinted toward the abutment of the fallen bridge. She threw herself onto her stomach and slid out toward the edge. She whipped her head from side to side, looking for a body in the debris at the bottom of the canyon.

Finnerty was right behind her now, very pissed off. "You're going to get yourself killed, or worse, you're going to get me killed."

Whitney spun and glared at him. "The bridge fell. This is my husband and daughter we're talking about. What would you have me do, suck my thumb?"

"I'd have you stay alive long enough to get your husband and daughter back," he retorted.

"Only two tracks going out of here on this side, boss," Two-Elk called out. She was working her way up the flat rim of the canyon with the alacrity of a bird dog on a hot scent. "One of the inmates. And the girl."

"Cricket?" Whitney sprang to her feet, adrenaline coursing through her blood. "You're sure it's not Tom with her?"

"He's wearing those air-bob soles like she is, right?" Two-Elk asked.

Whitney nodded.

"The ones with her are lug sole, Vibram, size eleven. I saw their shoe sizes in the reports. It's Kelly."

Whitney flashed on the brief profiles of the inmates Finnerty had shown her before they entered the cave. "The strangler?" she cried. Her hand traveled to cover her open mouth. She looked down over the edge of the canyon and almost tottered. Everything that mattered was disintegrating. She looked across the canyon to the gaping wound in the wall where Tom must have gone. She thought about the cave ahead on this side of the gorge, did a quick computation in her head, then bolted off, running north along the rim of the narrow canyon.

"Son of a bitch!" she heard Finnerty growl behind her. A hundred yards later, she felt the marshal's hand catch her beneath the elbow and spin her around. "Stop! We can't go after them like this, half-cocked."

Whitney ripped away from his grasp and snarled, "My daughter's out there forty minutes ahead of me with some sick fucking bastard who likes to kill people with his bare hands. So, no more creeping, Marshal. No more stalking. We're gonna run and we're gonna close the gap and we're gonna rescue my daughter. Okay?"

The skin on Finnerty's face tightened toward fury, then he got a puzzled expression that broke over into a smile. "You remind me of my wife," he said, shaking his head and scratching his temple, "always telling me what to do and most of the time right. Okay, Mrs. Burke, you lead. But when you think you're getting close, you slow us down and we take over. Whatever we do, we don't want an uncontrolled firefight in here. You could get killed. Your daughter could get killed."

Whitney's jaw set. She broke into a hard jog out along the rim of the canyon, knowing that somewhere on the other side, Tom would be driving himself unmercifully to get to Cricket. She would, too.

9:27 A.M.
TOWER RIDGE OUTFLOW
FURNACE RIVER

Swain was pummeled, punched, and flipped end over end. The current tore into his rain jacket, sucked him under, spun him around and around; and for one heart-stopping moment he thought he might not reach the surface again. Then the flow arched around some invisible object deep in the river's bed, and the physicist felt himself thrust up and out into the air and the pouring rain just in time to see the wall of the next haystack rushing at him. Chester was already flailing up and over its crest.

Rather than fight the river, Swain opted to go with it. He rolled over into the classic bodysurfing position—feet together, back arched, arms extended perpendicular to the body, hands cupped like a rudder. He coursed up the back of the wave, crested it, and saw that he had gained on his nephew, who was sputtering and thrashing his way down the wave's face.

"Hold on, Chester!" Swain cried. "I'm coming!"

The river drowned the boy's scream of reply. He went flying through the trough and up the side of the next haystack with his uncle twenty yards behind him. By the time the physicist reached the crest of that standing wave, he and his nephew were ten yards apart. Chester went down the front of the wave backward, his face a study in hysteria. He spun as he hit the trough at the bottom of the wave and was sucked under.

Swain knew that river kayakers called these sluicing pits "washing machines" because they could trap a man in an endless spin cycle and drown him.

"God, no!" he bellowed, throwing both arms straight out in front of him and ducking his head so he might accelerate down the wave's face. Then he porpoise-kicked and dived.

The river whirled him around and around and around, forcing brackish water up his nose. Branches and other debris lashed his torso. Still tumbling he collided with a solid, padded object. Instinctively his fingers reached, found the nylon straps of Chester's flotation vest, and held tight. Their combined mass was enough to counter the spinning action. In the next instant they were thrown to the surface far to the right of the fourth haystack. Chester had lost his glasses and his eyes were rolled back in his head. His skin was deathly gray and water drained from his nostrils.

"No," Swain sobbed. "You're not dying on me. Not now. Not now."

He laced his fingers deeper into the webbing of his nephew's vest and swam with all his might. The river grabbed at them and threatened to drag them under once more, but Swain kicked and fought with his free arm. They bounced off submerged boulders and twice were almost flattened by floating logs.

At last Swain got them almost to the far side of the river, but the shore was eroded and impossible to climb. They swept farther downstream. Ahead, along the bank Swain noticed an uprooted oak tree lying half submerged in the river. He aimed toward it and they crashed into its branches and became entangled there. The physicist knew he had to get his nephew up onto the shore to get his lungs cleared. He tried to hoist Chester up into the branches, but couldn't. The tree began to shift as if it might break away under the flood's insistent force. Then, above the roar of the river, came the grind of an outboard engine.

"Here!" Swain screamed and waved. "Boulter, we're here!"

The state police captain brought the bow of the whaler in almost to the crown of the tree so that Swain could grab the rope hanging from the stern. Boulter revved the engine and dragged them toward shore. When the hull struck bottom, he jumped out and tied off the bow, then waded back to where Swain still foundered in the current.

"Help him," the physicist sobbed. "Help him before it's too late."

Boulter took one look, yanked the unconscious teenager up onto the shore below the base of the cliff on Tower Ridge, and began administering mouth-to-mouth resuscitation in the pouring rain. Swain stumbled to his knees next to the trooper and Chester, blubbering, "It was my idea to put him in college so young. He was always so goddamned brilliant It seemed the right thing to do. I never knew he couldn't swim. How could I have not known? How could I have not taught him? How could I have not—?"

Chester coughed and puked up river water. He struggled and puked up more, then took a deep breath, choked, and vomited a third time. For a second there was no movement on his part, then he began coughing violently, but taking deep, raspy breaths between each cough.

"Thank God," Swain sobbed. "Thank you, God, for saving my boy."

Ten minutes later, Chester was weak but sitting up, his back resting against his uncle's chest. "I'm sorry, Chester," Swain said.

"For what?" Chester managed to say.

"For everything," Swain replied, his voice choked with emotion. "For pushing you so hard when you were a kid. For never taking the time to be there for you other than academically. For thinking that immortality is something that is achieved, rather than given. You were my immortality, Chester, and I just couldn't see it. I couldn't and I'm sorry. I feel like I stole your childhood from you."

His nephew was silent for a long time, then he said, "No, Uncle Jeff, you didn't steal it. Mom's death was the real thief. You just tried to make me better in the only way you could. Yeah, I may have lost a childhood, but I'd have to say my late adolescence has been pretty exciting so far."

Swain looked down at his nephew and almost chuckled.

"Think you can move now, kid?" Boulter asked.

Chester nodded. The trooper reached down and lifted him to his feet like a wet rag doll. Swain got up and together he and Boulter helped Chester toward the whaler. As they approached the riverbank, Boulter asked, "Where's the sensor? We've still got to take those readings."

Chester reached inside the neck of his now-tattered rain jacket, but his hand did not emerge with the device. "Must have torn free in the river," he moaned. "I failed you guys."

Swain was reaching out to pat his nephew on the back when out of his peripheral vision he caught sight of a bright yellow nylon cord tangled in the limbs of the half-submerged oak tree. He let go of Chester, waded out unsteadily into the water, and, at last, grabbed the cord and pulled up the sensor. The golden infinity symbol was swelling to ten times its normal size. The multicolored bar graph showed a huge data response. Swain stared at both of them as if he could not believe what he was seeing.

"We've got 7.5 megavolts with low photon surge, and incredible neutron exchange and quark decay," the physicist screamed with joy, pointing up the face of the fog-obscured cliff. "You found it, Chester! Gregor's stone's right here! Right inside this god-damned beautiful hollow mountain!"

9:45 A.M.
SPAGHETTI WORKS
BAILEY'S-PARKER'S CONNECTION ROUTE
LABYRINTH CAVE

"Which way now?" Kelly growled. "And don't you fuck with me, little girl."

Cricket shrank from the swarthy inmate. For the past hour they'd been moving fast through flat, monotonous passages. Every moment since leaving her dad had seemed distorted by the harsh pyramidal glare of her headlamp beam. Now she looked at the fork in the passage, then down at her compass, which trembled in her right hand, trying to remember exactly what her father had said. "We go down this left passage," she said.

"Better be right," Kelly snarled. "I ain't there to get my share, I'm gonna be a right angry man. You don't want to see me when I get pissed, now, do you?"

"No." Cricket turned away before he could see her chin quiver and set off to the north down a long oval tube floored with loose gravel. She squinted and stared about, trying to take it all in, trying to imagine what her dad would do in her place. But this was the first time that Cricket had ever tried to navigate alone in a cave she'd never been led through before. I'm only fourteen! Then, to her chagrin, she remembered herself saying, I'm not a child anymore, Dad. I'm a young woman.

She wished suddenly that her mother were there, to seek her advice, to tell her that she understood about the way life can change in a brutal instant. Then, for a long panic-stricken moment, all she could think of was that she going to die. She had seen Kelly's temper and she was going to die. She found herself wishing she could somehow whistle Kelly to death, then go rescue her dad from Gregor and Lyons.

They passed a slit in the cave wall where crystal-clear water bubbled and seeped into a basin before spilling out in a gossamer cascade that drained into cracks in the rock. Cricket caught sight of her reflection in the basin water and barely recognized herself. It was the same face. But older. For the past two years that's all she'd wanted to be—a person everyone realized was old enough to take care of herself. Now she suddenly did not want to be older. She wanted to be a child snuggled tightly between her parents in the soft glow of fireflies.

Cricket wondered whether she knew who she was anymore. She'd never in her life thought about hurting someone and here she was wanting to kill the man behind her, the second man she'd wanted to kill in the span of less than two days. She swallowed hard at what felt like a smooth stone lodged in her throat

Then she heard that strange voice in her head again, that voice that she recognized as her own, but more mature, tougher, certain. The voice was telling her that sometimes, to survive, humans had to act in ways that weren't human. She had a right to live—a right that trumped all others. In the end, what mattered was that she and her dad emerge from the cave and find her mom. Kelly did not matter. Neither did Gregor or Lyons. She told herself she had to accept the strangeness of her reflection in the basin water; like it or not, she was no longer little Cricket Burke, gifted athlete, struggling student, still aching to be taken seriously. Orphaned from one parent and then the other, these past few days had somehow christened her into a different person, someone acutely aware of love and evil and loss. For a second, she almost broke under the weight of it all.

She flashed hard on images of her parents, then shrugged under the load and found she could bear it. Play to your strengths, she thought. The cave was hers, not Kelly's. She moved better than he did. He was strong no doubt, but she was faster; she could see that just from the way he was built—no real top-end speed.

A moment passed and then an idea blazed through her mind. Her breath caught at the brazenness of it. She looked down her legs to her boots, then glanced back at Kelly. He was rolling along behind her. His pistol was shoved in the band of his pack. The belly belt transmitter dangled at the end of his simian right arm.

"I need some privacy," she said.

"You peed back there half an hour ago," Kelly retorted.

"I'm getting my period," Cricket replied, shoving her jaw out at him.

Kelly's eyes narrowed and his lip curled. "You're shitting me."

"No," she said, pulling out a tampon from the top flap of her pack. "I have to put this in or I'm going to be bleeding everywhere."

"Ah, Jesus Christ, spare me the details," Kelly groaned, then his face hardened and he gestured ahead. "Go. Do it then. Up around the bend there."

"You'll need to unlock the belt," she said.

Kelly studied her. "You better not be messing with me, kid."

She remembered something a friend of hers had said when she got her period for the first time. "I'm soaking through my panties," Cricket said.

"Oh, what the fuck!" Kelly groused. He brought out a key and unlocked the belt. "You keep your headlamp pointed back in this direction and you talk to me, hear?"

Cricket nodded, then slowly, her heart beating in her throat, she turned and walked away from Kelly. The belly belt was still buckled but hung loose on her hips. She rounded the curve in the passage.

"Keep talking!" Kelly yelled. "Point your headlamp back this way."

Cricket thought quickly. She reached deep into her pack and tugged out her spare flashlight. She dimmed her headlamp and shone the flashlight's beam back toward the curve in the tunnel.

"I'm stopping," Cricket said, easing back another twenty yards. Trying hard not to tremble, she put the flashlight on top of a two-inch outcropping of the cave wall and aimed it back toward Kelly. "I'm taking off the belt. I'm unzipping my jumpsuit."

She kept walking backward, unloosening the straps of the belt as she went. It fell to her ankles and dragged in the sand. She stepped out of the electronic constraint. She could breathe fully now without the belt digging at her waist. She took a second to look around for somewhere to throw the device, somewhere Kelly wouldn't find it. But the passage was smooth and void of broken rock; there wasn't anyplace Kelly wouldn't see it. She would have to take it with her. She picked it up by one of the fabric loops that hung off the back near the energy supply.

"One more minute," she called.

For a second, Cricket hesitated. She remembered how she'd felt going to the starting line at the Kentucky State 400 finals. All the older girls had tried to intimidate her with their looks. She'd ignored them, done what her father had said—focused on the moment and believed in herself—and darn near won the race. That's what she had to do now—focus on the moment and believe in herself. She looked down at her compass. Trend north-northwest. That's what her father said. North-northwest.

"Zipping up my suit," she yelled. She eased off a few more gentle steps, turned, and took one last look back in Kelly's direction.

The flashlight rolled off the ledge and clattered across the cave floor.

Cricket made a break for it, still holding the belly belt. Her legs drove up and forward. The treads of her boots dug into the hard, dry sediment. In seconds, she was a hundred yards down the tunnel and opening her stride, reaching for her helmet and the light. She snapped it on highest power and chased the beam up a slight rise, accelerating the whole time.

Behind her, Kelly roared with fury.

10:02 A.M.
ENDLESS CRAWL
BAILEY'S-PARKER'S CONNECTION ROUTE
LABYRINTH CAVE

Tom came down a slope crowded with boulders like a skier bouncing in moguls, launching himself from one to the next, a dancer on the edge of ruin. He was using every athletic instinct, every last bit of cave skill, and every ounce of energy to one end: to get to the dry passages high in Parker's Ridge as fast as possible so he could begin backtracking toward Cricket.

He jumped off one last boulder into a bowl of moist black sand, then went to his knees before a horizontal gash in the stone wall. His headlamp shone into a crack about twelve inches high and so long and wide that he could not grasp its dimensions. The ceiling was blackish. The floor as far as he could see was that same black sand. It was like looking out into a vast desert landscape where the night sky was clouded.

He steeled himself for the grueling nature of what lay ahead, then immediately splayed his legs and stretched out on his belly and elbows. He stuck his head in the crack and began to wriggle his way in. Lyons grabbed Tom by the ankles and yanked him back.

"Slow the fuck down, you're gonna kill him," he snarled, gesturing at Gregor, who was bent over and gasping with exertion.

"He said he wanted to get to his stone fast," Tom said. "I'm taking him there, fast enough for me to get my daughter back."

Lyons grabbed Tom by the collar. "You don't get it, do you, man? Without him there is no stone."

"I don't care," Tom said struggling.

Lyons cuffed him across the side of his helmet, shook him, and hissed into his face, "There's a lot of people a lot more important than you who do care about that stone. So you understand this: You keep pulling this shit, you're never gonna see your daughter again."

"You need me a lot more than I need you," Tom roared back. "Without me, you and Gregor are lost. That's my only child up there. My only link with a life I once had, and I'm not losing her, for you, for him, or for that fucking stone."

At that, Gregor and the pall he cast grew larger, as if his anger were a shadow that enveloped him like a cowl. "Go as fast as you want, Burke. I'll stay right behind you."

Tom shook himself free of Lyons, then ducked down, splayed his arms and knees, cocked back his head, and drove forward into the crawlway, scrambling, pulling, kicking, and spitting his way through that gritty place. He told himself that now was the moment he'd been waiting for. A chance to exhaust Lyons and Gregor, to destroy them physically and mentally.

The crawlway went on for nearly six hundred yards, dark, oppressive, a vast wafer of an opening in the rock with very little peripheral information. Negotiating these kinds of passages seemingly without horizon struck Tom as similar to what ancient sailors must have done on cloudy nights in a stormy sea; they navigated by dead reckoning.

The enormity of his situation fell in around him then. What if he never saw Cricket or Whitney again? He felt for a moment as if the interior of his rib cage no longer contained lungs or heart, and his thoughts sprayed at him like the wake of a power boat, so fast, so final, and tinged with so many regrets, so many things left unsaid and undone. He was stunned at just how much his family—not science, not the cave, not NASA, not the whole scope of his career—meant to him. Everyone thought Whitney and Cricket relied on him. The truth was they were his supports, the arches of stone on which he leaned. He realized how abandoned he would be without them. Part of him wanted to lie down and cry, but he would not let himself. He looked back. Lyons and Gregor were gasping and fighting their way along behind him. Gregor gripped the belly belt transmitter in one hand. Lyons pushed along his shotgun.

Tom kept thinking about the belt. It dawned on him that he knew more than they did about the way radio waves traveled in caves. Without a repeater, the belly belt would be rendered useless if it was separated from the transmitter by more than a quarter mile. That's all he needed—to somehow put a quarter mile between himself and his captors. If he could do it, he'd be free to find and rescue Cricket. Together they could reach the surface.

A quarter mile. Four hundred forty yards.

10:14 A.M.
SPAGHETTI WORKS
BAILEY'S-PARKER'S CONNECTION ROUTE
LABYRINTH CAVE

"Bitch!" Kelly bellowed.

Cricket sprinted the rise in short, choppy, wide-stanced strides. She crested, found level ground, opened her gait, and poured it on.

She heard a strange crackling noise and glanced to the belly belt bobbing off the cloth loop around her wrist. Inside the girdle, from the metal nubs that faced both hips, the belly, and the base of the spine, corkscrews of blue-white electricity unwound and sparked. Kelly was jamming his thumb on the transmitter trigger over and over again.

But he was falling behind. Cricket could hear the off-kilter pounding of his footsteps fading. The ground dropped away again. She sensed that the cave was getting damper, and the slope a steeper grade than she'd first anticipated, but the slickness did not register until it was too late. The entire floor of the descending passage was coated with a whipped chocolate of mud mixed with sharp gravel. In midstride, Cricket's right foot kicked out from behind her and she was cast forward in a long spinning fall down the slope toward a puddle that filled the passage side to side.

Her cheek glanced off something hard and sharp. The belly belt tore from her wrist. She cartwheeled. Her left leg whipped down and struck the slope flush. She heard something in her knee go *pop*, then she cartwheeled again and splashed into the puddle.

For a second she lay there stunned, her knee a searing rush of pain. "No," she moaned. "Not now."

Then she heard the huff and slap of Kelly running. The first flickers of his headlamp showed on the ceiling of the cave upslope. She scrambled out of the puddle, trying to get to her feet, aware of a bitter salty liquid seeping into her mouth. She spat it out. Blood. She put her hand to her cheek and felt the seams of a long gash. Cricket forced herself up, spitting out more blood, trying to see how her knee would do. It held weight but felt destabilized, as if she'd torn something in there.

Kelly crested the ridge in a low running crouch, holding the belly belt trigger in his left hand like a baton. He caught sight of her hobbling away from the puddle and howled with the confidence of a predator that has sensed wounded prey, "You in big trouble now, girl!"

But Kelly too misjudged the greasiness of the terrain, and both his feet flung out from under him parallel, like a gymnast working the horse in a pike position, and he went down hard on his right hip and shoulder with a cracking noise. His pistol yanked free of his pack belt and spun into the puddle. The belly belt transmitter went flying from his hand, across the puddle, and landed next to Cricket. She reached out and grabbed it as a weapon even as Kelly, bleeding from jagged bits of gravel that scored his chin, was rising to his feet, rubbing his shoulder.

Below his headlamp beam, his slate-colored eyes blazed. He looked at the belt trigger she held. "What do ya think you're gonna do with that?"

He tore off his gloves and cracked the knuckles on his great gnarled hands, then held them before him like a Greco-Roman wrestler. "Ever seen what a python does to pigs down there in the Amazon?" he said. "Way it wraps 'em all up and hugs 'em tight?"

"No!" Cricket sobbed.

She turned and made to run, but with her knee she was no match for him. Kelly splashed across the puddle in two leaps and grabbed her by the back of her neck, then reached around the front with the other and lifted her in a swinging, throttling arc. For a second, Cricket hung in his grasp, choking for air. Her eyes felt so much pressure she was sure they would pop. Her spine stretched toward snapping.

"Gonna have to teach you a lesson 'bout being an inmate," Kelly growled in her ear. "Rule number one—guard's always right."

Cricket saw spots before her eyes. She felt the weight of the belly belt trigger in her hand. She swung back and drove it butt first into the gap between the angle of Kelly's jaw and the muscles of his neck. The blow hit some kind of nerve gathering there and Kelly grunted, shifted his feet, and dropped her. His head swung low and dazed like that of a ram that has just butted horns. Cricket cocked back her good right knee and rammed it as hard as she could straight into his groin. Kelly buckled over. She kneed him in the face. He stumbled backward and sat down hard in the puddle, cupping his testicles with one hand, his bleeding nose with the other. He sat there stunned for a second, then his eyes focused. "Fucking bitch!"

Cricket turned to run again, but her feet got caught in the girdle of the belly belt lying there in the muck beside the puddle. She looked at it, then up at Kelly, who was still grimacing in pain, but getting to his feet, the dripping pistol somehow in his hand. His lips drew down tight against his teeth and he seethed. "You, my friend, are about to have a serious attitude adjustment."

Cricket kicked the belt into the puddle beside him. Kelly looked at it, puzzled, then his eyes got wide in understanding and he jerked his head back up.

"Attitude adjustment's all yours, asshole," she said. She punched the trigger.

Fifty thousand volts coursed out the belt's contact points and electrified the puddle at Kelly's ankles. The strangler convulsed, fired the pistol with a deafening roar, was thrown three feet through the air, and landed in a heap up the greasy slope.

A nauseating stench filled the air.

11:00 A.M.
SPAGHETTI WORKS
BAILEY'S-PARKER'S CONNECTION ROUTE
LABYRINTH CAVE

"We should have caught up to them by now," Whitney said, stopping and bending over to take deep gulps of air. She hadn't run like this since the accident.

Two-Elk and Finnerty were blowing hard as well. They'd been going at a strong jog for more than an hour and a half and still had not caught up with Cricket. The tracker went forward, sweeping her headlamp across the floor, coming to rest on Cricket's flashlight, then flicking ahead to reveal tracks and deep gouges in the sand.

"She's running!" Two-Elk cried. "Cricket's got the electrical belt off and she's running!"

They were all sprinting now, the marshals holding their machine pistols and Whitney's head blazing with fear and wonder at the gall of her daughter's escape. They came over the rise and Two-Elk saw the steep slope and the polished places where Cricket and Kelly had fallen. She skidded to a halt. Whitney tried to surge ahead, but Two-Elk caught her. "You hold up and let me do my job now, ma'am," she said. "Caves may be your world. But the tracks are mine."

Whitney wanted to argue, but nodded.

Two-Elk eased her way down to the puddle, swinging her head back and forth, reading the cuts, grooves, and wedges in the wet banks around the puddles, reading the smoky tendrils of silt in the water.

"What happened?" Whitney cried out in desperation.

"They fought here and from the looks of it your daughter won," Two-Elk replied, shaking her head in admiration. "She hit Kelly with something and he's bleeding. He went down hard. So hard he shit his pants. Literally. There's feces there."

"He's got to be in shock of some kind," Finnerty said, fingering the trigger guard on his gun. "Where'd he go?"

"That's what I'm trying to figure out," Two-Elk said. She crossed the puddle and went up the bank to where the passage began to rise again. "Dammit, she's hurt, too."

"What!" Whitney cried. She ran down the slick hill, feeling herself on the verge of tears, then forded the standing water to where the tracker crouched. "How hurt? Is she bleeding?"

Two-Elk did not reply for nearly a minute as she studied the evidence left in the sediment. "A little, but it's not gouts of it, probably a blow to her mouth," the tracker said. "But her knee's injured. She's limping badly and—"

Her face screwed up in concern.

"What?" Whitney demanded.

"Kelly's up again, slowed, but he's still after her, and from the looks of it, he's moving better than she is."

Finnerty raced by Two-Elk, his gun raised before him, then shouted at his deputy, "Permission granted to shoot to kill!"

11:45 A.M.
SPAGHETTI WORKS
BAILEY'S-PARKER'S CONNECTION ROUTE
LABYRINTH CAVE

Cricket gritted her teeth at the pain. In the bottom of her pack she found a rectangle of dense foam called a SAM splint, used to immobilize ankles and sprained wrists. She sliced the foam in two, then cut off strips of her undershirt and tied the foam pieces to the sides of her knee, making a simple brace to help stabilize it. The device worked after a fashion, but every once in a while as she forced herself along, step by painful step, she felt a sickening slip and the threat of buckling.

It was more than an hour since she had escaped from Kelly, and she was worn down by fatigue and pain and the stress of constantly being afraid. She knew she had to keep going north-northwest until the passage dropped, then she would change her course to west-southwest. She glanced behind her, knowing that Kelly might be back there. She had taken his pistol, but at the moment of truth had been unable to pull the trigger. She had left him there on the bank moaning, sick, the stench of shit all over him.

Now the passage ceiling lowered. Cricket winced in anticipation of the pain, but went to her knees. She told herself she had to be deep in the connection route now. Soon the way would begin to rise in elevation, and when it did she'd be within an hour of finding her father.

However, after fifty yards of knee walking, despite her every effort to keep going, her weariness and the throbbing in her joints became overwhelming and she had to lie down and close her eyes. Just for a minute, she told herself. Just for a minute. She shut off her headlamp and fell into an uneasy sleep.

She dreamed of home. She saw the door to her parents' bedroom open and her mother come out.

It was dark and Whitney had her hands raised out in front of her, feeling her way toward a door she recognized that led to her own bedroom. Her mother opened the door and looked inside. The bed was empty and the window was open and her mother began to cry, "Cricket! Cricket, where are you?"

"Here Mom," Cricket mumbled. "I'm here. Right here."

She startled awake in the darkness, aware of the echoes of rocks snapping against one another somewhere not far behind her.

Terror stricken, Cricket turned on her headlamp to a weak glow, then scrambled forward, feeling her knee pound horribly, finding herself at the top of a stone staircase that dropped two stories to a three-way intersection of passage. Time to go west-south-west. The left passage. Get to it.

She scrambled down, wincing in agony at every step. Her knee had stiffened while she slept. She couldn't run.

Behind her, toward the top of the staircase, she saw the beam of a headlamp coming. He'd be on her in seconds. She had the pistol, but she still didn't think she could use it. Think. Think.

Cricket looked again at the sandy floor. She hobbled forward as fast as she could for ten yards, then walked backward in her own prints and eased up onto the stone flange below the middle and right passages. She hesitated for an instant, then whimpered to herself, "Please, please let this work"

She limped into the far right gash in the rock, the passage leading northwest, away from her father, away into the complete unknown.

1:04 P.M.
SOUTHERN PARKER'S RIDGE
LABYRINTH CAVE

Tom arched his back and extended his boot, gripping the outcropping, nosing the steel toe up and over onto the parapet of stonework that led into Grand Boulevard, an awesome arched cavity that ran north-south the entire length of Parker's Ridge, high in the guts of the geological mass, just below the caprock.

He got over onto the rock and lay flat on his belly, his arms and legs racked with spasms. Gregor came over the top and lay beside him. He was worn down, but to Tom's dismay nowhere near beaten; indeed, his skin had a rosy, healthy patina to it now.

"Something kind of sh-shifted inside me back there," Gregor announced, rolling his head around with his eyes closed. "Haven't felt this strong in years."

Lyons boosted himself up beside them. His face was dusted salt white. His eyes were irritated and red. He'd rolled up the sleeves of his cave suit to expose his massive forearms.

Tom got to his feet and Gregor sat up. "Which way?"

"Cricket will be coming toward us from the north," Tom said. "So we go north to find her and Kelly."

Gregor appraised Tom. "Is that the direction we need to get to Tower Ridge?"

"No," Tom said.

"Why are we backtracking, then?" Gregor demanded, anger suddenly in his voice.

"Because that's my daughter back up that passage."

Gregor's face soured. "I don't give a shit about your daughter."

"I figured that out," Tom said, growing more furious by the moment, but forcing himself to contain it. "But here's the deal. We can either go look for her or we wait right here for her. Either way, I'm not taking you west until I find her."

Gregor leaned back as if to backhand Tom across the face, but Lyons caught the scientist's wrist. Gregor wriggled against the powerful grip but could not wrestle free. "Let me go, Lyons. Let me go or you'll get nothing. Nothing!"

"We're gonna help him find his kid," Lyons said. "Then we go get the stone."

"You're not in ch-charge here."

"The fuck I'm not, you little physics dick," Lyons said, shaking him. "We don't help him get his daughter, we don't get to the stone. You under stand, Mr. Ph.D.?"

Gregor hesitated, then turned sly, like a cornered rat fighting for escape. "Two hours. We give him two hours, then we turn around."

"Can live with that," Lyons said, lowering the scientist's wrist. He looked at Tom. "Two hours, my friend."

For the next hour and forty-five minutes, Tom led them north nearly three miles along the far reaches of Grand Boulevard, his headlamp scanning, his eyes straining for any sign of Cricket. She had to be there. She could not fail, could not be injured or lost or…

His mind almost seized up as these thoughts spun in on him from all sides. Was this what Whitney had felt seeing Jeannie Yung in those last moments before the flood took her? Like she was trapped in a whirlpool, spun in ever-accelerating ever-downward spirals? Regret seared through him, true regret for what his wife had had to endure the past thirteen months and what she must be enduring now, frantic on the surface, praying for their survival; but most of all regret for every moment he had worked on the Artemis Project when he should have been with her in the aftermath of the accident. He vowed that things would be different if he just got the chance.

"Fifteen minutes," Gregor said. "Then we turn around."

"The other passage out of Smith's is just ahead," Tom said, jogging forward. He emerged into a large domed cavern that put him in mind of the ruins of the Colosseum in Rome, with an abruptly rising grandstand of stone. Set in the grandstand were the mouths of nearly a dozen converging passages.

"Cricket!" Tom called into the vast reaches of the cavern.

No voice came in return, and Tom called again and heard nothing but the fading tremor of his own voice. He turned and looked blankly at Lyons. "She should have been here by now."

The guard's normally granite face softened by several degrees. "How long ago?" he asked.

"Hour, maybe more."

"I'm f-f-feeling sick," Gregor said, and indeed, the glow that had bussed his cheeks in the southern passages of Bailey's Ridge was gone. His skin had turned once again to that waxy pallor. "I want to turn back. I need to go back. Lyons, you agreed."

"We're waiting right here," Tom insisted.

"No, we're not," Gregor said, suddenly beside himself with agitation. He plucked the pistol out and aimed it directly at Tom.

Tom knelt and held his arms up, palms out in front of him. "Go ahead, you stupid fanatical bastard. Shoot. I just don't fucking care anymore."

1:45 P.M.
NORTHERN PARKER'S RIDGE
LABYRINTH CAVE

"That's the wrong way!" Whitney exclaimed, staring into the black hole that marked the cave passage heading northwest.

"Just telling you what she did," Two-Elk replied. "Real smart kid, real tough kid, walking backward like that in her own tracks. It threw Kelly, at least for a while."

"Where does it go?" Finnerty demanded.

"No one's ever explored that passage," Whitney replied. "I don't know."

"How far behind are we?" the marshal asked.

"Half hour behind the girl," the tracker replied. "Maybe twenty minutes behind Kelly."

"Which way's your husband?" Finnerty asked.

"Back there, to the south, I'd expect," Whitney said, gesturing toward the far left passage. She hesitated, looking from one black hole to the next, horrified at the choice she was having to make—go after her daughter or her husband. Then she made her decision and hardened herself to it. She turned toward the passage Cricket had taken.

"You're sure?" Two-Elk asked as she passed.

"I know Tom, he'll survive," Whitney said. "Cricket is just a little girl."

Two-Elk looked at Finnerty, whose attention lingered on the passage going southwest. "Let's go, boss."

Whitney's senses immediately heightened. Every nerve in her body felt ignited by the danger of not knowing the way. She groped into the earth, seeing Cricket's tracks in soft sand here, a smudge of a displaced rock there. She tingled, then broke out in a sweat, reading the direction of the scalloping in the walls, bringing all her skills into play to anticipate where the cave might lead them. She imagined the underground rivers, streams, and creeks that had once coursed through these passages.

She imagined Cricket passing these walls, which had never seen man, not thirty minutes ago and began to run again.

2:15 P.M.
PARKER'S RIDGE
LABYRINTH CAVE

Seven hundred yards to the west, Cricket navigated the cave, hearing echoes of her father's and mother's teachings, echoes that gradually faded to murmurs as she heard that new voice, her own voice, the one that seemed to be getting sturdier with every painful step. Still, it was creepy being there in the cave alone; the water scribing on the roof was so tight and undulating it looked like the surface of the brain of a fetal pig she'd had to dissect the month before in biology class.

She reached the bottom of a breakdown pile that stretched up nearly four stories. She craned her neck to shine her lamp up its face, seeing what appeared to be a gouge in the rock heading west-southwest. That was good, she thought. The passage was trending back roughly in the direction of her dad.

Cricket jammed her fingers into a tight crevice and hoisted herself up, kicking and wincing and doing everything she could to keep her left leg on stable ground. She'd gotten no more than twenty feet up the side of the rubble pile, however, when a cramp seized up both sides of her lower belly and down the insides of her thighs. She doubled over, gritting her teeth, then felt herself go faint and she had to fight off the urge to throw up. At last the cramp ebbed and she straightened at an insistent warm, sickening pressure building below her navel and then boring down between her hips.

She knew.

Here of all places. Now of all times. She flashed on her mother, wishing she were there to guide her. She wrestled out of the coverall and dug into the bottom of her pack for the tampon. She got it in, then struggled her way back into her coverall, still more than a bit uneasy at the feeling of it all, when she heard again the sound of rock against rock somewhere in the passages behind her.

Then Kelly's loathing, taunting voice burst from the darkness: "You're up this way somewhere, ain't you, you little bitch!"

Cricket twisted, saw his headlamp cut the gloom, and started clawing her way up the hill, her knee threatening to snap again with every jerked action. She got up over the top of the hill. Ahead twenty yards, there was an opening facing south.

A crash of rock froze her. Kelly was already on the breakdown pile, the belly belt itself hanging from his pack. He climbed like a gorilla, legs spread wide, shoulders bowed, arms swinging and grasping and tearing rock, all the while glaring up at her, his bruised face cavitating with wrath.

"My ankles are burned!" he roared. "My nose is broken. I shit my fucking pants! Now you're gonna pay!"

Cricket threw her good foot against a boulder poised at the top of the bank and kicked it free. The rock bounced and cracked toward Kelly, causing him to dodge and lose his pace and balance. But it did not strike him, and after a moment's pause he came on even faster.

She kicked free two more stones, then got up on her feet and faltered and straight-leg strode her way under the arched opening in the wall. The passage was shaped like a cane resting in a corner, handle down; she descended it into a tight swale and confronted a smooth, slanted wall about fifteen feet high that had the consistency of moist chalk. She got her fingers and boot tread into the surface and began to climb up it in a watch-gear, back-and-forth motion.

She was nine feet up the side of the chalk cliff when Kelly raced into the chamber beneath her, leaped, and swatted. She felt his fingers brush against the sole of her boot like a flame.

"No!" she screamed, throwing her arms up and over, wrenching and kicking herself one-legged up the side of the precipice. Showers of moist clay balls struck Kelly in the face and had him wiping at his eyes and nose. Six, maybe ten feet above Cricket, the ceiling opened up into another passage.

Kelly cleared his vision and with a grunt tried to plaster himself onto the wall. His stance was too narrow. He slid and crashed. Cricket gained another two feet on him. Then he figured out the strange motion needed to ascend the chalk cliff and he spidered his way up a quick eight feet. Cricket fought off the urge to give in. She reached and pulled and her head thrust up through the hole in the ceiling into a barrel of a head-high passage with a dry sandy bottom.

Kelly batted at her boot again. With one great effort she pulled herself up and over into the sand. She rolled twice to create distance, snuffed out her headlamp, then dug into her pack and came up with the pistol. She aimed it shakily at the hole. Just as the top of Kelly's helmet appeared twisting right and left, she yanked on the trigger. The explosion felt like nails being pounded through her eardrums. Kelly's headlamp disintegrated.

She lay there panting in the pitch darkness, listening, wanting so desperately to hear silence. Then she heard him curse. She'd shot the light off his headlamp and succeeded in sending him on a quick slide to the bottom of the moist clay incline. But he was not dead. A light quickly showed in the hole. He'd found his flashlight. He was coming again.

Cricket looked at the gun and spun the cylinder. Empty.

She struggled to her feet, snapped her headlamp beam on again, and threw the pistol down the hole. Kelly dodged it, then grinned and kept climbing. Cricket dragged herself down the tube, sensing that it would open into a vast space just ahead.

"Got you now," Kelly bellowed. He rolled over the lip of the hole in the floor of the barrel passage and sprang to his feet, brow hooded and shoulders sloped, insane with rage, coming right after her.

Cricket looked over her shoulder. Kelly sprinted behind her, driving his body low like a linebacker preparing for tackle. She reached the entry to an expansive cavern shaped like an arena. Her leg buckled and she stumbled forward and down, hysterical with fear. Kelly planted one foot solidly, preparing to dive and drop his shoulder and forearm squarely on her chest

Cricket caught a blur of motion in the shadows. Lyons lunged out from behind a boulder, his left arm extended straight out, catching Kelly square across the throat. The strangler's feet kicked straight out in front of him and he landed stunned on the dense sand floor.

Tom dived onto Cricket and gathered her in his arms. "Oh, oh my, thank you," he said. "Thank you for being safe."

Cricket blinked, unbelieving, then the smell of her father broke through to her and she collapsed in sobs.

"It's okay, we're gonna be okay," he said, tears seeping down his cheeks. Cricket let herself melt into her father's arms, thinking she could sleep there forever, heal and mend there forever. "We heard the shot and the sounds of running and Lyons ordered us to turn off our lights and wait. But we're together again, Cricket. Together."

"Enough of the family reunion," Gregor snarled. "We move."

"She's hurt." her dad said. "She needs rest."

"She can't be that hurt or that tired," Gregor said, playing his headlamp over Kelly, who was slowly coming back to consciousness. He looked thrashed, with a purple nose grossly distorted, burn marks circumscribing his shins, and a livid bruise at his Adam's apple. He stank of shit.

"I can get along on it, Dad," Cricket said. "I just have to be careful rolling to the outside of my foot. Running hurts. Down climbing, too."

At the sound of her voice, Kelly's eyes focused and he made to get up and attack her. Lyons put his boot in the middle of Kelly's chest holding him to the floor. "Where the hell do you think you're going?"

Kelly's rough paws closed round Lyons's ankles and he attempted to throw the guard. Lyons flipped the shotgun off his shoulder and held it an inch from Kelly's nose.

"She fucking escaped," Kelly seethed. "She shot at me. She used the belt on me. Burned me. Broke my nose. Made me shit my pants!"

"Yeah, we can tell," Lyons replied.

Kelly's oily face turned ruby. "You listen, Lyons, I'm gonna get my due with her."

"Not now you're not," Lyons growled.

"All things in good time, Kelly," Gregor said. "Let's push for the stone before it's too late."

Kelly hesitated, then the greed showed in his face again. He glanced from the scientist to Cricket huddled in Tom's arms. "How far?"

"This time tomorrow, it will be yours to hold," Gregor said.

Kelly pointed at Cricket. 'This time tomorrow, you and me got a date. Meantime, put her in the belt again. And I'm carrying the goddamned transmitter."

3:14 P.M.
PARKER'S RIDGE
LABYRINTH CAVE

Somewhere in the distant cave ahead, Whitney heard the whoosh and the thud of what sounded like a gate slamming. It echoed all around them, over and over and over.

"Gunshot," Finnerty murmured, then he looked at Whitney. "Be calm. I'm sure she's okay."

"Quiet!" Two-Elk demanded. "The echoes, boss. Listen for the last one. It will tell us the direction."

The echoes slowed and the last one sounded and died. All three of them pointed south. Two-Elk and Finnerty got out front, their guns poised before them, headlamps barely glowing. Whitney felt beside herself with frustration. She wanted to grab one of the guns and go after Kelly and the hell with the marshals and their slow, methodical approach. This cave was her ground, not Fmnerty's, not Two-Elk's. She should be leading.

Moving again in that caterpillar fashion, it took them nearly twenty minutes to reach the bottom of the breakdown pile and another twenty to climb it and reach the chalk cliff, where Kelly had tried to grab Cricket by the ankle. Two-Elk picked up the spent pistol lying in the sand on the floor of the cave and looked all around. "No blood. He could have just dropped it from his pack and it discharged."

"Or he missed," Finnerty said.

"Or Cricket did," Whitney said.

They ascended the wall and soon emerged into the cavern that resembled the Colosseum. There was no sight of Tom or Cricket, and Whitney felt despair begin to settle over her like a fog. Two-Elk passed down the slope, studying the cave floor. She looked up at Whitney and beamed. "One good thing: Your daughter's back with your husband!"

Whitney rushed to the tracker and stared down at the two pairs of air-bob-sole tracks side by side in the sand. She felt a flood of conflicting emotions. She was overjoyed that they were together again. But it was also so unfair, so cruel, so grueling to be going on and on like this, seeing the story of her lost family written in footprints and suggestion and supposition. She sank to her haunches and held her head in both hands.

"Whitney, I know this is tough for you," Finnerty began. "But..."

"You want to know where they're going," she replied wearily.

"That's right," he said softly. "I won't give up."

She looked up at him, saw sincerity and determination in his expression, and she thought that he was very much like Tom, an essentially good man who did not quit, no matter what the odds arrayed against him.

"They're heading south, Marshal, toward the connection into Nyrens Ridge and the second cache," she said. "It's an easy-walking cave for many miles. Depending on Cricket's condition, they could move quite rapidly through that part of the ridge. We could keep pushing the pace, trying to catch up, but it hasn't worked yet."

"What do you suggest then?"

"I suggest we creep along as best we can until we get to the confluence of those two rivers Tom described on that digital video back at cache one," Whitney replied. "If Two-Elk says they've gone through toward Tower Ridge, we keep following. If Tom's led them off course, we do what he wanted us to do in the first place—we wait in ambush."

Finnerty thought for a moment, then nodded. "How far to the two rivers?"

"Three, maybe four hours."

"I'll take point," Finnerty said to Two-Elk

"No," Whitney said. This is my cave. I will."

7:50 P.M.
HERMES RESERVOIR

Helen Greidel clutched the lapels of her bright red rain parka, which flapped and billowed in the howling wind and whipping rain. Behind her, in the glare of headlamps, men in slickers emblazoned with FEMA across their backs passed sandbags up the steep bank of a levee. Beyond the levee, a vast body of water churned with whitecaps.

"It has been a story of wild reversals of fortune here in day three of a subterranean drama that has gripped the world," Greidel shouted into the camera. "In the most remarkable of those turns of events, NASA has just announced that it has regained signal contact with two separate groups of people trapped deep inside Labyrinth Cave.

"Nearly two days ago, in the wake of a devastating earthquake that sealed the entrances to the largest cave in the world, NASA lost signal contact with fugitive inmates holding Tom Burke and his daughter Cricket hostage and with a rescue team composed of U.S. marshals led by Burke's wife, Whitney," Greidel went on. "No one on the surface knew whether they were dead or alive. Now NASA is telling us that they are receiving clear signals from Cricket and Tom Burke, who appear to be accompanied by only three of the four captors who took them hostage in a deadly attack involving an experiment designed to help man mine the moon. NASA says it is also receiving strong locator signals from Whitney Burke and two of the three marshals who entered the cave nearly three days ago as part of a daring rescue attempt."

Greidel paused, pressed her earpiece to her head, and nodded. "NASA officials are refusing to speculate on what has happened to the missing marshal or the missing escaped convict, but they are now saying that both groups trapped inside the cave appear to be moving westward toward Nyren's Ridge, about an hour apart.

"While all this is welcome news indeed, a new threat to those trapped underground appears to be building here some twenty miles to the northwest of the cave system." Greidel turned and gestured to the FEMA workers toiling behind her.

"That is the Furnace River, the river that drains Labyrinth Cave, and is also fed by this fourteen-hundred-acre reservoir. Federal disaster workers and a team from the Army Corps of Engineers have been mobilized out of fear that the reservoir's dam, damaged in the earthquake, might now breach, sending hundreds of millions of gallons of water downstream and thrusting floodwaters high into the interior of the hollow mountains where those trapped are already engaged in a life-and-death struggle."

The screen switched to a shot of a flatbed truck diving through the night. Squatting on the truck was a giant rock-drilling machine.

"NASA, meanwhile, has confirmed that it is building a road for a huge machine called a tunnel borer up the side of Tower Ridge, site of the collapsed entrance closest to those still alive underground. NASA says it hopes to begin an effort to reenter the cave in a second rescue attempt within hours."

Indeed, twelve miles to Greidel's southeast, high on the flank of Tower Ridge, Jeffrey Swain watched as skidders and bulldozers churned up mud and knocked down trees, trying to flatten a way for the hulking metal torso of the boring machine, which was being winched slowly up toward the rubble pile that was once the Virgil Entrance to Labyrinth Cave.

"The kid's got the sensor running," Boulter said, and the physicist turned to see Chester, who had refused to go to the hospital, now crouched in front of the thousands of tons of rock and dirt that blocked the way into the mountain. Swain's nephew was colorless and haggard, still showing the physical effects of his near drowning earlier in the day. But as the analog and digital readouts fountained across the screens of the sensors he held, Chester's face became so animated that the physicist could not help but smile.

"It's in there, Uncle Jeff, no more than a mile," he crowed.

"You're sure it's that close?" Swain asked, coming closer.

"Look at the scans," Chester replied. "We're fluctuating between seven and nine megavolts. Low photoionization, relatively weak neutron and gamma-ray production. And look at the quark decay. Just incredible."

Indeed, the golden infinity symbol was expanding and contracting in even larger pulsations than had been present at the outflow on the Furnace River, and the peak of the bell graph was almost off the charts.

The state police captain knelt to get a better view of the screens and said, "I still don't understand why we didn't get these readings when we came up here two days ago."

Chester shrugged. "Maybe Gregor's got it on a timer and it wasn't running then."

Swain shook his head. "More likely the cave-in had the place sealed up tight," he said. "But the earthquake dislodged enough of the impacted debris that the stone's unique electromagnetic signature must have begun to escape and be registered."

"They're heading this way!" a voice cried out from the stormy twilight.

Swain stood and looked downslope to find the pit bull figure of Angelis scrambling his way up through the muck, his arm still in a sling. When the NASA mission commander reached them, he explained about the signal transponders suddenly resurfacing on the cave map and the approximate location and direction in which the two groups were heading.

"Gregor's coming for the stone," Chester said.

"We've got to get in there first," Swain agreed. "Gregor can't be allowed near it. How long until they can get that tunnel borer up here?"

Angelis looked down the hill. "At least another two hours."

But Boulter was barely listening. "You're sure about Sanchez?" he asked Angelis.

The mission commander sobered and nodded. "I'm sorry, Captain. There's no signal showing."

Swain watched the trooper hang his head in stunned silence and felt anger build within him. So many people had died over this moon rock: Carson MacPherson, the three guards from Eddyville, the woman at the Laundromat, the missing inmate, the deputy marshal. Chester had almost been the eighth casualty. He knew the stone could mean so much good for mankind. But that was just a concept. Now he was beginning to see the rock as a symbol of death and lies and greed and—

The physicist stopped in midthought, attracted to and bewildered by the sight of a half-dozen military tanks and armored personnel carriers emerging out of the rain and fog from behind the tunnel borer. Soldiers began pouring out of the carriers. The tanks chugged by the bulldozers and skidders and ground to a halt twenty yards away.

A short, barrel-chested officer in his late forties with a scar that reached from his chin across his cheek to his ear strode up the hill. His epaulets carried two gold stars.

"I'm Major General Lyman Hayes," he barked. "I'm taking over this operation at the direct order of the President of the United States."

Final Connection

8:30 P.M.
CONFLUENCE OF FORGOTTEN AND NO RETURN RIVERS
NYRENS RIDGE
LABYRINTH CAVE

Filthy, bruised, reeling from lack of sleep, able to go on solely because of the energy his reunion with Cricket had generated, Tom trudged out onto a terrace above a crescent-shaped plaza through which sluiced a river some fifteen feet in breadth. The river was flanked on the north by a bulwark of pillar and cleaved block that supported the terrace. Dazzling salt crystals coated the buttress all the way to the rock flat that banked the river. At the southern end of the cavern, the river split east and southwest under an archway with several feet of headroom. Cricket limped behind him, locked once again in the belly belt.

Tom glanced at her. He knew she was battered with fatigue and pain, but not once in the last five hours had she complained. She had the right to feel defeated being back in the belt, but instead she seemed so filled with resolve that he studied her for a moment. There was something different about her; she was firmer and yet more resilient. He'd always known she was a tough kid. How many children raised in a family like hers, in this environment could fail to be physically rugged? But it was something more, something he just could not place at first other than the fact that right then she reminded him so much of Whitney. Then it hit him. He was looking at her the way he would an adult. As someone he could depend on: as a peer, as an ally.

Lyons eased alongside, followed by Kelly, who kept glaring Cricket's way. Gregor brought up the rear. Despite his waxen skin and his gaunt, crooked build, the physicist was acting as if he'd been up for an hour with two cups of coffee under his belt after a long night's sleep. Nervously alert.

Tom blinked and yawned. Then he realized where he was and shook himself alert. The message he'd left on the computer at the first cache said to expect him here, at the confluence of Forgotten and No Return Rivers, at midnight tonight. It dawned on him that if the message had reached the surface, a second rescue team, apart from the one they'd heard back in Munk's Ridge, could have entered the cave from the west. He began to crane his head, peering into the shadows, trying to make out human forms among the rocks and crevices of the bulwark below him. But there was nothing.

"Where now?" Gregor asked.

"Cricket needs to rest awhile," Tom said, trying to stall in case the first rescue team was still somewhere behind them. "I need to rest, too."

"Need twenty myself," Lyons said. The large man climbed down over the pillars to the floor of the lower hallway. He threw his sack on the floor about ten feet from the riverbank and laid his head down on it, resting his shotgun beside him. "Everyone take five."

"How can you even think of sleeping, Lyons?" Gregor cried. The hairless man's bearing fairly sizzled now. "We're getting close. I can feel it in my bones."

"You've been giving us that crap the past two days," Kelly retorted dully.

"So you had a rough go with the girl," Gregor sneered at him. "None of your suffering matters. None of my suffering matters. Some of the greatest minds of the ages have sought the stone—Aristotle, Magnus, Aquinas, Bacon, even Jung. Don't you understand? We're only hours away from beholding its magnificence."

"I just wanna see the gold," Kelly said.

Lyons said nothing. He closed his eyes and in seconds his breathing turned deep and raspy. Tom watched him, thinking that people who have the ability to just shut down like that had to be accustomed to stress. He wondered if he'd been in the military before becoming a prison guard. Or was he just so exhausted that sleep was the only thing that mattered right now?

Cricket sat down next to her father and laid her head on his shoulder. "So tired, Daddy," she said.

"Go to sleep," he said. "I'll be right here when you wake up."

She snuggled into his arms and closed her eyes.

Tom looked around. Still no sign of their would-be rescuers. He had to give them time to get here. With the high ground above the rivers, this cavern was the best possible place for an ambush in the entire cave system. If he led his captors away from this cavern, he would have to lead them back. He glanced downstream toward the second cache site and the connection route through Pluto's River into Tower Ridge. Then he turned his attention to that overhang from which the tributaries of the No Return River flowed. He'd run several sonar soundings up the hole over the years but had never explored that part of the cave. Could he take the chance of leading them off that way? What if they hit a dead end?

Cricket trembled and jerked in his arms. Tom watched her for the longest while, taking hope from the fact that she had been returned to him as a sign that they might indeed survive this trial. Then he thought of Whitney that first time they'd kissed in the hemlock glen below the cabin. He remembered the moonlight in her hair. The sweet smell of her skin as he nuzzled her. The soft brush of her lips. The rush up his spine as they molded to each other.

He reached up and turned off his headlamp, seeing Whitney as if she were in front of him in the moment after they'd broken their first embrace. "I promise you we will get back to you," he mumbled as his head began to droop toward sleep. "I promise."

Twenty minutes later, Gregor kicked Cricket's boots and then her father's. "Get up. We've delayed enough."

Cricket yawned, stretched, and groaned at the ache in every muscle in her body.

"Loosen your splint, then tighten it," Tom said. "And eat something. We've got another long walk ahead of us."

Cricket nodded, then unwrapped the splint and let her fingers dig into the swollen flesh around her knee. She found the tender spot and cringed. It was so sore she almost teared. Then she closed her eyes and told herself she could go on. She had to go on. There was no choice. If she collapsed now, they would leave her. She rewrapped the strips around her leg, then dug out a food bar from her pack. It was a dry chocolate raspberry that made her aware of how parched she was. Her water bottles were empty. She got up and limped toward the river, water bottles in hand. Kelly sat with his back against the stone buttress, his legs sprawled before him, his upper lip twisting at the sight of her. He threw his own water bottles at her. "Fill mine first," he ordered.

Cricket bent down and picked up the bottles, avoiding his glowering stare. She turned, doing everything she could not to let him see the shaking of her hands. Every time he looked at her it was clear he intended to kill her when this was all over. That thought kept cycling through her head as she opened the top of Kelly's water bottle. She glanced at her feet and saw on the rock beside them the shards of what had been a plate of delicate salt crystals. She remembered her mother telling her that Native Americans had used the salts as laxatives and purgatives.

Cricket leaned forward, dipping Kelly's bottle into the cold water. Then she picked up a handful of the crystals and crushed them over the mouth of the bottle. There was a filter in the lid of the bottle designed to extract bacteria and other impurities. Cricket tore out the rubber gaskets that made the filters work.

"Where's my fucking water?" Kelly yelled.

"Leave the girl alone," Lyons growled.

"No," Kelly said. "I won't."

She screwed the top on, turned, and tossed it to Kelly. He snatched the bottle out of the air, regarded her for a second, then drank greedily.

It was nine-thirty by the time they had all eaten, drunk, and reshouldered their packs. Cricket turned to head north and downstream. She had never been to this part of the cave, but she had spent hours upon hours looking at the maps her parents had made of the Labyrinth. The way to Tower Ridge lay in this direction.

But her father grabbed her gently by her upper arm, then made as if to kiss her temples and whispered in her ear, "We need time for that rescue team to catch up with us. Rinky-dink, okay?"

Cricket nodded, but her heart began to slam. Her father was taking a big chance, but she followed him without hesitation toward the southern end of the cavern, then entered the water, wading forward toward the overhang that marked the passage into the unexplored regions of Nyrens Ridge. Her dad reached the overhang and started to duck. Gregor climbed into the water after Cricket, then halted as if an invisible cord were lashed to his chest.

"You're sure this is the way, Burke?" Gregor called out.

"Do you want to lead?" Tom replied, his face betraying nothing but confidence. "You seem to know something about this place."

Cricket watched doubt course through Gregor as he looked back downstream, then he studied Tom. "No. Go on then."

In the early going, the cave that contained the No Return River ran a serpentine course under a low ceiling that forced them to crouch to avoid hitting their helmets. They were in and out of the chilly water constantly. The cold actually made Cricket's knee feel better and she moved along quite well between Gregor and Lyons.

But what she was seeing all around her made her increasingly agitated. She knew that no one had ever been in this part of the cave before. Her dad could predict how a cave might open up before him as well as any man alive. But she understood a thing or two about caves herself, and the silt in the water, the muddy banks, and the wet ceilings did not bode well for navigation.

Forty minutes into the soggy march, Kelly got a desperate look on his face, then began to race back along the bank of the river the way they had come, tearing at his coveralls. It's working, Cricket told herself. The laxatives are working.

When Kelly returned, he'd lost all color and complained of thirst. He sucked down a third of the second contaminated bottle. They started moving again.

Ten minutes later, Gregor cried out, "The water's glowing!"

All their headlamp beams flared down on the surface of the underground river. Cricket saw it, too: tendrils of glimmering greenish yellow against the steel-colored limestone streambed, a flow within a flow. It reminded her of a fishing trip she'd taken with her parents off Cape Hatteras when she'd seen the warm turquoise waters of the Gulf Stream against the cold gray Atlantic. Seeing the Gulf Stream had given her great pleasure, but Cricket tensed at the sight of the brackish green plume in the cave water. She knew its source and braced herself for trouble.

Ahead she saw her dad squatting as if to more closely examine the phenomenon.

"Huh," he said as if he were puzzled. "Must be microbial."

"Whaddya mean, microbial?" Kelly asked.

"Cave bacteria that give off their own light, like underwater fireflies," Tom replied. "Bring your light close to the surface and the bacteria should glow even brighter."

Cricket's attention darted among the men staring suspiciously at the river water. One by one, they lowered their headlamps toward the surface. Shaking, she lowered her lamp as well. The stream seemed to turn almost iridescent, the plume of each tendril mushrooming as it moved with the current between her legs.

Cricket knew the phenomenon was not microbial but man-made, caused by a fluorescein dye. Each of the NASA cavers had carried ten grams of the dye in their packs. It was supposed to have been dumped back inside Smith's Ridge as part of a U.S. Geological Survey experiment to trace the cave's water transit time. Her father must have tossed it in the water as a signal to whoever might be following them.

Gregor's lip curled with distaste. "These microbes aren't poisonous, are they? I mean, we won't get sick by being in the water, will we?"

"Not that I've ever heard of, though I wouldn't want to drink it unfiltered," Tom said.

Kelly cringed and Lyons asked, "How much further to dry ground?"

Tom hesitated at the question. It was obvious to Cricket that he'd hoped to reach solid footing long before now. "The river's running higher than normal, but we can't be far now," he said.

Tom turned and began wading again through the glowing blue cloud. Cricket followed, watching as the plume became longer and wider, filling the channel bank to bank before passing around a curve behind them.

She prayed her father was right, that there were rescuers still following them, that the rescuers would see the dye and wait for them back there in the salt cavern.

10:00 P.M.
CONFLUENCE OF FORGOTTEN AND NO RETURN RIVERS
NYRENS RIDGE
LABYRINTH CAVE

"Which way did they go?" Finnerty called from the terrace above the joining of the two rivers.

Whitney watched impatiently as Two-Elk worked the sides of the underground streams. The tracker squatted and ran her good hand along the embankments, and then stood and shook her head, the beam from her headlamp whipping back and forth.

"There's disturbance here where someone broke off salt crystals," she said, "and over there on that spit of ground between the two streams and again down the common river a ways. Problem is, it's all flat hard rock. No gravel, no sediment, no sand, no mud."

"Which means what?" Whitney demanded.

"They could have headed in any of three directions—downstream or up either of those two tributaries," Two-Elk replied before turning to Finnerty. "Your call on whether we take the chance on waiting them out here."

The U.S. marshal's cheeks puffed. "I need more information."

"What about the sensor those physicist guys gave us?" Two-Elk suggested. "If they're going for the rock, they'll be heading in whatever direction the signal's strongest."

"Makes sense," Finnerty said.

The deputy unzipped the top of her jumpsuit and brought out the slender handheld instrument. She went to each of the upriver passages and triggered the device. The golden infinity symbol on the cobalt screen throbbed at each outflow. But when she aimed the device downstream the amplitude of the pulses was noticeably larger.

"The stone's that way," Finnerty said, clearly frustrated. He thought for a moment, then said, "Ultimately, Two-Elk's right—that's where Gregor's going, to this stone of his. Why don't we try to find it and wait for them there, Whitney?"

"Because I know my husband," Whitney replied firmly. "He risked his life to leave that message. He said he'd be through here around midnight. He'll be here."

Finnerty unsnapped his helmet squatted, and rinsed it in the river. "But what if they forced Tom and Cricket downstream?" he asked. "If we wait here until midnight we could find ourselves hours behind. I think we should at least make a reconnaissance in that direction. If we don't find their tracks, we'll come back."

He stood and put the helmet back on. The strain of the constant darkness and lack of sleep was carved around his eyes.

"What if Tom returns before we do?" Whitney asked. "We could end up running into them and having the uncontrolled firefight you keep saying you want to avoid."

"I guess I'll have to take that chance," Finnerty replied moodily. "We're heading that way, at least until the tracking conditions improve."

The marshal turned up the intensity of his headlamp beam as if emphasizing that his decision was final. Whitney felt her stomach sink. She turned, looking for something, anything, that would give them a clue as to where Tom and Cricket had gone.

"Let's go," Finnerty said. "We're going downstream."

Whitney took a deep breath and was turning to follow the marshal and his deputy when she caught sight of a glimmering blue-green cloud billowing in the water near the outflow of the east fork of the No Return River.

"The hell we are," she said.

They built a semicircular cairn of rocks along the northern rim of the terrace some thirty-five yards back from and forty feet above the confluence of the two rivers. The top of the cairn was arranged in the manner of a fortress wall with low points through which the marshal and his deputy could shoot. Finished, they sat on their packs behind the wall atop piles of flat stones. Finnerty and Two-Elk removed their helmets, set them on the ground, then tugged on gray balaclava hoods. The machine pistols rested in their laps.

"Just like sitting in the woods, waiting for deer," Finnerty said, satisfied.

Two-Elk rolled her eyes. Whitney felt herself coil with frustration, expectancy, and dread. From her angle, she could look through the port directly in front of Finnerty and see the overhang above the outflow of the No Return River. She realized that although she might see Tom and Cricket climb free of the water, she would lose sight of them as soon as they had taken several steps downstream. But by then, she thought, it would all be over.

"Kill the lights," Finnerty said.

Whitney looked at him. "I need to ask you something first."

"Go ahead."

"I asked Two-Elk this already, so I know you're married, but it's important—do you have children?"

At that she saw a cloud of sadness and uncertainty settle over the marshal. "Not yet," he said. "We're trying, but there have been—complications."

Two-Elk cocked her head at him. "You never said anything about that"

Finnerty reddened. "Aren't Natalie and I allowed some privacy?"

"Sure, boss," Two-Elk replied. "Sorry."

Whitney reached out and touched the marshal's sleeve. "Don't give up. Never give up on the idea of family."

Finnerty's eyes moistened, then he turned his head and looked away. "I won't," he said. "You don't either, okay? We're going to do everything in our power get Cricket and Tom back for you, Whitney." Then he reached down between his boots to where his helmet lay and twisted off his headlamp. "Total silence now. When you see their lights coming, Whitney, don't move. Don't make the slightest noise. Hold your breath if you have to. Let us handle it. This is what we're trained to do."

Two-Elk turned off her headlamp and rested the muzzle of her machine pistol in the break in the rock wall. Even though Whitney had little experience with guns, she wanted to be armed herself, to be part of it, to do something concrete to end this nightmare once and for all. But all she could do was turn over the fate of her family to these two people. She bit at her upper lip and twisted the knob on her headlamp.

Instantly, there fell a blackness so complete that she could not have seen her hand had it been an eighth of an inch in front of her face. Panic surged from deep in her stomach and it surprised her with its strength after so many hours, days now, inside the cave. Her throat seemed to close from the inside, as if she were going into some kind of allergic shock. She swore she could taste the water, the grainy liquid that had fouled her mouth when she had fallen into the flood with Jeannie's body and lost her light.

Then Whitney squeezed her hands into fists and shook her head violently in the darkness; she would not allow herself to come apart now, not when she was this close to Tom and Cricket. She summoned up pictures of them and pored over them in her mind. Over many minutes the panic gradually ebbed.

After a while, after she became used to the absolute blackness, she noticed her senses of hearing and smell becoming more acute. She heard the river babbling below her. She heard the quick shallow rhythm of her breath, the deep, slow, monklike exhalations of Two-Elk, and the sonorous rasps of Finnerty right beside her. She smelled them and herself and the stale onion odor of the cave.

It was dank above the rivers and she was glad for the heat packs she'd shoved down the back and front of her jumpsuit. The packs warmed her torso and gradually turned her drowsy. But every once in a while, one of the marshals would shift in the dark beside her and she'd jolt alert. At last, Whitney could stay awake no longer. Her head slumped onto her chest and she slept uneasily. In her dream she saw herself *crouched on the ledge of the flooding belltower in Terror Hole Cave, the terra-cotta water brushing against the soles of her boots. Suddenly there was a bubbling in the current, as if an obstruction downstream had dislodged and the flood came up a quick three inches. Then up breached the body.*

Whitney sobbed and tried to back away from it. But she slipped and fell from the ledge into the water. The body bumped against her as she struggled to get back up on the dry outcropping, bumped her again and again. Whitney threw out her elbow to push the body away, but succeeded only in rolling it over. Only this time it was not Jeannie's face on the drowned corpse. Or Cricket's. Or Tom's.

It was her own.

11:20 P.M.
EAST FORK, NO RETURN RIVER
NYRENS RIDGE
LABYRINTH CAVE

Mounds of sand banked the underground stream. The sand met a rough wall of limestone. The river did, too, and disappeared.

"Shit," Tom muttered. He flared his headlamp left and right along the seam of liquid, sediment, and stone, looking for a way forward. He sought a crack, a chink, some small hole, anything. But the water and sand filled every bit of opening in the rock.

He turned to his captors and, trying to look each one of them in the eye, said, "I don't understand it. The way is flooded. We'll have to turn back."

"Fuck," Lyons said, throwing down his pack and gun on the riverbank.

Gregor's entire body went rigid. "This isn't the way," he said. "Never was."

"It *is* the way, at least one of them," Tom insisted. "This route is shorter, but it floods sometimes. We'll just have to go back the way we came and take the higher, drier route into Tower Ridge."

"Liar!" Gregor said, the tendons in his neck vibrating. "We've been moving away from the stone ever since we started up this river. My body feels it."

"Double-cross," Kelly snarled as he stepped forward, holding up the belly belt transmitter. "Told you not to fuck with us."

Tom braced himself for the hot, electric pain. Instead, Cricket keeled over, half in, half out of the underground stream, her arms and legs jerking, her eyes bulging out of their sockets. It looked like a dozen knives were stabbing into her at once.

"No!" Tom cried. He splashed through the water, going after Kelly.

Gregor tripped Tom and he sprawled in the stream. Gregor put a boot on his back. "Don't you move, Burke," Gregor said. Then he looked at Kelly. "Teach him a lesson. Hit her again."

Kelly grinned, raised the transmitter, then doubled over. Sweat beaded on his forehead and he grimaced at the convulsion in his abdomen. In the last hour, he'd been stricken four times with bouts of diarrhea. With each attack he had grown progressively weaker and now the cramping appeared to threaten even his ability to stand.

Tom watched Cricket rise up on one elbow and look at Kelly through electrically glazed eyes. "Whatsamatter, Kelly, feel like you're gonna poop your pants again?" she whispered.

Kelly twisted his head so that the beam of his lamp reached her. Another cramp racked his body, but he fought against it and at last righted himself and said, "You put something in my water back there, you bitch."

Cricket glanced at her father, then back at Kelly, the fright showing everywhere about her. "Don't know what you're talking about."

"No?" Kelly said. He rammed his thumb down on the red button.

To Tom's horror, veins all along Cricket's hairline stood out and her tongue sought the back of her throat. Kelly hit the button a third time and she convulsed backward in a trembling arch.

"You'll kill her!" Tom screamed. He fought out from under Gregor's boot, trying to get up. But Gregor kicked him in the ribs and he fell onto the stream bank.

Lyons splashed forward as if to grab Kelly, but his foot snagged on something under the water and he went to his knees on the bank. Gregor pointed his gun at the guard. "Don't interfere, Lyons. We're not done with her yet."

A malevolent grin crossed Kelly's face as he prepared to hit Cricket with a fourth shock. Tom spun toward Gregor, desperate to get the attention off of Cricket. "Lyons isn't interested in the gold at all," he blurted. "He wants the stone. He told me he'll kill Kelly and you—he'll kill all of us once you've shown him where the stone is."

The guard's focus darted to the shotgun, then back to Kelly and Gregor. "Be cool now, boys," Lyons said, curling his fingers into the sediment along the stream bank. "Burke's trying to turn us on each other. He's been trying to do it all along."

But Gregor crouched and aimed the muzzle of his pistol toward Lyons's chest. "When did he say all this?" he asked Tom.

"Day before yesterday, after Mann died. He said the stone was what was important, not the gold."

Cricket rolled over, her body still shaking, and laughed bitterly. "And I heard Kelly trying to convince Gregor to kill you, Lyons. Why don't you all just kill yourselves and get it over with?"

"You two don't know what you're doing," Lyons yelled. "I'm the only hope you've got."

"Fuck you," Tom replied, then he looked back at Gregor. "He said as long as he got out of here with the stone, he'd make sure Cricket and I would be safe. He said you and Kelly wouldn't matter at that point."

Gregor went cold and lethal, like a snake about to strike. He cocked the hammer of his pistol. "Is that so?" he muttered. " 'Wouldn't matter'?"

The slightest twitch rippled through Lyons's normally impassive face. Then he rolled sideways, whipping his hands up and out. Sediment flew threw the air. The grit cloud got into Gregor's eyes. The physicist shot wildly, dropping the gun and staggering in the water. The blast and ricochet in that bound place made him dizzy and sick to his stomach. But he scrambled forward and dived onto Cricket to shield her body with his.

Lyons was up on his feet, rushing Kelly, who swung a beefy right arm in an arcing hook toward his attacker. The guard flung out his left hand, blocking Kelly on the inside of his elbow. Then he rammed his great shoulder into Kelly's solar plexus. Together they flew off the bank and into the water.

Lyons knelt on top of Kelly, holding him under. The guard was so caught up in the frenzy of it all that he didn't notice Gregor stagger to his feet with a football-sized rock from the streambed in his hands.

"Lyons!" Tom cried. "Watch out!"

But the guard got only half turned before Gregor brought the rock smashing down on the back of his helmet. Lyons crumpled, then collapsed to his right his lower torso in the stream, his chest and head sideways on the bank. Blood ran from his ears and nose. He spasmed, coughed, then lay deathly still.

JUNE 18, 2007
12:59 A.M.
CONFLUENCE OF FORGOTTEN AND NO RETURN RIVERS
NYRENS RIDGE
LABYRINTH CAVE

"Quiet now," Finnerty whispered. "They're coming." Muddled, still suffering from the effects of her nightmare an hour before, Whitney strained her eyes in the direction of the confluence of the two cave streams. It was faint at first, but unmistakable—a faraway light shining off the surface of the subterranean watercourse, growing stronger with every moment.

The light became a definable beam. Above the low gurgle of the streams, Whitney heard splashing then a figure appeared behind one of the headlamps, a heartbreakingly familiar form backlit by other headlamps. Her breath caught hard; she had imagined this so many times in the past few days that she wondered whether she was still in her dreams.

Tom waded out from under the overhang and stepped up onto the triangular spit of rock that separated the two rivers before their final joining. Whitney's hand flew to her mouth. Seen this way, at a remove of sixty yards and framed in the chromatic, elliptical shadow cast below his headlamp, her husband looked like a picture she'd seen of Marines near the end of the Bataan death march. His cheeks were sunken and filthy. Bags of skin hung below his eyes, which seemed to slump back in their hollows. But it was his posture that rattled her: shoulders forward, spine curved, legs without spring, a posture of being witness and victim to things so indelibly brutish that your body cannot help but be bent by it. A busted-down stance Whitney knew only too well. It was the way you handled yourself when you were on the verge of a breakdown.

Tom's lamp was now joined by that of a skeleton of a man Whitney recognized as Gregor from photos Finnerty had shown her. Despite the torn-up state of his body, he radiated force and menace. Finnerty slipped off the safety of his machine pistol. Two-Elk did the same. Then Cricket appeared behind Gregor, so ragged and befuddled that if Whitney had not recognized that lock of hair hanging down out of her helmet, she would not have known her. Cricket stumbled and splashed forward. Kelly came out from under the overhang and jerked her to her feet by the neck of her cave suit

"Keep moving," he said, dragging her with his right hand.

"Fuck you!" Cricket yelled, struggling against his grip.

"You want it again, kid?" he demanded furiously, waving the transmitter in her face. "I'll give it to you, that's what you want. Gregor says you get to live awhile longer. But it don't matter to me if I do it here or down the road. So keep moving or die."

Animals, Whitney thought. These men are total animals. Then she noticed Two-Elk holding a pair of fingers up for Finnerty to see and the marshal nodding. She understood. Four men had taken Cricket and Tom hostage. One had disappeared before reaching the first supply cache. Now a second was gone. What had happened?

She turned her head back toward the marshals. In the dim light given off by the headlamps below, she saw them using glowing green irradiated tritium sights to aim down the barrels of their automatic weapons. The scene was so unnerving, she wanted to hide her head between her knees. Tom swung his headlamp around the cavern, as if he anticipated the ambush. Whitney's fingers clenched in prayer, then her thoughts turned savage. Shoot them she thought. Blow them away. Tear their bodies apart if it will save my family.

"Burke's blocking me," Finnerty murmured.

"The girl's in the way for me," Two-Elk whispered.

For a beat Whitney was baffled. Then she snapped her attention back to the drama unfolding below her and saw what they were talking about: Gregor and Kelly stood behind Tom and Cricket. A clean shot was impossible.

"Keep moving," Gregor ordered. "Not one detour. Straight to Tower Ridge."

Tom's headlamp arced around the room one last time. Then, reluctantly, he put one foot in front of the other, leading them north toward Whitney and the marshals. Cricket limped along behind her father, a tight stoic expression on her face. The convicts kept their positions on the far side of Whitney's family. For an instant she lost sight of Tom. Then, through the shooting holes Two-Elk and Finnerty had constructed, she caught fleeting glimpses of him and Cricket. The marshals' guns swung after them.

Tom stepped clearly into the frame of her peephole in the rock wall, flanked by Gregor, both men right there in front of her at thirty yards, and then they were gone. Cricket came into her direct line of vision, paralleled by Kelly. And then they were gone, too, and there was only the slap and shuffle and echo of their footsteps.

Whitney listened in disbelief as the sound of their footsteps faded. They had to be yards from leaving the cavern now. She jumped up from her hiding position and, for a split second, saw them as distant and shadowed outlines silhouetted by the collective bloom of their headlamps. She opened her mouth to scream to Tom and Cricket to run.

A strong gloved hand clamped across her mouth. A forearm wrapped around her neck. Whitney threw back her elbows and felt them hit Finnerty in the ribs. The marshal grunted in pain but did not relax his grip, and Whitney felt herself being hauled backward and down.

She began to whimper into the glove, to whimper and whine like a child taken from its mother.

"Shhhh, Whitney," Finnerty whispered softly in her ear. "It's going to be all right. It's going to be all right."

7:00 A.M.
TOWER RIDGE
LABYRINTH CAVE

By dawn that day, the torrential rains had been falling on the highlands above the Furnace River for nearly three solid days. A data recorder, maintained by the U.S. Geological Survey, pegged total precipitation at nearly fourteen inches, with three more expected in association with violent thunderstorms throughout the day. The river, which normally ran at fifteen thousand cubic feet per second at this time of year, was now roaring at nearly ninety-five thousand cubic feet per second.

Shortly after seven o'clock, despite hundreds of man-hours of effort to shore up the dike, the waters of the Hermes Reservoir began to spill over the rammed-earth dam. Workers were evacuated to high ground and the warnings went out down-river—the Corps of Engineers expected the dam to be breached within the hour. FEMA was already declaring the region a disaster area.

Thirteen miles away, from a position nearly five hundred yards downslope from the Virgil Entrance to Tower Ridge, Helen Greidel was back on the job, doing a live report for the *Today* show, her back to two tanks and a company of soldiers guarding the road.

"In a stunning development in the ongoing Labyrinth Cave saga," she began, "an entire division of the Sixteenth Armored Cavalry based at Fort Knox, Kentucky, was deployed around Labyrinth Cave last night. Military spokesmen are telling us that the move came at the direct order of the President of the United States, but are giving us little information as to why the army has been called in.

"At the same time, federal earthquake researchers out of Memphis say they are being kept out of the area, known to be the epicenter of a massive temblor three days ago. The researchers say that the army is citing national security as their justification for not allowing them in to examine the fault lines. The army, NASA, and the White House have all refused to elaborate to the media gathered here and turning increasingly testy, but I can tell you that security and tension outside the largest cave in the world is the highest I've ever seen outside the Middle East."

From high behind the news anchor came a metallic shrieking noise that caused her to squint and shake her head before turning to point up the mist-shrouded ridge. "That noise you hear is a giant tunnel borer, which has been biting its way into the mountainside for the past several hours, trying to reopen a way into the cave so rescue workers can attempt to find those trapped and held hostage."

Up near the entrance to the cave, Swain stuffed cotton into his ears. Huge diesel engines mounted behind the massive drilling head of the shaft-boring machine powered a series of hydraulic arms that rotated a monolith of hardened steel bits against the solid caprock of the ridge. Chunks of rock splintered and broke up under the assault. Robotic arms shot down from behind the drilling head and cleared the rubble to a conveyor belt that led downslope to dump trucks waiting to haul.

"How long till we break through?" Major General Hayes shouted at Angelis and Boulter over the shrieking of the borer. "The President's orders are that we can absolutely not let this Gregor character get to that moon rock first. The President says failure is not an option here, gentlemen."

The NASA mission commander looked at Swain, who tapped Chester on the shoulder. The teenager was studying his three-dimensional map on a laptop set on a folding table under a tent awning that had been set up during the night.

"What do you think, Chester?"

"If my calculations are correct, Uncle Jeff, we've got to cut through another thirty meters of rock before we hit open cave. The Army Corps of Engineers said the borer cuts at nine meters an hour."

"So three more hours," Swain replied.

"Give or take," Chester said.

"What's the position of the people inside?" the general asked.

Swain looked over Chester's shoulder at the computer, then out into the mist toward the foggy silhouette of Nyren's Ridge. "They're still split up, two groups, no more than ten minutes apart, descending toward Pluto's River—the connection into this ridge."

"Can they get to the rock before us?" the general demanded, pounding his fist into his open hand.

"I don't know," Swain admitted.

"I'll say it again, Doctor: Failure is not an option."

"Everybody in the government has made that clear to me from the get-go," Swain said, trying to control the rising anger he felt.

"You have what you need to control that thing once we get in there?"

"We think so," Swain replied. "Again, General, as I've been saying since the beginning of this fiasco, we've never dealt with anything like moon rock 66095 before."

Angelis said, "You said it could destabilize if it was handled incorrectly."

The physicist nodded. "Gregor's log notes indicate the stone reacts mercurially in the presence of quick surges or lapses of energy. But I think we're okay as long as it doesn't receive any more big jolts."

"All you keep talking about is this stone," Chester shouted in frustration. "What about those people in there? Shouldn't we be thinking more about how to rescue them?"

At that, the general's expression turned icy. "My orders are clear, young man. The people trapped inside the cave are not the primary concern of the U.S. government. The rock is."

Swain's jaw dropped. "You can't be serious."

"Dead serious," Hayes replied, glancing at his watch. It was 7:20 exactly.

"This is outrageous," the physicist cried. "Nothing is worth those people's lives."

"No?" the general snapped. "Wasn't it you who told the President the rock could be the most important discovery since the splitting of the atom?"

"But those people—" Swain said.

"In the course of history, they will be nothing more than a footnote," Hayes said. "The United States in possession of the rock will be all that matters."

Swain made to protest, then turned and walked away, feeling used and sullied for his part in all that had occurred. He felt Chester's hand on his shoulder. "You couldn't have known, Uncle Jeff," he said.

"I should have known, Chester, and that's the awful part of it," Swain replied bitterly. "If I hadn't been so caught up in the science, in the glory of the remarkable discovery, I could have predicted what the politicians would do. They want it for its power. Nothing more."

A cool wind swept across the open slope below. Several miles to the southwest, jagged lines of lightning rent the sky. And above the caterwauling of the shaft borer came the explosive rumblings of thunder.

Upriver, emergency workers and engineers did not hear the thunder. It was drowned out by a great cracking and heaving as the earthen dam holding back the Hermes Reservoir exploded outward and millions upon millions of gallons of water, a rolling wall the color of nickel, bore downriver, obliterating everything in its path.

7:21 A.M.
NYREN'S-TOWER CONNECTION ROUTE
LABYRINTH CAVE

Cricket crawled along a greasy passage descending deep inside the seventh of the Labyrinth's nine ridges. Gregor was on all fours in front of her, creeping after her dad. Her knee was killing her, but she drove herself without mercy, doing everything to keep space between her and Kelly, who crawled behind her.

The roof of the cave rose suddenly to eight feet and she found herself in a low, rectangular cavern. The walls and ceiling were topaz in color and showed signs of heavy anastomoses—scores of small, winding tubes connected in a mazelike pattern that made the rock look like termites had been at it. The pocking was heaviest where the left wall of the cave met the roof, so heavy that it looked like an overlay in the way a sculptor might use latticework to effect bas-relief.

Cricket got to her feet and felt her knee give way. Her father caught her and held her while she moaned.

"Keep her moving!" Gregor exhorted.

"She needs to rest," Tom said in a flat monotone that surprised her. "Just give her fifteen minutes."

"Sure, what the fuck, take fifteen," Kelly slurred, a sleepy grin on his filthy, swarthy face. "Take a load off, Gregor. Eat a little."

Kelly's pupils were dilated, his irises watery. He opened a plastic container, shook out two white pills, and swallowed them. During the night, they had reached the second cache and restocked their supplies. In the medical kit Kelly had found thirty-five doses of Percoset, a narcotic painkiller, and had begun eating them, not only for the high but their constipating side effects.

"Ten minutes, no more," Gregor snapped. The stone's just ahead of us, Kelly."

Cricket leaned on her father, who helped her to a sitting position against a huge boulder near the center of the cavern. He sat beside her, staring down at the pocked rock between his legs. In that position, he reminded her of her mother in the aftermath of one of her waking nightmares, haunted, chewed up, and alone; and it shocked Cricket.

"You okay, Dad?" she whispered. "You look awful."

"I keep seeing you on that stream bank with Kelly jamming his thumb down on that button," he murmured. "I keep seeing myself unable to help you, Cricket. I keep seeing the blood trickling from Lyons's head. I keep wondering why no one was there at the two rivers. Can't seem to make those thoughts stop circling in my head. Can't seem to stop thinking that once we reach that stone, we'll be—"

"Fine," she said firmly. "We'll be fine, Dad."

He smiled, but it was a grim smile. He did not look at her and said nothing. She'd never seen him like this. This wasn't the man she knew as her father at all. This was someone beaten and Tom Burke had never been beaten.

"We're going to get out of here and see Mommy, right? Dad? Look at me. We're going to get out of here, right?"

At last he raised his head in her direction, and his rheumy, bloodshot eyes seemed to look right through her.

"Don't know, Crick," he said. "Just don't know anymore."

"But what about what Grandpa used to say," she pleaded. "With each other we can get through anything?"

"Don't know about that either," he replied dully.

7:30 A.M.
NYREN'S-TOWER CONNECTION ROUTE
LABYRINTH CAVE

Whitney, Two-Elk, and Finnerty, meanwhile, were less than a half mile behind Tom and Cricket, inching their way along a ledge above a horizontal chasm where the pewter-colored walls had been water sculpted into thin vertical flutes. They disturbed acrid dust that got into Whitney's eyes and nose and burned at the back of her throat. When they cleared the ledge, Two-Elk knelt in the dust, examining the footprints.

"How far ahead are they?" Finnerty asked.

"Can't tell," Two-Elk replied. "I'm having trouble understanding how the tracks change over time underground. We should slow down, boss, or we might bounce right on top of them."

"You already were on top of them," Whitney interjected bitterly. "Three days and you had them and did nothing!"

Finnerty turned to her and spoke with great restraint. "We've been over this, Whitney. We had no clear shot. And I was not about to jeopardize the lives of your husband and daughter by taking a risk like that."

"You keep saying it's about my family," she retorted. "But I've thought about it Marshal. Your job is recapturing fugitives. To you, that's the bottom line. Tom and Cricket could die and you could get those men and it would all be a success to you."

Finnerty's face contorted and he spat out his response: "Mrs. Burke, you have no idea what I think about how I consider my job, my life. No idea! I'd venture to say my wife has no idea whether I'm alive or dead. I'd venture to say Two-Elk's father and sister are in the same boat. As it stands, you know your husband and daughter are alive. You've seen them. Now you may hate me for making that decision back there, but I can live with that because I know I made the right choice. We'll make another attempt to save your family at the stone. Period."

They stood there, glaring at each other.

At last, Whitney said, "What if they get to that stupid rock and those inmates kill my family before we catch up?"

"I don't deal in what-ifs," Finnerty said. "I promise you, we're not done yet. Not by a long shot. Now they're getting farther away from us while you argue. Where do we go next, Mrs. Burke? Or do you just want to sit here and second-guess me until your family is dead?"

Whitney felt her jaw tighten, then she gestured at a passage that led down and to the right. "We crawl through that hole and descend toward Pluto's River. That's the final part of the connection route into Tower Ridge."

Two-Elk looked at the sensor. "That's where the rock's got to be, boss. Signal's getting real strong."

Finnerty did not wait for Whitney to lead, but dropped through the crevice in the rock going down into the tight passage that led into the deepest part of Labyrinth Cave. As Two-Elk disappeared behind him, Whitney told herself that no matter what the marshal said, if she got anywhere near Cricket and Tom again, she was going to scream at them to run. She was going to let them know she'd come for them. She would save them—or die trying.

Two-Elk's light faded and Whitney began to wriggle down into the crevice. Just before her shoulders twisted through the opening she swore she caught a flash of light sweeping through the darkness behind her. She whipped her head around, letting her headlamp explore the blackness, her heart pounding.

But there was nothing behind her but rock and shadow.

7:40 A.M.
NYRENS-TOWER CONNECTION ROUTE
LABYRINTH CAVE

Tom eased his way feet first down a steep, twisting cavity in the rock His head felt squeezed, as if it were in a vise that altered his senses. Everything seemed blunted: his vision, his touch, his taste. Then ahead he heard what sounded like the muffled clash of cymbals in a concert hall.

"What's that noise?" Gregor demanded.

"Don't know," he replied, genuinely confused. "Pluto's River is right ahead of us a couple of hundred yards. But I've never heard it sound like that before."

Indeed, in Tom's experience, the underground watercourse that marked the last 175 yards between Nyrens Ridge and Tower Ridge had never run higher than waist deep and always at a lethargic pace that produced a gentle gurgling. But when he emerged from the feeder passage onto a boulder above the subterranean river, he confronted a cataract of foaming bronze water, swirling and pounding against the walls of the cave. Less than two feet of air showed between the churning liquid and the roof. In a heartbeat, that viselike sensation left him and he felt his nerves go raw.

"The storm up on the surface must have the Furnace out of control, backing up into its tributaries," Tom shouted. "It's too dangerous to cross!"

Gregor looked from the river to Tom and back again. "Is this the only way to Tower Ridge?"

"Yes."

"Then we're going across."

"We'll drown!"

"The stone's right there on the other side. I feel it in every cell in my body. We're going. Now. Or we're dying here. Now!"

Kelly, who had been eating more of the pain pills, appeared unaware of the gravity of the situation. "Let's go, let's go," he slurred waving the belly belt device and Lyons's shotgun at Tom. "Time to take a dip, Burke."

Tom looked at Cricket. "At least let her stay. With her knee, there's no way she'll make it."

"No, Daddy," Cricket cried. "If you're going, I'm going."

Tom hesitated, then saw Kelly's thumb move toward the belly belt's transmitter. "Go," he said.

Tom climbed into the churning water. The river punched at the backs of his legs, spun him at the waist, made him stagger and almost go under. Then he spread his stance wide and got some semblance of balance. "The current's strong! We'll have to lock arms to cross!"

Cricket looked out at her father in the water, then down at the hand that Kelly offered with a narcotic grin. "I'd rather stick my hand in acid," she said.

The strangler's grin evaporated and he raised his hamlike fist. But Gregor got between them. "The girl stays with me," he said.

Gregor hooked his right forearm through Cricket's left elbow and tugged her toward the water. She took one awkward step. Cold, muddy water filled her boots. At the second step, the water surged against her knee and it almost buckled. She hopped ahead and plunged off into the deep water, which reached the bottom of her rib cage. Like her father, she almost went under. But Gregor proved extraordinarily strong and kept her upright. Kelly came into the water and grabbed Gregor's other arm, then her dad linked his with Cricket's and together they set off in a shuffling sidestep out into a current that changed every few feet, gyrating and buffeting them from all angles.

The beams from their headlamps were like those of lighthouses cutting back and forth across the flooding waters. By the time they had covered seventy yards, barely eighteen inches separated the surface of the river from the curved ceiling of the cave. At every step, the river beat at Cricket's shoulder, torso, and knee, turning her, floating her, threatening to topple and pull her under.

"This is what Mom must have felt in the Terror Hole," Cricket said.

"Worse," her dad said through gritted teeth. "She had no room to move."

The current suddenly surged and pulled her from her father's grasp. Her foot caught in a cavity in the riverbed. A hot knife of pain ripped through her knee, and despite Gregor's iron grip on her other arm, she lurched forward, flailing to stay upright. The water flooded into her mouth and made her gag. It broke over her helmet and gushed in at the neckline of her dry suit.

Her hamstring muscles, already so fatigued from compensating for her injured knee, now cramped at the effort of wading. Her father grabbed hold of her again and she got her balance. She plunged her hand under the water, trying to hold her knee steady, thinking it would not be possible to take another step. Then she saw her dad's headlamp angle toward the ceiling as if he were looking for a way marker. Cricket labored to get herself upright and shine her beam alongside his. Their lights revealed diagonal arches carved into the stone that made the roof look like the ribwork of an old ship's hull. And then their lamps found a long, jagged crack cutting at a forty-five-degree angle across the ceiling.

Her father smiled down at her with his old confidence. "We're gonna make it!"

He led them crosscurrent, tracking the fissure. Ahead fifteen yards, Cricket saw where the crack became a crevice that cleaved the ceiling nearly three feet wide, and within that crevice a series of ledges led to higher ground. She felt strangely energized by the chaos. She was thinking of survival now, hers and her father's and nothing else.

"Wait here," Tom said. "There's a deep hole in front of us. Let me swim across and get up in that fissure in the ceiling before you come."

With that he pushed off, stroking through the current, stopping to tread just below the widest point of the opening in the roof. He bobbed then reached up and tried to get a handhold so he might hoist himself out of the water. But the wall there was nearly vertical. Every time he tried for purchase, his gloves slipped. At last, Cricket saw him draw in a big breath, then drop totally under the water. A second later, he thrust upward, bursting out of the river even as he threw both arms up and to the side toward the walls of the fissure. He shook there for an instant in an iron cross position, then managed to kick his foot forward onto a tiny nub of support. Another two moves and he was up inside the gash in the ceiling of the river passage, feet braced against both sides, looking back at them, holding out his hand.

"Cricket first," he called.

"Not a chance," Kelly said. He let go of Gregor and swam. When he got beneath Tom, he thrust up his hand. Her dad caught it and hauled Kelly to safety. Gregor pushed Cricket away from him and began stroking. Without his weight to anchor her, Cricket had to fight with every ounce of strength to avoid being swept away.

"All right now, Cricket," her dad yelled when Gregor had been lifted into the fissure. "Your turn!"

Cricket took a deep breath, kicked off the bottom with her good leg, and stroked her way across the fifteen yards of spinning copper water toward his outstretched arm. The current was stronger, much stronger than she expected, like a riptide she'd once been caught in off Cape Hatteras. For a second, the idea that she wasn't going to make it flashed through her. Then she shook it off, clenched her teeth, and punched her arms up and over, up and over, focusing on her dad's hand. Nothing else mattered. Just the glove. Inches away now. And then she was right below it She tried to stand, but couldn't. The water was too deep. She treaded, then threw her right arm upward and just missed.

"Again!" her dad yelled.

Cricket felt her strength waning. But she took a deep breath and flailed upward with her right arm toward his outstretched hand. He caught her by her fingertips. Cricket threw up her other hand and caught his glove and grinned fiercely when she felt herself being lifted.

Her shoulders came free of the flooding subterranean river, then her torso and her thighs. Cricket could see the strain the move was putting on her father, so she tried to kick her good leg forward in the same way he had in order to get herself into the fissure. But instead of helping the situation, the jerking motion tore her dad's glove free of his hand and she felt herself break from his grasp and fall.

"Daddy!"

7:45 A.M.
NYREN'S-TOWER CONNECTION ROUTE
LABYRINTH CAVE

Whitney was concentrating so hard on squeezing herself sideways between the walls of sharp stone on the twisted route that wound steeply down into the west flank of Nyren's Ridge that the noise echoing somewhere in the cave below her did not register at first.

She slid free of the crack, took five steps after Two-Elk, then halted as the implications of the cacophonous sound curtain hauled back and pulverized her. Her tongue dried so fast she thought it would crack. Her vision wavered, then distorted toward hallucination when she stepped like a zombie around the last turn of passage and saw the raging torrent that was Pluto's River.

Finnerty and Two-Elk squatted on a projection of rock, casting their lamps on the bubbling, churning waterway. "Which way?" the marshal asked. His voice came to Whitney as if it had been fed through a synthesizer, slowed, stretched, and hollow. She felt her arm rise of its own accord and point downstream.

"Is there another way across?" Finnerty asked.

Her felt her head shake, No.

"This passage is gonna close," Two-Elk yelled. "We're gonna lose them."

"Lets do it then," Finnerty said. Both the marshal and his deputy jumped into the water and were swept fifteen yards downstream before they managed to get their footing and turn to wait for Whitney.

But she breathed in through her nose and that smell, that smell of decomposition that accompanies a flood, triggered a full-scale mental retreat. She curled down into a ball and rocked back and forth, hypnotized by the terra-cotta water bubbling and flashing in the beam of light cast by her headlamp.

Finnerty began making come-on motions, but Whitney ignored them and kept rocking. The marshal tried to fight his way back to her, but the flow there was too strong. Two-Elk gestured toward the sensor around her neck. Finnerty shook his head and tried again to get upstream to Whitney, but the current buffeted him, threw him backward. Two-Elk turned and began to swim downstream. Finally, with the horror of what he was doing painted all over his face, the marshal turned and followed her.

At some level, Whitney was aware that they were leaving her but did not care; her head buzzed as if thrust into a hive, and then she collapsed fully into the waking nightmare. She saw herself back in the belltower in Terror Hole Cave, understanding that this buzzing in her head was what Jeannie must have felt before the flood took her; and gazing at Pluto's River, Whitney had the overwhelming desire to follow Jeannie at last, to ease into the water and let it close over her head to stop the panic attacks forever.

Then, from far away over the river's roar, a piercing cry penetrated the buzzing haze.

"Daddy!"

Whitney blinked and turned her head toward it as a drunk might a distant police siren. Then she heard it again, faint but distinct

"Daddy! Help me!"

Whitney gazed beyond the bobbing headlamps of Finnerty and Two-Elk, already tapering from view.

"Cricket?" she mumbled. Then, shaking her head to clear the buzzing, she stood and screamed, *"Cricket! Cricket, I'm here!"*

For a stunned second, Whitney watched her headlight beam disappear into the darkness of the flooding cave and heard nothing. Then, from far off she heard Cricket's voice again, "Mommy!" And then Tom's voice, "Whitney!"

Whitney took a step toward the water and froze. Finnerty and Two-Elk had disappeared; their lights were gone. Her own headlamp showed that the river was seconds from reaching the ceiling and becoming a sump.

Rocks rumbled behind her. She twisted and found herself looking into a dying headlamp and under that frail light the unfixed eyes of Billy Lyons. His black skin was coated with a film of gray dust

Blood caked at his nose and matted below his ears and down his neck. He reached out a hand toward her. "Wait," he growled.

Whitney freaked and jumped out into the flood.

7:55 A.M.
PLUTO'S RIVER

Cricket fought her way back upstream. "Mommy!"

For a split second as she thrashed against the surging river, she saw the flicker of headlamps coming at her. Then they disappeared. "Mom! Mom!" Cricket stopped treading water and listened. But there was no reply. And no more sign of the lights.

She knew her mother was not coming, that she could not come; in the instant after their voices had reached each other, the river passage that linked Nyrens Ridge to Tower Ridge had flooded to a sump.

Cricket began to sob and hit at the water. "No! No!"

"Cricket!"

She tilted her head up in a daze, her headlamp finding her father still leaning down out of the crack. Gregor and Kelly were perched on rocks above him.

"Mommy was here," she said, bewildered. "She came for us."

"I heard her, honey," he replied, his face stricken with grief. "Give me your hand now, sweetheart. Swim across the current and give me your hand."

Cricket stared out at the point in her headlamp beam where the water met the roof. Her mom had conquered her fears and come for them. She had been in the cave the whole time, trying to rescue them. That must have been her making noise back on the underground mountain days ago. It all seemed so hopeless now that Cricket wanted to float away.

"C'mon!" Tom shouted. "Don't give up. Not now! Remember what you told me back there? With each other we can survive anything?"

"You don't believe it anymore," Cricket sobbed. "You said so. I saw it in your face."

"No," he said. "I do believe it. And so did Mommy. That's why she came. Believe, Cricket."

Crying, punching and slapping at the water, Cricket made her way crosscurrent to her dad's outstretched hand. She was barely aware of throwing her arm up, being caught and lifted into the fissure. Her thoughts were only of her mother and how much she wanted to be safe in her arms. And then Cricket found herself stumbling up the ledges after Gregor and Kelly, who were already climbing higher into the crack. Her teeth chattered. Her body quivered with cold. Her knee felt as if it had been bludgeoned with a hammer.

Forty feet up, the passage broke left. Cricket stopped and shone her light back down toward the river. Tom saw what she was doing and shook his head. "It's no use. No one could get through there, Cricket. Not even your mom on her best day."

Eighty yards to the south, Whitney slashed her way downstream. She looked over her shoulder and saw Lyons jump into the water after her.

"Wait!" he called weakly. "Please!"

Whitney came to where the roof of the cave and the surface of the river turned seamless. Cricket's and Tom's voices echoed through her mind. She looked around, then spoke to the cave itself: "Gimme a chance. That's all I'm asking. Just one chance."

She took a deep breath and plunged into the sump.

The chill water was like a slap to the face and Whitney became instantly aware of the implications of what she had done. Free diving into a sump, even one where you knew the way, was about the most dangerous thing a caver could ever do. Her potential for life was now measured in seconds. But rather than cripple her, that realization triggered a fight response and adrenaline coursed through her veins. The light cast by her headlamp bounced and refracted off millions of bronze-colored air bubbles. It was like having your head out a car window at night during a blizzard with the high beams on, disorienting, claustrophobic, damn near blinding. Whitney clawed at the lamp to weaken the beam. Then she kicked and swam her way into the swirl.

Ten feet. Twenty feet. Her lungs began to burn. A voice inside her head screamed at her to keep swimming or die. Thirty feet. Forty. The adrenaline petered out of her system. Her diaphragm spasmed. She had an almost uncontrollable urge to open her mouth and breathe. Forty-five feet. Fifty. Her muscles were on fire. She couldn't go much farther and knew it.

At last she couldn't swim another stroke. Twisting her head back and forth, she searched for something in the cold, frothing water, anything to give her hope. But there was nothing. She prepared herself to inhale and succumb at last to the waters and the darkness.

A swell in the current caught her, twirled, and thrust her upward. Her helmet banged against the roof of the flooded cave. The current sucked her back down a foot and then propelled her up again in a spiral action.

Whitney breached into an air pocket six, maybe seven inches high, just wide enough to accommodate her helmet and very long, close to the entire width of the passage. The current tried to tug her down again. She kicked against it, tilting her head back and sucking the sweet air into her lungs. She remembered when she and Tom had surveyed this passage years before. The roof of the cave was marked by so many deep grooves that it looked like the ribbed hull of an old wooden boat. She was up inside one of those grooves now; the river water must have risen so fast that the air was trapped.

Whitney took several more deep breaths, then told herself she had to find the fissure in the ceiling that marked the way into Tower Ridge. If her memory served her right, between here and the fissure, every three yards or so, another one of these grooves traversed the cave roof. Were they filled with air, too?

The current pulled at her again. Don't think, she told herself. Just go.

She filled her lungs one last time, let go of the sides of the groove, dropped down into the chill water, and arched herself backward. The flow shoved her straight up against the roof of the cave, which is what she'd hoped would happen; the pressure made her like a human fly, able to bounce along upside down against the cave ceiling. The headlamp illuminated every plane, every depression in the rock, and then the next groove.

Flooded.

One more chance. Just one more chance, she prayed as she pulled and scratched her way toward the next groove. She breached into a foot of air, sputtering, gasping, and panting. The sounds of her breathing boomed around her. Something bumped against her from behind. She looked over her shoulder and screeched bloody murder.

Not six inches behind her, bobbing in the air pocket, was the head of Two-Elk's drowned corpse. The deputy marshal's eyes were rolled back in her head. Grainy bronze liquid drained from her nose and mouth. Her machine pistol trailed from a sling around her neck. The sensor Chester Norton had given her floated out in front of her; the golden infinity symbol was bulging and thinning on that emerald screen.

Whitney's consciousness went kaleidoscopic. *Jeannie's body bobbed on the surface of the water in Terror Hole Cave. Cricket's body breached up beside it, followed by Tom's and then Two-Elk's.*

"No!" Whitney screamed. She kicked away from the deputy marshal's corpse, scraping her helmet along the sides of the groove, fearing she might faint or go completely mad.

Then, in the river below her, she felt a hand close around her ankle.

8:05 A.M.
TOWER RIDGE
LABYRINTH CAVE

"At last!" Gregor crowed. He spun in circles, his arms held wide, letting his headlamp beam course about the lofty cavern.

"I know you fancy yourself discoverer of this cave, Burke," he declared. "But you're not. My grandfather brought me in here when I was seven. An old Shawnee showed him the way in when he was a boy and swore him to secrecy. I was sworn to secrecy in return. I used to play in here all the time until ... "

Gregor fell silent, blinking at the ground, a tortured expression on his face.

"Who fucking cares about your shitty childhood?" Kelly said. "Everyone's got one. Let's get the gold, man. The gold!"

That seemed to bring Gregor back from some dark and private place. Without another word he sidled off toward the southernmost end of the cavern and a landslide of fallen boulders. Tom helped Cricket along. She looked like a cat that'd been kicked and left in the rain.

"Hold on, Cricket," he whispered. "Don't give up on me now. I'll think of something."

Cricket did not reply, and Tom raised his headlamp and gestured toward a cavity high on the side of the cavern wall. "If you're looking for the way out, it's up there," he said. "Or at least that used to be the way out. It's collapsed back up in there three hundred yards or so now."

"Guess what, Burke?" Gregor sneered. "You don't have a clue."

Gregor crouched, reached in between two of the boulders at the base of the slide, and, to Tom's surprise, withdrew a steel bar about four feet long. He walked eight feet to his left, fitted the bar into a worn slot underneath a rock about three feet tall, and threw his weight onto the lever. The boulder eased to one side, revealing a crawlway.

"The Shawnee used to come here to bury their medicine men," Gregor announced, shaking with anticipation. "This was the entrance to their sacred—"

The scientist stopped, hearing something in the distance. Then Tom heard it, too; a faint but distinct vibrational shrieking noise emanating from the rock somewhere high above them.

"They're drilling," Kelly said, shaken from his drugged stupor.

"They're after the stone!" Gregor cried. "Move!"

8:05 A.M.
PLUTO'S RIVER

Whitney screamed, sucked in water, and gagged. The hand let go of her ankle. Finnerty surfaced behind her.

"Thought I was toast!" the marshal sputtered. "I got a little air in a pocket back there. Saw your light underwater. Figured there had to be more air ahead and—"

He stopped suddenly, looking over Whitney's shoulder at Two-Elk's drowned body. "Oh, God, Lydia, no!" He smashed his hand against the rock overhead.

"My daughter! My husband!" Whitney said. "I heard them. They were just ahead of us."

"I heard them, too," Finnerty said, unable to take his eyes off his dead deputy. "Just before the whole passage flooded and—"

"I'm going after them," Whitney said. She turned and swam toward Two-Elk. She shuddered, then reached up and got the sensor from the dead deputy's neck and hung it around her own; then, almost as an afterthought, she took the machine pistol.

That startled the marshal out of his shock. "I better take that," Finnerty said.

"No," Whitney said. "This stays with me."

8:15 A.M.
SHAMAN'S CATACOMB
LABYRINTH CAVE

Gregor scrambled headlong down the secret passageway. Cricket and Tom followed, with Kelly urging them on with the shotgun. The cave walls were the color of tarnished brass. Designs had been worked into the stone with primitive chipping tools. The remnants of ancient bundled reed torches were strewn all along the floor. Three hundred feet down the shaft, the carvings petered out and the way hooked to the north. Here and there along the main route they passed small grottoes where skeletons lay amid ancient spears, bows and arrows, leather shields, and woven reed moccasins.

Tom knew he and Cricket were near the end of their long journey and therefore in more danger than at any other time since being taken hostage. But as a cave scientist, the extraordinary anthropological evidence was almost overwhelming to behold.

Then he smelled it. A chemical stench that gnawed at the lining of his nostrils. The fumes reminded him of a noxious smoke that had billowed down their street at home after an electrical transformer blew during a thunderstorm the summer before. Cricket cringed and sneezed, then pointed at the walls.

"Look Dad," she whispered.

"I see them," Tom said.

Where the baseboard would have been in a residential hallway, a ragged line of newly fissured rock showed. It appeared as if the layer of limestone that composed the upper part of the passage had been fractured during the earthquake and shoved eight inches to the west. And the brass cast that had made the upper portions of the passage so attractive was now marred by broad swatches of soot, as if the walls had been scorched.

With every step, the charring became more pronounced until the cave walls looked like the flanks of a recently erupted volcano. Tom reached out and ran his fingers along the rock and was flabbergasted at the pitted texture. Labyrinth Cave was composed almost entirely of limestone, a soft rock but this formation was as hard as volcanic stone, though it was unlike any basalt he'd ever seen or heard of before.

Gregor stopped and stared around at the igneous rock. He reached out and touched it too, appearing as befuddled as Tom.

"What's going on?" Kelly asked suspiciously. "This ain't gold."

"Don't worry," Gregor said. "There will be transmutation just ahead."

And indeed, within ten yards, the cave walls turned from pitted to riffled, like black ice formed under a sudden blast of arctic wind. Tom became aware of a powerful and resonant noise emanating from the cave ahead. The sound rose and fell in a wavelike pattern that put him in mind of the buzz of a barber's electric clippers, only magnified a hundred times or more.

"What the fuck is that?" Kelly demanded. For the first time, Tom heard uncertainty in the strangler's voice.

"The awesome rhythm of the universe at play, Kelly!" Gregor cried. "Hurry, we're almost there!"

The cave passage bent sharply right, and when Tom rounded the curve he was confronted with a painful strobe of light being generated from somewhere just ahead It was almost blinding after so many days of living in the soft columns cast by the headlamps, and all of them stopped for a moment, squinting letting their eyes adjust.

Then Gregor surged forward. Kelly began to move, too, but Tom held Cricket back. The quality of the light was unlike any he'd seen before and he was sure now that he had more to fear from Gregor's rock than from the mad scientist or the homicidal maniac who followed him. Twenty yards ahead, the passage dog-legged left and the light was most intense. Backlit by that dazzling, pulsing glare, the physicist's skin turned a sickly, gelatinous silver color. Kelly halted in his tracks, staring after Gregor as if seeing his hair-less, waxen skin and disease-ravaged body for the first time.

"Come on, Kelly," Gregor exhorted. "See what a poor white-trash boy from the backwoods of Kentucky discovered. Transmuter of elements. Harness of the creative force of the universe. The philosophers' stone!"

"It's running in there?" Kelly asked.

"Of course. I told you it would be."

Kelly shook his head. "I ain't going in there with it running."

"It won't hurt you!" Gregor cried. "Look at me!"

"I am looking at you," Kelly growled. "And I ain't going in there with it running."

"I need help to deactivate it," Gregor insisted.

"Take Burke," Kelly said. "I'll stay with the girl watch our backs."

Gregor raised his pistol toward Tom. "Let's go."

"No, I won't leave my daughter with him," Tom said.

"I don't need you anymore," Gregor said coldly. "If you and your daughter want to die now, so be it."

Tom looked from Gregor to Kelly to Cricket. "Stay here," he said.

"No, Dad," she whispered. "Not with him."

"I promise you, I'll be back," he said.

"Not with him, Daddy, please."

"We've got no choice."

Kelly grabbed Cricket by the upper arm and held her while Gregor disappeared around the corner. Tom held Cricket's gaze, sickened by the tears that gushed down her face, then he followed. He rounded the bend in the passage and immediately threw up his arm to shield his eyes from the brilliant throbbing light.

He stood at the entrance to a cavern perhaps twenty-five feet high, thirty yards wide, and again as long. Tom's first impressions were of the walls, the ceiling and the floor, how they all appeared to be composed of a slaglike metal that had been seared to a coarse, stygian pigment Three-quarters of the way across the cavern, a jagged wound ten inches wide rent the floor from side to side. The gash was so black it seemed capable of sucking light into itself. And it stank. The crack was the source of those caustic electrical fumes, now so strong and rank that Tom felt his throat begin to close and his stomach turn over.

Close to the gash in the floor, moon rock 66095 sat atop what appeared to have been some sort of burnished altar. A singed and blistered rubberized box rested at the base of the blackened pedestal. Heavily insulated cables ran out of the case to a geodesic cobweb of wires that encircled the stone. Within the cobweb, the visual effect was similar to pictures Tom had seen of total eclipses of the sun; the center of the rock appeared dark and solid, but there was a thin, electric-blue corona of light hovering just above the stone's many concave planes and extrusions. Spiking off the stone's surface were flares of energy like the flames of welders' torches gone amok. Each whipsaw was accompanied by that resonant buzzing that filled the cavern. The longer Tom stood there, the more he became convinced that the stone had to be throwing some exotic form of radiation. He had to get out of there.

Then he noticed that Gregor was advancing toward the stone, removing his helmet. A look of crazed ecstasy came over the scientist's face. He got within five feet of the flaring rock and stopped just outside the reach of the dancing fingers of energy. For Tom it was like looking at an X-ray picture; in the presence of the light, Gregor's skin turned an opaque aluminum, and Tom swore he could see the shades of his bones and the suggestion of his arteries and veins. Gregor's heart seemed to pump in time with the vibrations coming off the rock His blood moved through his capillaries like shadows on a tormented sea.

Gregor turned toward Tom and exulted, "It was worth every step getting here, wasn't it? I've done it Transmutation on a massive scale. Look at this place! Look at me! From the time of the great pharaohs, the adepts believed that the ultimate purpose of the stone was becoming one with the universe. You're my witness, Burke. Robert Gregor is consumed and reborn in fire, whole with the mystery at last!"

Feverish with accomplishment feeding on the mysterious energy pulsing off the stone and whatever bizarre theories he'd developed to explain the workings of moon rock 66095, Gregor struck Tom as suddenly vulnerable.

"All there is is burnt rock here," he snorted. "And you look like you just walked in from Nagasaki. Kelly will break your neck when he sees this."

"Those are transmuted ores!" Gregor cried furiously, waving his pistol at Tom. "I am a transmuted man! The scientific significance of this is overwhelming. The world will roar its applause!"

"Roar with laughter is more like it," Tom shot back. "All you created is black rock and a body savaged by radiation sickness. You failed, Gregor. You are a failure."

"Silence!" Gregor screamed, then pointed at the flaring stone. "They'll remember me like Newton. Like Galileo. Like Bohr!"

Tom took a careful step toward the physicist, his peripheral attention on the pistol in Gregor's right hand. "No one will remember you, Gregor. No one. They'll forget you, like they forgot your . . ." He remembered something Cricket had told him the night before, something about what Gregor had said as she'd brought him down the rope in Dante's Tubes. "They'll forget you like they forgot your mother, Gregor. In the history books, you'll just be an overeducated trailer-trash boy who went nuts and killed his supervisor. A failure like your mother. Buried in a pauper's grave."

Gregor began to quiver so hard with rage that Tom believed he was no longer aware of his surroundings. He saw his chance and rushed the physicist, his body bent low. He tackled Gregor at the knees and together they crashed to the floor of the cave. Gregor's pistol spun across the floor.

Tom swung his fist overhand, punching Gregor twice high in the ribs; then he closed his hands around Gregor's throat. The scientist writhed and struggled. Tom dug his fingers into the impossibly strong muscles of his neck. For a moment, he believed that he had him that he felt the life force beginning to drain out of this ravaged thing that used to be a man. Then there was an explosion in Gregor's eyes, as startling as the energy coming off the stone; he grinned evilly, then whipped his head left and bit Tom on the wrist. His teeth reached bone

Tom howled and released his hold. Gregor clubbed Tom's face with the butt of his fist. White spots flashed through Tom's brain and he felt himself fall to his side. There was a moment of confusion, punctuated by heated pain and the awareness that his wrist was gushing blood. Then his vision cleared. Tom rolled over and came up on his knees. Gregor sat with his back to the altar below the flaring rock, aiming the pistol at Tom, an expression of pure malice on his face.

"Everyone will remember me," Gregor said. "No one will ever remember you."

8:30 A.M.
VIRGIL ENTRANCE
LABYRINTH CAVE

On the surface, the wind blew to a gale, driving the rain in horizontal lines across the top of the ridge. The sky had turned an iron gray splotched with dark purple. Booming claps of thunder all but drowned out the wailing of the shaft-boring rig. Lightning struck less than a half mile to the west, above the narrow valley between Tower and Walker Ridges.

"Those strikes are getting damn close!" Angelis yelled.

"We better take cover!" Boulter screamed back.

Swain, meanwhile, was looking in the direction of the gaping hole the boring rig had augered into the hillside. White dust billowed and plumed from the shaft, mixed with the rain, and fell like wet chalk. A lightning bolt razored down from the sky and struck the ridge three hundred yards above the hole. At that the physicist panicked. If what Chester had hypothesized about the stone and lightning was true—?

"Uncle Jeff," Chester yelled. "Those men!"

"I know!" Swain cried, turning and running at Major General Hayes. "You've got to get those workers out of that hole! They're in great danger."

"Can't do that," the general replied. "We've got to get to that stone without delay."

"If one of these bolts grounds into the cave and reaches the rock it could be amplified and accelerated," Swain insisted. "They could all be killed. Everyone on this mountain could be killed."

"You know this for sure?"

"No, but… "

"I have my orders, Doctor."

"I'm holding you responsible for those men's lives, General!" Swain bellowed. "Too many people have died going after this rock!"

Hayes shook his head. "Leave if you wish, Dr. Swain. But we're going into that mountain the fastest way we can."

8:32 A.M.
SHAMAN'S CATACOMB
LABYRINTH CAVE

A gunshot rang out over the buzzing roar emanating from the cave ahead.

Cricket kicked Kelly in the shin, wrenched free of his grasp, and hobbled as fast as she could down the tunnel toward the pulsing metallic light.

"You fucking bitch, get back here," Kelly bellowed. "I've had it with you!"

Cricket rounded the bend in the passage and halted at the sight of the stone and the silhouette of Gregor standing over the prone figure of her father. Gregor yanked the trigger of the pistol over and over again, infuriated beyond reason by the dull clicking noise the gun made. He was out of bullets.

"Daddy!" Cricket screamed again and raced to her father's side. Blood and chips of bone oozed from a gaping wound above Tom's right elbow.

"Hey, sweetheart," he said weakly, trying to rise.

"Shoot him, Kelly!" Gregor barked. "Shoot them both!"

But Kelly was looking wildly from the flaring stone to the walls of the cavern. "There's no gold," he mumbled. "There's no nothing."

"Give me that gun!" Gregor yelled, coming at Kelly.

Kelly swung the shotgun around and jabbed the muzzle into the physicist's throat, backing him away from Tom and Cricket. "I'm gonna shoot you,

you fuck, you lousy lunatic fuck. There's no gold in here!"

"Who cares about gold?" Gregor croaked. "It's the science!"

"I don't give a rat's ass about the science." Kelly was now pressing Gregor against the cave wall. "I risked my life for—"

The convict flipped off the safety on the pump-action and began to squeeze the trigger. Cricket watched Gregor stare down the gun barrel in complete disbelief, then his eyes darted left, passed, returned, and locked.

"There!" he crowed. "In the cracks, Kelly. It's there!"

The strangler hesitated at the trigger, then aimed his headlamp along Gregor's line of sight.

Cricket looked, too. So did her father. And now they all saw for the first time that the grotto was not completely blackened, but webbed with minute veins of a hundred different alloys. Some had the consistency and patina of hammered silver. Others were liquid, reflective, almost like mercury. But every few feet or so, there were set in the slag intricate capillaries of a metal so beautiful that it took Cricket's breath away. Richer than opal, paler than gold, more lustrous than platinum, it was an ore that looked as if it had been shot through with moonlight.

Kelly clicked the safety back on and drew back the shotgun's muzzle from Gregor's throat. He stepped to the wall and ran his fingers with unbridled desire over the alluring veins of the precious metal.

"You see?" Gregor said, rubbing his throat. "I told you. Rarer than gold. More valuable than gold. Like nothing ever seen before on Earth."

"It's true," Kelly whispered in rapture. Then he spun around, homicidal again. "But what good does this do me? You'd have to mine it. It would take months."

"The stone, you fool!" Gregor replied through gritted teeth. "Don't you see? This was only my first experiment with large-scale transmutation, and look at the results! Look at it! Help me get the stone out of here. We can take it far away. We can do it again. We can turn whole rooms into that lovely metal. We'll be the richest, most powerful men in the world!"

Kelly's attention jumped to moon rock 66095, then to the ore in the blackened wall, then back to Gregor. He eased the shotgun to his side. "They're drilling above us," he said. "They got to be guarding all the entrances, too."

"Doesn't m-m-matter," Gregor said, gesturing to the far side of the grotto and the beginnings of a crawlway that was as scorched as the crack in the floor. "My grandfather said there was another way out of the cave, the way the Shawnee believed the souls of the dead left. We'll escape this cave with the stone and go overland from there."

Gregor went by Cricket and her dad to the rubberized box at the altar's base and opened it to reveal a half dozen wet-cell batteries. He reached past them and brought out a handheld computer linked between the batteries and the coils of wire that surrounded the stone. He began punching in a series of codes on the keypad.

"What about them?" Kelly asked.

Gregor looked over his shoulder and shrugged. "You've suffered enough at their hands. They're yours."

Kelly turned the shotgun toward Cricket. Then he seemed to think better of it. He set the gun down, reached into his pack, drew out a pocket knife, and snapped it open. "I want this to hurt."

"Please!" Cricket said, shielding her father. "You've got your stone. Let us go!"

Kelly scowled and advanced toward them. "I still got dung in my pants, you little cunt. Your time has come."

"*Not before yours does, bastard!*" Whitney yelled.

Kelly twisted to find Whitney and Finnerty crouched in the archway of the grotto, each with a machine pistol trained directly on him.

"U.S. marshal," Finnerty barked. "Drop the knife. Move away from the girl."

"Mommy!" Cricket cried.

"Whit!" her dad gasped.

"I've come to take you both home," Whitney said.

"Drop it Kelly," Finnerty said, easing into the room. "Do it now. And you, Dr. Gregor, get away from that box."

Cricket saw Kelly's eyes narrow to slits, then he let his arm down and his hand relax. The knife dangled at his fingertips. Gregor took a step from the box toward the stone. For a split second, Finnerty's attention left Kelly for Gregor. That was all it took.

Kelly flicked his wrist and dived. The blade rotated through the air and buried itself beneath the marshal's left clavicle with the sound of a pillow being plumped. Finnerty grunted and spiraled down, losing control of the machine pistol just before he crashed to the cave floor. The gun twirled crazily through the air, bounced once, then slid to the edge of the dark crack in the cavern floor.

Cricket saw it, but was frozen by the events. Kelly rolled toward the shotgun.

"Shoot him!" Finnerty yelled at her mother.

Whitney stuck the automatic weapon out in front of her, her arm shaking as if she were about to bat at a hornet's nest with a broom handle. She closed her eyes and jerked the trigger. A long staccato burst of deafening explosions echoed through the chamber and the gun bucked under repeated recoil. The spray of .9 mm rounds tore through Kelly's torso just as he reached the shotgun. It raked along the floor toward Gregor. The physicist threw himself backward, but the barrage of bullets peppered the black box housing the power pack and controls of the electromagnetic source charging moon rock 66095.

Kelly convulsed at the bullet impacts, then sprawled on his side. The strangler peered down, bewildered by the multiple wounds in his chest and abdomen. He brought up his index finger and touched one. He looked right at Cricket as if expecting understanding. "It burns," he said. "Never expected fire."

Bright frothy blood bubbled up at Kelly's lips and choked off whatever else he had to say. His skin blued. His eyes went wide, then dulled, and he slumped.

Cricket hobbled toward her mom and dad. Whitney dropped the gun and embraced them both. "Thank God," she sobbed. "You're both alive. Both alive."

"Love you, Whit," Tom said. "Nothing more important than you. Ever."

Cricket started to cry, thinking it was all over. Then she saw Gregor over her mother's shoulder. Twenty feet away, the pale scientist rocked back and forth on his haunches, staring at the laptop computer, which had been gouged by the bullets. Sparks flew from the keyboard. The screen flashed a gibberish of numbers and codes. Fierce arcs of electricity leaped within the cobweb of wires surrounding the stone. The buzzing tone emanating from the moon rock changed, became shriller, more erratic. "You've ruined it!" he moaned. "My work! My life! Ruined!"

"Get him away from it," Finnerty gasped. "Swain said the stone could destabilize if it wasn't deactivated correctly."

The marshal had gotten himself up into a sitting position. The knife was embedded to the hilt in his chest so tight that it acted as a plug preventing the blood from gushing forth. Gregor heard Finnerty and looked around as if he were waking from a terrible dream. Then, out of the corner of his eye, he saw the marshal's machine pistol lying there on the other side of the cavern and went for it on his hands and knees, screaming, "I'll kill you all!"

"The gun, Mom!" Cricket yelled.

Whitney tore herself free of their embrace and scrambled toward the machine pistol, too. Out of the corner of her eye, Cricket caught a moving shadow in the entrance to the cavern. The shadow became a blur and Billy Lyons charged in like a wounded bull, soaking wet, his face a sculpture of violent intent. Gregor reached for the gun. Lyons rammed a knee into the scientist's stomach and knocked him flat. The guard snatched up the machine pistol, dropped, and rolled out into the sniper's prone position, the barrel of his weapon swinging among them all. "No one moves, no one dies!"

8:40 A.M.
VIRGIL ENTRANCE
LABYRINTH CAVE

High over tower ridge, a massive lightning strike erupted, a taproot of energy that hurtled toward the earth in a single stout trunk that grew limbs and then lesser branches, all of it curling toward the dome of the mountain like a willow tree canting in a storm. The canopy of electricity encircled the ridge for one terrifying instant that was wedded to a single clap of thunder as loud and destructive as an aerial bombardment.

The concussion hurled Swain, Chester, Boulter, Angelis, and Major General Hayes off their feet. Then the entire ridge began to fluctuate beneath them.

A two-hundred-foot chunk sheared off the mountainside like a slab of windblown snow avalanching. The landslide rumbled downhill, throwing mature oaks like javelins, flipping tanks and armored personnel carriers like they were toys.

Inside the tunnel the boring machine had dug, the walls disintegrated, crushing the massive drilling head as if it were aluminum foil. The diesel engine driving the borer ruptured, then exploded in a mushrooming ball of orange and scarlet flame.

8:37 A.M.
SHAMAN'S CATACOMB
LABYRINTH CAVE

"Hands up, lady," Lyons shouted at Whitney.

She hesitated, then raised her hands. "Please," she pleaded. "No more."

Lyons ignored her and pointed the muzzle of his weapon at Finnerty. "Identify yourself!"

"Damian Finnerty. U.S. marshal for eastern Kentucky."

Lyons relaxed a little. "Finnerty," he said. "They figured you'd be the one called."

"Who figured?" Finnerty grunted in confusion.

Lyons got to his knees and then to his feet. "President, his national security adviser, chairman of the Joint Chiefs of Staff. I'm a Marine major, special ops. Been watching Gregor ever since he was put in Eddyville."

"I don't buy it," Finnerty said. "You killed three guards."

Lyons shook his head. "None of those men are dead. It was staged. FBI got them out of there before you could examine the scene, am I right? The government was hoping Gregor would go for the stone if he had the chance, and he did." He gestured at the rock and smiled. "Now I'm returning this puppy to its rightful owner. The United States of America."

Whitney looked at him incredulously, angrier than she'd been in her entire life, then her hands dropped and curled into fists. "You *let them* escape! You bastard! You let Andy Swearingen be killed? You let my husband get shot, my daughter be tortured?"

At that instant, the gigantic lightning bolt encased the ridge above them.

From the blackened archway on the far side of the grotto, from the passageway the shamans' souls were said to use to leave the chamber, came a rushing, harmonic blast. The air in the archway rippled and blurred like wind over a desert floor.

The mirage pulsed forward, striking Lyons from behind and throwing him onto his face. It picked Whitney up and pitched her to her side. Finnerty was pounded against the cave wall, where he slumped to one side. Tom was squished into the floor.

The invisible force punched Cricket in the chest. She reeled backward and landed behind a large boulder. She reached up and held on to the boulder as a sailor might a mast in a gale. The squalling buzz emanating from the stone became so mighty it threatened to burst her eardrums. She lifted her head and felt a hurricane's wind buffet her cheeks. On the stone altar, she saw the moon rock's surface turn translucent and then molten and fiery as if it were filled with the sun's power.

"Its gonna blow!" Tom screamed at her. "Get down!"

Cricket saw her mother curl herself down into a ball and cover her head. But Cricket could not turn away. She squinted in awe as spinning electrical storms seemed to appear within the plasma inside the rock. One storm curled itself into a backward S that burst up out of the stone, turning into a brilliant coil of blue and yellow accelerated and amplified energy that arced and then whipped down toward the crack in the floor.

The crack and the floor around it instantaneously disintegrated into millions of glowing particles—fluorescent greens and blues and reds—all colliding and caroming off one another in complete and total chaos, all except for the thin spiral ones the golden color of a full moon at night. Those particles seemed to drill through the others, busting them apart.

Lyons tried to get up, to get to the rock. But the shaking inside the cavern became almost inconceivably violent. Chunks of rock burst from the ceiling. A fist-sized piece of debris struck his jaw, shattering it and knocking him out cold. A bigger chunk landed on top of Kelly's body, crushing it.

One last tremendous oscillation pulsed through the cavern, breaking moon rock 66095 free of the geodesic wire dome that encapsulated it. The stone tumbled across the altar, fell, and bounced across the floor.

The oscillations and the buzzing died. The fluorescent grains of matter around the chasm began to gather like bees swarming their queen, fusing together into atoms that in turn clustered into molecules that arranged themselves in slowing cooling ever-darkening patterns until, within a matter of moments, the walls of the crack in the floor had returned to that black and stinking abrasive slag. The gash had widened to nearly five feet across.

The stone landed next to her mom, who still held her hands over her head. Cricket could see the rock; it was no longer fiery and translucent, but slowly fading to a dull and unremarkable gray. Her mother raised her head and stared at it, perplexed, this thing from another celestial body, this simple object that channeled energy in a way never before seen by man, this mystery that had threatened to destroy their family, their place in the world, forever.

"Gun, Whitney," Finnerty croaked. "Forget the stone. Get your gun."

But Whitney kept staring at the rock and now she reached for it. Tom got up on one elbow. "Whitney, no! Don't touch it," he said.

"Get away from the stone!" Gregor bawled. "It's mine!"

Whitney looked up to see the materials scientist sprinting at her in an insane rage. Tom lashed out his foot, trying to trip him, but Gregor nimbly jumped it, and made for Whitney. "I'll kill you all, just like I killed MacPherson," he seethed.

"Mom, get away," Cricket screamed.

But Whitney grabbed the rock. Gregor lunged and got hold of the stone at the same time. Whitney held tight with both hands and they fought for it, battling in the black dust and the electrical smoke that choked the grotto. For an instant Cricket saw the stone sliding from Gregor's grasp and her mother turning her hips, trying to wrench it completely free of his fingers.

"Never!" Gregor screeched.

He rocked his head back and smashed it down against her mom's face. She grunted in agony, let go of the rock and fell forward, blood gushing from her nose and mouth. Gregor let loose a primal wail of triumph and brandished the stone high over his head.

Cricket flashed on the way Gregor had struck Lyons back there on the No Return River. He was going to kill her mother with it. That triggered some energy source deep inside her, an energy source more powerful and profound than any she'd ever felt before. It coursed through and electrified every cell in her body. At the same time, she heard that voice, that woman's voice that was her own, telling her to save her mom, that after everything that had happened, Whitney could not die this way. She surged upward, no pain in her knee now, and flashed across the grotto.

"Gregor!" Cricket screamed.

The scientist turned from her mother to face Cricket, still brandishing the rock.

"Cricket! No!" she heard her father yell.

But Cricket was no longer the naïve young teenager who had entered the cave nearly four days before. She was an entirely different person, consumed and driven by the mysterious energy that welled, accelerated, and now amplified inside her. She drove her shoulder square into Gregor's chest.

At impact, it was as if a shock wave of something primordial fluxed through Cricket; she felt as if she were coming apart into a whirling assemblage of particles that, together with Gregor, tottered for a beat on the brink of the black chasm that rent the cavern. Then they tipped, separated, and plunged over into darkness.

Surfacing

JUNE 19, 2007
11:46 A.M.
ICU
COLUMBIA SOUTHWEST HOSPITAL
LOUISVILLE, KENTUCKY

"Let me see boulter," Finnerty rasped. "Just for a minute."

"Absolutely not," his wife replied. "You're six hours out of surgery for a collapsed lung and have had a nasty dose of some exotic radiation."

The U.S. marshal for eastern Kentucky lay in a bed surrounded by beeping monitors. IV tubes fed into both arms. His skin was gray, his breathing labored, but he smiled. "Hey, you never know, babe: maybe it'll help my sperm count."

Natalie smiled in spite of herself. "You've got a one-track mind, you know that?"

"Just about you," he said. "Nat?"

"Yes, Damian?"

"I had a lot of time to think underground. What do you think about adopting?"

Tears welled in her eyes as she reached out to hold her husband's hand. "Why don't we get you better before we think about that, okay?"

"Okay," the marshal said, then he closed his eyes and drifted off again.

When Finnerty awoke, he was surprised to find Captain Boulter sitting by his bedside. "Natalie let you in?"

"Took a lot of arm twisting," the trooper said.

"Never works for me," Finnerty said, shifting uncomfortably. "You'll have to give me lessons."

"How you feeling?"

"Like there's a hot poker in my chest, but the doctors said they got the lung closed up tight," the marshal replied. He glanced over Boulter's shoulder at his wife standing in the doorway with her arms crossed. The commandant won't tell me anything about the others."

Natalie glared at him. "And he's not going to until you're better."

"Ignore that woman behind the curtain," Finnerty said. "Where are the Burkes? And the Marine, Lyons? I passed out in the cave after… "

"Tom Burke came out of surgery about the same time you did," Boulter said. "He lost the arm. His wife's heavily sedated and being treated for quark-decay exposure. Lyons was flown out of here by military helicopter. I have no idea where he is."

Finnerty licked his lips. "And Gregor? The girl? The stone?"

Boulter's expression tightened. "Still looking."

2:20 P.M.
TOWER RIDGE
LABYRINTH CAVE

Helen Greidel stood before armed sentries guarding the makeshift road up Tower Ridge. The landslide rubble was visible behind her. She held her hand to her earpiece, then nodded and looked into the camera.

"In the aftermath of a powerful and unprecedented second earthquake here in eastern Kentucky, soldiers are still searching the depths of Labyrinth Cave for survivors," she began. "Eight people, including six members of the Army Corps of Engineers who were operating a tunnel-boring machine when the quake hit, are known dead. Two people remain missing—Robert Gregor, one of the inmates who escaped and took refuge inside the cave, and Alexandra 'Cricket' Burke, daughter of Artemis Project leader Tom Burke and his wife, Whitney. They and two others were pulled from the ground late yesterday after a second boring machine was flown into the site by helicopter.

"Beyond basic information about the rescues, neither NASA nor the U.S. Army is granting interviews," Greidel went on. "That and the fact that security remains wartime tight here has raised serious questions about what really went on here not only within the media but among members of Congress, who are already calling for hearings. In other developments ... "

Deep inside Tower Ridge, Jeffrey Swain waded south along Pluto's River, which had receded over the past thirty-two hours to almost knee level. The physicist was clad in a white radiation suit. Five soldiers in similar outfits trailed behind him and Chester. Swain could see through the visor of Chester's helmet. His chunky nephew was gushing sweat and looking miserable as he watched the screen of the sensor he held before him like a shield.

"Anything yet?" Swain asked.

Chester stopped and held out the sensor for the physicist to see. "Nothing even approaching the signature," he said.

Indeed, the golden infinity symbol lay inert in its sea of deep turquoise. The bell curve of colors that measured the electromagnetic spectrum on the other screen was relatively flat. Only one bar—the one that noted quark decay—fluctuated at all.

"You ask me, Uncle Jeff, that stone's history," Chester said.

"We're not giving up," Swain replied. "That rock's in here somewhere and we're going to find it. We have to find it or this was all for nothing. Have you forgotten that transmuted cavern above us? I'm betting those metals in the walls up there are elements we've never seen before!"

Swain and his nephew had been in and out of Tower Ridge twice to examine the transmuted ores inside the Shaman's Catacomb and to search for the stone. On this third trip, Hayes's soldiers had brought collapsible cable ladders and they'd all climbed the sixty feet down through the gash in the floor from Shaman's Catacomb into this passage. They'd been working their way north, following the downstream course of the subterranean riverbed for nearly an hour.

"I know how you feel, Uncle Jeff," Chester replied. "So close, yet so far."

"That's not it at all," the physicist snapped, suddenly very agitated. "Carson MacPherson could be an asshole, but he was my colleague and research partner for more than twenty years. He lost his life over that stone. Ten other people died because of that rock. A girl not much younger than you died because of that rock."

Chester stopped and peered through his visor at his uncle. "That all that's bugging you?"

"No," Swain admitted. "I keep telling myself that I'm here because of the science, Chester. But I'm not. The truth is that I'm here because our government had an object that might have solved all our energy problems and then lost it. I'm here because of commerce and economic vitality, not science."

The physicist felt himself working up into a frenzy and he went on without a moment's pause. "Has that woman, Greidel, managed to broadcast that story to the world? No. Why? Because the government doesn't want the media to know that it had a rock that amplified energy, changed elements, and then disappeared. All they care about is saving face, recovering that stone, and then getting to the moon so they can find more. And I'm being used in the whole thing. Jeffrey Swain, the great hero who discovered room-temperature superconductivity. The hero who's a farce is more like it."

He threw up his hands in disgust.

"Why are we helping them, then?" Chester asked in a voice low enough that the soldiers behind them could not hear. "Why don't we just leave and go home?"

"I don't know," the physicist replied. "Maybe I just need to see the thing that cost Carson and all those other people their lives. Maybe by seeing it, I'll get some sense of closure."

"You'll be okay," Chester said as he patted his uncle on the arm.

Swain nodded sadly and watched as his nephew turned and went forward under a low rock vault. He saw the teenager come to a quick stop and jut his head forward at the sensor. "I think we've got something," Chester said, holding out the device. The infinity symbol had begun to fluctuate ever so slightly.

Together the physicist and his nephew began to slosh through the water, casting their lights about the cavern ahead.

"It's here, Uncle Jeff," Chester said. "It's got to be—"

He stopped in midsentence, shining his headlamp among the rocks along the banks of the underground river. Swain leveled his headlamp that way, too, and his breath caught in his throat. Cricket lay there on her side, her cave pack still cinched tight around her shoulders and waist, her right leg splayed away below her hip at an unnatural angle. Gregor lay just beyond her.

Chester ran in front of Swain, dropping the sensor into the mud. Swain raced after him, calling over his shoulder to the soldiers, "It's them! The girl! Gregor! Come quick!"

Within seconds, one of the soldiers, a medic, was listening to Gregor's chest. "This one's gone." He turned to Cricket, leaned over her, then popped upright. "She's alive, but just barely! We got to get her out of here, now!"

The medic immediately applied emergency heat packs to her body, then wrapped her in a Teflon blanket. Three of the soldiers fashioned a litter and within minutes were rushing the girl back toward the gash in the ceiling that led back up to the Shaman's Catacomb. Two soldiers remained behind with Swain and Chester, all of them looking at the busted, ruined thing that had once been Robert Gregor.

"What a waste," Swain said, feeling a combination of hollowness and awe. "What a terrible waste of talent and promise. He could have changed the world, you know."

He turned to Chester. "Is it here? The stone?"

The physicist's nephew looked all around, then finally found the sensor lying in the mud. Chester picked it up. The infinity symbol had returned to its inert state. "It's not registering anymore, Uncle Jeff," he said. "Must have been a false reading."

Swain looked back in the direction in which the soldiers had taken Cricket. "Yeah," he said. "False reading."

JUNE 18, 2008
9:30 P.M.
14 VALLEY LANE
TARRINGTON, KENTUCKY

"And we'll pick up where we left off tomorrow night," Whitney said, closing the cover of the novel.

"Can't we read just one more page?" Cricket pleaded. She was curled about her pillow, wearing her favorite ratty blue nightgown. "I feel sorry for her and Duane."

"It's getting late, and you said you wanted to go watch the four-hundred championship tomorrow."

"I'm gonna be in the finals next year," Cricket boasted. "No matter what it takes."

Whitney smiled at her daughter's confidence. "How's it feeling?"

Cricket lifted her leg to show fading red scars that ran from her ankle to mid-shin and again from her knee to mid-thigh She rotated her foot, then bent her knee and straightened it. "Doctor says I'll be good enough to sprint in about a month."

Whitney got up from the side of the bed, marked the page, and set the book, Jim Harrison's *Dalva,* on the shelf next to one of Cricket's track-and-field trophies. Whitney had read the novel—the story of a woman who endures tragedy, loses her way, then ultimately refunds herself through family—during her stay in the hospital and thought that Cricket, too, might learn from the story.

She knew it was a strange thing for a mother to be reading aloud to her fifteen-year-old daughter, but it was something they had done every night since their ordeal in Labyrinth Cave had ended exactly one year ago. Reading at bedtime was something Whitney's mother had always done with her, right up until a week before she died; and reading to Cricket made Whitney feel as if she were a link in a long invisible chain stretching backward and forward through time and events, giving structure and coherence to her life. She also believed that the time she and Cricket spent reading and talking before lights-out was like layer upon layer of cement being added to the foundation of a relationship that had been badly neglected in the thirteen months following Jeannie Yung's death.

Whitney leaned down, tucked the sheet under Cricket's chin, and kissed her daughter on the cheek. "See you in the morning," she said. "Love you."

"Love you too, Mom."

Whitney paused at the door, looking back at her daughter. Cricket seemed so much a woman these days that it made her ache inside. But seeing her like this, tucked under the sheets, that strand of strawberry-blond hair hanging in her eyes, Cricket could have been three years old and lying in a field of daisies.

Whitney wandered back down the stairs past a framed photograph of her with Jeannie Yung. She thought how life is sometimes like a cave, a tortured, convoluted succession of byways that takes you down into darker places than can ever be imagined; a nether region where you are forced to search the shadows to find out what you hold real and true; a series of difficult passages to be negotiated with a faith in something greater than yourself so you might once again emerge into sunlight.

She had at last come to terms with her grief and guilt over Jeannie's death. But before she slept each evening she thanked her dear departed friend for watching over her family during their long nightmare and recovery.

Like everyone who had been in the Shaman's Catacomb, Whitney had been exposed to a brief but intense dose of quark decay and suffered a short sickness. She was still being monitored by government doctors, but these days she was the picture of health, physically and mentally. She had notified the university that she intended to take a temporary leave of absence from her teaching position so she could spend more time with Cricket. Her baby would not be at home much longer and Whitney wanted to spend as much time with her as possible.

Whitney lingered by the photograph of Jeannie, then crossed the family room toward Tom, who was pecking away at the computer keyboard. On the desk next to him was a card they'd received the day before from Damian and Natalie Finnerty announcing the birth of their baby daughter, whom they had named Lydia in Two-Elk's memory.

Whitney smiled, threw her arms around Tom's neck, and kissed him on the cheek "How's it going?" she asked.

"Gets easier every day," he replied, leaning back in the chair and nuzzling her.

Whitney kissed him on the cheek again and walked into the kitchen.

Tom sat there listening to his wife bustle in the cabinets and the refrigerator, musing as he often did these days about the aftermath of all that had occurred inside Labyrinth Cave.

In the months following Cricket's rescue, team after team of government researchers under the direction of Dr. Jeffrey Swain had secretly entered Tower Ridge. All of them were dumbfounded by the spectacular alloys imbedded in the slaglike walls of the Shaman's Catacomb. As Swain had predicted, that lustrous metal the one that looked like moonlight had been shot through it, was later shown to be a composite of three previously unknown elements with atomic weights greater than any measured before on Earth.

An autopsy of Robert Gregor's body revealed that he had died of massive blunt force trauma brought on by the fall. The coroner noted bizarre tumor growths in his organs, specifically his heart, kidneys, and liver. She also found dense concentrations of exotic heavy metals in Gregor's spine and brain, which she theorized had upset his chemical balance and contributed to his madness.

After much soul searching Swain at last defied the government's wish to keep the stone secret and went public in an exclusive interview with Helen Greidel. He told the complete and true story surrounding the death of Carson MacPherson and the discovery of room-temperature superconductors. It was time, he said, for him to come clean, give credit where it lay, and to inform the nation of the entire reason why the government was spending so much money to return to the moon.

In the wake of Swain's admissions, Robert Gregor, ironically, got his wish: He would be remembered for all time as the discoverer of room-temperature superconductors, quark decay, and full-scale transmutation. In its coverage, *Time* magazine characterized him as "part-Einstein, part-Frankenstein, a brilliant, troubled and yet tragic figure who embodied the best and worst of modern scientific research."

Congress convened hearings in October. The Burkes, Jeffrey Swain, Chester Norton, Jim Angelis, Mark Boulter, and Damian Finnerty were all called to testify. During two weeks of televised hearings that electrified the nation, the entire story came out.

The media star of the entire event turned out to be Major William S. Lyons, who caused an uproar appearing before the committee in the full-dress blue uniform of a United States Marine officer, complete with sword and white gloves. Lyons revealed that he was put in the Eddyville prison to watch over Gregor at the request of the President and under the direction of the chairman of the Joint Chiefs of Staff, both of whom considered the recovery of moon rock 66095 vital to the future of American technological and economic security.

Lyons explained that the guards—Wilcox, Jarrett, and Andrews—had all been given substantial bribes to participate in the staged escape. All three men had been wearing bulletproof vests and carrying fake blood capsules in their mouths when Lyons appeared to shoot them. The sheriff who "found" the bodies was also in on the charade.

At the climax of the hearings, Lyons coolly defended his actions and that of the executive branch against a barrage of intense cross-examinations regarding the intentional release of violent state prisoners, the deaths of LaValle Cox and Andy Swearingen, and his failure on many occasions to fully protect the Burkes.

"My orders were to get back the stone," Lyons testified. "Civilian casualties were expected from the outset. Where I could, I acted to help the Burkes. But keeping them safe, frankly, was not my mission."

"Did you get the stone?" the distinguished senator from Vermont asked snidely.

Lyons took a deep breath, then shook his head. "No, Senator, I failed. It's something I'll have to live with the rest of my life."

Indeed, all the testimony taken at the congressional hearings came down to one thing—even after tens of thousands of man-hours spent searching the lower reaches of Tower Ridge, moon rock 66095 had not been recovered.

The Artemis Project stalled during the investigations, but news reports the evening before indicated that despite all that had happened, Congress recognized the need to return to the moon to mine superconducting ores on the Descartes Highlands. And to perhaps find a second moon rock that behaved in the extraordinary fashion of 66095.

Tom looked down at the prosthesis that jutted out the sleeve of his shirt. Since the amputation, he had not been back inside Labyrinth Cave, or any cave whatsoever. Except for trips to Washington, D.C., to testify and to lobby in favor of establishing the nine limestone ridges near Hermes, Kentucky, as a national park he had spent the year in physical rehab. When he wasn't learning to use his new arm, he stayed at home with Whitney and Cricket.

In many ways, however, Tom thought, the past year had been the best of his marriage, and indeed of his entire life. Almost every morning since surviving the ordeal, he had taken to waking early, lying in bed next to Whitney, and studying the features of her face the way he once so passionately studied the geology of ridges. How, he always asked himself, had he ever stopped seeing her as the light that lit his way through the darkness?

And every morning Tom would rise silently and pad down the hall to ease open Cricket's door and see her sleeping there in the moonlight. Watching her like that consistently reinforced in him a belief in the possibilities of tomorrow and his hard-learned conviction that emotional connection was ultimately of more significance than any scientific discovery.

Whitney came back into the room carrying two glasses of chilled white wine. She grinned at her husband slyly and said, "You know, I can think of something much more interesting than dwelling in the past…something involving a slinky black negligee I bought for your viewing pleasure a long, long time ago."

Tom's eyebrow shot up. "Is that right?"

"Come upstairs, say good night to Cricket, and then I'll show you," she teased.

Together they climbed the stairs. Whitney tickled her husband in the ribs, then slipped into their bedroom. Tom went down the hall and stuck his head in Cricket's open doorway. "You should turn off the lights now, sweetheart. It's getting late."

Cricket held out her arms and smiled impishly at him. Tom laughed. "Still know how to twist your old man around your little finger, don't you?"

"Uh-huh," Cricket said Tom gave her a hug and kissed her on the forehead.

"Dad?"

"Yes, honey."

"You think they'll ever find it—the stone?" Tom glanced out the window at the half moon glowing brightly in the spring sky. "I've thought a lot about just that lately and to tell you the truth I sort of hope they don't."

"Really?" Cricket frowned. "Why not?"

"What it did to Gregor. The suspicions of what it may have done to the astronaut who found it. All the death and wrong that was done in pursuit of it. The way the government acted trying to get it back. I honestly don't think we're ready for it."

"Yeah," she said, looking down at the sheets while Tom stood and crossed the room back to the doorway. "Dad?"

Tom turned. "Yes, sweetheart?"

"I love you and Mom more than anything."

"We feel the same way," Tom said, clicking off her light "Get some sleep now."

The door shut and Cricket listened to her dad's familiar shuffling footsteps go down the hallway. The door to her parents' bedroom clicked shut and she heard her mother giggle. She got out of bed, padded to her door, and locked it. Then she went to the computer on her desk, went on-line, and called up her e-mail.

She found a note from Chester Norton. They had met during the congressional hearings, and despite their five-year age difference she could tell he had something of a crush on her, which she was doing little to discourage. His Uncle had taught him to swim during the past year and he practiced every day in a pool at the university. He'd lost a lot of weight since she'd first met him and looked trimmer and more handsome every time she saw him. And besides her dad, he was the smartest, nicest guy she'd ever met.

Chester's note informed her that Dr. Swain was still hard at work on a theoretical explanation of moon rock 66095. He went on to detail some of his uncle's thinking. Most of it was mathematical and went right over her head. Chester said he and Dr. Swain were planning a trip to Kentucky in the next few weeks and would like to interview her and her parents again about what had happened when the stone destabilized in the Shaman's Catacomb. Their recollections, he said, might yield clues to its physical properties.

Reading that, Cricket started chewing the inside of her cheek. She had not told anyone, not even her parents, the entire truth of what had occurred after she collided with Robert Gregor and they had spilled over into the abyss. She'd testified before Congress that she remembered falling, then hitting water, then nothing more until she'd woken in the hospital. Cricket wrote as much in her reply to Chester.

She sent the e-mail, then went and sat on her bed. She opened her window and peered out into the warm Kentucky night. To her delight, the first fireflies of the year were dancing and flickering outside.

Seeing the moon glow so spectacularly through the branches and leaves of the oaks, Cricket could not help but think of Gregor and what had really happened after they tumbled into the chasm. She closed her eyes. Some of the memories were murky, but others were so vivid it was as if they'd been welded into her mind.

Gregor pitched backward into the abyss, clutching the stone to his breast. Cricket flipped after him toward the far wall of the crevice and then, some thirty feet into the fall, a tremendous jolt passed through her hips. For a heartbeat, she dangled from a rock outcropping by a carabiner clipped to her cave pack.

The outcropping snapped off and she fell again. Her headlamp beam caught the reflection of oily water below her. And then nothing.

She came to consciousness in Pluto's River, which was rushing her downstream, batting her off submerged boulders, forcing her through tight spots. And there was an ungodly pain shooting through the entire length of her right leg.

Then she passed out again and awoke hours later to find herself in the pitch dark, half in, half out of the river. She managed to drag herself out of the water, then rummaged in her pack which was still cinched tight to her waist. She found a battery and installed it. She let the saber of light flash about the cave, then stopped, shocked by the sight of a boot almost directly in front of her. The boot was attached to a leg and then to the misshapen body of Robert Gregor, slumped against one of the boulders.

His skin showed the jaundice of death, yet he still lived. In his lap lay moon rock 66095, a simple gray rock with a vein of dark crystal running through its center. The scientist's saucer eyes winced at the light and Cricket turned the headlamp down until it was barely a candle's glow. She lay there looking at him, saying nothing and for several moments Gregor did the same in return.

"I hope in the end," he finally rasped, "you don't think I'm completely evil. Despite everything, despite all my hard work, I am fragile, too. Human."

Cricket did not know how to respond. She did not move closer, but watched Gregor as he labored for breath and cradled the stone the way a mother might a newborn.

"The stone was my discovery," Gregor said. "My conquest. My moment in time. The thing that changed me, made me whole and better than others in a way nothing ever had before. MacPherson was going to take the stone away from me, take credit for it I couldn't let it happen. Will history judge me so awful to want to unlock all of its secrets, to be the first to know everything it was capable of, to be its guardian?"

"Guess not," Cricket said.

"You saw it then," Gregor croaked. "The power of it?"

Cricket nodded. "Yes."

"Thrill you?"

"Yes."

"Scare you?"

"Yes."

"All great discoveries are like that." Gregor said. "They force us to completely change our way of thinking. Nothing is more exhilarating or terrifying than that kind of change."

He stopped, shuddered, and fought for air. Then he seemed to summon up his last strength and held out the rock toward Cricket. "Yours now," he said. "Keep it well."

There was a rattle in his chest and the life went out of him. The stone rolled from his fingers and landed in the mud.

Looking out the window at the moon from the comfort of her bedroom, Cricket pictured herself staring at the rock in the mud in front of Gregor's body.

Then, as she had almost every night since returning home, she came away from the window, went to her door, and checked once more to ensure it was locked. Satisfied, she moved to her closet, pushed aside an old milk crate filled with magazines, and found two loose floorboards. She took up a flathead screwdriver from the milk crate, fitted it into a crack between the boards, then pried them up. She reached down between the joists and retrieved a burlap bag She went to her bed, opened the bag and turned it upside down. A lead-lined pouch, the kind photographers use to shield their film from x-ray machines in airports, fell out. She opened that and watched in wonder as the stone that had been found on the Descartes Highlands of the moon nearly thirty-six years before rolled out onto her rumpled sheets and blankets.

Cricket hefted the stone, still amazed that a week after coming home from the hospital, she'd gone out into the garage on crutches and found the bin where her father always stored their caving gear. She'd picked up her pack and, to her astonishment found the stone still inside, buried at the bottom under all her gear.

No one, not the soldiers, not Dr. Swain, not Chester, not her parents or any of the doctors or government officials who had been swarming Tower Ridge, had ever thought to search her pack when she'd been carried from the cave. They had been concerned only with saving her life. And the longer their attention had passed over her, the more she had become convinced that the stone was better off hidden.

The doctors had said she'd been exposed to a serious dose of quark-decay, and there were times when she got nervous at the idea of keeping the moon rock. But she'd checked it with her father's old Geiger counter at least a hundred times in the past twelve months and gotten no reaction whatsoever. And during the bimonthly tests the doctors put her through, she'd shown no sign of additional quark-decay exposure.

Without the electronic matrix, moon rock 66095 was totally inert, nothing like the fiery transmitter of rare energy she'd witnessed in the cave. She knew, however, that in the long run she would have to give it to someone better suited to keeping it safe.

From time to time, Chester Norton would say or write something cryptic to her about moon rock 66095, and she wondered if he and Dr. Swain suspected she had it. But neither he nor his uncle had ever asked her outright and she had never told them. Perhaps she would someday.

In the meantime, she thought about the massive impact explosion of an asteroid hitting the moon that had somehow created this marvel billions of years ago and wondered whether that was God's intention. She thought about the many terrible things that had been done in an effort to possess and understand it and wondered whether that was God's intention, too. Then she thought about Dr. Swain and his mathematical explanation of its workings. She had her own theory about the rock, a theory she had been developing alone almost every night since coming home from the hospital. It had nothing to do with superconductors or quark decay or any of the other scientific terms used to describe the stone.

Cricket had come to think of the moon rock as a heart, a marvelous, dangerous pump that somehow magnified and speeded energy, the same way our hearts in our chests can speed and channel blood, the same way our hearts in our chests can speed and channel love.

A heart could recast three beings like Cricket and her parents back into one as easily as the stone could recast base ores into exotic alloys. Denied its presence in their lives, geniuses like Gregor could turn insane and murderous. In pursuit of it, men like Mann, Kelly, and even Lyons could turn their backs on their fellow human beings.

Her mother had seen horrible things happen to her best friend and so found herself lost in the darkest passages of her mind. But her heart had eventually guided her out. Her dad had more heart than anyone she knew. But there was that one moment in the cave when he'd lost his spirit and then, with her mother's help, regained it. That incident seemed to have made him stronger and yet more tender and attentive than he had ever been before.

Cricket smiled and held the stone up to the warm light of the moon. She marveled at how the spider veins of black crystal caught the moonlight, made it stronger, made it flash and sparkle like a mountain stream.

Then she clasped the rock to her breast, thinking how a piece of the moon and the events inside Labyrinth Cave had somehow transmuted her from a girl to a woman, someone who had learned that the invisible power of the heart could give her the means to survive anything life might throw at her.

If only she let herself feel its gravitational pull at every turn.

Acknowledgments

This book could not have been written without Roger Brucker, author, founding director of the Cave Research Foundation, and one of the world's greatest explorers of the underground. He took me under his wing introduced me to the remarkable world of deep caves, and patiently read drafts of the manuscript, offering his suggestions and insight. For all that, his humor, and his friendship I am forever grateful.

My deepest gratitude goes also to the other endurance cavers who helped me through the tight spots, especially Lynn Brucker, Kathryn Burgess, C. Philip Henry, Marty Brown, Douglas Alderman, John Armstrong, Rich Kline, John Logsdon, Anne Wesley, and Jeanne Guerney. Any mistakes concerning the technical aspects of deep caves and the methods of endurance cavers are mine alone.

What little I know of North American vertical rope techniques, I learned from Bruce Smith and Allen Padgett. Thank you.

Thanks also to Dr. Lawrence A. Taylor of the Department of Geological Science at the University of Tennessee for patiently explaining to me the composition of rocks from the Descartes Highlands, including moon rock 66095; and to Dr. Carlton Allen, Astro-materials Curator at the Johnson Space Center in Houston; and to Andrew L Chaikrn, author of *A Man on the Moon*, an amazing account of the Apollo voyages. Forgive me for altering history.

I am likewise indebted to Barry Bannister, deputy warden at the Kentucky State Penitentiary at Eddyville, for his patience in showing and explaining the intricacies of maximum security segregation units and medical transfer procedures. I take responsibility for any dramatic licenses.

My thanks as well to Ellen Wolf, Harold Miner, and Todd Harrington, who helped me understand post-traumatic stress disorder and the effects of claustrophobia. I hope I got it right.

I owe a huge debt to Alexandra "Pandi" Sullivan, for helping me understand the fears, aspirations, and longings of a fourteen-year-old girl.

Fellow writers Damian Slattery, Joseph Finder, and Daniel Silva kept me going through the tough times with their unfailing support

Linda Chester and Joanna Pulcini, my friends and tenacious agents, patiently read and reread the various drafts of the manuscript. It's a privilege and a joy to be associated with them. And finally, my thanks to the team at Atria Books, including Judith Curr, Tracy Behar, and Mitchell Ivers, my editor. Few authors have the luck to work with such professionals.

Made in the USA
San Bernardino, CA
04 December 2018